WELCOME TO T

New York Times B

JULIE JAMES

~A *Cosmopolitan* Red-Hot Read~
~A *Booklist* Top 10 Romance of the Year~
~American Library Association Reading List for Top Genre Novels~
~Best Contemporary Romance, *All About Romance* Reader Poll~
~National Readers' Choice Award Winner~
~RomCon Readers' Crown Award Winner~

"[JULIE JAMES] IS A MASTER"*
and her novels are...

"An addictively readable combination of sharp humor
[and] sizzlingly sexy romance."—*Chicago Tribune*

"Sexy fun. Romance fans will pop their corks."
—*Library Journal*

"Sparkling [and] sexy."—*Booklist*

continued . . .

Suddenly One Summer

JULIE JAMES

JOVE BOOKS, NEW YORK

JOVE

An imprint of Penguin Random House
375 Hudson Street, New York, New York 10014

SUDDENLY ONE SUMMER

A Jove Book / published by arrangement with the author

JOVE® is a registered trademark of Penguin Random House LLC.
The "J" design is a trademark of Penguin Random House LLC.
For more information, visit penguin.com.

ISBN: 978-0-425-27376-0

PUBLISHING HISTORY
Jove mass-market edition / June 2015

PRINTED IN THE UNITED STATES OF AMERICA

10 9 8 7 6 5 4 3 2 1

Cover design by Rita Frangie.
Cover photograph of waves © Katarina Stefanovic / Getty; photograph
of grass on sand dune © Asaf Eliason.

Penguin
Random
House

To Mr. James

Acknowledgments

First and foremost, I owe special thanks to my wonderful friend Kellie Cross for sharing her insight and experience as a family lawyer and for going above and beyond in answering all my pesky questions. Huge thanks, as well, to Pamela Clare, for graciously imparting her knowledge and experience as an investigative journalist, and to Amy Guth for helping me with some questions about the *Tribune*.

I'm also indebted to John Robertson, private investigator, for teaching me the ins and outs of Internet people searches, and to Kevin Kavanaugh and Brent Dempsey for their additional insight into the investigatory field. Thanks, also, to Beth Kery, for chatting with me about the therapy process and "difficult" clients.

Many thanks to my agent, the fantastic Robin Rue, to the entire team at Berkley, and to my editor, Wendy McCurdy, for all her support and creative insight, and for brainstorming with me when I needed to "talk out" this book. I'm also tremendously grateful to Elyssa Patrick, Kati Brown, Brent Dempsey, and "Mr. James" for beta reading the book—sometimes more than once—under tight deadlines and for their helpful critiques.

Last, but certainly not least, thank you to all the readers who take the time to reach out to me and let me know that my words put a smile on your face. The feeling is definitely mutual. ☺

Suddenly One Summer

Prologue

ALTHOUGH PEOPLE OFTEN said that divorce was an ugly business, Victoria Slade had a different perspective. Typically, by the time clients arrived on her office doorstep, it was the *marriage* that had gotten ugly. Divorce was simply the part where the truth came out.

In a cab on the way to her town house on Chicago's north side, Victoria leaned her head against the seat and thought about the case she'd wrapped up today. Her client, a forty-five-year-old stay-at-home mom, had been blindsided three months ago after being served with a divorce petition by her husband of fourteen years. According to the terms of the couple's prenuptial agreement, Victoria's client was not entitled to receive any portion of the sizable business empire her husband had amassed, throughout the course of their marriage, as one of the most successful celebrity chefs in Chicago. The three lucrative restaurants, the bestselling cookbooks, and the income derived from his Food Network cooking show had all been designated "separate assets" per the prenup and thus untouchable by his wife in the event of a divorce.

Unless, of course, Mr. Celebrity Chef violated the

no-cheating clause in the couple's prenup, thereby rendering the entire agreement invalid.

Knowing this, Victoria naturally had done a little digging.

She would say this for Mr. Celebrity Chef: he'd covered his tracks better than most cheating spouses she'd come across—and that was coming from someone who'd made virtually a cottage industry out of the unfaithfully wed. Most got caught after leaving a text message or e-mail trail, others because of suspicious activity on their credit card or bank statements. But this guy had been smart: he'd bought his twenty-six-year-old mistress a one-bedroom condo in the Ritz-Carlton Residences via a limited liability company that he'd created under false pretenses—supposedly a "food supply" company—to which his restaurants had made bimonthly payments in the amount of twenty thousand dollars.

Unfortunately for him, however, the forensic accountant Victoria had hired to comb through Mr. Celebrity Chef's books was even smarter.

And the rest was history.

Because of the diligent work of Victoria Slade & Associates, their client had walked out of this afternoon's settlement conference with significantly more money than the maintenance award she would have received had they not busted her husband with his hands in the metaphorical cookie jar. So to celebrate, Victoria had taken all six of her associates—and Will, her assistant and right-hand man—out for a well-earned evening of dinner and drinks.

Lots of drinks, judging from the tab Victoria had signed off on when leaving the restaurant.

She, herself, was basically sober when the cab pulled up in front of her three-story townhome. She enjoyed a good bourbon on the rocks as much as the next girl, but tonight she'd been wearing her Badass Boss hat, and as far as she was concerned, badass bosses didn't get falling-down drunk in front of their employees.

She tipped the driver an extra twenty when the taxi came to a stop. "Would you mind waiting until I get inside before you drive off?" She was playing it safe, of course, given the recent string of burglaries in the Lincoln Park and Lakeview neighborhoods. Not to mention the fact that it was one o'clock in the morning.

He nodded. "Sure. No problem."

After getting out of the cab, she crossed the sidewalk and headed up the front steps of the brick town house she'd lived in for the last ten months. Her first home. In truth, she probably could've afforded to buy the place a couple of years earlier given the success of her firm. But with childhood memories of "Notice of Foreclosure" dancing in her head, she'd wanted to be confident she wasn't biting off more than she could chew with the mortgage.

Victoria unlocked the front door, triggering the warning beep of her security system, and immediately punched her code into the keypad. When the alarm went silent, she turned around and waved to the cabdriver.

All clear.

She brought in the mail, deposited it on the kitchen counter, and headed upstairs. After rearming the security system from the keypad in her bedroom, she changed into a T-shirt and shorts, quickly scrubbed the makeup off her face, brushed her teeth, then climbed into bed. She debated whether to return some work e-mails, then decided—*nah*—that she'd earned a few hours off given the success of today's settlement conference.

With a satisfied smile, she snuggled into the covers and began to drift off.

BEEEEEEP.

Victoria shot up in bed when she heard the warning signal from her security system that the front door had been opened.

She heard the door shut downstairs, followed by the sound of footsteps.

Oh my God. Someone was in her house.

She slid out of bed and grabbed her cell phone from the nightstand. The alarm signal stopped, and the house fell silent again.

Her heart started thumping in her chest when she heard a man's voice downstairs.

"We're good to go," he said.

Victoria moved silently into her walk-in closet, a space almost as large as her bathroom. Her laundry hamper was tucked between the wall and a row of long dresses. Sliding past the clothes, she crouched down and hid behind the hamper.

Her hand was trembling as she dialed 9-1-1 on her phone. A woman's voice. "9-1-1, what is your emergency?"

Victoria whispered, her words coming out in a rush. "My name's Victoria Slade. I live at 1116 North Garner. Someone's broken into my house."

"Is the intruder in your home right now, ma'am?"

"Yes, I think there are two of them. I'm hiding in a closet upstairs and—" She paused, hearing something that made her palms sweat. "Someone's coming up the stairs. I can't talk—they'll hear."

"Ma'am, I'll stay on the li—"

Victoria turned the volume on the phone all the way down and covered the speaker with her hand. Through a small space in between the hamper and the wall, she could see the closet doorway.

She held her breath as the footsteps on the hardwood floors grew louder.

A man dressed in dark clothing came into view in front of the closet. He paused, and then reached for his hip and pulled out a gun.

"You sure she hasn't been home?" he called out to someone, in a gruff voice.

Another guy stepped in front of the closet. "Yeah, I'm sure. Why?"

"The bed's been slept in."

"So? You make your bed every fucking day? Come on, let's get to work."

She heard the second guy walk out of her bedroom, but the man with the gruff voice stayed where he was, gun in hand. From behind the laundry hamper, she watched as he moved toward the master bathroom across from the closet and turned on the light. He paused in the bathroom doorway, and then headed for the closet.

He reached in and flipped the switch that turned on the light.

As light flooded the small room, Victoria saw that he wore a black mask with openings at his eyes and mouth. He stepped inside the closet.

Her heart began to beat so hard against her rib cage she was afraid he might actually be able to hear it.

She stayed absolutely still, praying he didn't see her through the gap between the hamper and the wall.

A soft whirring sound came from the other side of the closet.

The man spun around, pointing his gun. Then he relaxed when he spotted a brown case, her automatic watch winder, sitting on a shelf. Tucking the gun into the holster at his hip, he walked over, opened the front of the case, and picked up her watch. He examined it for several moments, flipping it over in his hand, and then pulled a medium-sized cloth bag out of the front pocket of his black hoodie. After dropping the watch inside, he moved on to the jewelry box that sat next to the watch winder.

With his back to Victoria, he spent what felt like an eternity rifling through the jewelry box, then picked it up and dumped the entire contents into his bag. Something fell to the floor with a *clink* against the hardwood floors, and he crouched down to pick it up.

There was a loud crash downstairs.

Victoria started at the sound at the same moment the masked man shot up to a standing position. He shouted to his partner, "What the fuck was that?"

She heard a loud commotion downstairs. Someone shouted, *"Police!"* and then—

A gunshot.

Instantly, the intruder was out of the closet. Suddenly remembering the cell phone in her hand, Victoria put it to her ear. "Hello?"

"It's okay, Victoria. I'm still here. Help is on the way," the 9-1-1 operator said.

The unwanted memory washed over her with the force of

a tidal wave, carrying her back to a stranger's voice on the other end of a phone line, all those years ago.

Hang in there, Victoria. Help is coming, I promise.

Suddenly, she felt . . . off. The space between her and the hamper began to contract, closing in on her. The air seemed stifling hot, and she felt dizzy.

"Victoria? Are you there?"

The voice sounded faint, far away, and she couldn't tell if it was real or in her head. Past and present blurred together.

"Are you okay, Victoria?" the voice repeated, more urgently.

As her vision narrowed and darkness closed in, her last thought was *of course* she was okay. Victoria Slade could handle anything. She was tough, she was strong, she—

—was blacking out from her first-ever panic attack.

One

A month later

"**THOUGH I WALK** through the valley of the shadow of death, I will fear no evil; for thou art with me . . ."

As the priest wrapped up his homily, Ford Dixon's eyes fell once again on the photograph of his father that rested on a stand in front of the casket.

They'd gotten lucky with the photo. As he, his mother, and his sister, Nicole, had realized when preparing for this memorial service, John Dixon had posed for very few pictures by himself, particularly in recent years. Fortunately, they'd been able to crop a photograph taken just four months ago, one of him holding his granddaughter, Ford's niece, in the hospital after she'd been born. It wasn't a professional-quality photo—Ford had taken it with his phone—but his father looked happy and proud.

It was a good memory, one that he and his mother and sister could look back on without the uneasiness that clouded many others.

Any moment now, it would be his turn to deliver the eulogy. Never having given a eulogy before, the investigative journalist in him naturally had done his research. He was supposed to keep his remarks brief, but personal, and he was supposed to focus on a particular quality of his father that he'd admired, or share a story that illustrated something his father had enjoying doing.

Most of the people attending the funeral service knew that, in truth, there had been two John Dixons: the larger-than-life, gregarious man always up for a good time—who, sure, rarely had been seen without a beer in his hand—and the moody, angry drunk he could become when he'd had one, or four, drinks too many. Ford could wax poetic for hours about the first John Dixon, because that man had been his hero, the father who'd spent hours playing catch with him on weekends in the field next to their townhome subdivision. The man who used to make up funny bedtime stories with different voices for the characters. The man who'd organized water balloon fights for the kids at family barbecues, the cool dad who'd let him have his first sip of beer at a Cubs game, the guy always getting a laugh out of the crowd of parents sitting on the bleachers during one of Ford's Little League games.

But the other John Dixon?

That guy was a lot harder to warm up to.

Get away from me, kid. Don't you have any damn friends you can annoy?

Ford cleared his throat just as the priest looked in his direction.

"I think Ford, John's son, has some remarks he'd like to share with us today."

Ford stood and walked to the lectern located to the right of the altar. He looked out at the decent-sized crowd and saw a lot of familiar faces, a mixture of family acquaintances, relatives, and close friends of his and his sister who'd come to offer their condolences.

With a reassuring glance at his mother and sister, who sat in the front pew, Ford rested his hands on the sides of the lectern. He hadn't written any notes, planning instead to rely on the innate storytelling instincts possessed by all good journalists—instincts he'd inherited from the man who lay in the casket behind him, a man who, once upon a time, had woven epic tales about Ford's stuffed animals while tucking him in at night.

Today, that was the John Dixon he chose to remember.

"The Fourth of July when I was eleven years old, my father decided we had to have the biggest, most elaborate fireworks display in the neighborhood. Ah, I see some of you out there smiling already . . . You know exactly where this story is going."

AFTER THE FUNERAL service and subsequent lunch, Ford drove his mom back to his parents' house in Glenwood, a suburb north of the city. His parents lived—or now, he supposed he should say his *mom* lived—in a subdivision nicknamed "the Quads" because each square-shaped building contained four small townhome units stacked back-to-back. Although Glenwood was well known as a very affluent town—one of the ten richest in the U.S., according to *Forbes*—the particular neighborhood in which he'd grown up was decidedly blue collar, mostly families with two working parents who'd specifically chosen the subdivision because of its access to public schools ranked among the best in the state.

"I'm worried about your sister," his mother said as they drove along Sheridan Road, past the tree-lined side streets and multimillion-dollar mansions that, while technically part of his hometown, had always felt like a different world.

Ford glanced over, feeling a mixture of admiration, amusement, and frustration. The comment was so typical of his mother. She'd just buried her husband of thirty-six years, and of course here she was, thinking about someone else.

He reached over and squeezed her hand. "Nicole will be fine, Mom."

She gave him a no-nonsense look. "Don't *you* start giving me the grieving-widow platitudes. There've been enough of those these past few days."

That got a slight smile out of him. Fair enough. Unlike his father, with his wild mood swings, Maria Dixon had always been grounded and down-to-earth. "Fine. I'm worried about

Nicole, too," he admitted, despite being firmly of the belief
that his mother didn't need to be thinking about this today.

It wasn't exactly a secret that his twenty-five-year-old sister, Nicole, had been struggling as a single mom ever since
giving birth to her daughter, Zoe, four months ago. As a part-
time actress and a full-time instructor at a local children's
theater, she worked days, evenings, and some weekends, yet
still barely made enough to support herself in the city. Ford
had talked to her about seeking child support from Zoe's
father—some musician Nicole had dated for a few months
last year—but apparently the guy had freaked out when he'd
found out Nicole was pregnant, and had packed his bags for
L.A. without leaving her a forwarding address.

Ford hadn't met the shithead, but his jaw clenched every time
he thought about the way the guy had left his sister high and dry.

"I've tried talking to her, but she's so hard to get a hold of
these days," his mother said. "I'd been planning to visit her
at work this week, but then your father . . ." Her lower lip
trembled as her voice trailed off.

Oh, *man*. It killed him to see his mother fighting back
tears. No doubt, they were all reeling from the surprise of his
father's death. And while there was nothing he could do to
change the past—a fact that ate away at him given the way
things between him and his father had ended—there was, at
least, something he could do in this situation.

So when his car pulled to a stop at a red light, he turned
and looked his grieving mother in the eyes.

"I'll make sure both Nicole and Zoe are all right, Mom. I
promise."

A FEW HOURS later, Ford pulled into the parking garage of
his loft condo building in Chicago's Wicker Park neighborhood. He'd distracted himself with music during the drive
home, but once he turned the car off, there was nothing but
silence.

This was the moment he'd been dreading for the last few
days, when the deluge of funeral arrangements subsided and

he no longer had to be "on," nodding and making small talk and graciously thanking everyone for their sympathies. The moment when he was finally alone, with nothing but his thoughts to keep him company.

A man stepped in front of Ford's car and waved. "Hey, Ford."

Or . . . maybe this wasn't that moment.

Ford got out of his car to greet Owen, the guy who owned the condo next to his. "Sorry. Didn't see you walking over."

With a sympathetic expression, Owen shook his hand in greeting. "How'd everything go today?"

Ford appreciated that Owen had taken the time to drop by the wake yesterday. The two of them had been neighbors for four years, and had hung out occasionally. Less so recently, ever since Owen had moved in with his girlfriend and put his condo on the market. "It was a nice service, thanks." He was quick to move off the topic. "What brings you back to the old hood?"

"Just came by to pick up my mail." Owen gestured to the stack of magazines and letters he carried. "I saw you and thought I should mention that my real estate agent rented my place for the summer."

"You're renting?" Now that was a surprise.

"I know. Not my first choice." Owen shrugged. "But in this market, I wasn't getting any offers anywhere close to my asking price. So we thought we'd rent it for a few months, and maybe put it back on the market in the fall. Figured I should give you a heads-up in case you see a stranger coming out of my front door."

"Right." Ford nodded. A silence fell between them, and he realized he was probably supposed to say more.

"Her name's Victoria," Owen went on, "and she's some big divorce lawyer or something. I haven't met her, but from what I hear she just bought a condo in River North and needed a place to live until the sale closes at the end of August. Apparently, she was really eager to get out of her current home. Not sure what the story is there."

This was all interesting information, and Ford knew that Owen was just trying to be friendly. But these last few days of making polite conversation were starting to wear on him.

"Thanks for letting me know." He gestured to the door that led inside the condo building. "Unfortunately, there's some stuff I need to take care of . . ."

"Oh! Of course," Owen said quickly. "Don't let me keep you."

After promising to stay in touch, and assuring Owen that he would let him know if he needed anything—only the hundred-and-thirtieth time he'd made that pledge this week—Ford escaped and got into the elevator.

He exhaled as the elevator began to rise toward the fourth floor, and prayed that he wouldn't bump into any other neighbors—past, current, or future—before he got to his loft.

He got lucky.

His hallway was empty. He walked quietly to unit 4F, the loft all the way at the end. Key already in hand, he unlocked the door and let himself in.

In his bedroom, he yanked off the tie and black suit jacket he'd worn for the funeral. Pacing in his bedroom, he thought about these past few days and felt a stab of emotion.

This was not how things between him and his father were supposed to end.

Granted, their relationship had been complicated for a long time. But he'd always held on to a small hope that something would happen to bridge the chasm between them. Rehab would work one of these times, or there would be some sort of health scare—nothing too serious—that would inspire his dad to give up drinking for good.

Obviously, that had been wishful thinking.

The last time he'd seen his father had been two weeks ago, at his cousin's college graduation party. There'd been plenty of beer at the party, of which his father had consumed too much, and Ford had kept his distance, not wanting to deal with one of his dad's moods on what was supposed to be a happy occasion.

He couldn't remember what he and his dad had talked about that day. Certainly nothing of significance, none of the things Ford would've said if he'd known then that his mother would call ten days later, crying, to tell him that his father had dropped dead in the kitchen after suffering a massive heart attack while she was out grocery shopping. There'd been no warning. The doctors said there was nothing anyone could have done; his father's heart muscles had been significantly weakened, likely the result of years of excessive drinking.

So many things left unsaid. And now . . . that could never change.

Fuck.

All of the emotion Ford had been holding back suddenly boiled over. Without thinking, he grabbed the glass-and-cast-iron candle holder on his dresser and whipped it at the wall opposite him.

Seeing the glass smash into pieces was oddly cathartic.

There was, however, one small problem. Apparently, the iron candle holder had been a little heavier than he'd thought. At least, judging from the eight-inch *hole* he'd just put in his bedroom wall.

He surveyed the damage.

Well. At least this was one problem he could actually fix.

Two

BRIGHT AND EARLY the following Thursday morning, Victoria walked into the lobby of her downtown office building. She took an elevator up to the thirty-third floor, which her firm shared with two other tenants, a small consulting group and an engineering firm.

Back when she'd been looking for a place to hang her shingle, she'd been attracted to this particular office space because of its clean, modern lines, and great use of natural light. The bright, open feel of the place was reassuring to her clients, who were going through a difficult time in their lives. *You're going to be okay after this divorce. Victoria Slade & Associates will make sure of it*, said the sunlit, sophisticated décor.

After unlocking the fogged glass doors that bore her firm's name, she turned on the lights to the reception area. She liked being in before everyone else, so she could soak in those few moments when the office was quiet and just hers.

Her office had two walls of windows that framed a picturesque view of the city and the Chicago River. She settled in behind her desk and checked her e-mail while sipping the coffee that she'd picked up on the way in. About a half hour later, she heard her four associates trickle in, followed by Will, her assistant.

She heard a knock and saw Will standing in the doorway.

"Give it to me straight. How bad are they?" he asked, touching the rim of his new wire-frame glasses. He'd turned forty years old earlier in the year and, much to his displeasure, had been told by his eye doctor that he needed reading glasses.

"Ooh . . . I like them," Victoria said approvingly. "Very Gregory Peck."

"*Hmph*" was Will's sole response, although she noticed he seemed to have a little swagger in his step as he took a seat in front of her desk.

"Tomorrow's the big day. Is there anything else you need me to take care of?" he asked.

She smiled, knowing this was pretty much a rhetorical question. If there was anything else that needed to be taken care of, Will already would've thought of it himself. The man was a god when it came to organizing these types of things. "I think we're all set."

Tomorrow she would move into her temporary home, a loft condo in a converted warehouse in Wicker Park. She hadn't lived in an apartment or condo building since law school—her place before the townhome had been a duplex— and, as a relatively private person, she wasn't overly enthused to suddenly be sharing common space with a bunch of strangers. But this was her life now, at least for the foreseeable future, so she supposed she would just have to get used to it.

Ever since the break-in, she'd hadn't gotten more than three or four hours of sleep each night. Instead, she would lie awake in her bed, listening for any strange sounds and repeatedly getting up to check her security system—not that her security system had kept the burglars at bay before.

Scary thought.

From what she'd learned from the police—who, thankfully, had arrived quickly on the scene because of the 9-1-1 dispatcher—the masked men had staked out her place for most of the night, with the exception of a short break when the man with the gruff voice needed to use the bathroom at a convenience store a few blocks away because the White Castle sliders they'd grabbed earlier hadn't agreed with him.

Nice.

Apparently, his partner was a former employee of a home security company, and thus knew how to bypass certain types of alarm systems—including hers. The police had caught both men, one of whom had foolishly fired his gun at the cops and thus earned an attempted murder charge, along with a charge of home invasion. During questioning, they admitted being responsible for the string of burglaries in the neighborhood, and were expected to be in prison for a good, long time.

Victoria knew she should consider herself fortunate, at least as far as scary-ass home invasions by masked men with *guns* went. But when the two weeks of not sleeping stretched into three, and after Will walked in on her dozing off at her desk, startling her and making her face-plant against her open laptop, she'd decided it was time to face facts.

She wasn't comfortable living in a place that had more than one level.

She couldn't relax in her townhome, and feared she would always be tense at night, waiting for that *beep* of the alarm, and listening for the sound of footsteps on her stairs.

Once she'd come to terms with that, she'd immediately put her townhome on the market and spent a weekend condo hunting with Audrey and Rachel, her two best friends. She decided on a two-bedroom place in the Trump Tower, telling herself that the burglars hadn't *really* gotten the best of her if she was moving to a place with its own indoor pool and health club.

And it even has a spa, dickheads.

In her head, she had all sorts of sassy one-liners for the scary-ass armed men who'd broken into her place.

But there was one problem: the current owner of the Trump Tower condo couldn't close on the sale until late August. She'd been about to walk away from the deal—she needed to get out of her townhome ASAP before she made some sloppy mistake at work in her sleep-deprived state—but then her friend had saved the day. Rachel knew a real estate agent who was trying to rent her client's condo for the summer, and the place was available to move into immediately. Victoria signed the three-month lease the moment the agent faxed it over, Will found a company that would send in a team to pack up all of her stuff (she didn't even want to ask how much *that* cost her), and thus tonight would be her last night in the town house she'd proudly purchased as her first home.

Yes, she was pissed. She'd been chased out of her own place by the Burglar Dickheads, essentially, and that didn't sit well with her. On top of that, she'd just bought the town-home ten months ago, so she probably would have to sell it at a loss. But she needed to be practical here—she was a busy woman, the head of her firm, and she needed to be at the top of her game when it came to work.

And oh my God, she couldn't wait to finally get some darn *sleep*.

SHORTLY BEFORE NOON, Victoria waved at Will as she passed by his desk on her way out of the office.

On the phone, he covered the receiver with his hand and whispered, "Good luck."

She felt a twinge of guilt, because this was the first time in the five years she and Will had been working together that she'd lied to him. She'd told him she would be unreachable for the next hour because she had a dentist appointment, when in truth she had something else to take care of.

Not a big deal. Just this . . . teeny, tiny problem she'd been having ever since the break-in.

Her research into these types of teeny, tiny problems had led her to Dr. Aaron Metzel, supposedly one of the top cognitive-behavioral psychologists in the city. His office was located in the Gold Coast neighborhood, a quick cab ride from downtown.

Victoria adjusted the lapel of her jacket as she rode the eleva-tor up to Dr. Metzel's floor. She wasn't quite sure what to expect from this appointment—it had been over twenty years since she'd last seen a psychologist—but she'd deliberately worn her favorite gray tailored suit and snakeskin heels. It was a suit that made her feel particularly put-together and confident.

There was a small, private waiting room adjacent to Dr. Metzel's office, with a sign on the interior door that said "Please make yourself comfortable." Thinking that "comfortable" was a bit ambitious—she was here only out of necessity—she took a seat in one of the empty chairs and distracted herself by checking e-mail on her phone.

A few moments after she sat down, the interior door opened. A balding, fortysomething man dressed in a blazer, khakis, and button-down shirt smiled at her.

"Victoria?" He held out his hand as she approached. "Aaron Metzel. Nice to meet you." He gestured to the adjacent room. "Come on in. Have a seat wherever you like."

"Thanks." She looked around curiously as she entered his office. The blinds were pulled down, but angled open, allowing a good amount of natural light to come in. It wasn't a massive office, but enough to accommodate a desk and book-shelf in front of the windows, a couch along one wall, and two leather armchairs in the center of the room. She chose the armchair closest to the door and took seat. Not sure where to put her purse, she set it on the floor.

She watched as Dr. Metzel—or was she supposed to call him Aaron?—grabbed a notepad and pen from his desk. They made brief small talk—Yes, she'd found the office just fine; No, thanks, she didn't need anything to drink—before getting down to brass tacks.

Seated across from her, Dr. Metzel crossed one leg, set-tling into his chair. "Let's talk about what brings you here. I know from our telephone conversation that you're having some issues with panic attacks."

Whoa, whoa. It sounded like somebody was getting a little ahead of himself here. "Actually, there's been just the *one* panic attack, the night my home was broken into." She felt it was important to emphasize this.

He clicked his pen open. "Tell me about that experience."

"Well, I remember suddenly feeling very light-headed, and hot, and then I guess I just fainted."

"Has that ever happened to you before? A loss of consciousness?"

"No."

"What happened when you came to?" he asked.

"There were two police officers hovering over me, asking if I had a medical condition. And it took me a moment to answer them, because at first I didn't know who or where I was." She took a deep breath. "But then, after a few seconds, everything came back to me."

"Does it make you uncomfortable, thinking back to that experience?"

"Of course," Victoria said, thinking this would be self-evident.

"In what way?" he asked.

"For starters, it was embarrassing, lying there on the floor like that. And scary. Like I said, I've never blacked out before. But I understand why it happened. My heart rate was escalated, I had a decreased oxygen intake, and I was under intense emotional stress."

Dr. Metzel's lips curved. "Somebody's been doing some research."

Heck, yes, she'd done her research. And she'd also quickly learned that looking up symptoms on the Internet was the quickest way to convince herself that she had *every medical condition in existence.* "Logically, I understand that I fainted during the break-in because of the extreme circumstances."

He waited. "But . . . ?"

"But ever since that incident, occasionally I'll find myself in some sort of situation—a normal situation—and I'll start to worry about having another panic attack."

Dr. Metzel wrote something on his notepad and then looked up. "Can you give me an example?"

She nodded. "So the first time it happened, I was riding the subway, heading home from work. The subway was packed, and it was warm and stuffy. You know how it gets. And the stuffy air reminded me of that night in my closet when I fainted, and, thinking back to that, I suddenly began to feel . . . off."

"Off in what way?"

"Nervous. Dizzy. My heart started racing, like the time in the closet."

"What was going through your head during that moment? Do you remember what you were thinking?"

"I was thinking that there had to be at least twenty people between me and the exit door, and that if I *did* have another panic attack right there on the train, it was going to cause a huge scene."

More note taking.

"So what did you do?" Dr. Metzel asked.

Victoria shrugged. "I basically said, 'Screw it.' At the next stop, I bulldozed my way to the door, got off the train, and took a cab the rest of the way home."

"Have you ridden the subway since then?"

She tried to downplay this with a smile. "A nice air-conditioned cab ride home isn't all that expensive. I figured why bother with the subway while it's so hot?"

From the way Dr. Metzel furiously scribbled something down on his notepad, she had a feeling she'd failed that question.

Crap.

She shifted uneasily in her chair, not enjoying the feeling of being so . . . scrutinized.

"Any other incidents?" Dr. Metzel asked.

"Well, I also walked out of an exercise class the other day." She blushed, a little embarrassed to admit these things. Not to toot her own horn or anything, but as a lawyer, she had a reputation for being fearless and tenacious in the courtroom. Heck, she'd been called a "ballbuster" by more than one irritated male opposing counsel. Yet here she sat, admitting she couldn't ride the subway or take an exercise class.

Dr. Metzel cocked his head. "What happened in the exercise class?"

She shrugged. "Basically the same thing that happened in the subway. About twenty minutes in, I noticed how hot the room was getting and everything just spiraled from there. I kept thinking, 'Uh-oh, am I feeling a little light-headed?' And, 'Oh, crap, what if I faint in the middle of this class,

because that's going to look really weird and cause a scene.'
That kind of thing."

He raised an eyebrow. "Have you been back to the exercise
class since that experience?"

"If I say no, are you going to start scribbling on your notepad again?"

Indeed, apparently he was.

When Dr. Metzel was done writing, he looked at her.
"What if you *had* fainted? Dropped right there in the middle
of the class and everyone saw. Would that be such a terrible
thing?"

Victoria shuddered at the mere thought. "I don't think anyone wants to cause a scene like that, do they?"

He acknowledged this with a nod. "Probably not. But I
notice that you keep talking about 'causing a scene' and looking 'weird.' Is that something you consider important, how
other people view you?"

Well.

That seemed like a bit of a loaded question.

"Um . . . maybe, I guess," she said, not sure how this particular line of questioning was relevant.

"Can you expand on that?" Dr. Metzel asked.

Do I have to? "I suppose I try to present myself a certain
way in front of other people. But doesn't everyone do that?
The point is, Doctor"—when he didn't correct her, she
assumed it was okay to call him that—"I run a successful law
practice and have a professional reputation to maintain. I can't
be running out of the courtroom because I'm suddenly feeling woozy or worried about having another panic attack."

He nodded. "I understand."

Good. Now they were getting somewhere. "I fully recognize that these lingering . . . fears"—she hesitated over the
word, debating whether it was too extreme—"are obviously
all in my head. And I'm sure they'll go away as more time
passes from the burglary. But since they're kind of, well,
annoying, I was hoping you might have some tricks to help
speed up the process. You know, breathing techniques, relaxation exercises, things of that nature." She went for a joke.

"Feel free to order me to visit a spa or get weekly massages as part of my treatment."

Dr. Metzel chuckled. "I'm not sure about the spa part, but certainly both relaxation and imagery techniques can be very helpful in the treatment of panic disorder. Now, one thing I'd—"

Wait. "Did you say 'panic *disorder*'?" she interrupted.

"Yes. Panic disorder."

She sat back in her chair. But . . . she didn't have a *disorder*. She was just having a few small panic *issues*. Clearly, the good doctor here needed to get with the program.

Then she realized what was going on. "Ah. Sorry, I should've mentioned this up front. I'm not fishing around for some kind of diagnosis in order to get insurance coverage. I'm fine paying out of pocket for these sessions."

"That's good to know," he said. "And, admittedly, this is just an initial assessment. But based on what you're telling me, I'm comfortable diagnosing panic disorder at this time."

Huh.

Having deposed and cross-examined several psychologists, her lawyerly instincts took over. "If you don't mind my asking, what, exactly, are you basing that diagnosis on?"

"I don't mind at all," Dr. Metzel said patiently. "In a nutshell, panic disorder is the fear of having a panic attack. Your fear of causing a scene, or looking 'weird,' and the changes you've made in your behavior—no longer riding the subway and stopping your exercise class—are all very classic symptoms."

Completely caught off guard, Victoria tried to process this. "But . . . I don't have any history of anxiety." Not that Dr. Metzel would know this—because she hadn't intended, and still didn't intend, for these sessions to be an all-access pass into certain things from her past, but she was about as mentally steady as they came. *She* was the rock. Hell, ever since she was ten years old, she'd made a point of demonstrating just how unflappable she was.

"In your case, the break-in was the catalyst for your initial panic attack," Dr. Metzel said. "And as you said, that's not a wholly atypical physiological response, given the extreme stress you were under at the time. But as for why that incident has now brought on your fear of having additional panic attacks . . . well, that's something we'll want to explore in therapy."

Therapy.

Aw, *criminy*.

Once upon a time, after The Incident, Victoria had gone through therapy at her mother's insistence. Two years of it, in fact, "just in case" there was anything she wanted to talk about. So she had a pretty good idea what to expect: all the talking, and the dissecting of her every thought and emotion.

Going through that ordeal again sounded about as much fun as stapling her tongue to the carpet.

"Can't you just patch me up with some breathing techniques and send me on my way?" she asked, trying to charm her way out of this.

Dr. Metzel returned the smile and clicked his pen. "Are weekends better for you? I have an opening for Saturdays at one P.M."

She took that as a no.

Three

"IT'S ME—YOU know what to do at the beep."

At the sound of the familiar greeting, Ford grumbled under his breath. Per the promise he'd made to his mother, this was the second time in three days that he'd called to check up on his sister and Zoe. Both times, his call had gone straight to voice mail.

"Hey, Nic. Just checking in to see how everything's going. I thought I might swing by sometime this weekend—maybe take you and Zoe out to lunch. Call me." After hanging up, he looked at the phone for a moment, and then turned back to his computer.

A week had passed since his father's funeral and at times, it felt a little surreal how most things just went back to normal. He'd taken a couple of days off from work to help his mother go through his father's things, a process that had hit him harder than he'd expected. But he'd buried his emotions down deep and had stayed focused on the tasks at hand—both for his mother's sake and, admittedly, his own. He felt better when he stayed busy. Doing something, anything, felt good and productive.

Especially when the alternative—sitting around his loft and ruminating—resulted in an eight-inch hole in his bedroom wall.

Not his finest moment.

Fortunately, right then, he had work to distract him. It was a typical Friday afternoon in the *Chicago Tribune* newsroom, mostly quiet except for the sound of clicking keyboards and occasional conversation as people got up to get coffee. The newsroom was large and open, with no walls separating the desks, and the air pulsed with a feverish beat as everyone raced against the clock to make their deadlines.

Today, he was finishing up a piece that was part of a series in which he'd exposed a multimillion-dollar bribery scheme involving a city transportation official and the company that had won a contract to supply Chicago with its red-light cameras. He'd worked for over a year on this particular series, and the corruption scandal was now the subject of an FBI investigation. He took particular pride in that—like many investigative journalists, he enjoyed seeing that his work had actual impact, and contributed to rectifying a wrongdoing or injustice.

After wrapping up the red-light piece and e-mailing it off, he met with his managing editor, Marty, to discuss an idea for a new story he'd been developing over the last couple of weeks.

"The April Johnson murder? You're a little late to the party, Dixon. We covered that three weeks ago."

"Not from this angle," Ford said. Last month, April Johnson, a seventeen-year-old honors student and artist, had been shot and killed by a gang member a block away from her high school grounds. Because the girl had recently visited the White House and met the First Lady as part of her school's successful participation in the Department of Education's "Turnaround Arts" program, her killing had been widely covered in all the Chicago media.

Mostly, the press coverage had focused on the victim—rightfully so, given the tragic circumstances. But Ford had done a little digging, and wanted to explore another aspect of the crime. "Everyone's focused on how Johnson's death is a symbol of this city's problem with gang violence, or using it as a platform to discuss gun control. But I've been looking into the nineteen-year-old shooter, Darryl Moore. Apparently, a year ago, he'd been arrested and sentenced to two years probation for illegally carrying a firearm. And get this—a criminal records check shows that the guy got arrested *three* more times after that. Did the probation department even know about the arrests? Did they know, but fail to take any action? I'm thinking somebody dropped the ball there."

Marty considered this. "Might be worth checking out what's in the probation department's records on Moore."

"Glad you think so." Ford grinned. "Especially since I requested the file yesterday."

Marty shook his head. "Of course you did. All right, run with it."

Ford worked on the new story for the rest of the afternoon, getting lost in his research. He called it quits for the day at five thirty, and then took a cab from the *Tribune* building to Home Depot, where he picked up the remaining supplies he needed for his weekend project. He planned to patch the hole in his bedroom wall, and also had decided to mount some book-shelves. Working with his hands would hopefully burn off some of the restless energy he'd been feeling since the funeral.

He checked his phone during the cab ride home. His friends clearly were in Check-On-Ford mode—a coordinated effort, he suspected, seeing how Charlie and Tucker wanted to get together tonight, and Brooke for dinner on Saturday. He texted them all back with a yes, appreciating the gesture and the not-so-subtle attempts to keep him company.

When the taxi pulled up in front of Ford's building, he spotted a large moving truck.

Ah, right. He remembered now that today was the day his temporary next-door neighbor, Victoria the Divorce Lawyer or Something, was moving in. Seeing that she'd reserved the elevator for the movers, he lugged the two bags of supplies he'd bought at Home Depot, along with his messenger bag, up the four flights of stairs.

When he spotted her open front door, he figured he should do the neighborly thing and introduce himself.

"Hello?" Not getting an answer, he stepped inside and found two movers in the dining area of the loft, carefully lowering a round, expensive-looking table to the floor. "Sorry, I was walking by and thought I'd pop in. I live next door." Still holding the bags of supplies, he gestured awkwardly in the direction of his place. "Is Victoria around?"

One of the movers shook his head, brushing off his hands after setting down the table. "She just left to make a run back to her old place."

"I'll catch her later, then. Thanks." On his way out, Ford stole a glance around the loft and saw that the rest of his new neighbor's furniture looked as expensive as the dining table. Judging from the elegant cream sofa with its many accent pillows, her taste was sophisticated and decidedly feminine. And he also immediately concluded that she was single.

No man could ever get comfortable watching Monday Night Football with all those damn throw pillows.

"SO, I'M THINKING I'll go with a barn theme for this new project. Instead of chairs, everyone will sit on bales of hay, and we'll bring in actual livestock—cows, pigs, maybe a few chickens—that can roam free in the restaurant while people eat. You know, really emphasize the farm-to-table aspect of the menu."

Victoria jerked her eyes open, having just caught what Audrey was saying. "Wait. You want to have *chickens* walking around the restaurant?"

When both Audrey and Rachel smiled, she caught on. "All right, all right, you got me." So she'd closed her eyes for just a second. In her defense, she hadn't slept for more than four hours a night in over a month. Not to mention, the bar they were in was filled with cozy, ambient candlelight that practically invited a girl to curl up in one of these big leather chairs and catch a few quick winks . . .

She sat up straight and gave herself a mental face-slap.

"You're exhausted, Vic. Maybe we should call it a night," Rachel suggested.

"Nope, I'm good. I promised you guys drinks in exchange for helping me unpack, so drinks we will have." Victoria grabbed her cocktail—an old-fashioned, the specialty of the house—and tipped it in gratitude. "And by the way, thank you again for that."

Her friends had been amazing today, coming over to help unpack her stuff. Audrey and Rachel had tackled the living and dining area, the movers had handled the kitchen, and she had taken on her bedroom and bathroom. Between the team of people in her condo, they'd had everything unpacked by eight o'clock with the exception of a few boxes of odds and ends that would probably just go into storage for the summer.

To show her appreciation, she'd insisted on taking her friends out for drinks. They'd chosen The Violet Hour, *the* place to be on a Friday night in Wicker Park—at least according to Will, who, naturally, already had done the research for her. Located just a couple of blocks from her loft and described as a modern-day speakeasy, the bar had a fun, *Alice in Wonderland*–like feel, with handmade cocktails poured by bartenders dressed in bow ties and suspenders, dramatic floor-to-ceiling velvet curtains, and high-backed blue leather chairs grouped around cocktail tables.

Determined not to be sidelined by a little drowsiness on her first night out in her new neighborhood, Victoria chatted with her friends for a while about work. Audrey, an interior designer, told them about the pitch she was planning for a new restaurant scheduled to open next spring, and Rachel, who owned a boutique clothing store, had just found out that her shop was going to be featured in *Chicago* magazine.

Rachel was momentarily distracted by something to Victoria's left, and then she leaned in conspiratorially. "Okay, I found a good one for you tonight," she said to Victoria, with a challenging gleam in her eye. "The hottie at your nine o'clock. Dark hair, navy shirt. He was checking you out, by the way. Let's say his name is . . . Carter."

It was a game they'd been playing for the last few years, ever since Victoria had told Rachel and Audrey during a mutual friend's bachelorette party that she didn't see herself ever getting married. Rachel, a staunch believer in happily-ever-after, would find some guy at a bar and make up an elaborate backstory about him, trying to convince Victoria that her Mr. Right might be out there.

"All right. Let's hear about Carter," Victoria said.

Rachel thought for a moment. "He's a firefighter."

"Rescues people. Love it."

"He grew up with three sisters, and he calls each of them once a week just to see how they're doing. He gets along with his parents, particularly his mother, who he adores," Rachel continued. "Has a dog that he rescued from a shelter—"

"Of course."

"—named after some poet. Like . . . Emerson," Rachel said.

Victoria raised an eyebrow. Somebody was laying it on a little thick tonight.

"His last serious relationship was three years ago, which ended amicably when he and his ex realized they were better off as friends. And he has *no* commitment issues," Rachel added, with a flourish.

Audrey laughed. "That's cheating."

Rachel looked at Victoria daringly. "So. Husband material or not? But before you answer, you really should look at the man in question."

"Which guy are we talking about?" Audrey asked.

"Dark hair, blue shirt," Rachel said.

Audrey angled in her chair, then her eyes widened. "Holy smokes, that is one good-looking man. Vic, you have to check him out."

Victoria shook her head. "Nope. Don't need to."

"I don't care how cynical you are," Rachel said, with a satisfied smile. "We're talking about a hot firefighter with no commitment issues who loves his mom."

"And he sounds very lovely to date. Probably too lovely for a jaded person like myself, but I'd give it a shot, anyway. But as for marriage . . . nope. Not for me."

"You don't know that," Rachel said in exasperation.

"Oh, but I do. Because in my line of work, I've seen all the ways your wonderful scenario here can go wrong."

"Like what?"

Victoria paused, debating whether to go down this route. Then she rested her arms on the table. "All right. Here's how I see this potentially shaking out."

"Here we go," Audrey said.

"Let's say this Carter the Hot Firefighter and I get married. It's good in the beginning, all new and exciting, and we decide to buy a house together so we can have more space. This is where we hit the first bump in the road. See, up until now, he's been saying that he's okay with the fact that I make more money than him. But when I want to look at houses that would be outside his budget, because *I* can cover the mortgage, suddenly the money becomes an issue. At first, he makes jokes about it, referring to me as his 'sugar mommy.' But then we start fighting about how much to spend on vacations. And birthdays. And how much my shoes cost. And he begins making snide comments about feeling emasculated, and before you know it, *all* we do is fight about money. The hot sex we used to have five times a week? Gone. We haven't slept together in months. Which leads to the second bump in the road." She paused dramatically, getting into her story now. "The ex-girlfriend he's stayed so friendly with. See, he's been telling her about our marriage problems, and suddenly they're meeting for coffee, and then drinks, and then he remembers how much she used to understand him, more than I ever have, and how easy it is to talk to her, until one day I leave work early to surprise him on his day off and find the two of them going at it like jackrabbits on our dining room table—the expensive antique table he's always hated because we bought it with 'my' money," she added for extra embellishment. "As for the three sisters and the mom, yes, he does adore them. And in our divorce settlement conference, he'll spitefully tell me how they secretly always hated me, because I work too much and didn't put family first, and because they never thought I was good enough for him in the first place."

Victoria finished her speech with a flourish—*And that is that, my friends*—and then noticed that Audrey and Rachel looked a little . . . surprised.

Uh-oh.

That may have sounded a touch too cynical, even for her. She sometimes forgot that not everyone had a front row seat, day in and day out, as marriages died their slow, painful deaths.

"Or . . . maybe we'll have two kids, a summer home in Michigan, and be happily married for fifty years," she said, quickly covering with a joke. "Heck, where is this future husband of mine?"

She glanced over her shoulder to look at the man who'd inspired their whole debate, this dark-haired guy in a navy shirt who undoubtedly was not a fireman, or named Carter, or even—

Ho-ly crap, he was gorgeous.

Slightly unruly dark brown hair, a strong, chiseled jaw that even Superman would envy, and piercing eyes—Victoria couldn't make out the color from where she sat, but it didn't matter. He wore a short-sleeved shirt that showed off the toned muscles in his arms and broad chest, and she'd bet that every inch of his body not currently on display—*boo*—was just as delicious.

She blinked, and turned back to her friends. "Wow."

"I know." Rachel leaned in. "And he's been checking you out this whole time."

"Maybe he and his two friends will come over." Audrey sized them up with a scrutinizing air. "The one with the hat has a cute hipster thing going on. I could work with that."

Unable to resist, Victoria sneaked in one more peek.

When his eyes met hers across the bar, boldly holding her gaze, she felt a thrill of attraction zip through her body.

The corners of his lips curved in a smile, as if to say, *Yeah, I felt that, too.*

Victoria was just thinking about her next move, or how she might respond to *his* next move, when an attractive woman with short blond hair sat down in the seat next to him and whispered something in his ear.

Ah. Well. So much for that.

Victoria turned back to her friends.

Audrey rolled her eyes. "What a jerk. Totally checking you out while he's here with another woman."

Rachel, ever the optimist, was quick to jump in. "Now, now, we don't know what the situation is. Maybe that's his . . . sister."

"Ah, yes, one of the three sisters he adores and calls every week." Victoria cocked her head. "You know what? Let's go with that. If we never talk to him, then we'll never find out that he isn't perfect. He'll always remain as lovely in our fantasies as Rachel says he is."

Audrey grinned and raised her glass. "I'll drink to that."

"Me, too," Rachel seconded.

They clinked their glasses together in cheers.

CHARLIE AND TUCKER would probably skin him alive if he didn't say yes.

At a table near the back of The Violet Hour, the blond woman who'd just taken the seat next to Ford had a question for them. She was at the bar with her girlfriends as part of a bachelorette party, and they wanted to invite Ford and his friends to join them for a round of drinks. The blonde had pointed out the table where her girlfriends sat, and the group had waved back enthusiastically—ten or so women, all dressed up and each one looking cuter than the next in their Friday-night outfits.

Needless to say, Charlie and Tucker were *in*.

Ford, however, had his eye elsewhere. A short while ago, he'd caught sight of the brunette sitting across the bar, the one who had her long, chestnut hair pulled back into one of those sexy high ponytails. She wore dark jeans, killer red heels, and a loose-fitting red top that dipped down on one of her shoulders, exposing bare skin.

A few minutes ago she'd launched into a speech, speaking passionately about something to her two girlfriends. The investigative journalist in him had been intrigued, wondering what it was that had her so fired up.

And he was also intrigued by that bare shoulder. Where was the bra strap? *Was* there even a bra?

Inquiring minds wanted to know.

Then she'd glanced his way and held his gaze when she'd caught him watching her. A few moments later, she'd looked again.

He'd been contemplating his next move when the blonde from the bachelorette party unexpectedly sat down next to him, and the brunette in the red heels hadn't looked at him since.

Crap.

"We'd love to join you for a drink," Charlie said enthusiastically, answering the blonde on behalf of the three of them.

"Hell yes, we would," Tucker concurred wholeheartedly.

"Great! I'll let everyone know you're coming," said the blonde, before rejoining her friends.

Tucker watched as she walked back to the table of women, and then spun around in his chair to face Ford and Charlie. "Bachelorette party—*sweet*." He did a fist pump.

"Very subtle, Tuck," Ford said.

"I can't believe you hesitated," Charlie said to Ford. "Dude. If someone asks if you want to join a bachelorette party, you say *yes*."

Tucker leaned in. "I bet they dared the blonde to come over and talk to us. They do things like that at bachelorette parties, you know. Games. *Dares*. Like . . . someone has to buy a guy a drink, or convince him to give her his underwear."

He paused.

"Trying to remember what underwear you put on this morning?" Ford asked.

"Trying to remember *if* I put on underwear this morning." Tucker grinned slyly. "I guess one of you boys will have to field that one."

"And . . . that just shot to the top of the list of things I did *not* need to know tonight." Charlie polished off his drink and set it down. Then he turned to Ford. "You ready?"

Ford's eyes flickered back to the brunette in the red heels. "Why don't you guys go ahead? I'll settle up the check and join you in a bit."

Maybe.

Charlie stared at him, flabbergasted. "What has gotten into you? There are ten women over there whose collective goal tonight is to get wild and crazy as they celebrate the beauty and power of being female."

"Ooh . . . the redhead in the black dress just licked a lollipop shaped like a penis. Seriously, why are we still sitting here?" Tucker followed Ford's gaze, spotted the brunette in the red heels, and grinned. "Ah, another hen in the henhouse."

Ford watched as the brunette laughed and shook her head at something one of her friends said. Then his eyes roamed lower, liking the way those skinny jeans fit her curves.

"So . . . you appear to be set here," Charlie said teasingly. "I guess Tuck and I will see you later, then."

Just then, the brunette and her two friends stood up from the table and made their way to the front door.

Sitting in the back of the bar, Ford felt a flicker of disappointment as he watched her leave.

Tucker commiserated with a shrug. "Well, you win some, you lose some."

"Or in Tuck's case, you lose some, and then you lose some more," Charlie said.

Tucker shot Charlie a glare, and then pointed to the table of women who'd invited them over. "On the bright side: bachelorette party."

Ford considered this. Having been friends with Charlie and Tucker since their freshman year of college, he suspected this fascination with the bachelorette party was, in some part, their attempt to distract him and have fun after everything that had happened with his father last week. And, seeing how he was more than happy to *be* distracted, he settled up their tab and followed his friends over to the table of women, who cheered at their arrival.

There definitely were worse ways to spend a Friday night.

Four

VICTORIA GOT BACK to her loft shortly after ten o'clock that night. Deliberately ignoring the remaining unpacked boxes—she would deal with them later—she headed straight to her bedroom. After stripping out of her bar clothes, she changed into shorts and a T-shirt and practically rubbed her hands with glee as she eyed her bed.

She couldn't wait to crawl in.

She made quick work of brushing her teeth and scrubbing off her makeup. Out of habit, she grabbed her e-reader as she climbed into bed. In her old place, to deal with her insomnia, she'd often distracted herself from listening for strange noises by reading. But tonight, she felt safer in the smaller space of her loft, protected not only by the alarm system for her unit, but also by the security of the building in general. There was an upside to being surrounded by neighbors—with all the people in the building awake on a Friday night, it made an extremely unappealing target for anyone on the outside.

With that in mind, she set the e-reader on her nightstand, next to her trusty phone. She turned off the lamp and pulled up the covers, feeling more relaxed and comfortable in bed than she had in a month. As exhausted as she was, she could probably sleep right through to Sunday.

She drifted off with a smile, thinking that would be just fine.

A DOOR SLAMMED shut.

Victoria shot up in bed when she heard footsteps on hardwood floors. Disoriented by the relatively unfamiliar surroundings, it took her a moment to remember that she was in her new place, the loft. She heard muffled voices, several of them, and instinctively reached for her phone.

Then she realized the sound wasn't coming from inside her place, but rather through her bedroom wall, the wall she shared with the unit next to hers.

She flopped back down onto the bed and exhaled in relief.

The footsteps on the hardwood floors sounded like high heels, several pairs of them, and she could hear both men and women talking and laughing. She hadn't met her next-door neighbor yet—someone named "F. Dixon" according to the mailbox next to hers in the lobby—but from the sound of things, he or she was having a late-night get-together.

As if on cue, the acoustic guitar intro of Peter Gabriel's "Solsbury Hill" began to play, and a woman—who sounded more than a little tipsy—yelled out, "I LOVE this song!"

Victoria covered her head with a pillow and tried not to weep.

It wasn't that the music was overly loud. And, admittedly, the voices were muted; presumably F. Dixon and Co. were hanging out in the living area of his/her loft—which, yes, they were perfectly entitled to do. But it was two A.M., and Victoria had just been in the middle of the longest stretch of sleep she'd had in a month.

"Who wants a penis pop?" someone shouted.

And . . . that was her cue to take her leave.

She had no clue what a "penis pop" was—although it sounded kinky and quite possibly a little painful for all parties involved—but these were not things she needed to be musing over at two A. M. With a huge sigh of annoyance (not that the people next door could hear her given all their damn racket), she grabbed her pillow (yes, she was fussy and couldn't sleep without her special pillow) and dragged herself out to the living room. She flopped onto the couch and tried to get comfortable.

Then tried some more.

Granted, when she'd bought the couch, she'd been going for style. Silly her, to not have presumed that one night she'd need the Edwardian-era sofa with its low-rolled arms and arched back for a campout in her living room because her neighbor would be throwing a raucous late-night sex soiree complete with penis pops.

She tossed the sofa's too many damn throw pillows to the floor in frustration.

Then she got up and grabbed her iPad to Google "penis pop" because, seriously, what *was* that?

Ah . . . *lollipops*. Got it.

After tossing and turning for nearly an hour on the couch, she heard a door shut, and then several voices out in the hall-way. When the voices faded, she got up to check on the situation in her bedroom.

Silence.

Thank God. With a spring in her step, she quickly grabbed her pillow from the living area and crawled back into bed. She snuggled in under the covers and had just begun to doze off when she heard a woman laugh.

Victoria's eyes opened.

Next she heard a man's deep voice—his words muffled—followed by the sound of something bumping against the other side of the wall. A headboard.

The woman moaned.

Oh . . . that was just *great*.

Not needing to hear any more, with an angry huff, Victoria carted her special pillow back into the living room, flopped onto the couch, and hunkered down for a long night.

* * *

EARLY THE FOLLOWING morning, grumpy and bleary-eyed after a less-than-ideal night spent sleeping on her sofa, she went on a quest in her new neighborhood for some much-needed coffee.

Fortunately, she didn't need to walk far. Just around the corner from her place she found a café called The Wormhole that looked promising enough. She opened the door and blinked in surprise when she saw all the 1980s movie posters on the walls, as well as an actual DeLorean—yes, the car from *Back to the Future*—parked on the loft upstairs.

Wow. It was safe to say they took their '80s seriously in these parts.

Charmed by the kitsch of the place, she ordered a large coffee and grabbed a seat at the table underneath the *Raiders of the Lost Ark* poster. She checked the morning news and her e-mail on her phone, in no rush to get back to her place.

So, her first night in her new loft hadn't gone exactly as planned. Granted, she'd probably cobbled together around six hours of sleep, which was more than any other night this past month. But she hoped that last night had been an aberration, and not a sign of what she could expect from her neighbor in unit 4F during the course of this summer.

If not, she and this "F. Dixon" person were going to have some serious words.

Fueled by caffeine, she left The Wormhole and headed back to her place. After riding the elevator up to the fourth floor, she got halfway down the hallway when the door to the condo next to hers opened.

Ooh . . . the mysterious F. Dixon, she presumed.

A thirtysomething woman with shoulder-length brown hair stepped out, wearing a black skirt, sleeveless aqua top, and black strappy heels.

Fiona Dixon? Faith Dixon? Victoria silently mused over the possibilities. Eager to establish a good rapport with the person with whom she would be sharing a bedroom wall for the next three months, she smiled as she approached.

"Hi there. I'm Victoria—your new neighbor." She gestured to her own front door. "I just moved in yesterday."

"Um, hi." Looking flustered, the woman in the aqua shirt blushed. "Actually, I don't live here. But hey—congrats on moving in."

Victoria chuckled as they passed each other in the hallway. "Thanks." Feeling a little awkward—*Note to self: don't ambush innocent bystanders in the hallway*—she grabbed her keys out of her purse. When she got to her front door, she looked up and caught the woman glancing over her shoulder, at F. Dixon's place.

The woman smiled, looking decidedly pleased.

Ah, understood. Victoria had the feeling, from the looks of that smile, that someone had just spent a very enjoyable night with the owner of unit 4F, presumably the man with the deep voice.

After the woman in the aqua shirt got on the elevator, Victoria contemplated knocking on F. Dixon's door to introduce herself. But then she decided it would be a little strange to drop by right after his overnight guest had left. So instead, she unlocked the door to her own loft and put her caffeine-fueled energy to good use by tackling the remaining unpacked boxes.

That took her all the way until lunchtime, when she broke to grab a quick sandwich at a deli down the block. When she got back to her loft, she took a look around for any unpacked boxes that she'd missed, and then happened to notice how quiet the place was right then.

A slow smile crept across her face.

Kicking off her sandals, she armed the security system for her unit and headed into the bedroom. She drew the shades and climbed into bed, feeling rather decadent to be napping on a Saturday afternoon. Undoubtedly, she had plenty of work she should be focused on—her firm would hardly run itself—but after the night, and month, she'd had, she figured she'd earned a little siesta.

She fell asleep almost the instant her head hit the pillow. A wonderful, deep sleep.

That is, until she was woken by the sound of someone *sawing* through her bedroom wall.

What. The. Hell?

Victoria opened her eyes, expecting to find dust and drywall falling all around her. She rolled over in bed and stared at her wall. On the upside, no one was actually coming through it. But from the sound of things, for some inexplicable reason, the owner of unit 4F had chosen this moment—during her much-needed nap—to saw a hole into his side of the wall.

Of course he had.

Things went silent for a few moments, and then Victoria heard the whirring of an electric drill and someone whistling. She sighed and muttered a few curse words—not that he could hear her, again, over all the noise.

So far, F. Dixon was turning out to be a real pain in the ass.

Five

FORD SMILED WHEN he opened his front door and saw the woman standing before him. "You're early. Sorry, the place is little messy."

Brooke Parker, his closest friend since fourth grade, walked in. She looked around, taking in the spare piece of drywall, paint bucket and brushes, and various tools he had spread out around the living room and kitchen area, which he was currently using as a workspace. "Wow. What's going on here?" She stepped over two large boxes that contained the factory-style oak-and-steel shelves he'd picked up this morning.

"Fixing a hole in my bedroom wall. Then I decided to put up a few bookshelves. Beer?" he offered.

"Sure."

He headed into the kitchen, opened the refrigerator, and grabbed a bottle for each of them.

Brooke used a bottle opener to open her beer. "A hole in your bedroom wall, huh? How did that happen?"

"I, uh . . . sort of threw a candle holder at it the other day."

"Ah." She took a sip of her beer and then checked out the

boxes stacked on his kitchen island. "And the . . . Campaign Faucet set in brushed nickel?" she asked, reading the label.

He shrugged. "Thought I'd update the fixtures in the powder room while I was at it. Maybe put in a new vanity, too." When she raised an eyebrow—fine, maybe he had gone a little overboard in Restoration Hardware today—he changed the subject. "What's Morgan up to tonight?"

Looking every inch the happy newlywed right then, she smiled at the mention of her husband, Cade Morgan. "He's out shopping for crampons with Vaughn and Huxley."

"Sounds intimate."

Chuckling, she took a seat in one of the barstools in front of the granite island. "It's for their Mount Rainier climb. I told you they're doing that next month, right?"

"You've mentioned it." Several times, actually.

"I was thinking about flying out to surprise him after he finishes the climb. Hopefully get a photo of him in all his mountain gear." Brooke cocked her head when she saw him fighting back a grin. "What?"

"It's cute, seeing you with your smitten, my-husband-is-so-hot-he-even-climbs-mountains glow."

"Well, my husband *is* hot. But don't ever tell him I said that. Because that man's ego is already healthy enough." She frowned, reached underneath her leg, and pulled out a purple, penis-shaped lollipop. Two inches long, and curved upward in a semierect state, it was a surprisingly realistic rendition, complete with veins and two testicles.

"Interesting," Brooke said, looking amused.

"Don't ask," Ford grunted. Those damn lollipops kept popping up everywhere—that was the third one he'd found in his loft today.

Holding it by the stick, Brooke wagged the purple penis pop in front of him. "Yeah . . . there's a zero percent chance I'm *not* going to ask about this, so you might as well start talking."

"The short version is that I ended up entertaining a bachelorette party last night."

The corners of her mouth twitched. "Are you moonlighting as a stripper now?"

Ford threw her a look. *Cute.* Well aware that the quips and running commentary wouldn't end unless his friend got the information she wanted, he proceeded to tell her about last night.

Tuck, Charlie, and he had hung out at The Violet Hour with the bachelorette group until nearly closing time, when someone—and by "someone" he meant Tuck, who clearly had been trying to buy more time with the redhead—had the bright idea that they should continue the party at Ford's place, since he lived right around the corner. And although Ford had come to the conclusion, somewhere around midnight and his third drink, that at age thirty-four he was probably a little too old for these kind of "Bachelorette party—whoo-hoo!" antics, he'd gone along with the plan for Charlie's and Tuck's sakes.

Big mistake.

When they got back to his loft, one of the women, a brunette named Charlotte, made it abundantly clear she was into him. Actually, if anything, she came on a little *too* strong, breaking out the dirty talk in his kitchen while everyone else was partying in the living room. Nevertheless, when she stuck around after the others left, stripped off her top and skirt, and headed for his bedroom, wearing nothing but a thong, high heels, and a coy smile, he'd followed without thinking much about it.

Hey, he was a single guy. Of *course* he'd followed the woman wearing nothing but a thong and high heels into his bedroom.

But when they got there and began fooling around, something felt off. Yeah, his body was responding in a physical sense, and, no doubt, some part of him kept thinking, *Hey, asshole, you have a dirty-talking, half-naked woman in your bed—what's the damn hang-up?* But mentally he just . . . wasn't completely into it.

He was hardly a saint when it came to sex. He'd always had an easy time getting along with women, probably the product of having a female best friend, a sister, and a mother he respected the hell out of. He *liked* women, enjoyed talking with them, flirting with them, charming them, and yes, sleeping with them. He hadn't had a lot of luck with long-term relationships—and, admittedly, he rather enjoyed the alternative—but he never lied, he never cheated, and he was always careful to make sure no one got hurt.

And he'd never used anyone for sex.

But he realized in that moment, as he and Charlotte fell onto the bed and his eye caught sight of that stupid hole in his wall, that most of the evening he'd been going through the motions, trying to let his friends, and the bachelorette party, and alcohol distract him so that he wasn't just sitting at home thinking about the regrets he had about his dad. And while he didn't need some deep, emotional reason to have sex—hell, sex was fun, who needed more reason than that?— he also prided himself on not ever having sex for a *bad* reason. Like sleeping with a woman he wasn't even into just because he could.

So with that in mind, he'd told Charlotte that he thought they should slow things down.

This . . . did not exactly go over well.

She was surprised at first, and then her eyes filled with tears as she began pouring out her story to him. How this was her first night out since breaking up with her boyfriend, whom she'd been with for six years. How he'd panicked about getting married and had dumped her, which had totally wrecked her self-confidence, and so tonight she'd wanted to do something fun and wild, like picking up the hottest guy in the bar so she could say *screw you* to her ex and feel back in the game again.

Naturally, Ford had felt like shit after hearing her story. So to compensate, he drew on the primary thing he'd learned while being best friends with a woman for over twenty years.

He'd simply listened while Charlotte talked.

Somewhere along the way, she began asking for his opinion, as a guy, about the situation with her ex. Thinking this was a great way to keep them in the friend zone and ease over the earlier awkwardness, he stayed up for two hours chatting with her, and then covered her up with a blanket after she passed out on his couch. In the morning, he woke up to hear her rustling around in the living room. Embarrassed, she immediately apologized for falling asleep, so to be a nice guy, he made her a cup of coffee and acted like this kind of thing happened all the time. And when she cheered up after that and asked if he'd like to get together sometime for drinks and talk more, in order to not hurt her feelings, he'd said sure.

This was the part of the story when Brooke interrupted by thunking him—literally *thunking* him—on his head.

"You just said you aren't even into this girl," she said incredulously.

They'd moved out onto the deck while Ford had been telling her all about his adventures the previous night. Leaning against the brick ledge, he rubbed his head. "First, *ouch*. Second, just because I'm not into her doesn't mean I have to be a dick."

"I guarantee she left your place this morning thinking you're interested in her."

He waved this off. "No way. After I said we should slow down, we just hung out and talked. You know, like you and I do."

She rolled her eyes. "You men can be such boneheads about these things. She doesn't know you the way I do. She's vulnerable right now. Her ex turned out to be an asshole and then you come riding in—"

"There was no riding."

"—being the good guy, looking the way you do"—Brooke gestured to him—"wanting to talk and slow things down and be all sensitive with your coffee and your little blanket. What woman could resist that? My God, why didn't you just cuddle a puppy shirtless while you were at it?"

He mentally filed away that seduction technique for future reference. "So, you're saying I was supposed to just toss the crying, heartbroken woman out of my condo in the middle of the night?"

"Of course not. That would've made you an asshole."

Ford considered this for a moment. "So, from the female perspective, basically anything I could've done last night to get myself out of an awkward situation would've resulted in me being either a bonehead or an asshole."

She smiled, patting him on the shoulder. "Now you're catching on."

"You know, Parker, these male-female heart-to-hearts of ours are just so helpful."

She laughed. "Somebody has to keep you in your place. You're too charming for your own good."

She ruffled his hair, and a comfortable silence fell between them as they leaned against the brick wall, sipped their beers, and looked out at the view of the Chicago skyline.

Then she looked sideways at him. "About all these home improvement projects of yours . . . how long are we going to pretend this isn't some male angsty excuse for you to bang on things and work out your grief and frustration?"

"Probably when I'm done remodeling the kitchen."

She half-smiled at the joke, but then the look in her eyes turned serious. "I'm here anytime you want to talk. I love you, you know."

He put his arm around her shoulders and pulled her in close. "I know." When he and Brooke were kids and his dad was in one of his foul moods, he used to hang out at her house whenever he'd needed a break. During those times, he hadn't said much about the situation with his dad—talking about feelings was hardly his forte—and he didn't say anything further right then, either.

After a few moments she broke the silence in typical Brooke fashion. "So, about this sex problem you're having . . ."

Seriously.

"There is no sex problem," he growled, fully aware that she was teasing him in order to lighten the mood. But still. "Just the wrong girl at the wrong time." He cocked his head, suddenly remembering something. "But you should've seen this brunette in red heels that was also at the bar last night. She was . . . something." He grinned. "With a girl like that, there would never be a wrong time."

"Aw, it's cute, seeing you with your smitten, I-just-saw-the-most-beautiful-girl-across-a-crowded-bar glow," Brooke said.

He brushed off her teasing. "I don't do smitten." That kind of vulnerability and willingness to put himself out there to be rejected by someone . . . well, that was something he'd never been able to do. Never had any desire to do. Instead, he kept things light and casual in his relationships, never getting too close to anyone, always just having fun.

And his entire adult life, he hadn't seen anything that had made him want to handle things any differently.

VICTORIA FLIPPED THROUGH her mail as she rode up the elevator to the fourth floor. Seeing how her plans for an afternoon siesta had been interrupted by the ubiquitous Mr. F. Dixon and his saw and drill, she'd gone out for a walk in her new neighborhood. She had a quiet evening planned—assuming a certain someone didn't have any more drywall to tear down or raucous penis-pop parties planned—and figured she'd order pizza and veg out on the couch with a movie.

Once inside her loft, she tossed out the junk mail and set the rest on her kitchen counter. She'd just pulled out her phone to look up Piece Brewery and Pizzeria, a restaurant she'd discovered during her walk that seemed promising, when she heard a man's voice out on her balcony.

She froze at the sound, her heart pounding, until she saw through the sliding glass doors that her balcony was clear.

Right. The man's voice wasn't coming from *her* balcony, but the one next door.

She exhaled—holy crap, that had freaked her out—and then realized something. If the man's voice was coming from the balcony next door . . .

It had to be F. Dixon.

Between her run-in with the woman who'd left his place this morning with a satisfied smile, and the way he kept intruding into her space in the less than forty-eight hours she'd lived in the building, she was a little curious to get a look at the guy.

Okay, maybe a lot curious.

She tiptoed to the sliding doors of her balcony—before realizing that was a touch overdramatic since he couldn't hear her, anyway—and peered through the glass.

Not seeing anything at first, she had to readjust her position to get a better angle. Then she spotted him on the balcony next to hers: a tall man wearing a baseball cap. He leaned against the ledge with his back to her, and even when he angled to the side he had the baseball cap pulled down too low for her to see much of his face.

But what she *could* see was that he wasn't alone.

A woman with long, blond hair stood side by side with him on the balcony. She held a bottled beer in her hand, and looked at F. Dixon with a serious expression. From their body language, there was no mistaking the fact that the two of them were close.

Victoria couldn't help but wonder if the blonde had any clue about the brunette who'd just spent the night at his place.

"I love you, you know," the blonde said to him.

Victoria would take that as a no.

She couldn't make out his response, but, really, it didn't matter. After eight years of being a divorce lawyer, she knew his type—men who wanted to have their cake and eat it, too, when it came to women. They led women on, they lied, they cheated, and in the end, people got hurt.

Sometimes really hurt.

Are you still there, Victoria? Help is coming, I promise.

Shoving the memory aside, she tried not to gag as F. Dixon put his arm around the blonde's shoulders and pulled her in close. Aw, wasn't he so sweet and affectionate? Why, he looked so *caring*, one would never guess that just last night, he'd had another woman in his bed.

The jerk.

Thinking that she'd seen enough of her neighbor for one day, she stepped away from the sliding glass doors and headed back into her kitchen to order that pizza.

Six

AMAZINGLY, OVER THE next four days, the ubiquitous
F. Dixon actually allowed Victoria to get some sleep.

How gracious of him.

Oh, sure, there were minor annoyances. Like his nighttime
routine. From the low din of television she could hear through
her bedroom wall, he liked to watch the news at night, followed by sports. At least, she assumed these were sporting
events he was watching, judging from the shouts of *Yes!* and
Aw, come ON! and *What the hell was that?* that permeated her
wall while she tried to read a book in bed.

Either that, or F. Dixon had a strangely critical way of dirty
talking.

The sounds coming from his bedroom weren't overly loud,
and they always ended by eleven thirty P.M., when she went
to sleep. And, yes, she knew that neighbor noise was simply
part of condo living. Still, reading in bed was her way of
relaxing at the end of a busy day, often the only peaceful thirty
minutes she ever got. So, rightfully or wrongfully, this nighttime routine between her and F. Dixon just . . . irked her.

Normally, there'd be an easy solution: she could buy a

white-noise machine. But that was out of the question after the break-in at her townhome. She felt safer in her new place, but nevertheless, she didn't want to do anything that would impair her ability to hear strange sounds at night.

So for now, she supposed she would have to grin and bear it.

Or at least, frown, mutter sarcastically under her breath, and bear it.

On the upside, she was now clocking in a luscious *seven* hours of sleep per night, and holy crap did it ever feel good. She felt more energized, more like herself than she had in over a month. So much so, in fact, that she'd begun to wonder whether she needed to continue her therapy sessions with Dr. Metzel. True, she still wasn't riding the subway or attending her exercise class, but in the grand scheme of things, weren't these minor inconveniences? Mankind had, after all, invented taxis for a reason. And, really, who needed to exercise indoors when one lived in a city where the weather was nice . . . at least twenty days out of every year?

Denial ain't just a river in Egypt, girlfriend.

Great. Suddenly her subconscious was a psychotherapist, too. And kind of a little sassy.

Victoria mulled over these thoughts while walking back to the office after court Friday morning. From the looks of things in the lobby, someone in her building was hosting a workshop or some kind of conference, because there were nearly thirty people milling around the elevator bank wearing nametags. Not thinking much about it, when the elevator arrived and one of the men in the group gestured politely in her direction—*After you*—she stepped into the elevator and moved to the back.

And then about fifteen people crammed in after her.

When the doors closed, and the elevator began to rise, she began to feel uncomfortable with all the people pressed against her. Maybe she was imagining it, but the air in the elevator suddenly felt stuffy and warm. She was essentially trapped—a realization that made her heart beat faster.

Just stay calm, she told herself. This sudden onset of anxiety was all in her head. She knew that.

Or was it?

After all, she'd blacked out just a month ago in circumstances a lot like this. What if that happened again? What if she felt light-headed and needed to get off the elevator and nobody moved out of her way and everyone stared as she . . .

She took a deep breath and exhaled. As people chatted around her, she stared up at the floor indicator, counting down the seconds until she was free. Her mouth was dry, she felt hot and flushed, and her heart was pounding, but she could do this, she was going to make it—*thirty, thirty-one, thirty-two*—

The doors sprang open at the thirty-third floor.

"Coming out!" she said, a tad too vehemently. To cover, she smiled as she slid past the other passengers—*Nothing to see here*—trying to appear normal and casual as she hurried out.

Then she stood in front of the glass doors marked Victoria Slade & Associates, and exhaled as the elevator doors slid closed behind her.

"Hey, you."

She jumped at the sound of the voice, and saw Will waiting for an elevator heading down. "Hi." Her voice sounded unnaturally bright.

Will cocked his head. "Are you okay?"

"Yes. Sure." She realized she was sweating a little under her suit jacket. *Lovely.* "I, uh . . . was in a rush walking back from court. I have that conference call at eleven, right? Didn't want to miss it."

"The call is at eleven thirty."

Dammit. For once, couldn't the man *not* be so organized and on top of her schedule?

"Right. Eleven thirty," she said. "Well. Guess I didn't need to rush, after all, heh, heh."

The chuckle was probably overkill.

Luckily, Will's elevator arrived, so with a casual wave she headed through the glass doors, nodded hello at the receptionist, and strode down the hallway to her corner office. She smiled as she passed by her associates' offices, deliberately exuding confidence—*yes, I am still your fearless leader; no, I did not just freak out trying to ride a stupid elevator*—and

then she shut the door when she got to her office and sank
down into her desk chair.

After that experience, it looked like she'd be spending
tomorrow afternoon with the good doctor, after all.

KNOCK, KNOCK.

The noise, coming from the front door, immediately woke
Victoria. She sat up in bed and quickly got her bearings.
According to the clock, it was nearly one A.M. Who the heck
was knocking at her door?

When she couldn't come up with an answer, her heart
began to beat faster.

Dangerous intruders don't knock, she reassured herself.
Unless . . . what if this was some kind of trick to see if she
was home, and maybe if she didn't answer the door, whoever
was outside would break in to steal stuff?

Another knock.

Victoria hopped out of bed, scooped her phone off the
nightstand, and shoved it into the pocket of her pajama pants.
Then she grabbed the baseball bat she kept underneath her
bed and carried it with two hands into the living room, feeling a rush of both fear and adrenaline. *The hell with this.* This
was *her* place and she was sick of weird stuff happening at
night and she was not going to end up trapped and helpless
in a goddamn closet this time.

The hallway outside was lit, and she saw a shadow move
in the light filtering in underneath her front door. *On second
thought* . . . She pulled the cell phone out of her pocket, keyed
in 9-1-1, and positioned her thumb to hit send. With the bat
still in her right hand, she crept carefully to the front door
and peeked through the peephole.

A woman stood outside.

Victoria exhaled in relief. Upon closer examination, she
realized it was the brunette she'd seen coming out of F. Dixon's
apartment last Saturday morning. The woman raised her hand,
as if to knock on the door again, then paused and bit her lip.

Instinct took over. Thinking perhaps the woman needed some kind of help, Victoria deactivated her security alarm. She set the baseball bat against the wall, and opened her door.

The other woman was dressed for a night out in a black top, skirt, and heels. She teetered slightly and blinked when she saw Victoria. "Wait, I know you. You're his neighbor. Are you two hooking up already?" She paused, and her eyes widened in realization. "Oh my God, you're the *neighbor*. I knocked on the wrong door, didn't I? Crap, I'm so sorry. I was looking for Ford."

Ford.

The mysterious F. Dixon finally had a first name.

The brunette continued to apologize and explain, her words slightly slurred. "I thought I would surprise him . . . Last week we talked about getting together again, so I was out with my friends and thought, 'What the hell?'" She paused, and then gave Victoria an embarrassed smile. "You know, I was a lot better at this kind of thing in my twenties." She got a little teary-eyed, and cleared her throat. "Well. I should let you get back to sleep. Sorry again." She looked unsure which direction to head in as she turned first left, then right.

Victoria pointed. "He's that way," she said, not unkindly. Yes, it was one o'clock in the morning and this woman had woken her up and scared the hell out of her, but still. She looked a bit . . . lost.

"Thanks." The other woman smiled appreciatively, and then headed down the hallway in the direction of unit 4F.

Victoria closed her door, but not all the way. Because, naturally, she planned to eavesdrop.

She heard a knock, and after a few moments of silence, there was the sound of a door opening.

A deep voice, gravelly with sleep. "Charlotte . . . wow, hey. I wasn't expecting you."

Victoria wondered if he had the blonde cozily stashed in his place at this very moment, or perhaps yet another, heretofore unseen woman—since he seemed to have them coming out of the woodwork.

If so, somebody was going to have some 'splaining to do.

She tilted her ear toward the crack she'd left open in her doorway, trying to hear whatever the brunette was saying.

No dice.

Enunciate, people—if you're going to wake me up in the middle of the night, at least make sure I can hear the darn show.

"It's okay. Come on in," Ford said.

A few seconds later, Victoria heard the click of a lock. The hallway now silent, she closed her own door and reactivated the alarm. She went back into her room and glanced at the wall she shared with Ford Dixon as she climbed into bed.

Seriously, the man should just get a revolving front door and spare everyone a lot of trouble.

THE NEXT MORNING, Victoria dragged herself into the shower and yawned underneath the spray. After last night's unexpected visitor, it had taken her a long time to fall back asleep. She'd gotten out of bed twice, the first time because she couldn't remember if she'd armed the alarm, and then twenty minutes later, when she'd realized she'd left the base-ball bat by the front door.

Coffee was definitely in order.

She had a few hours to kill before the dreaded appointment with Dr. Metzel, so she decided to catch up on some work at The Wormhole coffee shop. She grabbed her laptop and stuffed it into the tote bag she used on weekends, then grabbed her keys.

She opened her front door and nearly barreled right into a man's broad chest.

"Oh!" Startled, she looked up and found herself staring into a pair of piercing light blue eyes. Eyes that belonged to a man who had his hand raised, as if about to knock on her door.

Victoria blinked.

It was *him*.

The hot guy from the bar last Friday, the one Rachel had made up the backstory about, the one with whom Victoria had been exchanging looks until the blond woman with short hair sat down next to him.

He was here. On her doorstep.

"It's you," he said, breaking into a smile.

And when he smiled like that, the strangest thing happened to Victoria. Even though she was cynical and jaded, even though she didn't believe in "the one" or soul mates or any of that kind of crap, for a split second her heart did this little skipping thing when she thought—oh my gosh—he *had* felt something that night in the bar and he'd tracked her down so they could meet, like something out of a romantic comedy movie.

"And it's you." Impossibly, the guy was even more attractive in the daytime. Those *eyes*. She cocked her head. "What are you doing here?"

He chuckled, a warm, rich sound. "This is the craziest thing. I'm Ford." When she blinked, not getting it at first—*Ford, Ford*, why did that seem like a name she was supposed to know?—he pointed in the direction of unit 4F. "Your next-door neighbor."

Oh . . . *right*.

Ford.

The ubiquitous, womanizing, saw-wielding, TV-yelling Mr. F. Dixon.

Ah, yes. Fate, that sneaky little trickster, was undoubtedly giggling proudly over this one.

Victoria peered across her doorstep at the man who, in the span of eight days, had given her sexy looks at the bar while talking to another woman, spent the night with Charlotte the Brunette just hours later—and possibly last night, too—and had a *fourth* woman, the blonde on his balcony, tell him that she loved him. All while merrily sawing through his drywall during her nap and throwing late-night soirees with penis pops.

She rested her hand on the doorjamb. "Seems like you've had a busy week, Mr. Dixon."

Seven

IT REALLY WAS the craziest thing.

His new next-door neighbor, the woman renting Owen's loft, was none other than the brunette in red heels that he'd seen last Friday at The Violet Hour. Currently there were no actual red heels—not that he had any objections to this weekend-casual look she had going on. Wearing a cotton zip-up and black yoga pants that made her legs seem as long as sin, she had her long, glossy, chestnut-brown hair pulled back in a ponytail.

He assumed the comment about his busy week had something to do with Charlotte's surprise drop-in last night. And, as it happened, that was the reason he'd come by. To apologize. "The woman who showed up at my place last night said she knocked on your door by mistake. I'm really sorry about that. I had no idea she planned to come over." He flashed her a playful grin. "Any chance you were still awake at the time, so I can feel like less of a jerk here?"

Her eyes were a warm chocolate brown, framed by thick lashes. "Dead asleep."

Damn.

"Ah. Well, I promise that won't happen again." Last night, he'd had a nice but honest conversation with Charlotte in which he'd made it clear that they were not looking for the same thing. She'd apologized for dropping by uninvited, and had sheepishly joked about feeling like she was in college again, using alcohol to make her bolder when it came to men and inevitably making the wrong decisions. And Ford got that—she certainly wasn't the first person to make a bad decision while drinking. But seeing how that definitely wasn't a situation he wanted to get dragged deeper into, he'd called her a cab, waited with her downstairs to make sure she got in safely, and wished her well when he'd said good-bye.

Figuring the less said about that awkward topic, the better, he focused instead on the woman standing in front of him— the very cute and seemingly single woman with whom he shared a bedroom wall. He held out his hand to make the introduction official. "Your name is Victoria, right? I hear you're a divorce lawyer."

She nodded as she slid her hand into his. "I run a family law firm here in the city."

Interesting—her own firm. He knew her last name was Slade from the mailbox next to his, so he made a mental note to Google her later. "Let me guess. You're off to squeeze in some work right now." He pointed to her laptop bag and winked. "I have several friends who are lawyers, so I know the drill. You guys are always working."

"Actually, I *was* just heading out to do some work." She stepped into the hallway, putting them very close to one another as she turned and locked her front door.

"So how do you like the building so far?" Ford asked conversationally.

She turned to face him once again. "Oh, like any place, it has its positives and negatives."

Perhaps he was reading her wrong, but he got the distinct impression from her pointed look that she was including *him* in this assessment.

So . . . he was one of the "positives," was he?

Suddenly, he had a feeling that Victoria the Divorce

Lawyer or Something was going to be a *great* addition to the building.

He stepped a little closer, his tone teasing. "If you're on the fence, you obviously haven't seen all the building has to offer. I mean, you really haven't lived until you've experienced the wonder that is our common storage room."

That got a slight smile out of her. "I'll keep that in mind."

"Just be sure to watch out for the guy in 4B," he warned.

That caught her attention. "Why? What's wrong with the guy in 4B?"

"He's a *borrower*," Ford whispered. "Pots, vacuum cleaners, stepladders, heck, the guy's even got two patio chairs of mine. And you'll never see it again, except maybe on eBay." He paused, sensing that he had her hooked. "But that's nothing compared to the people in 3A."

She waited. "What's the situation with the people in 3A?"

"Long story. I should probably fill you in over coffee sometime."

It took her a half second, and then she smiled. "Ah . . . I see what you did there. That's pretty clever, sneaking in the coffee invite that way."

He grinned, guilty as charged. "So, is that a yes?"

"No."

Ford waited for the punch line. *Kidding!*

Then he waited some more.

And . . . now this was getting a little awkward.

He cocked his head, seeing no reason not to be direct. "Sorry, but last Friday at the bar, I thought we had a vibe going."

"We did." Her tone was surprisingly pleasant for someone who'd just rejected a guy without a second thought. "But unfortunately, I'm not interested in joining the cavalcade."

"The cavalcade?" No clue what that meant.

"Of women coming in and out of your place."

He smiled, because, well, that was a bit of an exaggeration. Obviously, he needed to clear the air here. "That cavalcade. Look, I'm not sure what you—"

She held up her hand. "Don't get me wrong, I have nothing against casual dating. I'm a big believer in it myself, actually. Between the blonde, the brunette, and the redhead you undoubtedly have on deck for tonight, it looks like you've got a nice arrangement for yourself here. And under different circumstances, I'd probably say, hey, rock on with your frisky self. But as the person who has to share a *wall* with you, these antics with the partying, and the penis pops, and the late-night hookups showing up on your doorstep—and mine—are starting to wear a touch thin. And frankly, it all seems a little . . . juvenile."

Ford blinked.

"But hey—to each his own, right?" With a smile, she gave him a wave in good-bye. "See you around the building, Ford. And thanks for the tip about the guy in 4B."

Without so much as a second glance in his direction, she headed for the stairwell, pushed her way through the door, and disappeared.

Ford stood there, taking a moment to digest the fact that yes, that had just happened. Some perfect stranger who didn't know jack-shit about his personal life had just given him a smug talking-to.

All of a sudden, Victoria the Divorce Lawyer or Something didn't seem like such a great addition to the building, after all.

WANTING TO GET some writing done that morning, he grabbed his messenger bag from his loft and then texted Brooke on his way to the coffee shop. Just yesterday, during dinner, she'd asked what his new neighbor was like. At the time, he hadn't yet had the pleasure of meeting Ms. Victoria Slade, Esquire, but now he could give his friend a full update.

Just met the new neighbor. She SUCKS.

He shoved the phone into his bag, Victoria's speech still ringing in his ears.

Fine. Perhaps bringing the bachelorette party back to his place wasn't something he would do under normal circumstances. Admittedly, he'd been off his game that night, not wanting to be alone. And yes, he did feel a little guilty about the situation with Charlotte. As soon as he'd seen her on his doorstep last night, he'd known that Brooke had been correct, and that he had, indeed, given Charlotte the wrong impression. But in his defense, he'd been *trying* to be a gentleman last weekend and not hurt her feelings. As he'd learned the hard way, having any response other than "Hell, yes" to a woman who strips off her clothes in one's living room was some damn tricky business.

But . . . juvenile?

Hardly.

He got along just fine with women. He'd never had any complaints when it came to dating, at least not in recent years—although, admittedly, he generally kept things superficial enough that there was never much to complain about. And, granted, he was pretty careful about the women he went out with. Either they were like him and not looking for anything serious, or they were women who were in the market for commitment, marriage, and kids, but who were also savvy enough to understand that *he* was the dating equivalent of a layover. A brief, hopefully fun, pit stop on the way to their final destination.

It wasn't that he'd entirely ruled out marriage for himself. Or, at least, living with someone. But he'd learned in his twenties, from his short forays into semi-real relationships, that women expected more than what they got from him on an emotional level. They wanted—probably not unfairly—an openness and trust that he just couldn't deliver.

He'd attended more than one Al-Anon support meeting, and he knew that his so-called difficulty with intimate relationships and trust issues were, at least in part, the product of growing up with an alcoholic parent. And while he supposed it was nice to know that he wasn't alone in his screwed-up-ness, at the end of the day all that self-awareness did was make him more careful not to drag anyone down into a likely dead-end relationship with him.

"You hear yourself, right? You're trying to control your feelings and the feelings of others," Brooke had said one night during their junior year of college when she'd come down to visit him from the University of Chicago. They'd been out at the bars that night, and somehow had gotten into a long conversation about relationships. "That's so common in adult children of alcoholics."

In response, he'd told her exactly where she could stick her Psych 300 analysis.

But, seeing how she was a woman, he'd naturally said it with a lot of charm.

He walked into The Wormhole and smiled at the female barista, determined to put his encounter with Victoria out of mind. "I'll take a twelve-ounce of your darkest roast."

As he waited, he got a text message from his sister. Finally.

Sorry I've been MIA. It's crazy here. Can't do lunch tomorrow b/c I'm teaching a lesson, but we need to talk. Are you around monday?

He texted Nicole back—I should be home from work by 6—then grabbed his coffee and headed to his regular table underneath the *Ghostbusters* poster. Settling in to knock off some work, he pulled out his laptop and read through the file he'd obtained from the Cook County probation department on Darryl Moore.

As he'd suspected, the probation department had completely fallen down on the job—and April Johnson, seventeen-year-old honors student who'd planned to go to Drake University in the fall, had paid the ultimate price. Her killer, who was obligated to report to his probation officer once a month, stopped showing after two meetings. On top of that, probation officers dropped by his home on *nine* occasions, never once finding him there despite the seven P.M. curfew the judge had ordered as part of his sentence. Over the course of the next five months, Darryl Moore managed to get arrested three more times—including for criminal trespass at the high school just a block away from where he shot April Johnson. Yet, according to their records, the probation department knew nothing about any of his arrests.

Not surprising, Ford thought dryly, given the fact that the probation department had wholly failed to maintain any sort of contact with the guy.

So much for the "supervised" part of supervised release.

He made a note to call Moore's former probation officer—a veteran with twenty-eight years on the job—to see if he'd agree to an interview. Then he checked the clock on this laptop and saw that it was nearly time for him to meet Charlie and Tucker at the gym.

As he was packing up his notes and computer, he spotted her. Victoria.

She sat at a table near the back of the coffee shop, underneath the *Goonies* poster, with her cappuccino mug and laptop in front of her as she read through some documents.

He slung the messenger bag over his shoulder, not thrilled to see her leisurely hanging about in *his* coffee shop. He debated whether to simply ignore her and leave, but ultimately decided, since she seemed to be so interested in his personal life, that there was something he would like to say on the matter.

She looked up from her laptop when he stopped at her table. From the flicker of surprise that crossed her face, he gathered she hadn't realized he was in the coffee shop.

"For what it's worth," he said, without preamble, "the blonde is just a friend, and the most intimate thing the brunette and I shared last night was polite conversation before I walked her downstairs to a cab. As for tonight, there's no redhead currently in the lineup, most unfortunately, but given your proclivity for spying, I'm sure you'll be the first to know if that changes."

Victoria threw him a wry look. "I wasn't *spying*. The brunette knocked on my door, and you and the blonde were out on your deck, which happens to be the one next to mine."

"Huh." Ford rubbed his jaw, pretending to consider this. "See, it's funny, because I've been inside your place. Owen and I used to hang out. And if I remember correctly, if you're standing inside, it's not exactly a direct line of sight to my deck. You have to sort of press yourself against the glass door"—he leaned against the table, demonstrating—"and then crane your neck to the side in order to see anything. See that?" He repeated the move. "Press, and then *crane*. Now some people, Ms. Slade, might call that 'spying,' but you're right—it's unfair of me to make that assumption when we don't even know each other. For all I know, you often spend your Saturday evenings just hanging out, smooshed up against your sliding glass door. If you ask me, that sounds a little uncomfortable, but hey—to each her own, right?"

In response to his speech, she said nothing at first. Instead, she took a sip of her cappuccino and then set down the mug. "Point made."

From her begrudging tone, Ford got the distinct impression that Victoria Slade, Esquire, didn't enjoy being proven wrong about anything.

Score one for the juvenile.

"WHAT ARE THE odds?" Victoria paced in front of one of the racks in Rachel's shop. The boutique was only a few blocks away from The Wormhole, so she'd dropped by to tell her friend that the man they'd been ogling last weekend just happened to be her new neighbor.

And to vent.

"You should've seen him with his little press-and-*crane* routine. As if *I* am the person who overstepped boundaries here, when he's the one sawing through walls and has women coming and going at all hours of the night, waking me up and knocking on my door." She caught Rachel's look. "What?"

Standing behind the counter while folding jeans, Rachel appeared amused. "I think the whole thing's hysterical."

"Yes, well, you don't have to live next to the guy."

"We are talking about the same man from the bar, right? Gorgeous, dark hair, a smoldering gaze that promises hours of dirty, mind-blowing sex? Yeah, it's a real hardship having to sleep ten feet from him."

Victoria shot her a wry look as she passed by a dress rack. "You forgot annoying, smug, and— Ooh, I *love* that dress." Her attention temporarily diverted, she checked out a red, polka-dotted, vintage-inspired shirtdress.

"We're flying through that one," Rachel said. "I don't have your size in the store, but we should be getting in more next week. Want me to put one aside for you?"

"Have I ever mentioned how much I love having a best friend who owns a clothing store?" Victoria checked her watch. "Shoot. I have to get going. I have this . . . thing this afternoon." She was deliberately vague, not wanting to get into the whole Dr. Metzel, Girl-You-Have-a-Panic-Disorder saga.

Not that she was embarrassed to tell Rachel and Audrey about the teeny, tiny issues she'd been having ever since the break-in.

Okay, she was a little embarrassed.

Rachel raised an eyebrow, her tone sly. "A go-home-and-pretend-not-to-ogle-your-hot-neighbor thing?"

Ha, ha. "Not happening. Trust me, my press-and-*crane* days are over as far as that man is concerned."

Forty minutes later, Victoria sat in Dr. Metzel's office, in the same leather chair as last week.

"I couldn't help but notice last time that you seemed hesitant when we talked about including psychotherapy as part of our sessions," Dr. Metzel led in, after the obligatory chit-chat part of the appointment was over.

And so it begins.

Now he would want to know why she didn't like psychotherapy, and whether she had any experience with it, which would naturally lead into a discussion about her parents' divorce and the aftermath.

"It's not a process that comes naturally to me," she acknowledged. "Putting all my feelings out there to be dissected and analyzed." Ever since she was ten, she'd been pretty guarded with her emotions. Even when something was wrong, she'd sucked it up and kept her feelings to herself. Frankly, she hadn't had much choice.

"Well, here's the thing, Victoria," Dr. Metzel said. "I want you to be as comfortable as possible during these sessions. So if having your feelings 'dissected'—as you put it—isn't something you're ready for, why don't we table that for now? Today, let's focus instead on some breathing techniques and relaxation exercises that can help the next time you feel a potential panic attack coming on." He smiled. "Sound okay?"

She hadn't expected him to say that. The last time she'd

done therapy, at her mother's insistence, she'd felt pressured to talk even though the whole time she'd wanted nothing more than to move on.

She smiled slightly, exhaling in relief. "Okay."

"Good." Dr. Metzel folded his hands in his lap. "To start, we're going to entirely change the way you've been breathing your whole life."

All right. Now *that* she could handle.

THE NEXT MORNING, as Victoria sat on her bedroom floor, putting on her shoes to go for a jog, she heard a faint beeping sound.

She cocked her head, trying to place the noise. There it was again—coming from the direction of the wall she shared with Ford. She got up and climbed onto her bed, listening.

Beep.

Had the man left his alarm clock on? The beep didn't sound quite that loud, although it would nonetheless be annoying if she had to listen to it all day.

The room fell momentarily quiet, so she pressed her ear up against the wall.

Huh. Nothing.

Suddenly, there was the loud *whir* of an electric drill right at her ear. With a yelp, she leapt off the bed and checked—no holes in her head, always a plus—and then glared at the wall.

Twenty seconds later, she knocked on the door of one Mr. F. Dixon.

After a brief pause, he threw open the door. Wearing a white T-shirt that stretched across his broad chest, jeans, and a tool belt slung low around his lean hips, he looked her over. "Ms. Slade. What a pleasant surprise."

In response to his dry tone, she gave him an ultra-sweet smile. "I was hoping we could have a conversation about your home improvement projects. As in, how long you expect them to last."

"Sure, we can have a conversation about that." He lifted the bottom of his T-shirt to wipe sweat off his brow, revealing—*hello*—a six-pack of perfectly sculpted abs. "As long as we can also have a conversation about your hair-drying routine."

She put a hand on her hip. "What's wrong with my hair-drying routine?"

"You mean, other than the fact that it wakes me up at the crack of dawn every weekday morning and goes on forever?"

Please. "Six thirty A.M. is not that early on a weekday." She considered this, looking him over. "You do have some sort of actual job, I take it?"

He grinned lazily, drawling, "Nah, no time, Ms. Slade. Not with the cavalcade to entertain."

All right, so somebody had his boxer-briefs in a bunch over the "cavalcade" comment. "Look, maybe I was wrong in my assumptions about the blonde. But the brunette? I ran into her in the hallway that morning after she left your place. It seemed pretty obvious that she liked you."

Something flickered in Ford's eyes—guilt, perhaps? Then it was gone, and he cocked his head. "How long did you say you'll be in Owen's place?"

"All summer."

"Funny. That's exactly how long my home improvement projects are going to last." He returned her fake smile.

And then shut the door firmly in her face.

Eight

MONDAY MORNING, VICTORIA sat in Judge Bogg's chambers as her opposing counsel argued on about what a neglectful father Victoria's client was.

At issue in today's pretrial conference was the emergency Motion for Visitation that Victoria had filed on behalf of her client, Nate Ferrara. He and his wife, Heather, had jointly filed for divorce last December and had agreed to alternate the weeks that their two children, ages seven and ten, lived with each of them. Last Sunday night, however, Mrs. Ferrara had called her soon-to-be ex-husband and told him "not to bother" picking up the kids for his visitation week, and also said she wanted to amend their agreement so that he saw them only on alternating weekends.

"Mr. Ferrara isn't around enough, Your Honor," argued Greg Jaffe, Victoria's opposing counsel. "Ever since he was promoted at his company, he travels one or two nights every week, and, even when he is in town, he barely makes it home before the kids' bedtime. The real person taking care of these kids when they stay with their father is the nanny he hired to watch over them. And while she sounds like a capable enough person, there's no reason for the children to be in her care when they have a mother who they can be with instead."

"What Mr. Jaffe is basically arguing, Your Honor, is that my client has less of a right to see his children simply because he's a working parent," Victoria said.

"No, I'm saying that given the facts in this particular case, it doesn't make any sense to have these kids raised by a babysitter during the weeks they're supposed to be with their dad."

"My opposing counsel exaggerates the circumstances," Victoria told the judge. "The facts are that unless he's out of town, Mr. Ferrara drives his children to school in the mornings and makes a point to be home before they go to bed—even if it means he has to bring work home and finish it while they're sleeping. He has attended every parent-teacher conference—even before he and Mrs. Ferrara separated—he checks the kids' homework every night and recently helped his son build a diorama for a classroom presentation. He and the kids also take an indoor family rock-climbing class on the weekends, and just last month, when his daughter came down with the stomach flu, *he* was the one who stayed up all night and took care of her—not a nanny. Yes, Mr. Ferrara's work schedule has become more demanding since his promotion, Your Honor, but lots of parents have demanding work schedules. The fact remains that he is a meaningful part of these children's lives and shouldn't be punished because he can't always make it home in time for a family dinner."

The judge considered this, and then looked at the other attorney. "Any response to that, counselor?"

Five minutes later, Victoria walked out of the judge's chambers and smiled at her client, who'd been waiting anxiously in the courtroom.

She felt good about today's victory—if one could call it that. In her line of work, there were seldom any true "winners," particularly when children were involved. But that didn't stop her from always doing her best to ensure that her clients' interests were protected as much as possible throughout the divorce process.

She'd been fortunate in her career. In the beginning, she'd simply been in the right place at the right time: about six months after opening her firm, a former law school classmate passed along her name to a woman, someone in her book club, who was looking for a divorce lawyer. That woman turned out to be the wife of an extremely wealthy riverboat casino owner who had done some *very* un-husbandly things with eighteen-year-old prostitutes in his casino hotel. When the wife walked away from the divorce nearly fifty million dollars richer in a high-profile case with significant local media attention, Victoria Slade & Associates instantly became one of the go-to family law firms for Chicago's rich and famous.

Because of her success, Victoria now had the luxury of being selective in the cases she took on. Her clientele tended to be mostly women, although not always. Regardless of gender, she believed that her primary responsibility as their lawyer was to help her clients feel empowered during the divorce process. She was blunt and didn't sugarcoat, and she asked each prospective client the same question during their initial meeting: "What do you need in order to move on from this marriage and start building your new life?" If the answer was something she thought she could deliver, she took them on as a client.

And then she fought like hell to get the job done.

After returning from court, the rest of Victoria's workday was spent bouncing between meetings with her associates, and on phone calls with either clients or opposing counsel. She left the office around six o'clock—early for her. But she'd been trying to shake a headache all afternoon and figured the best way to do that was to set the laptop and cell phone aside, pour herself a glass of wine, and have a long, relaxing bath.

Per usual, she avoided the subway, opting for a cab home instead. It began to pour about a mile from her building, but fortunately she had her umbrella as she darted from the cab into the small lobby. She grabbed her mail, flipping through it as she rode the elevator up to the fourth floor.

When she stepped out of the elevator, she saw someone at the end of the hallway—a woman leaning against the door to Ford's condo. In her midtwenties, with shoulder-length, light brown hair, she wiped her eyes, obviously crying, as she pushed a baby stroller back and forth.

Oh, boy. What now?

Ever since her run-in with Ford at the coffee shop, a nagging voice in the back of Victoria's head had been asking whether she had, perhaps, rushed to judgment about her new neighbor and whatever situations, frisky or non-frisky, he had going on with the women she'd seen coming and going from his condo. But now here they were, just two days later, and the guy had a crying woman with a *baby* on his doorstep.

At this rate, they were going to have to set up a damn number dispenser and a waiting area outside unit 4F.

The younger woman's eyes were puffy and her cheeks blotched. She tucked a lock of hair behind one ear, appearing embarrassed by her obvious state of distress as Victoria approached.

"Sorry. I'm just waiting for my brother to get home." She cleared her throat and peered down at the stroller, continuing to push back and forth.

Oh. She was Ford's *sister.* Victoria had assumed . . . Well, whatever. She paused in front of her door, keys in hand, and watched as the younger woman brushed away more tears.

Just keep moving. It's a family matter. She'd paid the price once for sticking her nose into Ford's business, with that little press-and-*crane* routine of his. She wasn't about to do it again.

She put her key into the lock, just as the other woman sniffed and did that shaky-inhale thing people did when trying to stop crying.

Aw, hell.

She stuffed the mail into her briefcase and walked over. "I'm Victoria. Ford's neighbor. I don't mean to intrude . . . but are you okay?"

The woman looked her over. "Are you Owen's girlfriend?"

"No, Owen moved out. I'm renting his place for the summer."

"Oh." The woman cleared her throat. "I'm Nicole." She gestured to Ford's door, as if feeling a need to explain. "My brother's on his way. He texted and said he got stuck in traffic. I guess he was on the south side, doing an interview for work."

"Ah," Victoria said, as if this information made sense. In truth, she had no clue what Ford did for a living. They hadn't gotten that far in their brief, mostly insult-based exchanges.

She watched as Nicole continued pushing the baby stroller back and forth.

"If I stop moving, she wakes up," Nicole explained. "The only time I can get her to nap is when she's in the stroller." She blinked back more tears, and tried to cover with a more lighthearted tone. "Sorry. I'm a little sleep-deprived."

Victoria stepped around so she could peek inside the stroller. She was far from an expert on babies, but guessed this one to be somewhere around four months old. Wrapped in a pink and lime green blanket, and with a little bit of dark brown fuzz on her head, she slept with a pacifier in her mouth. "She's adorable. What's her name?"

"Zoe."

"That's pretty." Victoria gestured to her front door, the words coming out of her mouth before she even thought about them. "You're welcome to wait inside my place until your brother gets home." She nearly thunked herself on the head— *For Pete's sake, Slade, what happened to minding your own business?* Really, she didn't need to be getting involved with whatever the problem was here.

"Oh, no," Nicole said. "That's nice of you to offer. But we're okay out here. I wouldn't want to impose."

Back and forth with the stroller.

And more sniffles.

Victoria sighed to herself, thinking about the quiet evening she'd envisioned, the glass of wine and the hot, relaxing bath she'd had planned. "Are you sure you don't want to come in and sit down?" She went for a joke. "Because I'm getting exhausted just watching you push that thing."

Nicole hesitated. "Well, if you're sure you don't mind . . . actually, it would be nice to sit down for a few minutes." She managed a slight smile in return. "Thank you."

"Of course. It's not a problem." Victoria let them inside her condo, holding the door open so Nicole could get in with the stroller. She shut the door quietly, being mindful of the sleeping baby. "Make yourself comfortable. Can I get you something to drink? I have Diet Coke, water, iced tea . . ."

"A glass of water would be nice, thanks."

Victoria headed into the kitchen, and set her umbrella and briefcase off to the side. Watching as Nicole took a seat on the living room couch, she cracked open a bottled water and poured it into a glass with ice.

Okay . . . a little awkward here, having a perfect stranger—with a baby—in her home. A crying stranger, no less. Not exactly sure what to say, she set the glass of water on the coffee table in front of Nicole, and then smiled as she sat down in the chair next to the couch.

Nicole continued to push the stroller back and forth across the hardwood floors. "Thanks. I should probably text my brother to let him know that I'm here."

Victoria wondered how that message would go over, seeing how she and Ford were hardly on the most neighborly of terms. With one hand, Nicole pulled her phone out of her jeans pocket. "Would you mind pushing the stroller while I type?"

"Oh. Sure." Victoria took hold of the handle and slowly pushed it back and forth, imitating Nicole's pace. She peered down at Zoe, all nestled in her blanket next to some giraffe toy that was clipped to the side of the stroller.

If anyone had told her that she would be rocking a baby to sleep in her condo today, she would've said they really needed to cut back on the hallucinogenic drugs. Not that she had anything against babies, but if she went down that road at all, they weren't in the schedule for another good four or five years.

Soak it up while you can, girls, she told her hormones.

Nicole finished typing and then looked around the loft. "This is a nice place." She checked out Victoria's suit. "Are you a lawyer?"

Victoria smiled. "Is it that obvious?"

"My brother's best friend is a lawyer. You remind me a little of her. What kind of law do you practice?" Nicole's phone buzzed with a new text message. She checked it, then looked up at Victoria quizzically. "You said your name is Victoria, right?"

"Yes."

"That's what I told Ford. He seems really surprised that I'm with you." She typed a quick reply to her brother. "'Yes, your neighbor, *Victoria*,'" she typed, in a tone that was equal parts annoyance, mocking, and affection. Then she put her phone down and gestured to the stroller. "Thanks. I can push again." She took over from Victoria, then brushed her hair off her face with one hand. "Sorry, you were saying something about your law practice?"

"I'm a family lawyer. I run my own firm, actually."

Nicole paused, then reached for her glass of water. "Huh. That's interesting. So . . . do you handle child support cases, then?"

"Child support is certainly part of a lot of my cases, yes."

Nicole leaned forward in her chair. "How does that work in situations where the mother and father were never·married? Say, hypothetically speaking, that a woman wants to collect child support from the guy who got her pregnant. What does she have to do?"

Victoria glanced down at Nicole's left hand. No ring. "Well, first she would file a petition for child support. Assuming we're talking about someone who lives in Illinois"—and, given Nicole's very interested look, Victoria had a sneaking suspicion they were—"there are guidelines for what the father will pay, based on his income and the number of children. She'd want to make sure he's being truthful in his financial disclosures and not hiding anything. Also, she can request separate contributions toward the child's education, medical expenses, and extracurricular activities."

"I didn't realize you could ask for those kinds of things."

"A good lawyer would help with all of that. As well as any custody and visitation issues that might arise."

Nicole's eyes darted toward Zoe. "Custody?"

Victoria treaded delicately here. "I'm not sure what the situation is between the mother and father in this particular hypothetical, but if you ask a man to support a child financially, he very well may want to be a part of that child's life."

"Right. Or . . . maybe he won't care at all." Tears welled up in Nicole's eyes again.

Victoria went out on a limb. "Nicole, we're not really talking about a hypothetical here, are we?"

After a moment's hesitation, the other woman shook her head. "I shouldn't be bothering you with this—I don't even know you. It's just that you mentioned you're a family lawyer, and lately, I've been thinking a lot about these things. It's what I planned to talk to Ford about tonight, actually." Her lip began to tremble. "I'm just not doing so well, raising Zoe all by myself."

That confession out of the way, her words began to flow faster. "I didn't know how *expensive* everything would be—the diapers, the formula, not to mention day care. I mean, I'm already back at work, because my job doesn't have paid maternity leave, and I'm barely getting by. So I'm picking up extra work, giving private guitar lessons to kids in the evenings and on weekends, but that cuts into the little time I have with Zoe, and I feel like I barely see her, and I'm always so exhausted when I *do* see her that I find myself counting the minutes until her nap or her bedtime. And I feel so horrible admitting that, but it's true and . . ." She shook her head, trailing off.

The family lawyer in Victoria felt compelled to ask, "So you've tried making arrangements with Zoe's father? And he's refused to take on any financial responsibility?"

Nicole bit her lip. "Well, here's the thing: I don't exactly know who Zoe's father is."

Oh. "Meaning, there's more than one guy who could've gotten you pregnant?"

"No, it's definitely the one guy. I just don't know who he is." Nicole blushed. "It was a one-night stand. My girlfriends and I went out for my twenty-fifth birthday, and I got really buzzed. I started talking to this guy and one thing led to another and we went back to my place, and—*surprise!*—a few weeks later I realized I was pregnant. Which is crazy, because I know we used a condom. But maybe there was a second time, or the thing slipped, I don't know. 'User error.'

That's what my OB called it." She glanced over at Zoe. "I thought about not keeping the baby, but . . . I just felt this bond with her from the moment I found out I was pregnant. And it's not like I thought being a single mom was going to be easy." She looked at Victoria with tired eyes. "But I didn't realize it would be *this* hard, you know?"

The words took Victoria back to a memory of her own mother, lying in a hospital bed looking tired and frail.

I just didn't know what to do. I didn't know it would be so hard.

"So, what's the plan here?" she asked Nicole, rather bluntly. "You asked me about child support payments, but I'm thinking you need to know who the father is first. Courts are sort of sticklers about that."

"Well, I do know his name," Nicole said. "Peter Sutter. Hopefully with that, I can find him somehow. That's why I want to talk to Ford. He's an investigative reporter—he has access to all sorts of people-search databases and stuff. I figure he can help me find Peter Sutter, then . . . I'll just tell him about Zoe and demand that he help out financially. She's his responsibility, too—it takes *two* people to make a baby, after all." She said this without hesitation, as if the whole plan was settled.

Right.

From both personal and professional experience, Victoria had a slightly more realistic view of things.

"And when, assuming you can find this Peter Sutter, he tells you to take a hike—what then?" she asked Nicole. "When he refuses to take the paternity test, because he doesn't remember you, or because he doesn't want to be a dad, or because he's married with three kids and he was cheating on his wife when he hooked up with you and doesn't want to get busted—what happens after that? Or maybe you do manage to prove that he's the father, but then he lawyers up and fights back against every child support payment, because he's a deadbeat, or because he doesn't think he should have to pay his whole life for one 'mistake,' or because he's some rich asshole who thinks you're a gold digger who's after his money. The point is, Nicole, this guy could be anyone, he could be broke, or just a selfish jerk who doesn't care one bit about his responsibilities. And it may be a long time before you see any money from him—*if* you do find him—which means you can't count on this man to solve your problems. *You* are going to have to find some way to do this on your own. I know it's tough being a single mother, but you are all your daughter has, the only person she can depend on, and she needs you to be there. She needs to know, no matter whatever else is going in her world, that *you* can do this. So you're just going to have to suck it up, pull it together, and figure out how you're going to make this work even if you never get one dime from the guy."

Nicole blinked in surprise.

Victoria paused, equally surprised.

Oh, shit.

That whole speech had just spilled out, way too vehemently. Realizing she needed to say something fast, she pointed, covering. "And *that* is exactly the kind of tough-love speech I would give you if I was the lawyer handling your case."

Nicole looked confused for a moment, and then she broke into a wide smile. "Wait—you want to take on my case?"

Uh-oh. "Well, I said *if* I was the—"

"This is so great!" Nicole clapped her hands in excitement.

Before Victoria could clarify the misunderstanding, Zoe woke up with a start. She opened her eyes, looked around the room for a second, then spit out her pacifier and let out an indignant wail.

"Oops. Sweetie, I'm sorry. I didn't mean to wake you up." Nicole made a face at Victoria as she reached into the stroller. "Duh. That was dumb of me." She scooped up Zoe and held her against her chest and shoulder, rubbing the baby's back with a *Shh*.

Zoe kept right on howling.

"She's probably hungry." Looking flustered, Nicole began digging around in a diaper bag strapped to the stroller handle while balancing Zoe with one arm. She pulled out a bottle and a yellow packet of formula.

"Would you mind taking her for a minute while I mix this?" she asked Victoria.

Little Zoe, with her red, scrunched-up face, looked less than enthused about this idea. Still, it wasn't like Victoria could refuse. "Of course." Naturally, she could hold a baby for a few minutes. She used to babysit back in high school; it wasn't as though she'd never held an infant before. Just . . . not in a really long time.

Nicole's left hand was full so she couldn't just plunk Zoe into Victoria's arms, so Victoria reached over and semi-awkwardly lifted the baby into her lap.

Okay. That wasn't too bad. She could do this.

"Hi," she said, smiling down at Zoe.

Zoe let out a yell of outrage.

Nicole rushed over to the sink to fill the baby bottle with water. Victoria tried bouncing, and then some rocking. She even cooed, "Mommy will be right back," but nothing worked; Zoe was in a mighty pissed-off mood and apparently determined to let everyone in the building know it.

Nicole dumped the formula into the bottle and shook it—by this point Zoe had worked herself into a full-fledged fit, rather like a wailing police siren—then hurried back to Victoria and scooped the baby up. She settled Zoe on her lap, plunked the bottle into Zoe's mouth, and literally mid-howl the crying just stopped.

Silence.

"Wow." Victoria chuckled, a combination of shock and awe. "Is that always how she is when she's hungry?"

"And when she's tired, or has a wet diaper, or dropped her pacifier, or she's too warm or too cold . . ." Nicole peered down at her daughter. "She's a little pistol, all right." She gently stroked her finger across Zoe's cheek, wiping away a tear.

In that small moment, Victoria saw the full range of Nicole's emotions. She saw the exhaustion in the other woman's eyes, the frazzledness, the uncertainty, but also the love and adoration she felt for her daughter.

She could help this woman; she knew that.

Nicole's case was both unusual and complicated, and she would need a good family lawyer, someone who would make sure that Nicole wasn't railroaded or taken advantage of in court. A lawyer who would ensure, first and foremost, that Zoe's interests were protected.

Victoria looked down at the baby, who now drank content-edly from the bottle, as if nothing had ever been amiss. A little pistol, indeed.

Good for you.

She got up from the couch and took a business card out of her briefcase. "Here," she said, putting the card on the coffee table in front of Nicole. "Call my office tomorrow and we'll talk about where to start with your case."

Nicole read the card out loud. "'Victoria Slade and Asso-ciates.'" She cocked her head and looked Victoria over, taking in her designer suit. "It's really nice of you to offer to help. But honestly? I doubt I can afford a lawyer like you."

"We'll figure something out." The truth was, Nicole almost certainly could not afford a lawyer like her, at least not at Victoria's standard hourly rates. But she had taken on pro bono and reduced-rates matters in the past. That was one of the advantages of being the boss—she had the freedom to basically do whatever she wanted.

And the more she thought about it, she *did* want to help. This past month, she'd been feeling unsettled about a lot of things: the break-in, the panic attacks, and the flashbacks about her mother. But this situation here, with Nicole and Zoe, was something she could fix.

She may not have been able to ride a damn subway car, but the law was her wheelhouse.

Suddenly, there was a knock at the door.

Nicole's eyes widened. "That's probably Ford. You can't say anything about this yet—not until I've had the chance to talk to him tonight. He doesn't know the truth about Zoe's father. I was too embarrassed to tell my family the real story, so I made up an ex-boyfriend who ditched me when he found out I was pregnant."

"I won't say a word." Victoria winked at Nicole as she got up to answer the door. "That's attorney-client-privileged information now, right?"

And as far as she was concerned, the less said to Ford Dixon, the better.

Nine

FORD WENT STRAIGHT to Victoria's place from the parking garage—still carrying his messenger bag—thinking his sister and niece would need to be rescued as fast as possible from the clutches of his cranky, meddlesome neighbor.

Victoria opened the door, looking every inch the high-powered lawyer in her sleek black suit. "Mr. Dixon. How nice of you to grace us with your presence," she said faux-politely.

"I hear you're harboring my sister. More of your apparent quest to be all up in my business, I take it?" His smile was as pleasant as hers, his words just as dry.

"Something like that." She stepped back, giving him room to come inside.

He saw Nicole sitting on a couch in the living room, feeding Zoe, and could tell that she'd been crying.

Surprised, he shot Victoria a quick glance, and then headed over. "Nic. What happened?"

"Oh, you could say it's been a bit of a rough day. But luckily, your neighbor here is a saint."

Ford stole another look at Victoria, who had moved into

the kitchen to give them space. Her rich, dark brown hair fell forward as she typed something on her cell phone.

A saint? Clearly, he was missing something.

First things first. "Are you and Zoe okay?" he asked Nicole.

"Why don't we go to your place and talk?" she suggested. "I think we've intruded on Victoria for long enough."

His big brother protective instincts went on high alert, hearing this reference to some "talk" he and Nicole needed to have. Still, she was right—they should wait until they were alone. "Sure. I can push the stroller, since you have Zoe." He looked over at his niece, who gripped the bottle between her two tiny hands. Her head was turned as she drank, and she stared right at him with those big brown eyes.

Reaching over, he tickled her chest, getting her to smile and kick out her legs. "There's my smile."

Nicole rolled her eyes. "Of course she smiles for *you*. Is there any member of the female species who doesn't adore you?"

From the kitchen, Victoria cleared her throat loudly. She looked over and gestured vaguely with an innocent smile. "Sorry. Must be dry in here."

Ford threw her a look. *Ha, ha.*

Carrying Zoe, Nicole walked over to Victoria. "Thanks so much for letting us hang out while we waited." She lowered her voice. "I'll call you tomorrow, then, about the thing."

His ears perked up. What *thing*? Something obviously was going on with his sister, and he didn't like being out of the loop. But he stayed silent, holding back his questions until he and Nicole were alone.

"You're welcome. I'm glad I could help." Victoria brushed her finger against the back of Zoe's hand. "Later, kiddo."

Perhaps by reflex, the baby grabbed her finger.

"Aw, look at that. I think she likes you," Nicole said.

"Of course she does. She's obviously a very smart girl." Victoria wagged her finger, comically shaking Zoe's hand in good-bye. Then she caught Ford watching and blushed. Gently, she extricated her finger from the baby's grip and walked in the direction of the front door.

He took that as his cue to leave.

Victoria held open the door for Nicole and Zoe, nodding in good-bye. Ford followed behind, pushing the stroller. He paused in the doorway and raised an eyebrow. "A saint?"

She gave him a sweet smile. "I believe the words you're looking for are, 'Thank you, Victoria.'"

Always with the sarcasm.

But on this occasion—as much as it killed him to admit it—she happened to be right. He had no idea what had transpired here between her and Nicole, but nevertheless, she'd taken in his sister and niece and for that . . . he owed her his gratitude.

Most unfortunately.

"Thank you, Victoria."

She raised an eyebrow, as if waiting for the punch line, and then looked surprised when none came. Shifting uncomfortably in the doorway, she gave him a dismissive wave. "Whatever, you're welcome."

It was a funny thing, he thought. When she wasn't being snarky or throwing barbs at him, there wasn't anything to deflect his attention away from the fact that she was a beautiful woman. Like right then, the way her full lips curved upward as she peered up at him with those warm, chocolate-brown eyes.

"So, we're just . . . hanging out here in the doorway, I guess?" she said.

Yep, so much for that moment.

ONCE INSIDE HIS place, Nicole took a seat on the couch and settled in to finish feeding Zoe. Ford bided his time, changing out of his work clothes and throwing on a T-shirt and jeans. When he came out of the bedroom, he found Zoe lying on a blanket in the middle of his living room while Nicole rinsed out the baby bottle in his sink.

He got down on the floor next to Zoe, shaking the giraffe toy above her chest. Her eyes widened and she reached for it, trying to grip it with her hands.

"You should've seen the meltdown she had at Victoria's. It was pretty epic," Nicole said from the kitchen.

Ford could easily believe it. The last time he'd been over at Nicole's apartment she'd been trying something called "sleep training"—which, if all the crying and hollering was any indication, Zoe had been none too thrilled about. "Mom would probably tell you it's payback. You weren't exactly an easygoing baby, either."

Nicole put the clean bottle into the diaper bag and sat down on the floor next to Ford and Zoe. "Have you talked to Mom this week?"

"I drove out and saw her yesterday afternoon."

"How's she doing?"

"You know Mom. Keeping herself busy. She gave me a box of Dad's things that she thought I might like to have. She has one for you, too." Ford had stashed his box in the closet, but hadn't looked at it yet.

Wanting to get down to the business at hand, he nodded in the direction of Victoria's place. "So? Want to tell me what was going on in there? Mom's worried about you. We both are. I've been trying to reach you ever since the funeral."

"I know, I'm sorry. Things are always so crazy, I feel like I never get a chance to catch my breath. Between balancing work and Zoe, I just . . ." Nicole swallowed, and her eyes filled with tears. "I think I'm doing a terrible job at everything. Especially being a mom."

Ford's voice softened, seeing his sister cry. "Nic . . . that's not true. Why didn't you come to me earlier about this? You don't have to stretch yourself so thin with work. I can help you out with money until things settle down." He wasn't rich, but he certainly made enough to help out his niece and sister.

"I know. But a temporary fix isn't the solution. It's not like you're going to support Zoe forever—nor would I want you to. And it's not just about the money, anyway." She looked at him. "Obviously, I've been thinking a lot about Dad ever since the funeral. The things you said in your eulogy . . . it really hit me hard, hearing those stories. I spent so much time being angry with Dad, or fighting with him, or being resentful that he just couldn't get his shit together, that I'd forgotten about a lot of those good moments. Like, remember how great he was with Zoe that first day he and Mom came to see her in the hospital? He held her practically the whole time, just talking to her and telling her stories about the days you and I were born. But instead of simply enjoying the moment, the whole time I kept thinking, 'Why can't he be this way *all* the time?'"

"I know." The truth was, Ford had been thinking exactly the same thing that day at the hospital. He'd spent nearly his whole life only partly able to enjoy good moments like that with his dad, because he'd always been waiting for the other shoe to drop.

Nicole looked down at her daughter, who was happily gumming the giraffe toy. "Zoe has a father out there. Maybe he'd be a good father, maybe he wouldn't. But after losing Dad, I feel like I owe it to her to at least give her the chance to have some nice moments like that."

Ford was all for making his sister's ex-boyfriend accept financial responsibility for Zoe. Hell, he'd been pushing Nicole to sue the jerk for child support since the day Zoe had been born. But beyond that, for both his sister's and Zoe's sakes, he needed to be a voice of reason here. "He fled the state when you told him you were pregnant, Nic," he said gently. "As good as your intentions are in wanting Zoe to have a relationship with him, it doesn't sound like he's exactly a stand-up guy. Financial responsibility is one thing, but you can't make a man be a father."

Nicole took a deep breath. "Okay. So, you have to promise that you won't get all big brother judge-y when I tell you something about me and Zoe's dad."

He was a little offended by whatever she was implying. "Hey, give me some credit here. My best friend is a woman—I think I'm pretty damn enlightened when it comes to relationships and the female of the species. I promise you, nothing you say will be something I haven't heard come out of Brooke's mouth."

"I got pregnant after a one-night stand, and I have no clue who my baby's father is."

Except that.

Nicole folded her arms across her chest, practically daring him to be shocked and appalled.

Ford exhaled—yes, fine, he didn't deny that he needed at least a moment to process this information. "All right. Tell me everything." He chucked her under the chin. "And this time, you dope, make it the truth."

She went misty-eyed again and pointed to her tears. "My God, it never *stops*." Then she told him about going out with her girlfriends to celebrate her twenty-fifth birthday, meeting Peter Sutter, and bringing him back to her place.

"He was gone when I woke up the next morning. And I have no idea how to track him down." She paused when she saw Ford glowering. "Remember, you promised. No judgment."

"I said I wouldn't judge *you*. But I'm thinking that the asshole who slept with my sister, got her pregnant, and then sneaked off without so much as a good-bye is entirely fair game."

"Not defending the guy, but in fairness, it's not like he had a reason to think he got me pregnant. I know for a fact we used at least one condom, because I found it—"

Ford held up a hand, cutting her off. "Really don't need to know that. Ever."

She smiled tentatively at him. "I thought, with your *Trib* resources, that maybe you'd be able to help me? Find Zoe's father, I mean."

As if she even needed to ask. "Of course I'll help you. That's kind of what big brothers—and supercool uncles—do. But there's one thing I need to ask first." He looked her right in the eyes. "How concerned should I be that you were obviously pretty drunk the night you met Zoe's father?"

"It's not like Dad. Promise. I just partied a little too hard on my birthday."

He studied her for a moment. "Okay." Satisfied, he got up to grab a small notebook he kept in the kitchen, ready to get down to business. "Now, anything you remember about this Peter Sutter can help me find him. Age, hair color, even the name of the bar you met him in."

Nicole nodded. "Sure. Okay."

When Ford sat back down, he suddenly remembered something. "By the way, what's the mysterious 'thing' that you need to talk to Victoria about tomorrow?"

"Oh! That." Nicole spoke excitedly. "Did you know that she's a family lawyer?"

According to his research, she was a big-time divorce lawyer with a client list that read like the Who's Who of Chicago. "I may have heard something to that effect."

"Well, guess what? She offered to take my case. She said that I need a good lawyer to handle all the child support details and also any custody and visitation issues that might arise. And, how awesome is this—she suggested that she'll cut me a break on her rates."

Ford sat back. "Really."

Nicole cocked her head. "Why do you say it like that? What's going on with you and Victoria, anyway?"

"I assure you, nothing is going on with me and Victoria." The woman was far too smug for his tastes. Judgmental. Not to mention, snarky. He could go on and on, except, really, it wasn't worth his time.

Oh—and prickly, too.

Presumably, Nicole caught his dry tone. "Ford, you *will* play nice with the smart, kind-hearted lawyer who offered to take on my case."

He snorted. "Kind-hearted? Are we talking about the same neighbor?"

"Uh-huh. The very pretty one living about ten feet away."

"Is she pretty? I hadn't noticed," he said vaguely.

His sister smiled. "Oh, you noticed."

A HALF HOUR later, he walked Nicole and Zoe to the door.

"I have one condition for tracking down this guy for you: that you talk to your doctor about all the stress you've been under." He knew jack-squat about post-partum depression and "baby blues"—maybe Nicole was simply going through the

same stress all new moms experienced. Still, he'd feel better
if she talked to someone.

She pulled him in for a hug, her voice thick. "You never
could resist telling me what to do."

He watched as she and Zoe strolled down the hallway to
the elevator, and then his eyes fell on the door next to his.

*She offered to take on my case. And, how awesome is
this—she suggested that she'll cut me a break on her rates.*

Perhaps it was time that he and Ms. Victoria Slade, Esquire,
had a little chat.

Ten

VICTORIA CLOSED HER eyes, relaxing as the hot water and steam surrounded her. She had Norah Jones piping through the bathroom speakers—*It's just the nearness of you*—and a glass of zinfandel on the marble ledge of the tub.

Heaven.

This was the moment she'd been looking forward to all day. No more thoughts about work, or crying strangers with crying babies. Simply a few minutes to unwind and get in some alone time, just her and her cucumber-scented bubble bath and—

Knock, knock.

—some jerk knocking on her front door.

"Go away," she muttered under her breath, thinking whoever it was would get the hint when she didn't answer. And indeed, that seemed to work. There was a second knock, which she also ignored, and then silence.

Peace at last.

Except . . .

Now she was wondering *who* had knocked at her door. Nicole, perhaps? Had she left something behind? Or maybe it was Ford. He was basically the only person Victoria knew in the building, so it had to be one of the two of them. Unless some random person had just knocked on her door. Some stranger who wanted . . . what, exactly?

She shifted uneasily in the bathtub.

The logical part of her knew that this was not a question she needed to stew over. People knocked on apartment doors all the time. At some point, she was going to have to stop being so hyperalert about these kinds of things.

Get over yourself, Slade. It's all in your head.

That decided, she eased back in the tub and got on with the relaxing. Realizing she'd missed her favorite song, she grabbed her phone from the ledge and used the app that controlled the sound system to skip back.

It's not the pale moon that excites me, Norah crooned.

Feeling better, Victoria took a sip of her wine and then closed her eyes, once again succumbing to the hot water and steam, the heady scent of the bubbles, the soft, sultry music— *It's just the nearness of you—*

Another knock at her door.

Son. Of. A. Bitch.

Muttering under her breath, she climbed out of the tub and quickly dried off. After wrapping the towel around herself, she headed into the living room and looked through the peephole on her door.

Ford stood in the hallway.

She groaned in annoyance, half-shouting through the door. "What?"

He blinked at the unceremonious greeting, and then cocked his head. "What are you doing in there? I can see your lights on through the balcony—you're obviously not sleeping."

Oh, really? Who was spying on whom now? "I was *trying* to take a bath."

"Oh." He paused, as if considering this. "All right, I'll come back. What do you need, ten minutes?"

"Ten minutes?" She rolled her eyes. *Men.* "That's hardly enough time to—" Feeling stupid arguing through the door, she sighed in frustration. "Just hold on." Figuring she might as well get this over with, she grumbled under her breath and went into her bedroom to throw on jeans and a T-shirt. On her way back to the door, she removed the clip she'd used during her bath and shook out her hair.

She threw the door open and got right down to it. "So. To what do I owe this pleasure, Mr. Dixon?"

His lips twitched at the corners. "That's an interesting way to wear eye makeup."

Victoria stepped back and checked out her reflection in the foyer mirror, and saw that she had two big black raccoon-like smudges of mascara under her eyes. *Oh, for Pete's sake.* She gestured impatiently for him to enter. "Well, come in already. I'll be right back." She left him standing there and went to the bathroom to grab her makeup remover, then scrubbed her face clean and headed back out into the living room.

She found Ford standing by the couch, checking out a photograph of her and her mom from law school graduation.

"I know someone else who went to Northwestern Law. Cade Morgan. Two years ahead of you, I'm guessing?"

Clearly, somebody had been doing a little research on her, if he knew what law school she'd attended. "I know the name. Listen, I have a tub of steaming hot water and a nice jammy zinfandel waiting for me. Maybe we could cut to the chase?"

Ford turned to face her. "My sister said you offered to take on her case."

"That's true." And if he'd come here tonight to tell her he had a problem with that, unfortunately, he'd just have to get over it. She may have stumbled unintentionally into being Nicole's lawyer, but now that she'd made a commitment, she was all in.

"She also said you'd mentioned cutting her a break on your rate."

"Also true."

He studied her. "Why would you do that? You don't even know my sister."

Victoria leaned her hip against the back of the couch. "She needs help. I can help her. It's not all that complicated."

He came around the couch, moving closer. "I looked into you, you know. Your firm appears to be quite successful."

"I do all right."

He stopped in front of her, shifting uncomfortably. "So, if someone with your . . . seemingly acceptable legal skills"— he looked slightly pained by the acknowledgment—"has decided to help my sister, I suppose I shouldn't get in the way of that. Even if it does mean we have to work together."

Victoria, who'd been rather enjoying seeing Ford stumble his way through this begrudging, quasi–thank you, blinked at this last part. "I'm sorry. Did you say, 'work together'?"

"Trust me, I'm not thrilled about it, either. But seeing how you're Nicole's lawyer, and I'm the one who's going to track down Peter Sutter, I figure we're pretty much a team now."

A *team*? Oh, now that was cute. But, unfortunately, not the way she operated. "Right. I remember Nicole saying something about you using your resources at the *Trib* to find Peter Sutter." Victoria waved this off. "That won't be necessary anymore. I plan to hire a private investigator to handle that."

He folded his arms across his chest. "But I already told Nicole I would do it."

"Well . . . *un*-tell her, then."

He raised an eyebrow.

"It's nothing personal," she said. "Okay, yes, fine, it is personal. You and I hardly mesh well. But on top of that, I don't subcontract out the investigative work in my cases to relatives of clients. Period."

Ford considered this. "How much will a PI charge you?"

She thought back to the last time she'd worked with a private investigator. "Around a hundred an hour. Maybe more."

"And you'll just pass along that cost to my sister, despite the fact that she has someone who's offered to do the work for free?"

Victoria bristled at the implication. "I didn't say that."

"Then . . . what? Your firm eats the cost of the PI? All we have is a name and the bar where Nicole and Peter Sutter met. Do you realize how long it could take to find this guy? We could be talking about thousands of dollars here. *I* can save you that expense."

The practical businesswoman in her paused at that.

But.

"I just don't think you and I working together is a good idea."

He met her gaze boldly. "I can handle it if you can."

"I never said I couldn't handle it." And the truth of the matter was, technically, Nicole had every right to use her brother to track down Peter Sutter, whether Victoria liked it or not. She didn't have to give Victoria the go-ahead to use a private investigator for that.

"Then it's settled," Ford said.

Not seeing how she had much choice—most unfortunately— she wanted to get one thing straight from the beginning. "If we do this, we do it my way. I want to be kept fully in the loop with everything you're doing. I can't be worrying that you're running around knocking on the door of every Peter Sutter in town, demanding to know whether he knocked up your sister."

"Just so I know, is it your plan to be this bossy the entire time we're working together?"

She smiled sweetly at him. "You're welcome to walk away anytime."

"This is my sister we're talking about." He took a step closer. "Which means you're stuck with me, Victoria. Like it or not."

She'd had a bad feeling he was going to say just that.

TWO DAYS LATER, Ford was at his desk in the *Tribune* newsroom, finishing up the first part of his series on the Cook County probation department. Fueled by the second cup of coffee he'd had that morning, he wrote for nearly three hours straight, banging out the entire story before lunchtime.

Just as he was finishing up with some editing, his phone rang. He checked the caller ID and saw that it was Nicole.

"Unfortunately, no luck," she told him.

"You're sure?" Yesterday, he'd begun his search for Peter Sutter. They didn't have much to go on, just the name and a vague description—brown hair, between the ages of twenty-five and forty—but Nicole believed she would recognize him from a photograph.

Ford hoped she was right about that, because if she couldn't ID the guy, this was going to be a hell of a lot more complicated than it already was.

His first step, on the off chance they'd get lucky, had been to check Facebook, Twitter, and LinkedIn. He'd run searches for all Peter and Pete Sutters in Chicago, and then had e-mailed Nicole profiles of the three guys with brown hair who'd popped up.

"I'm sure," she told him. "Do these men honestly look like the type I'd go home with? Even when drunk, I have my standards."

"This isn't Match.com, Nic," he said. "I don't care whether they look like your 'type,' just whether they might look familiar. Besides, for all you know, these guys are totally cool in person."

"The second one's Twitter profile says, 'Angry son of a bitch. Don't like what I say? Go fuck yourself.'"

"Okay, not him."

"Call me stuck-up if you want, but I'm telling you, we're looking for a Peter Sutter who is *cute*."

"Cute. Got it," Ford said, pretending to take notes. "Eye color, height, address, phone number, and profession all unknown. But definitely a hottie. Based on that, I should have the case cracked by dinner."

Her tone was sweet. "Have I told you how awesome you are for doing this?"

"Yeah, yeah," he grumbled. "Save it for when I find the guy."

He hung up with his sister and wrapped up his probation department piece, then headed out to grab a sandwich. It was a warm and sunny late-June day, so he decided to walk across the river to one of his favorite delis. He grabbed a table outside and caught up on e-mail as he ate, not realizing until he'd finished his chips that he was only half a block away from the law offices of the illustrious Victoria Slade.

He could easily picture her in some sleek, sophisticated office, doing . . . whatever the heck high-powered divorce lawyers did on a Friday afternoon. Probably sassing someone, if their interactions thus far were any indication. Undoubtedly while wearing another one of those sexy suits she seemed to like so much. And high heels.

Hmm.

Actually, now that he thought about it, he really should drop by and update her on his plans for phase two in the search for Peter Sutter. Seeing how she'd been so worked up about being kept in the loop and all.

That decided, he threw away the remnants of his lunch and headed along the river. Her office was located in a glass skyscraper, and after checking the tenant listing, he took the elevator up to the thirty-third floor.

He saw the door marked with her firm's name in bold gray letters, and walked into a sunlit, elegant lobby with white leather chairs, hardwood floors, and floor-to-ceiling windows.

A receptionist greeted him from behind a curved white desk. "Can I help you?"

"Ford Dixon. I was hoping to see Victoria. I don't have an appointment."

The receptionist nodded. "Let me see if she's available."

Ford walked over to check out the view of the Chicago River while he waited. Moments later, he heard footsteps coming from the hallway behind the receptionist. He turned around and saw a man with wire-framed glasses and dressed in a slim-cut navy suit heading his way.

The man held out his hand in introduction. "Mr. Dixon? Will Coffer, Ms. Slade's assistant. I was told you wanted to speak to her." His gaze was polite but sharp. "Ms. Slade doesn't generally take walk-ins. Can I ask what this is in regards to?"

"I'm working with her on a case and thought I would stop by to give her an update."

"Dixon . . ." Will cocked his head. "As in, the Nicole Dixon matter?"

"That's the one."

"You must be the brother. Victoria's new neighbor." He suddenly appeared quite curious as he looked Ford over. "She's very busy today. But follow me—I'll see what I can do."

He led Ford down a hallway, passing several offices along the way. The place buzzed with an energy that was palpable—not unlike the newsroom before deadline. Phones were ringing, one lawyer paced in her office while practicing some kind of speech or argument, and a younger man, probably an intern or paralegal, hurried by them carrying a stack of files almost as tall as his head.

At the end of the hallway was a second, smaller waiting area outside a large corner office.

"Feel free to have a seat," Will said. "She's with someone right now, but I'll let her know you're here."

From his vantage point in the waiting area, Ford could see Victoria in her office. He'd guessed right about her outfit—today she wore a camel-colored suit with a white silk blouse and high heels.

She leaned against her desk as she spoke to a woman in her midtwenties who was also dressed in a suit.

He watched as Victoria nodded encouragingly as she talked, looking surprisingly . . . approachable. Friendly, even.

Then she turned as the associate left her office and spotted Ford sitting out in the waiting room.

She folded her arms across her chest. "You are not my one thirty appointment."

So much for friendly.

He stood up and walked over. "I was in the neighborhood. Thought we could talk."

She looked over at her assistant. "How much time do I have?"

"Mr. Ulrich just arrived," Will said.

Ford peered down at her. "Guess I'd better talk fast."

"*Quite* fast," she emphasized.

Her office was large and airy, with a bold glass-and-steel desk and a view of the city and the river. He took a seat in one of the chairs in front of the desk, wanting to get one preliminary matter out of the way. "Nicole mentioned that she dropped by your office yesterday to sign a retainer agreement. She said you agreed to take on the case pro bono. I thought this was going to be a reduced-fee arrangement."

"Isn't a no-fee arrangement even better?"

For some, maybe. But having grown up as one of a handful of working-class kids in a very affluent suburb, there was some pride at stake here. "I can help Nicole with the legal bills. You don't have to take this on as a charity case."

Her expression softened a bit. "If it makes you feel better, I benefit from this, too. My firm has made a commitment to take on a certain number of pro bono cases each year. And your sister's case seems like a worthy cause to me."

When she said it like that, Ford almost believed that was all this was—a high-priced lawyer needing to do a little charity work for PR reasons. But his instincts said that there was more than met the eye when it came to the woman sitting across from him.

Still, he tabled that issue for now, since he was up against the clock here. "So, I struck out with phase one in my search for Peter Sutter."

She leaned back in her chair. "And phase one was . . . ?"

"Social media searches. I'd thought maybe I'd find the guy on Facebook or Twitter, but no such luck. Which brings me to phase two of my search . . . but phase two is more complicated and will take me longer to explain. And you have a Mr. Ulrich waiting."

"I do. But I think my Monday schedule is a little better." She turned toward her computer, as if about to check her calendar.

"Monday?" He laughed at the ridiculousness of that. "You live ten feet from me, Victoria. I'm not making an appointment to see you next week when we can easily talk this weekend."

"Who said I'm even around this weekend?"

"Well, are you?" When she didn't immediately respond, he smiled, knowing he had her. "Remember, the hair dryer doesn't lie."

"I suppose I could stop by your place tonight, after work." She paused, her lips curving up at the corners. "That is, if I can squeeze my way in between the cavalcade."

"Couldn't resist getting that in one more time, could you?" He stood up. "You know, you are going to be so disappointed when I turn out *not* to fit into whatever 'womanizing player' box you've put me in."

"I haven't put you in any box." When he gave her a look, she cheekily made a small square with her fingers. "Okay. Maybe a little one."

SITTING AT HER desk, Victoria leaned to the side and watched as Ford strode down the hallway to the exit.

Of course he would show up, unannounced, at her office. The man clearly had no sense of boundaries. Not to mention, he was entirely too confident with his little I'm-not-making-an-appointment-to-see-you edict. And also just generally irritating.

Great ass, though.

Broad shoulders, too. Lean hips. A bit of a swagger in his step that made a woman think—

"So? Did I hear you're meeting him tonight?"

Startled by the voice, Victoria jumped and quickly righted herself in her desk chair. She looked at Will, who grinned knowingly from the doorway.

"It's not like that," she said, cutting him off at the pass.

"Hmm, isn't somebody quick with the denial. I was simply wondering if I should block off an hour for your meeting tonight. Or do you need more time to conduct your business with the ruggedly Adonic man who sleeps ten feet from you?"

She threw up her hands in frustration. "Why does everyone feel the need to keep pointing that out? I'm well aware of where the man sleeps."

"I bet you are." Will's tone was sly as he left her office.

Clearly, she needed to start being more Badass Boss–like in their relationship, if she was actually *paying* to be mocked like this. "And I don't think 'Adonic' is actually a word," she called out, determined to at least get the last word in.

Five seconds later, Will e-mailed her the link to Merriam-Webster.com.

Damn, that man was good.

Eleven

SHORTLY BEFORE SEVEN o'clock, Victoria knocked on Ford's front door. She'd run late with her deposition that afternoon, and then had stopped at her condo to drop off her briefcase. While there, she'd debated whether to change out of her suit and heels, and then had thought better of it. Yes, it was a Friday evening, but after her conversation with Will, she felt it was important to underscore that this was a *work* meeting. She would simply pop into Ford's place for a few minutes, get the lowdown on the search for Peter Sutter, and then be on her way.

To her surprise, however, it wasn't Ford who greeted her.

Instead, a thirtysomething man with a shock of spiky, jet-black hair and dressed in a T-shirt and workout shorts answered the door. One of the guys who'd been with Ford that night at The Violet Hour, if memory served.

His eyes widened when he saw her. "Wow. I picked the wrong building to live in. And I just said that out loud, didn't I? Shit."

"Said what out loud?" Victoria asked, deadpan.

It took him a moment, and then he grinned. "Ooh . . .

you're funny, too." He held out his hand faux earnestly. "Hi, I'm Tucker. Will you marry me?"

"Don't you think it's time you retired that lame line? You've been using that since college," said a man from behind him.

"It's not *lame*, it shows off my wry sense of humor and makes a good icebreaker." Tucker turned back to Victoria for agreement. "Right? Good icebreaker?"

Before she could answer, a second man, holding a bottled beer, appeared in the doorway—the guy in the hipster hat whom Audrey had been eyeing at The Violet Hour.

"Hello, Ford's new neighbor," he cheerfully greeted her, extending his hand. "I'm Charlie. We hear you're a divorce lawyer or something." He cocked his head. "Huh. Have we met before? You look familiar."

"I was just thinking the same thing," Tucker said.

"I think we were at the same bar two weeks ago," Victoria said. "The Violet Hour?"

Charlie pointed. "That's it! You're the girl Ford was checking out." He tapped Tucker on the shoulder. "Remember, right before we joined the bachelorette party?"

Tucked nodded. "Oh, yeah. Man, he was really into you that night." He paused. "Probably, I wasn't supposed to say that out loud, either."

"So. That's some coincidence, huh?" Charlie asked her. "You two living next to each other now."

"Like a freaky, kismet kind of thing," Tucker agreed.

Charlie snorted. "Kismet? Who uses that word anymore?"

"Um, lots of people," Tucker shot back.

"Yeah, lots of people like my grandmother."

"Well, then your grandmother must be cool as hell, because Kismet happens to be the name of a comic book character. Marvel *and* DC," Tucker emphasized victoriously.

Charlie rolled his eyes, then turned to Victoria. "Anyway."

"Yes. Anyway," Tucker said, looking a bit peeved.

Both men stared expectantly at Victoria.

"So, just to clarify . . . is Ford actually home?" she asked.

"Right. That." With a chuckle, Charlie pushed open the door. "He's in the shower—we just got back from the gym. He didn't know what time you'd be stopping by, so he asked us to hang around until he got out."

Victoria stepped inside the loft, checking out the place as she followed Charlie and Tucker. Layout-wise, the condo was the mirror image of hers, and the kitchen granite and shelves were basically the same, but that was about where the similarities ended.

"Wow," she said, both surprised and impressed. Clearly, he'd invested a lot of time and effort into the place. Half of the open floor plan was designated as a living space, with a leather couch and chair, brick walls, and a sliding door that led out onto the terrace. But the other half appeared to be a combination dining/work space, with a striking reclaimed-wood-and-steel table and matching stools, and two entire walls of built-in reclaimed-wood bookshelves.

It was a great space, masculine and urban and yet also warm and inviting, too. The wall shelves were various heights and filled with a mixture of books, artwork, framed photographs, and other interesting odds and ends: an antique clock, a sculpture of a hand, and something that looked like a replica *Star Wars* blaster.

She walked over to take a closer look. Good thing this wasn't a date, because if it had been, she would've been tempted to spend a good, long time examining all the nooks and crannies of those bookshelves, trying to discover what they said about the man who owned the place. "This is nice. Really nice."

"Try not to sound so surprised," said a dry voice.

Victoria turned and got her first look at the shower-fresh version of Ford Dixon. Gorgeous as ever; six-foot-plus inches of incredibly blue eyes; wet, mussed hair; low-slung jeans; and a T-shirt stretched across his broad, solid chest.

And bare feet.

She heard the tiny cry of a hundred unfertilized eggs as one of her ovaries exploded.

She cleared her throat, pointing to the wall shelves. "Did you do this yourself?"

"I did."

"With our help," Charlie said, waving from the kitchen. "Well, mostly Tuck and I just drank beer and held a few boards. Speaking of which . . ." He tossed his empty beer into a recycle bin under the sink and opened the fridge. He grabbed another beer, then stopped short when he saw Ford staring at him.

Charlie looked between Ford and Victoria, then smiled innocently and put the beer back. "I'm guessing you two have work you want to get to."

"What are you guys working on, anyway?" Tucker asked. "Is this something for the *Trib*?"

"It's a project for one of Victoria's clients," Ford said ambiguously, giving Victoria a subtle look.

"Huh. Sounds very . . . boring." Tucker pointed a finger at each of them. "Well. I guess we'll let you two worker-bees get down to it. Shall we, Charles?" He headed to the door with Charlie, then turned and walked backward the last few steps. "Victoria, it was a pleasure." Putting his thumb and pinky to his ear, he mouthed *Call me* as Charlie yanked him by the back of the T-shirt and pulled him out the door.

"Yep. That would be Charlie and Tuck." Ford turned to Victoria. "Nicole asked me to not say anything to my friends about the fact that she doesn't know who Zoe's father is. That's why I was vague about what we're working on tonight." He went to the couch and pulled his laptop out of his messenger bag. Absentmindedly, he ran a hand through his hair, giving it a rakish, finger-combed look.

One stubborn, errant lock fell across his forehead.

He caught her looking at him. "What?"

For some reason, she couldn't resist teasing him. "Your friends said you were quite taken with me that night at The Violet Hour."

He walked over, moving in close. "My friends say a lot of things. I learned a long time ago to ignore ninety-nine percent of them."

She smiled to herself as he strode over to the table, laptop in hand.

That wasn't a denial.

"SO TONIGHT, WE come up with our list of baby-daddy contenders," Ford said, setting his laptop on the table.

Victoria took a seat on the stool next to him. "Great. How do we do that?"

"That's what I'm about to show you, Ms. Slade." He typed in the Web address for Tracers Info Specialists, and entered the log-in and password he had via his status as a *Tribune* reporter. Then he angled the computer toward Victoria so she could see what he was doing. "This is a people-search database. From here, we can generate a list of all possible Peter Sutters in Chicago."

"Are we even certain the guy lives in Chicago?"

Good question. "Nicole said he mentioned being a Cubs fan. So keep your fingers and toes crossed that he's somewhere in this city, or we're essentially screwed." Next, he clicked on the link to run a new search. "First, we enter the information we do know." He typed in the blanks he could fill—all two of them. "Name: Peter Sutter. City: Chicago."

When Victoria leaned in closer to watch, Ford noticed her perfume. Something light and feminine. And kind of sexy.

"How do we know that's how he spells his last name?" she asked. "What about S-u-d-d-e-r? Or just one 't'?"

He blinked, refocusing. "Nicole remembers him making a joke about being nicknamed 'Peter Butter' and 'Peanut Butter' when he was a kid. So I think we should start with a double 't' spelling and then try other options if we strike out." He clicked "search" and, within seconds, onto his screen popped a list of approximately twenty Peter Sutters and their respective info. "Okay. Now we have something we can work with." He pointed to the screen. "This gives us dates of birth. Nicole said she thought her Peter Sutter was between twenty-five and forty years old, so let's be overcautious and go with an age range of twenty to forty-five. That means we take out anyone with a birthday before 1970 and after 1995."

"The first guy on the list is out," Victoria said. "And the second."

Ford removed the eliminated candidates as they scrolled through the entire list. When finished, he sat back as Victoria did a quick count.

"Eleven men left," she said.

"Yep. One of these Peter Sutters is likely the dickhead who had sex with my sister, got her pregnant, and then sneaked out while she was sleeping."

She gave him a sideways look. "This is probably a good time to reiterate my don't-do-anything-stupid-and-screw-up-my-case speech."

"Maybe it is," Ford growled. Because right then, he was trying to remember all the reasons he shouldn't give Peter Sutter a swift kick in the ass when he found him.

Victoria leaned her elbow on the table, angling her body to face him. "Okay, so I can see you're going into caveman mode or whatever. But remember, we agreed that we would do this my way. That means the *professional* way. So while it's sweet that you're protective of your sister, if we're going to do this, you have to take off your big brother hat and simply be an objective investigator."

Like that was even remotely possible. "Do you have a brother?"

She sat back and looked at him, as if already aware of what he was going to say. "No," she conceded.

"Okay, your father, then. Think about how he would feel if he was in my shoes."

"I haven't seen the man in over twenty years, but fine—I get the point you're trying to make. But can you at least fake being objective while you're out and about and doing . . . whatever it is you're going to do to track down the right Peter Sutter?"

He gave her a look that said, yes, he could be cool. He wasn't dumb enough to do anything that might cause trouble for Nicole. "I can manage that." He turned back to his computer and continued on. "All right. For each of the eleven remaining Peter Sutters, this report gives us a home address, phone number—which could be home or mobile, depending on what he's provided to credit agencies—and a social security number. And with those social security numbers, I can run additional searches that'll tell us all sorts of interesting things."

She appeared amused. "You're getting into this, aren't you?"

"Hell, yes. I'm a journalist. Information is my currency." He saw her smile. "What?"

"Nothing. I'm just picturing you at your desk at the *Tribune*, typing away with a little 'Information Is My Currency' sign framed on your desk."

"Cross-stitched and everything."

She laughed. "Really?"

"No, not really." He raised an eyebrow. "But if these hot-reporter fantasies are something you have often, Ms. Slade, we could always explore that in more detail . . ." He smiled innocently at her withering look. "Or maybe we should just get back to the search."

"Good plan."

Hands hovering over the keyboard, he paused and looked over. "I'm going to begin typing now, so you might want to brace yourself for the onslaught of sexiness."

"I'm braced."

Rather enjoying himself now, he turned back to his laptop. "So, like I was saying, with the social security numbers, we can run additional searches for all these guys. I'll go ahead and pull one up . . ." Using the first Peter Sutter as an example, he clicked on the link for "Premium Profile" and scrolled through the various categories. "Okay, so here we can see if he has an arrest or criminal record. Also, whether he's ever filed for bankruptcy, has an eviction record, has ever had any judgments filed against him in a civil case, holds any professional licenses, is a registered sex offender, has any tax liens against him, and any outstanding warrants."

"And people say there's no privacy on the Internet." When he didn't immediately answer, she looked over. "What's wrong?"

Ford frowned. "It says that this guy—Peter Sutter Number One—has a criminal record." He went ahead and ran the search, which pulled up the man's criminal history. "He served a three-year sentence for felony battery . . . Oh, and he also has *two* class B misdemeanor convictions for possession of a controlled substance." His tone turned dry. "Ah, what every man hopes for in his sister's baby-daddy."

Leaning back in the barstool, he sighed. *Great.* Now he had to worry about whether he might be tracking down a criminal and bringing him into his sister's and niece's lives.

"It's probably not him, Ford," Victoria said reassuringly. She pointed to the computer. "For all you know, Zoe's father is . . . Peter Sutter Number Six. And Peter Sutter Number Six is going to turn out to be a really good guy. He'll be one of those dads who drives his daughter to ballet practice every Saturday morning while singing Disney songs in the car."

"God, anything but that."

She laughed, and their eyes held for a moment. Then she looked away and turned back to the computer. "This is great stuff, by the way. But how do you plan to figure out which one of these eleven guys is the right Peter Sutter?"

"Nicole thinks she could ID the guy from a photo, so I guess I'll have to go to their home addresses and somehow get a picture of each of them. I'm not a professional photographer, but I know my way around a camera well enough."

It took her a moment. "Meaning, you're going to *stake out* these guys?"

He shrugged. "I don't have much choice. Although first, I want to check out the bar where Nicole met the guy, to see if anyone knows a Peter Sutter. Maybe he's a regular there and we'll get lucky."

"Huh."

She was giving him a look he couldn't read. "What?"

"Nothing," she said. "I mean . . . it's not *un*-interesting, this idea of going on stakeouts and doing all this snooping around."

His tone turned coy. "Having another hot-reporter fantasy? There's always room in the car for two during a stakeout, Ms. Slade."

Yep, that got him another withering look.

* * *

AFTER VICTORIA LEFT, Ford did a sweep of his loft and began packing up the Restoration Hardware boxes. The hole in his bedroom wall was patched and the shelves were installed. Now that Victoria was helping his sister and niece, he figured the least he could do in exchange was temporarily dial back the rest of his noisy home improvement projects. He'd probably gone a little overboard with that, anyway.

Besides, he wasn't going to have time to start a new project right now—this search for Peter Sutter would likely soak up most of his spare time for the next few weeks. Not that he was daunted by the task. In fact, it felt good to be helping his sister and actually *doing* something. Still, he planned to reach out to an acquaintance this weekend, an FBI agent who was a friend of a friend, to see if he had any suggestions about ways to make the search for Sutter easier.

He stacked the boxes in the closet in his master bedroom, thinking that a trip to the storage room might be in order. While shifting things around to make more room, he pulled out the box his mom had given him, the one with his dad's things. He held it for a moment, debating, then set it down on his bed and opened it.

It was a mixture of stuff—photographs, some school yearbooks, an old stamp collection he remembered his dad showing him when he was a kid. Wrapped in tissue paper was a picture frame, one that held a photograph of him and his father at the Illinois football game on Dad's Weekend his junior year of college.

He remembered that day well. His fraternity had been tailgating in the stadium parking lot, and his dad had commandeered the grill, joking around with all Ford's fraternity brothers and the other fathers as he cooked up burgers and brats. He'd been in a good mood then, the life of the party, hamming it up for the crowd and proudly sharing his grilling secrets.

One flip. You gotta let the meat do its thing.

Two hours and six beers later, he was "asked" by security

to leave the stadium after starting a fight with an equally drunk fan of the visiting team.

Ford set the picture frame aside. He dug a little deeper into the box and smiled when he found something else—a model rocket he and his dad had built together when he was nine.

Ah, now *that* had been a great day.

He pulled the rocket out of the box, turning it in his hands and recalling the weekend he and his dad had spent building and painting it with painstaking care. Afterward, they'd launched it in the field next to their townhome, and all the neighborhood kids had gathered around to watch as it flew over five hundred feet into the air. His dad had high-fived him when the parachute released, and then the two of them had stood in the grass, his dad's arm over his shoulders, watching as the rocket floated gracefully to the ground and landed without a scratch.

Clearing his throat, Ford set the rocket aside and repacked the rest of his dad's things into the box. While stacking it in the closet, he realized he'd left one small box in his bathroom, the new towel rack he'd planned to install. He went into the bathroom to grab it and heard the sound of running water coming from the other side of the wall.

Victoria was filling her tub.

He shook his head. What was with this woman and her damn baths? Was she part mermaid? He could just picture her right then, pouring herself another one of her "nice, jammy" zinfandels as she waited for the tub to fill. Probably piling her long, chestnut hair on top of her head . . . and then slowly stripping off her clothes, one item at a time. Closing her eyes in hedonistic bliss as she stepped in the tub, perhaps even moaning softly as she eased into the water and slid her hands over her naked, wet skin.

Ten feet from him.

With an irritated grunt, Ford grabbed the towel bar box and hauled it into his bedroom.

Looked like he picked the wrong day to stop hammering away his frustrations.

Twelve

HER EYES CLOSED, Victoria took a deep breath and exhaled, listening to the sound of Dr. Metzel's voice.

"The key is to breathe from your diaphragm," he reminded her. "Try putting one hand on your chest and the other hand on your stomach, above your waist."

As she had when they'd first started practicing these exercises during their last session, she felt a little silly and self-conscious, sitting in his office with her hands on her chest and stomach. But according to Dr. Metzel, "diaphragmatic breathing" was the core foundation for the relaxation techniques that would help with her tiny panic problem (she still refused to call it a *disorder*), so she went ahead and did it anyway.

"As you inhale, the hand on your chest should move less than the hand on your stomach," he said. "Now exhale, allowing all of the tension in your neck, shoulders, and back to drain away. Good. Remember, this is something you can do anytime you find yourself in a stressful situation. Speaking of which . . . you're getting homework this week. I'd like you to start facing the things that trigger your panicky feelings—like the subway."

Nervous butterflies danced in her stomach. "Are you sure I'm ready for that?"

"We'll start slow. Pick a time when you know the subway won't be crowded. Ride it for two stops, get off, and ride it back. And while you're riding, here's what I want you to do."

Dr. Metzel walked her through another exercise, one that involved relaxing different parts of her body while silently repeating a certain phrase. *I feel quiet. The muscles in my forehead are relaxed and smooth. My shoulders are loose. My legs and feet feel warm and heavy.*

She studiously tried to memorize every phrase. She liked this technique—for the first time, she felt like she had a weapon in her arsenal to fight back against the anxiety issues that had been plaguing her since the break-in.

"Don't worry, I'll give you a handout that lays out all of this so you can practice on your own," Dr. Metzel said. "If possible, I'd like you to spend fifteen minutes a day repeating this exercise."

More homework? Good. That meant more progress. She mentally doubled the time to thirty minutes per day, thinking the faster she could whiz through these exercises, the faster she'd be back to her old footloose and panic-free self.

When they'd finished running through the exercise, she opened her eyes. "Well, that wasn't so bad."

Dr. Metzel smiled. "Glad to hear it." He folded his hands on his notepad. "Now, with the time we have left, how would you feel about digging a little deeper into what might be behind these panic attacks of yours?"

Balls. She'd spoken too soon.

He must've seen the less-than-enthused look on her face. "It's your choice, Victoria. But I really do think that exploring these issues would be helpful to your treatment."

She considered this. The good doctor was smart, using her desire to be cured as fast as possible like a carrot on a stick that he dangled in front of her. So she agreed—reluctantly. "Okay."

He appeared pleased with her decision. "I think a good place for us to start is with that first panic attack you had during the break-in. Take me back to that night, when you were hiding in the closet. I believe you said the 9-1-1 operator told you that help was on the way, and then you suddenly began to feel 'off.'"

"That's right."

"What were you thinking about? Walk me through that moment."

"Well, I heard a gunshot downstairs, and the guy who'd been raiding my closet ran out. Then I started to talk to the 9-1-1 operator, and . . . she said something that triggered a flashback."

Dr. Metzel sat up in his chair, looking particularly interested in this new, unexpected information. "A flashback to what?"

So. Here they were.

Victoria had been hoping not to get sidetracked with things from her past that had been long since resolved—happily, she might add. But seeing how her only other choice was to *lie* to her therapist, she figured she'd just get it out there so they could move on to the business at hand. "To the 9-1-1 call I made when I found my mother after her suicide attempt."

Clearly not having expected that, Dr. Metzel simply looked at her a moment. "Oh."

Victoria pointed to the pen and notepad on his lap. "I'll wait while you go to town with that one."

HER PARENTS' DIVORCE had started off like so many cases she'd handled over the years. Her father, an American Airlines pilot, had an affair with a flight attendant eleven years his junior, and had decided to leave Victoria's mother when his mistress discovered she was pregnant. Worried about supporting two families at the same time, her father—to put it bluntly—had turned into a cheap son of a bitch during the divorce proceedings, challenging her mother and her mother's less-than-stellar lawyer over everything. Suddenly, Renee Slade had found herself looking for a job for the first time in ten years, while simultaneously having to fight for every alimony and child support payment to which she was entitled.

Eventually, the fight had just left her.

Her mom had struggled with depression for years—Victoria could remember several occasions on which she'd come home from school to find her mother still in bed, with the shades drawn. The "bad times," as Victoria had thought of them when she was a child, would last anywhere from a couple of days to a week or two, but then they'd go away, and things would be normal for a while.

She'd known that something was off leading up to That Day, six months after the divorce had been finalized, when she was ten years old. She'd noticed that her mom had started taking a lot of days off of work, had heard her crying in her bedroom when she thought Victoria was asleep, and had seen the bills piling up on the kitchen counter, along with the letters from the bank warning her mother that she was delinquent on her mortgage payments. She'd tried talking to her dad about it during their decreasingly frequent phone calls, but by then his second wife's baby—also a daughter—had been born, and he always seemed preoccupied with his new family.

Still, despite it all, Victoria had been in a good mood when she'd arrived home from school on that particular afternoon. She'd been invited to her first slumber party, at Denise Russo's house, and had raced excitedly into her mother's bedroom to tell her the news. At first, finding the shades drawn, she'd just assumed her mother was sleeping again.

But when she'd seen the empty bottle of sleeping pills tipped over on the nightstand, she knew instantly that something was very wrong.

Hang in there, Victoria. Help is coming, I promise.

The voice, from all those years ago, faded away as she looked at Dr. Metzel, feeling the need to set the record straight.

"Before we go down some unnecessary path, you should know that I had a lot of therapy after my mother swallowed those pills. Two years of it, in fact. So I think I'm good there. A-OK on that front."

"Yet you just had a flashback to that day a little over a month ago, triggering your first panic attack."

Well, that. "That's just because of the similarity in the 9-1-1 calls. It's not like I'm thinking about my mother's suicide attempt when these other panic issues have popped up on the subway or during my exercise class."

He considered that. "Okay, what *are* you thinking about during those moments, then?"

"Mostly that I don't want to faint or have another episode in public."

"We touched on that before. Your concern about what other people might think if you had a panic attack in front of them. To not look 'weird,' as you put it. Is that something you've always been focused on?"

She considered this. "I suppose it's something I've paid attention to for a while."

"Where do you think that comes from?"

She had a sneaking suspicion where he was going with this and decided to cut to the chase. "Are you asking if it's something that started after my mother's suicide attempt?"

"I think it's possible there's a connection. But I'd like to know what *you* think."

She sighed. So much for not going down this path. "Suicide is unsettling. It's morbid. People don't know what to do or say when they hear about something like that. And believe me, everyone knew what had happened with my mom: the neighbors, all the kids and teachers at school, even the parents. Some kids teased me, others went out of their way to be extra nice, and some just looked at me weird and ignored me. But no one simply acted normal. So *I* acted normal, hoping that, eventually, everyone else would do the same."

"And now, as an adult? Why do you think you still feel that same desire to appear 'normal,' as you put it?"

She shrugged. "I like the way people see me. They see a strong, confident person. What's so bad about that?"

"Nothing. But there's a difference between wanting people to perceive you as a strong, confident person, and being fixated on it to the point that it manifests itself in a panic disorder."

Victoria fell quiet, not quite sure what to say in response.

"Maybe we should switch gears for a moment," Dr. Metzel said after a pause, likely sensing her unease. "Let's talk about your personal relationships."

Any topic of conversation that didn't involve the words *fixate* or *manifest* or *disorder* was just fine with her. "Okay. What do you want to know?"

"Do you date?"

"Sure." She was a single woman in her thirties, living in a fun, vibrant city. Of course she dated.

"When's the last time you were in a serious relationship?"

"Define serious."

"It's hard to quantify, but let's say a relationship that lasted more than three months."

Victoria thought about it. "Marc Joyner."

Dr. Metzel readied his pen. "And why did things end between you and Marc?"

She laughed, not seeing how this was even remotely relevant. "It wasn't like it was some big, tragic breakup or anything. He was heading off to UCLA, while I was going to Duke, and we both realized a long-distance relationship wouldn't work."

Dr. Metzel did a little scrunchy thing with his eyebrows. "Are you saying that your most recent relationship to last three months was in *high school*?"

She shifted in her chair. "Well, if we're getting technical . . . it carried a couple weeks into the summer *after* high school."

Man, did the good doctor ever have a field day scribbling away in his notepad after that one.

VICTORIA LEFT HER session with Dr. Metzel convinced she was the most screwed-up person in the world.

She caught a cab outside his office, gave the driver her address, and took a deep breath as the car began moving. All right, fine. So she had some issues about marriage and long-term commitment. If it wasn't enough that the demise of her parents' marriage had *literally* nearly killed her mother, every day at work she was reminded of just how sad and painful it could be when two people had to untangle themselves from the life they'd made together.

Marriage was a gamble. And so far, she hadn't seen anything that made her want to put her own chips on the table and give that big old roulette wheel a whirl.

As for these panic issues . . . So what if the idea of losing her shit in public bothered her more than it might bother others? They didn't have her history; they hadn't grown up seeing how people had stared at her mom in the grocery store, or at parent night at school, like they'd expected her to have a nervous breakdown right there. She'd grown up in a relatively small community, and people had whispered about her mother for years after the suicide attempt—the "crazy" lady who'd once freaked out and tried to kill herself. *Her daughter is the one who found her, you know. Can you imagine? That poor kid.*

Even though the sympathy had been well meant in many cases, it had only made Victoria feel worse. *Stop looking at me and my mom, we're fine!* she'd wanted to scream when she was younger. So now, the good doctor would have to excuse her if she was a tad more sensitive, perhaps, to the idea of losing control in a public place and having everyone once again staring at her and wondering what the hell was wrong.

Victoria slammed the cab door a little harder than necessary when she climbed out, then turned and gave the driver a sheepish wave. *Sorry, my bad. Got a shrink up my ass and it's making me a little peevish. You know how it is.*

She brushed her hair out of her face and took a deep breath. Probably, this would be a good time to practice those "calming" exercises Dr. Metzel had been so jonesed about.

Fortunately, she was in a better mood by the time Rachel showed up at her place a few hours later.

"Is that what I think it is?" She pointed excitedly to the garment bag her friend held.

"Yep. It just arrived today." Rachel stepped inside and pulled the red vintage-style shirtdress out of the bag with a flourish. "It'll go perfect with those red heels you have that tie at the ankle."

Twenty minutes later, Victoria, her new red dress, and Rachel made their way to the elevator. They planned to take a cab to RM Champagne Salon, where they were meeting

Audrey for dinner and drinks. As they walked down the hall-way, Rachel talked about the date she'd gone on the night before.

"I liked him. *Really* liked him," she said.

Of course she did. Whenever Rachel liked a guy, she *really* liked him. Always so hopeful, her friend was. "Look at you smiling. Tell me everything," Victoria said, as they stepped into the elevator.

"Hold the elevator," called a voice from down the hallway.

"Oh!" Rachel, who was closest, hovered her finger over the buttons, looking for the door-open button.

The elevator doors began to close, but then a man's hand reached in, blocking them. When they slid back open, Victoria found herself face-to-face with Ford.

"Ms. Slade. Fancy meeting you here," he said.

Speaking of things that made her peevish.

"Ford." She nodded in greeting as he stepped into the elevator and stood next to her.

"Sorry about the doors," Rachel told him. "I couldn't find the button."

Victoria made quick introductions. "This is my friend Rachel. Rachel—Ford."

"Victoria and I share a bedroom wall," he explained, in a mischievous tone that made this sound illicit.

"So I've heard," Rachel said.

Victoria shot her a pointed look, but it was too late.

"You've been talking about me to your friends?" Ford looked up at the floor indicator, his mouth curved. "Interesting."

Refusing to take the bait, Victoria stepped out when the elevator reached the ground floor and gestured to the building's main entrance. "Are you grabbing a cab?"

He pointed in the opposite direction. "Driving. I'm hanging out with this girl tonight, at her place."

Oh.

Well, of course. That's what single men often did on Saturday nights.

"Really cute," he continued. "She has these big brown eyes.

Adorable smile. Although she does tend to cry a lot when she wants attention, and the last time I saw her, she spit up all over my couch. So it could be an interesting evening."

Victoria grinned. "Zoe."

Ford shrugged. "I thought my sister could use a night out with her friends, so I offered to babysit."

Hearing that, something inside her softened.

That was a sweet thing to do for his sister. Really sweet.

"Now, seeing how you like to keep track of my Saturday-night comings and goings, I should warn you that it's probably going to be a late night," he said. "I'd hate for you to wait needlessly for me for hours, smooshed against your sliding glass door."

And . . . so much for that moment.

"SO WE'VE ESTABLISHED that he's single, right?" Audrey asked at the restaurant after they had sat down at their table and Rachel had told her about the elevator encounter with Ford.

"He's single." Victoria took a sip of her sparkling rosé, then felt the need to clarify something. "Not that it matters."

"Please. I was there, Vic. There was definitely something in the air between you," Rachel said.

"Sure. Aggravation . . . irritation . . ."

"Flirtation . . ." Rachel added.

Victoria rolled her eyes. *Flirtation.* Please. "I hesitate to tell you guys this, out fear of adding more fuel to the fire, but Ford and I are sort of working together on this legal matter for his sister."

"How did that happen?" Audrey asked.

"Long story. The point is, his sister is now my *client*," Victoria emphasized.

Both Audrey and Rachel waited for more.

"And . . . so? There's no rule that says you can't hook up with the brother of a client, is there?" Audrey said.

Well, wasn't everyone suddenly a legal expert? "Fine. He's also my neighbor. Very bad idea, hooking up with a neighbor."

"Technically, he's only your neighbor for the summer," Rachel noted.

"And think of the upside," Audrey said. "You could knock on his door, have great sex with a gorgeous man, and be home in less time than it takes to get a mani-pedi."

Victoria opened her mouth to scoff at that, but then paused. *Well, when you put it that way . . .*

Then she shook off the thought and refocused. "Look, I get that he's good-looking. But he has this way of getting under my skin, and on top of that he's . . ." She searched for the right word.

"He's what?" Rachel beckoned with her hand. "Come on, let's hear it. I'd like to know what snarky comment even you could possibly make about the good-looking man who gives you smoking-hot looks across a bar, makes you smile—yes, I saw that when you two were standing outside the elevator— and who *babysits his niece* on a Saturday night so that his sister can go out with her friends."

Victoria thought about that for a moment, and then finally answered. "He's named after a car." *There.* She nodded. *Take that.*

Rachel smiled. "Sweetie, if that's the best you've got, you're in serious trouble."

Thirteen

THE NEXT MORNING, when Ford's alarm clock went off at seven o'clock, he reached over and swatted it blindly until it went silent. He fell back asleep, thinking, after the night he'd had, that he could treat himself to a snooze.

Or four.

When his alarm clock sounded for the fifth time, someone pounded on the other side of his bedroom wall. Ford's head shot up from the pillow and he blinked at the sound of a muffled, annoyed female voice. He couldn't catch the entire speech, and probably that was for the best, but he was pretty sure he heard a *Shut the damn thing off!*

"You know, Owen was never this fussy," he called out loudly. Granted, for the last year Owen had lived nearly full-time at his girlfriend's place, but still.

For a moment, there was a silence on the other side of the wall. Then a single thud. *Kiss off.*

Of course she had to get in the last word.

Awake now, most reluctantly, he made his way into the bathroom and stood under the shower spray for over ten minutes, trying to remember why he'd ever thought it was a good idea to schedule a coffee meeting for eight thirty on a Sunday morning. Then again, at the time he'd made the appointment, he hadn't realized what he was in for when he'd offered to babysit Zoe.

"It's really important that you stick to the schedule," Nicole had said last night, as she'd walked him through Zoe's nighttime routine. "Bottle at six thirty. Keep her upright for at least twenty minutes; the pediatrician says that helps with the acid reflux. Read her a book at seven fifteen, and then put her down at seven thirty. She gets two pacifiers, one in her mouth and the other in her hand, or she won't fall asleep. Oh, and she just started rolling over onto her tummy, but once she gets there she doesn't *like* being on her tummy, and she hasn't figured out how to roll back. So she cries when that happens and . . ." Nicole trailed off, and bit her lip. "Maybe this is a bad idea."

"Nic. I've got this," Ford had said, lifting Zoe up and getting a big smile out of her. How hard could it be? They were talking about one small baby who couldn't even crawl yet.

No problem.

"I'm just saying, no one other than me has ever put her down before," Nicole had said uncertainly.

"Go have fun with your friends. We'll be fine."

And for the first hour and a half, he and Zoe indeed had been just fine. As promised, he dutifully followed *the schedule*—Nicole having mentioned the importance of that only about twenty times. He did the bottle and the book, got Zoe zipped into some wearable blanket that looked like a potato sack, threw in a "Twinkle, Twinkle, Little Star" for good measure, and then put her down in the crib to sleep.

Eight minutes later, all hell broke loose.

Zoe began crying, so he checked the monitor and saw that she'd flipped over onto her stomach and, like Nicole had said, couldn't roll back. Zoe seemed royally pissed about that, too, judging from all the yelling and the way she kicked her legs in the potato sack. Not knowing what else to do—since he was pretty certain that babies were supposed to sleep on their backs—he went into her room and rolled her back over.

Big mistake.

For the next two hours—yes, gasp, they strayed from *the*

schedule—they played this game. Zoe would be quiet for ten or fifteen minutes, then she'd flip onto her stomach and scream bloody murder until he went back into her room.

"Listen, you," he told her after Take Seven. "See here? It's embroidered right on your potato sack. '*Back* to Sleep.' You don't like being on your stomach? Then stop rolling over."

She chucked one pacifier out of the crib, unimpressed with the lecture.

After that, Ford decided to try a new approach—this "self-soothing" thing he'd heard his sister talking about. The next time Zoe flipped over onto her stomach, he let her cry. But after fifteen minutes he caved, because the crying was god-awful and he felt guilty as shit, and certainly no one in the damn apartment building was going to be *soothed* by that racket. So they went back to the flipping game. Eventually, it got to be so late that they'd moved into the time when Nicole had said Zoe might wake up for a feeding.

Figuring she might be hungry—hell, he certainly could use a snack after all the drama—he fed her. She fell asleep mid-feeding, so he seized the moment and put her down in the crib, being careful not to wake her up.

That was Big Fucking Mistake Number Two.

Ten minutes later, he heard Zoe coughing on the monitor and realized that he'd forgotten to keep her upright after he'd fed her. He ran into her room and scooped her up just in time for her to throw up all over both of them, a full-out, volcanic-style heaving that spewed out of her mouth and nose. Which was doubly disconcerting because, (A) holy shit, no one had ever warned him that something so tiny and cute could puke like a drunken frat boy who'd just gorged on a double-stuffed burrito, and (B) now Zoe was hollering like a banshee—*Who left the dumbass in charge of me? Help!*—as he hurried around trying to find clean sheets and pajamas and a new potato sack for her to sleep in. His shirt smelled like baby vomit, so he stripped it off and said screw it to both *the schedule* and the self-soothing crap; he was getting this baby to sleep come hell or high water. So he gave her the two pacifiers, and rocked her in the chair until finally she dozed off.

He even managed to sneak her back into the crib, but as he rinsed his shirt in the kitchen sink, he started thinking about the drunken frat boy heaving, and worried that Zoe might do it again and choke.

And thus, an hour later, when his sister came home around one A.M., she found him passed out on the floor in front of Zoe's bedroom, one hand wrapped around the baby monitor, shirtless, and smelling like throw-up.

He woke up to see Nicole standing over him, looking as though she was trying really hard not to laugh.

"How'd it go?" she asked.

He raised a thumb in exhaustion.

"Piece of cake."

AFTER THAT ADVENTURE, Ford was more determined than ever to find Zoe's father. Who knew if the guy would end up being much help to Nicole, but it was worth a shot. If he hadn't before, he now fully appreciated how difficult it must be for his sister, trying to balance work, Zoe, getting some sleep, and having some semblance of a life. Hell, he'd been on baby-duty for seven hours and felt like he needed a vacation.

With that in mind, he grabbed his messenger bag and keys, and headed out the door. He walked to The Wormhole and ordered two large coffees, then took a seat at one of the tables in the back, where he could speak privately with the FBI agent he'd reached out to—a friend of a friend who specialized in undercover cases. He was hoping, at the very least, that the agent could help him eliminate at least one of the eleven Peter Sutter candidates.

A few minutes later, Special Agent Vaughn Roberts walked into the coffee shop and headed over.

"Why did we ever agree on eight thirty on a Sunday morning?" he asked, gripping Ford's hand in greeting.

Ford grinned. "I told you—I was happy to meet closer to your place."

Vaughn waved this off as Ford slid the second cup of

coffee across the table. "Gives me an excuse to visit the old neighborhood." He, too, had lived in Wicker Park up until nine months ago, when he'd moved into his fiancée's Gold Coast town house.

"How's Sidney?"

"She's good." Vaughn smiled. "Poked her head up as I left just long enough to mumble something about bringing her coffee. Not a morning person, that woman." He took a sip of his own. "By the way, this better not be for a story. If I see anything by you in the *Trib* tomorrow that quotes an 'anonymous FBI source,' we will have words."

Ford chuckled. Despite the fact that he and Vaughn knew each other well enough—a by-product of the fact that his best friend, Brooke, was married to Vaughn's best friend, Cade—there tended to be an inherent distrust between reporters and the FBI. "You're safe. This isn't for work. It's a personal matter."

"All right. Tell me more."

Ford took a piece of paper out of his messenger bag and slid it across the table. On it, he'd written Peter Sutter Number One's date of birth, social security number, and last known home address. "I was wondering if you could get me a copy of this man's mug shot. He was arrested four years ago for felony battery, served a two-year sentence at Stateville. When I ran a search, the mug shot came up as unavailable."

"He probably paid to have it unpublished." Vaughn looked at the information, then tucked the paper into the pocket of his jeans. "Shouldn't be a problem. I can pull it up tomorrow when I'm back in the office. I take it this Peter Sutter is someone you're looking for?"

"Actually, it's the opposite. I'm hoping this *isn't* the Peter Sutter I'm looking for." Without mentioning his sister or niece, Ford explained the situation and said that he was helping to track down Sutter for a friend. "I have the list narrowed down to eleven men. Hopefully, after seeing the mug shot, we'll be able to eliminate this guy as a possibility. For the rest, I'll have to do some legwork to get their photographs."

"The kind of legwork you're talking about works best for someone who lives in a single-family home or a two- or three-flat," Vaughn said. "You stake out the home, say, in the morning before work hours, and if you're lucky you'll get a shot of him coming out the front door. Or, you might catch him pulling his car out of the garage, so you follow him to work and get a shot of him exiting the vehicle. But even that's going to take time."

"I don't mind putting in the time on this."

"Fair enough. But if any of your Peter Sutters live in a large condo or apartment building, it's going to be a lot trickier to snap a photo."

Ford had already considered this, which was precisely why he planned to tackle the men living in single-family homes and two-flats first. Still, he had a Plan B if that didn't pan out. "I can get license plate and VIN numbers from their social security numbers." Which, in turn, would tell him the make and model car driven by each Peter Sutter. "If I have to, I can wait outside the parking garage, wait until the right car comes out, and then follow the guy from there."

"This must be for someone important, if you're willing to go through all that."

Ford said nothing, merely took a sip of his coffee.

Vaughn chuckled. "Look, all these stakeouts might work. But depending on the address, some down and dirty undercover work could be a lot more efficient."

Ford liked the sound of anything that could save time. "Such as?"

"You get a partner. Someone who could knock on a front door for some plausible reason and ask the guy if he's Peter Sutter. Meanwhile, *you* are stationed somewhere nearby where you can snap a photo. If you can, I'd recommend a female partner for this kind of thing." Vaughn pointed with his coffee cup. "A tall, built guy like you comes around asking questions, and people get their guards up. But both men and women are inherently less suspicious when it's a woman looking for information." He thought about that. "Maybe Brooke could help you out."

"I don't want to get Brooke involved in this." Because Brooke, naturally, would want to know *why* they were tracking down eleven Peter Sutters, and Ford had specifically promised Nicole he wouldn't share that information with his friends.

"Maybe one of your female co-workers, another reporter?"

The problem, Ford knew, was that any reporter he dragged into this would undoubtedly ask a lot of questions, and this was a personal matter. But . . . there was one woman who already knew all about the situation with Nicole. A woman who, as it so happened, had vehemently insisted that she be kept fully informed about the search for the missing Peter Sutter.

Ford looked at Vaughn. "I think I know just who to ask."

AFTER LEAVING THE coffee shop, he walked to the corner of the three-way intersection of Milwaukee, Damen, and North avenues, and waited for the light to change. A Blue Line train came roaring toward the elevated platform on the opposite side of the street.

His eyes drifted up, drawn in the direction of the noise, and he saw a handful of people waiting for the train. Then he noticed—*well, hello*—that one of those people happened to be the very woman he'd just been thinking about.

Victoria.

Dressed in jeans and a T-shirt, she took a step back as the train entered the station and slowed to a stop. The doors opened, and she remained where she was on the platform, seemingly hesitating, until the train chimed.

Doors closing, said the automated voice.

As if propelled into action by the words, she sprinted onto the train, just beating the doors.

Ford watched as the train pulled away, having no clue what that was all about.

Another curious development in the mystery that was Victoria Slade.

Fourteen

FLUSH FROM THE high of her success, Victoria walked into her loft feeling like a victorious woman, indeed.

She had ridden the Blue Line a whole *three* stops and back, without incident. Granted, the train cars hadn't been crowded, which was the very reason she'd chosen to ride on a Sunday morning. But it was progress, nevertheless.

In a celebratory mood, she pumped Alicia Keys through the loft's speakers. *This girl is on fire*. She kicked off her shoes and headed into the kitchen, singing along with the lyrics. *We got our feet on the ground, and we're burning it down*. She was no singer, far from it, but who cared? She had *done* something about her tiny panic issue. She could report back to Dr. Metzel, and for once he'd be able to scribble down an A+ in that little notepad of his.

The song finished when she was halfway through the banana she was slicing for a smoothie. Almost immediately, there was a knock at her front door.

She wiped her hands and crossed the room, checking the peephole.

Ford.

Great. She opened the door, wondering how long he'd been standing there.

"It *is* a catchy song," he said, the corners of his mouth twitching.

Yep. Long enough.

With a sigh, she put her hand on the door. "Do you think it would possible for me to get just a bit of privacy once in a while?"

"That's loft living for you. The sound proofing is terrible in this place."

So she'd noticed.

He took a step toward her, his blue eyes warm with amusement. "I have a proposition for you."

"What kind of a proposition?"

"Invite me in and I'll tell you."

Hmm. Not sure what this was all about, she kept one eye trained on him as she stepped back to let him inside her place. He followed her toward the kitchen.

"By the way, I like what you did with the space." He looked around at her furniture. "Is the condo you bought also a loft?"

She went to the blender to finish making her smoothie. "No, it's a more typical two-bedroom layout. Probably about the same square feet as this place, though."

Ford helped himself to a seat at the counter. "Where at?"

"The Trump Tower."

"That's hardly a 'typical' two-bedroom."

She smiled in acknowledgment. "Maybe not." She turned on the blender and mixed the strawberries, banana, and orange juice together. "So. About this proposition of yours," she prompted him as she poured the smoothie into a glass.

"I wanted to see if you're free for dinner tonight."

She blinked, not having expected that, and felt a strange flutter in her stomach. "You want to have dinner with me?"

"Yes. At Public House."

It took her a second. "That's the bar where Nicole met Peter Sutter."

He nodded. "I talked to an FBI agent today about the situation. Based on some things he and I discussed, I think it would be helpful if you check out the bar with me."

"Me?" She laughed. "What am I now? Your sidekick in this?"

"Not a sidekick. I need a front man. See, I thought about it: what if, when I go to the bar and ask around, Peter Sutter *is* a regular? Maybe the bartender will know him, and he'll want to know why I'm asking. I can come up with some excuse, but it would be less suspicious to have a woman doing the asking." He waited as she considered this. "Think of it as an adventure. An adventure that would help *your* client, the struggling single mom who's really hoping to catch a break with this."

"Now that's just playing dirty."

He grinned and stood up from the counter. "I'll pick you up at six. Wear something cute—like you'd wear on a first date."

Her eyes met his archly. "I didn't say yes."

He peered down at her, his voice a little huskier than usual. "You didn't say no, either."

A FEW HOURS later, Ford knocked on Victoria's door. When she answered, he was rendered momentarily speechless.

She looked drop-dead gorgeous in a black pencil skirt, short-sleeved white shirt with a scoop neck, and the hottest pair of high heels he'd ever seen—black, with a strap that wrapped around her ankle in a way that had him thinking all sorts of naughty, decidedly *non*-platonic-neighbor thoughts.

"I knew it," she said at his silence. "It looks like I'm trying too hard, right? I hate dressing for first dates—even fake ones." She held out her hands reassuringly. "Don't worry. I have a backup outfit."

She turned around, but he caught her hand and stopped her.

Over his dead body would she change that outfit.

"Leave it." His voice was so low it sounded like a growl.

Her lips quirked in a smile. "*Okay,*" she said, imitating his growl. "*Let me just grab my purse.*"

Seemingly, a comedy routine was going to be part of their amateur sleuthing tonight.

In his car, they went over their plan as they drove to the bar. Ford managed to mostly keep his mind out of the gutter, except for one brief moment when she crossed her legs, hiking up her skirt and exposing several inches of bare thigh.

"So I'm supposed to pretend I'm nervous about a blind date and trying to get intel on the guy before he shows up." She pointed to the traffic signal ahead. "Green light."

The cars behind Ford laid on their horns.

Christ. He hit the gas, forcing himself to concentrate on the task at hand. "Yes. Act chatty. Casual. Tell the bartender your date mentioned that he's been to the bar a few times, so you thought he or she might be familiar with him and could give you some insight."

"Let's say worst-case scenario here. What if the bartender *is* friends with him, and he's like, 'I don't remember Peter saying anything about having a date tonight.'"

Ford shrugged. "Play it off. Say you just texted him back confirming the date a half hour ago. Or, act flighty and say you must've gotten the day wrong. A male bartender isn't going to think you're suspicious. Men are always clueless about what's really going on in a woman's head."

"True enough. But what if it's a female bartender? What if I say I'm meeting Peter Sutter for a date and Peter Sutter is her boyfriend?"

He thought about that. "Then you'd better run."

"Run?" She looked appalled. "That's your suggestion?"

"And you're not going to get far in those heels, so I hope you know how to throw a decent punch." He grinned when he caught her look. "I'm kidding. Look, think about what we do know about Peter Sutter. He's good-looking, and he's the kind of guy who ditches a woman while she's sleeping after picking her up at a bar. Sounds like a player to me—odds are, he doesn't even have a girlfriend." Seeing a parking spot on the street about a half block away from their destination, he pulled to the side and reversed in.

He turned off the car and angled in the seat to face her. "Don't be nervous."

"I'm not nervous. Just . . . out of my element."

He smiled, having a feeling that was a rare occurrence for her. "You'll do great, Victoria."

She tilted her head to the side, as if considering this. "Probably, yes." Then she gave him a little smile to say she was joking. "Okay. Let's do it."

They both got out of the car, and he walked over to feed the parking meter. She leaned her hip against the hood, watching as he put the receipt on the dashboard.

"I'll walk in ahead of you and find a spot away from the bar," he told her. "Wait for my text, then you go in. If the bartender does know Peter Sutter, you'll have to improvise a bit. Don't seem too eager, but try to find out where he lives. Anything that we can cross-reference against our list. Say something like, 'I think he mentioned that he lives close to here,' that kind of thing."

Victoria blew out a breath of air. "Okay. I just thought of another worst-case scenario."

He hid a smile, thinking she was kind of cute when out of her element. "Technically, I think there can only be one worst-case scenario."

"What if I walk in and ask about Peter Sutter, and the bartender points to some guy and says, 'Sure, that's Pete, right over there!'"

Hell, they should be so lucky. "Not exactly sure what'll happen then. But it'll probably include me saying a few four-letter words to the dickhead."

That settled, Ford strode off in the direction of the bar.

LOCATED IN THE heart of the River North neighborhood, Public House, a so-called gastropub according to the online research Ford had done, was bigger and trendier than most sports bars he'd frequented. Sure, there was the requisite wood paneling and TVs on the walls, but the crowd seemed more "urban professional hoping to hook-up" than actual sports fan.

He told the hostess he was meeting someone and asked for a quiet booth away from the bar. Once seated, he surveyed the scene. There were two bartenders working that evening, a man and a woman, and only a couple of open seats at the bar.

A waitress stopped by his table to take his drink order.

Bypassing the self-serve beer taps built right into the booth, he ordered a bottle of Robert the Bruce.

All set, he texted Victoria after the waitress left. Take the open seat on the left side of the bar. From there, he would have the quickest access in case he needed to step in, in the highly unlikely event that anything went awry once she began asking questions about Peter Sutter.

Moments later, she walked in.

Ford pretended to be distracted by his phone, but out of the corner of his eye he watched as she took a seat at the bar and crossed one high-heeled leg over the other.

The female bartender approached Victoria and took her order. After she walked away, Victoria checked out the other patrons seated at the bar, pretending as though she was looking for someone. After her drink arrived—something in a cocktail glass—she began chatting up the bartender. Ford couldn't hear what was being said, but from Victoria's smile, and her gestures, and the way the female bartender chuckled and nodded along, the conversation appeared to be going well.

He guessed the moment Victoria mentioned Peter Sutter's name, judging from the way the bartender furrowed her brow as if thinking and then shook her head. Then the female bartender gestured for the male bartender to come over, and there was more gesturing and explaining the situation, and more smiles from Victoria, and then the male bartender shook *his* head.

The waitress, who'd been standing at the bar to pick up an order, joined the conversation, and although she, too, shook her head *no* at what Ford presumed to be the Peter Sutter question, she launched into some story that had all of them laughing. Then she headed off in the opposite direction, carrying a tray of drinks, and the bartenders got back to work.

Victoria pulled out her phone, as if checking her messages. A moment later, Ford's phone chimed with a new text.

No luck.

He wasn't surprised—it had been a long shot, but a lead worth checking out nevertheless. He set his phone on the table and looked up, just in time to see the male bartender moving closer to Victoria. The guy gestured to her phone, making a big show of looking indignant, and Ford had to restrain himself from rolling his eyes. He could only imagine the lame line the guy was giving her. *Where is this Peter Sutter, anyway? What kind of jerk leaves a beautiful woman like you waiting?*

When Victoria smiled in return, Ford decided to head over. Time for this twentysomething bartender with the spiky blond hair to go . . . make a gin and tonic or something.

He tapped her on the shoulder. "Excuse me. Are you Victoria?"

She turned around and gave him a curious look—they hadn't discussed this part of the plan. "I am."

Ford held out his hand and smiled. "I'm Peter Sutter."

Fifteen

CARRYING HER DRINK, Victoria followed her "date" back to the booth and took a seat across from him. "Peter Sutter, huh?"

Ford appeared pleased with himself for the joke. "We hadn't discussed a specific exit strategy, so I improvised."

They paused when the waitress came by to drop off two menus at their table. She winked approvingly in Ford's direction. Staying in character, Victoria smiled back—*Yep, I hit the blind-date jackpot with this one.*

"So. We struck out," Ford said, after the waitress left. "Although, on the upside, you didn't have to hightail it out of here in your heels."

This was true. Both bartenders and the waitress hadn't seemed at all suspicious about her story; in fact, they'd been quite friendly. "None of them knew a Peter Sutter, or even any regular customer named Peter or Pete. So we're back to our list of eleven candidates."

"Ten, hopefully, after tomorrow. I have a contact at the FBI office who's going to pull Peter Sutter Number One's mug shot for me."

"An FBI contact—aren't you resourceful?" She raised an

eyebrow when Ford handed her one of the menus. "Are we actually staying for dinner?"

"Of course, it's part of our cover." He gave a subtle nod in the direction of the bartenders. "They think we're on a date, remember?"

Hmm. Interesting, how that had worked out. But, seeing how it was dinnertime and the bar's menu had a Wagyu brisket dip on a butter roll, she decided to go with the flow. Just this once.

When she looked up from the menu, she saw that Ford was studying her. "What?"

"I've been wondering something. Where's *your* cavalcade?"

She wasn't following. "What do you mean, *my* cavalcade?"

"When we first met, you said you're a big believer in casual dating. Yet, I haven't seen one guy come around since you moved in. This isn't some all-work-and-no-play kind of thing, is it?"

She gave him a look. "No, it's not an all-work-and-no-play kind of thing. It's just . . . been an off couple months for me."

"How so?"

"For starters, back in May, two guys broke into my town-home while I was sleeping."

Ford frowned. "Did they hurt you?"

"No. But regardless, I didn't feel comfortable living there afterward, so I put my townhome on the market, bought the condo in the Trump Tower, and then moved into the loft. Between all that, and work"—*and starting therapy for this little panic problem*—"I guess my social life has been on the back burner."

"I didn't know about the break-in," he said after a moment.

"Why would you? Besides, it's in the past now." With the exception, of course, of the tiny, aforementioned panic problem—a subject that most definitely would not be coming up tonight.

He seemed about to say something, then changed his mind. "All right. But how about pre-break-in? Just how casual of a dater are we talking here? Heartless love-'em-and-leave-'em type, or more a serial monogamist?"

Victoria took a sip of her cocktail. "You're awfully curious tonight."

"It's the journalist in me."

So they were doing this now, getting personal. Okay, good. Come to think of it, after these couple of weeks of living next door to each other, she was a little curious about him, too. "How about option C, neither heartless love-'em-and-leave-'em type nor serial monogamist? I like keeping things simple and fun. No obligations, no expectations, no endgame of a marriage, two-point-five kids, and a minivan in the suburbs. I have self-selected out of the happily-ever-after rat race, so to speak."

"You don't believe in marriage?"

"I don't think *every* marriage is doomed. But these days, you've got as good of odds as a coin flip of finding one that will go the distance. And in the eight years I've been a divorce lawyer, I haven't seen much that inspires me to try my luck."

Ford was giving her an amused look.

"What?" she asked in exasperation.

"I've just never had a woman say that before on a date."

"It's a *fake* date. And welcome to 2015."

He laughed. "You're just so . . ." He trailed off, his expression a mixture of frustration and something else she couldn't read.

"Beguiling? Irresistible?" she offered.

"Not exactly the words I had in mind."

They were interrupted when the waitress dropped by to take their orders. Starving after her first foray into undercover work—and a darn good performance, if she did say so herself—Victoria ordered the hand-cut fries with dips as an appetizer along with her brisket sandwich.

"Make that two," Ford told the waitress, then picked up right where their conversation had left off. "Okay, so marriage doesn't inspire you. What about kids? Is that something you're considering down the road?"

"Maybe." Victoria shrugged. "I don't know how I'll feel in a couple years, so I've taken precautionary measures to keep that option open."

"'Precautionary measures'? What does that mean?" He took a sip of his beer.

"I had my eggs frozen when I was thirty."

He paused, mid-sip, and then set his beer bottle back down. "That's . . . very forward-thinking."

"Maybe it seems that way now, but I predict that in five, ten years, it's going be an option a lot more women consider." She leaned in. "Let's be honest, it's an advantage you men have in the dating game, a chip you wield over us—our biological clocks. How many times have I seen a woman, like me, single in her thirties, successful in her career, but she's in a near panic when it comes to her personal life because she wants kids and she's done the math: she has to meet a guy by the time she's this age, so she can get married by this age, and pregnant a year later. I say the hell with that. *I* will decide if and when I'm ready to have kids. I'm not about to cede control over that to Fate, waiting around for Mr. Right to show up on my doorstep." She paused, catching that.

Metaphorically speaking, of course.

"Wow." Ford rested his arms on the table. "I can't decide if I'm frightened by you on behalf of the entire male gender, or really fucking turned on."

She flashed him a grin. "All part of my allure." Taking another sip of her cocktail, she decided it was time to turn the tables. "So what about you? Why are you still single?"

"Maybe I'm no one's idea of Mr. Right."

"I'm not even going to stroke your ego by responding to that."

He gestured vaguely. "You've heard it all before. Afraid of settling down, don't want to lose my freedom, enjoying playing the field . . . the usual stuff."

Yes, Victoria had heard it all before. But with several years' experience deposing people and cross-examining them on the witness stand, she'd gotten pretty good at sensing when someone was holding back. And there was something about Ford—perhaps that touch of wariness lurking in the depths of those blue eyes—that made her think there might be more to his single status than this rote list of thirtysomething male commitment angst.

She tabled the issue when their French fries and dips arrived. After asking Ford about work, she learned that he'd discovered an interest in writing in college, and had started as a beat reporter in the *Trib*'s metro department after graduation. From there he'd worked his way up to the position of investigative journalist.

"It's a different way of approaching a story," he explained. "Beat reporters tell you what happened—the straight-up facts. For example: so-and-so got arrested for such-and-such crime. An investigative journalist, on the other hand, might look at how the arrest was handled, or why this person was arrested when there doesn't seem to be much evidence, or why the police aren't looking at this other guy over here."

"Basically, you're just nosy."

"I like to think of it as asking the bigger questions. Digging a little deeper to find the real story." He gestured. "Take you, for example."

She pulled back in surprise. "Me?"

"Sure. I've been trying to figure you out for a couple weeks now. Then you made that comment the other night about your father, that you haven't seen him for over twenty years."

"So? What does that tell you?"

"For starters, I'm guessing your parents were either never married or got divorced," he said.

"Divorced."

"And can I also assume that your mom raised you?"

"She did."

"See? There's the story," Ford said. "Divorce lawyer, raised by a single mom yourself, you go out of your way to help my sister, also a single mother. Do you know what that tells me?"

Probably, she didn't want to know. "I didn't go out of my way," she scoffed. "Your sister was crying in the hallway while pushing a baby stroller. I asked if she wanted to wait for you in my place, and everything spiraled from there." She pointed a French fry at him. "You want your story? You Dixons have invaded my life, that's the story."

He shook his head. "I think you have a soft spot, Victoria Slade."

Something about the way he was looking at her made her think of Audrey's comment the other evening.

You could knock on his door, have great sex with a gorgeous man, and be home in less time than it takes to get a mani-pedi.

Still not a good idea.

But when he looked at her that way, it took her a moment to remember why.

IT WAS DARK outside by the time they left the bar and drove home. In their parking garage, Ford asked when she'd started her own firm, which led into a conversation about one of her very first cases.

"They were two of the most stubborn people I've ever met in my life," she said, as they walked to the elevator. "The husband and wife both refused to move out of the house while the divorce was pending, so they drew a line down the middle and each stayed in their respective half."

Ford laughed, punching the up button. "Get out of here. That's like something out of a sitcom."

"I'm completely serious. They used painter's tape on the floor to make the line and everything."

"How does that even work? How do you divide a kitchen in half?"

"Oh my God, the kitchen . . . No, you can't divide it in half, so we had to negotiate a schedule of the hours each of them could use it. The other lawyer and I spent two days fighting over things like who got to eat breakfast first, or the wording of clauses that required each party to be responsible for cleaning up his or her own dishes." They stepped into the elevator. "It's funny now, but at the time I kept thinking, 'I did not work my ass off in law school for ridiculous shit like this.'"

She smiled at the memory as the elevator doors closed, and leaned back against the wall. Then she noticed Ford was watching her. "What?"

"Just thinking how different things might have been if the blond woman hadn't sat next to me that night at The Violet Hour. Right at the moment you looked over."

"How so?"

"For starters, I wouldn't have ended up hanging out with

the bachelorette party. And there wouldn't have been any Charlotte, nor any Charlotte waking you up in the middle of the night a week later and getting you all cranky with me."

"Who knows? Maybe everything would've happened exactly the same way."

"Doubtful. I was about ten seconds away from walking over to you before the blonde sat down, and if that had happened . . . Well, let's just say I'd planned to be pretty charming."

The elevator reached their door. "Awfully confident there, are you?" she asked, as they stepped out and began walking down the hallway.

"You've already admitted there was a vibe between us."

"True. But in this alternate universe where you walked up to me that night, the odds are that you still would've found some way to annoy me."

"Maybe. But, deep down, there would've been a part of you that would've been attracted to me, nevertheless." He slowed down as they reached her front door. "Which means you would've said *yes* when I asked to walk you home that night, and we would've ended up right here, on your doorstep. With you wondering if I was going to give you a good-night kiss."

Her pulse began to race when he took a step closer.

Stay cool, Slade.

"Actually, I probably would've said that a kiss isn't such a good idea, with us being neighbors."

"And I probably would've said that you're overthinking things." He put one hand on the wall next to her, trapping her in.

Wow, had his eyes suddenly gone all sexy and smoky.

She fought to keep her voice steady, despite the fact that her sassy subconscious had just jumped up and screamed *Yes! Finally!* and now was eagerly waving Ford in with two lit air-traffic control beacons. *Straight ahead. Keep it coming, big boy.* "And that probably would've annoyed me."

His lips curved. "Probably." He bent his head, his voice turning husky. "But I would've kissed you anyway."

She closed her eyes and sucked in a breath when his mouth brushed over hers in a teasing caress that shot a thrill of antici-pation down to her toes. Momentarily forgetting everything else except her need to feel more of him, she slid her hands up his toned, solid chest and curled her fingers into his shirt.

He growled softly and pressed her lips open, pushing her back against the door. When his tongue wound hotly around hers, she moaned and arched against him. He cupped her cheek with one hand, kissing her so thoroughly that they both were breathless as he slid one thigh between hers, his other hand gripping her hip possessively and—

A door opened farther down the hallway.

They immediately sprang apart. Victoria turned and pretended to be searching for her keys in her purse as Ford shoved his hands in his pockets and gave a nonchalant nod over his shoulder. "Hey, Dean."

"Hey, Ford."

Her cheeks flushed both from the kiss and from nearly being caught, Victoria looked up and smiled at Dean, her neighbor in unit 4A, as he walked into the waiting elevator. She unlocked her door and stepped inside her loft, then turned around.

When it was just the two of them again, Ford leaned against the doorjamb, peering down at her with eyes that were a warm, heated blue. "I think it's safe to say that if things had gone differently at the bar that night, that would've been one hell of a kiss."

"Maybe." She stepped closer. "But this would've been the part when I would've said good night to you anyway."

His lips curved as he held her gaze. "Good night, Victoria."

After watching him walk down the hallway to his place, she closed her front door and leaned against it. Alone in her loft, she touched her fingers to her lips.

Irritating and overconfident, no doubt.

But goddamn, did that man know how to kiss.

Sixteen

AT WORK THE following morning, Ford met with his managing editor, Marty, to discuss a possible idea for a new story.

As was his ritual, he'd watched the local news on TV before falling asleep the previous night, and had seen something that had gotten his journalistic fires going. "The kid is only nine years old. Apparently, his father had come home from a bar and started a fight with the boy's mother. The boy jumped in to help, so his father put *him* in the hospital instead."

Marty shook his head. "It's terrible, I know. Martinez covered the father's arrest yesterday," he said, referring to one of their criminal courts reporters. "But how is this a story for you?"

"They said DCFS previously had been out to the family's house twice because of claims of abuse, but decided both times that there wasn't enough evidence to support the allegations. I'd like to know what was in those DCFS reports. And I'd also like to know how many other kids in this city have been victims of abuse or neglect *after* their families were already involved with child protective services."

Marty leaned back in his desk chair. "Sounds very similar to your story on Darryl Moore and the probation department."

Ford met with Marty on almost a daily basis to discuss potential stories. That was part of the job; a good investigative journalist always had a lot of ideas. But this story, in particular, had struck a chord with him, and he was eager to run with it. "I think that's a good thing, given the interest in the probation department piece. Maybe we make it a series. A whole exposé on negligence in government agencies that are responsible for protecting the innocent. That kind of thing."

Marty considered that and nodded. "Well, as long as you're pissing off government bureaucrats, you might as well add DCFS, too."

Later that morning, there was a development on another front: Vaughn e-mailed over Peter Sutter Number One's mug shot and Ford immediately forwarded it along to his sister.

"It's not him. No way would I leave the bar with this guy," she said, calling him during a short break she had at work. "Look at that blank stare. Seriously, you take this dude home and you'll wake up strapped to a table wrapped in cellophane."

"It's a mug shot, Nicole. You're not supposed to smile and play pouty for the camera. Try to picture him looking more approachable."

"It's not him. The Peter Sutter I met looked normal."

"'Normal.' Truly, it's great how much you're giving me to work with."

She chuckled. "But the good news is, I'm more confident than ever that I'll be able to ID the right guy from a photo."

The next morning, Ford woke up at the crack of dawn and hit the road for some light espionage. He wanted to scope out the home addresses of the ten remaining Peter Sutters, just to see what they were dealing with.

Three addresses in, he had to agree with Vaughn—sitting outside these places and hoping to get shots of the various baby-daddy candidates coming out their front doors would be extremely inefficient. First, it was going to be tough to find a place to park his car in several of the neighborhoods. Street parking in many areas of Chicago was at a premium, and often the neighborhoods were zoned for residents only. All he needed was for some nosy neighbor to call the cops on him because he didn't have the right permit, or because someone decided that a lone man sitting for hours in a car while staring at a house was, in fact, pretty suspicious and creepy. *It's cool, Officer, really. I'm just waiting to see if the guy living here is cute and normal. Why yes, that is a camera with a zoom lens in my messenger bag. Funny story.*

Probably not the best strategy.

On top of that, there was also the problem of alleys. In the city, the garage of virtually every house, two-flat, and multi-unit condo building was located in the back of the property, not the front. Which meant that even *if* he was lucky enough to score a parking spot in front of the home, *and* no one called the cops on his creepy-looking ass, there still remained the very real possibility that Peter Sutter Number Whatever would exit his home through a garage and alley in the back.

All of which led him to conclude that Plan B was the way to go.

Later that day, he stopped at an office supply store on his way home from work. He carried the bag of materials down the fourth-floor hallway of his building, and made a pit stop at Victoria's front door.

He held up the bag in his hand when she answered. "I come bearing gifts."

She checked it out. "Office supplies? Ooh, you really do know how to charm a girl, Dixon."

Cute. "These aren't ordinary office supplies. They're props."

"Props for what?"

"Our next mission."

She laughed at that. "'Mission'? I'm not going on any mission with you. I have work . . . a life . . . things to do other than play amateur sleuth with you."

"But you're so *good* at it. Watching you in action on Sunday at Public House, that was seriously quality stuff. Hell, I was there with you, and even I forgot you weren't actually there for a blind date."

"This is your plan? To flatter me until I say yes?"

Actually, yes. But he also had other tactics in his arsenal. "Remember, it's for your client. The struggling single mom with the adorable four-month-old baby who really would like to meet her dad one day."

"You are shameless."

He'd prefer to call it *persistent*. And right then, standing on Victoria's doorstep and looking at her in that sexy black skirt suit and with the memory of their hot-as-hell kiss burned into his brain, he was beginning to suspect there was more than one thing he wanted out of this mission. "It'll only take a couple hours."

She folded her arms across her chest. "Look, I can't today. I have a hearing in the morning that I need to prep for tonight." She paused, making a big show of trying to sound begrudging. "But I suppose I could be free tomorrow evening."

"Tomorrow. Okay." He held her gaze. "Thank you."

She caught his look and pointed, getting all huffy. "You say one word about some alleged 'soft spot' and I'll dry my hair at five thirty in the morning for a month. "

He bit back a smile. "Wouldn't dream of it, Ms. Slade."

WHEN SHE DROPPED by his place the following evening, Ford had just finished preparing the last of their props.

"You didn't say what the plan is. Is this casual enough?" she asked as she walked into his loft. She'd sent him a text message earlier in the day asking what kind of attire was required for their "mission."

He looked over her sleeveless white top and summery skirt, and then his eyes held on her strappy sandals. "As long as you can run in those."

"Ha, ha." As they headed into the kitchen, she shot him a sideways glance. "You are joking, right?"

"Sure. Mostly." He grinned when she poked him in the shoulder.

She followed him to the island in the center of his kitchen, where he'd put together large padded envelopes addressed to five of the Peter Sutters. "So, these are the guys who live in single-family homes, townhomes, or two-flats with a front door that's visible from the street," he explained. "Here's the plan: you knock on the door and ask for Peter Sutter. Tell him you live a block over and that a package addressed to him was mistakenly delivered to your place. Meanwhile, I'll be waiting somewhere close by, ready to snap his photo as soon as he comes to the door."

She considered that. "All right, that could work. But what if someone else answers the door, and Peter Sutter isn't home?"

"Depends. If it's another guy, say that you're a neighbor, that you have a package for Peter, and try to find out when he'll be back. You're cute. A male roommate—at least a straight, single one—will be happy to have you drop by again. But if a woman answers the door and she offers to take the package, just give it to her to avoid suspicion. We'll move on to Plan C for that particular candidate."

"What's Plan C?"

"All questions about Plan C will be answered after the conclusion of Plan B."

"Meaning, you don't actually have a Plan C yet."

"This is true. But when I do, it'll be genius."

Shaking her head, she picked up one of the packages addressed to Peter Sutter. "There's actually something in here. What are you sending these guys?"

It didn't matter, he'd just needed something to fill the envelope and make it look legitimate. "Pens."

She laughed. "Pens? Aren't they going to wonder why they're randomly getting pens from someone named—" She checked out the return address on the envelope, then raised an eyebrow at him. "N. Drew?"

So he was having a little fun with this amateur detective mission. "It doesn't matter what these guys think. By the time they open the package, we'll be long gone."

She looked at the spread on the counter before them, then took a deep breath and nodded.

"All right. Let's go deliver some pens."

Seventeen

JUST FOR THE hell of it, Ford decided to start with Peter Sutter Number Six since Victoria had randomly mentioned him in an earlier conversation.

For all you know, Zoe's father is Peter Sutter Number Six. And Peter Sutter Number Six is going to turn out to be a really good guy.

Here was hoping.

This particular Peter Sutter lived on a tree-lined street in a single-family home in Roscoe Village, a neighborhood on the north side of the city. There were no street spots available within camera range—even with his zoom lens—so he double-parked the car across the street.

Ford grabbed his digital camera from his messenger bag and lined up the shot. There were steps leading up to Peter Sutter Number Six's front door, providing the perfect angle for a picture. Satisfied, he showed Victoria. "Now, when you get to the door, make sure you stand off to the right side, so you don't block my shot." He pointed on the screen. "See? You want to stand here."

She leaned in to get a better look at the camera, moving closer.

Christ, she was wearing that sexy perfume again. While practically sitting in his lap.

"Right side. Got it." She pulled back, her hand accidently brushing against his thigh.

Kill him now.

"And remember, you're supposed to be his neighbor, so walk to the end of the block and head west when you're done," he said, forcing himself to stay focused. "I'll pick you up on the next street."

"Sounds good." She reached into the backseat and grabbed the envelope addressed to Peter Sutter Number Six. "Wish me luck."

Victoria climbed out of the car and got her game face on. She crossed the street and headed up the front steps of the house, a brick three-story set on an extra-wide lot. Being careful to stand off to the right side, she took a deep breath and rang the doorbell.

Here goes nothing.

After a moment, the door flew open and she found herself looking down at a boy wearing a baseball cap, whom she guessed to be around seven or eight years old.

He could be Zoe's half brother, she realized.

His attention drawn to the handheld game device he played with, he barely spared her a glance.

She smiled brightly. "Hi, there. Is . . . Peter home?"

"Dad!" the kid shouted over his shoulder. "He's in the bathroom." Engrossed in the game, he walked away, leaving the door open.

Thanks for sharing. But then Victoria realized—holy shit—Peter Sutter was home. She was actually doing this, like *now.* Moving a few inches farther to the right, she looked around, as if admiring the yard.

"Can I help you?"

She turned and got her first look at Peter Sutter Number Six.

Average height and build, in his late thirties, he had light blond hair that was thinning at the top. Victoria smiled and held up the package. "I think this belongs to you. I live one street over and it was delivered to my place by mistake." Given his hair color, she had a feeling this wasn't Nicole's Peter Sutter. Nevertheless, she paused for a split second before handing over the envelope, so Ford could snap his photo.

"Oh, sorry about that. Thanks for bringing it by." Peter smiled and took the envelope from her.

"No problem." She turned and headed down the steps, just as Ford's car pulled away. Around the corner, she found him waiting for her as promised.

"It worked," she said excitedly, while climbing into the passenger seat. "Did you get a photo?"

"Sure did." Ford held out his camera and showed her on the screen. "But it's not going to be him. The hair color is wrong."

"Still, that's now two Peter Sutters out of the eleven that we can eliminate." She looked over approvingly. "You may actually find this guy, after all."

Unfortunately, they struck out with the next two addresses. No one was home at Peter Sutter Number Eight's place, and a woman answered the door on behalf of Peter Sutter Number Three—his wife, Victoria guessed, given the wedding band she wore.

After that, they drove to the Edgewater neighborhood, where Peter Sutter Number Eleven lived in a two-story row house with a wide front porch. Parking was easier to find in this neighborhood, and Ford scored a spot directly across the street.

"I just thought of another worst-case scenario," Victoria said. "What if someone sees you snapping photographs and charges the car, demanding to know what you're doing?"

"On the off chance that happens," Ford said, while adjusting the zoom lens to line up his shot, "I'll show him my *Trib* ID and say that I'm a photographer, getting photos for a Home and Garden feature we're doing on the neighborhood." He grabbed the envelope out of the backseat, handed it to her, and winked. "But it's really sweet that you're worrying about me."

She didn't bother responding to that as she exited the car.

Well familiar with the drill by now, she headed up the steps to the front door, got into position, and rang the bell. No one answered, so she rang again to be certain.

No luck.

With a shrug, she turned to go, and made it halfway down the steps when the door opened.

"Sorry," the man said, out of breath. "I was running on the treadmill and had earbuds in." He flashed her a perfect smile. "Luckily, I heard the doorbell between songs."

Chiseled jaw, striking light blue eyes, African American, he was shirtless and sweaty with a towel thrown over one shoulder, and had muscles rippling *everywhere*.

Victoria blinked, vaguely remembering something about a mission. "Are you Peter Sutter?"

He nodded. "Sure am."

She held up the envelope. "I live on the next block. This was delivered to me by mistake."

"Those tricksters at the post office—always keeping us on our toes." He headed down the steps to take the envelope from her. "Thanks for bringing it by."

"No problem." She walked away and met Ford at their rendezvous point around the block.

"Nicole said that her Peter Sutter is white?" she confirmed, climbing into Ford's car.

"Yep. It's not him." Ford watched as she shut the car door. "And I think you left your jaw on the steps back there."

"Oh, was he attractive?" she asked faux innocently. "I hadn't noticed."

He grunted as they drove off, muttering something about her walking to Peter Sutter Number Two's house.

It was their final stop of the evening, a garden-level condo in Lakeview. Victoria waited at the front door, ringing the bell three times for good measure, and then finally gave up.

Still, both she and Ford were in a good mood as they headed back to their building, having narrowed down the field of contenders to eight. "Do you plan to circle back to the three guys we missed today?"

He nodded. "At least for the two no-shows. I'm thinking we wait until Saturday—maybe we'll have better luck on the weekend."

"'We'll'?" she repeated. "As in, you and me?"

"Yes, you and me." He looked over while driving. "Come on. Tell me you aren't curious to find this guy. I see the gleam in your eye every time we pull up in front of a new place."

Okay, fine. So she'd gotten sucked into the Mystery of the Missing Baby-Daddy. "Maybe I am a little curious. It's a different kind of case for me. Normally, I see families as they're falling apart. I've never had the chance to bring one together before."

"Wow. That is an unexpectedly beautiful way to describe what we're doing here, Victoria."

"Go away."

He laughed, then cocked his head. "I couldn't do what you do. Seeing families fall apart, as you put it. It's too depressing."

"Divorce isn't always a bad thing. In fact, a lot of times, it's the end of a bad thing. Besides, it's not like your job is all sunshine and rainbows. That piece you wrote, about the teenage girl who was killed by that guy on parole? *That* was depressing."

He shot her a sly look. "You've been reading my stuff."

"I read the *Tribune*. Your stuff happens to be in there."

"Hmm." He pulled to a stop at a red light and looked over. "Have you had dinner? I was going to order a pizza, if you want to join me."

She could say no, obviously. She could go home to her empty loft, the same as she did every night, pour herself a glass of wine, and settle in with her book and her bath and have a nice, quiet evening.

Or she could choose door number two, an evening with the irritating-but-occasionally-funny-and-not-entirely-intolerable man who'd actually made her *moan* on her doorstep the other night from just a kiss.

"My treat, for helping me out today," he added, with a smile.

Well, a girl did have to eat.

A SHORT WHILE later, Victoria sat with one leg tucked underneath her at Ford's reclaimed-wood table, eating pizza and drinking a double-oaked bourbon on the rocks.

"So I've been thinking about those five Peter Sutters who

live in condos and apartments without an exterior front door," she said.

"You really are getting into the Mystery of the Missing Baby-Daddy. Is this a 'Victoria Slade always gets her man' kind of thing?"

She smiled. "Exactly."

"Not even going to pretend to be modest there, are you?"

"Anyway, after today, I was thinking that we don't necessarily have to get their photographs on the first pass. There are bound to be other guys, like Peter Sutter Numbers Six and Eleven, who don't even meet the general description we have. Why don't I just try the package-delivery ruse with them, too? I could say I live in the building, and that the envelope was delivered to the wrong floor. Sure, you won't be able to snap a photo right there in the hallway, but maybe we can eliminate a couple of these guys on our own, just on sight."

He grabbed another slice of pizza. "I'd been thinking along those same lines. But the problem is, those types of buildings are likely to have a doorman or a security desk—and if that's the case, we wouldn't get past the first floor. Not to mention, in a large condo building, there's usually a mailroom or someplace where the residents go to pick up their packages."

She sat back, discouraged. "That's true."

"But, I was thinking I could try to bribe a doorman. Slip him fifty bucks and tell him that I'm a reporter from the *Trib* trying to track down a Peter Sutter for a story. Then I ask if he can at least tell me whether the Sutter who lives there is Caucasian with brown hair." He flashed her a wicked grin. "You're welcome to tag along. Maybe watching me flash my press ID will inspire a few more of those hot-reporter fantasies of yours."

"Been waiting for a chance to sneak that in again, have you?"

"A whole week."

Her lips curved up when she saw him studying her with those keen reporter eyes. "You're about to be nosy again, aren't you?"

"Did you know in law school that you wanted to be a family lawyer?"

"I had a pretty good idea that's what I wanted to do, yes."

"Because of your parents' divorce?"

"Because I knew I'd be good at it."

His knowing look said he hadn't missed the fact that she'd dodged that question. "How old were you when they got divorced?"

"You know, I've taken depositions that didn't involve this many questions." She took a sip of her bourbon. "I was ten."

"Was it just you and your parents?"

"At the time it was just me. Now I have two half sisters, the older of whom was born seven months after my parents separated."

"Ah. So that's why . . . ?"

"Yep, that's why. My father had an affair, then married the other woman when she got pregnant."

"Are you close to your half sisters?"

She felt a pang of something that stung, but quickly covered it. "Actually, I've never even met them. After my parents got divorced, my dad moved his new family to Miami, where he'd grown up. My grandfather and several of my aunts and uncles on my father's side are very active in the Cuban political community. I think my dad had wanted to get back there for years."

Ford cocked his head. "Slade doesn't strike me as a particularly Cuban name."

"It's not. I'm only half Cuban—I took my mother's last name when I graduated from high school. By that point, I hadn't seen my father in seven years, and it seemed like the right thing to do." Thinking she'd shared enough, she redirected the conversation. "What about you? Have you and Nicole always been close?"

"Sure, I guess. Although when we were younger, with the nine-year age difference, it was more of a protective older brother–little sister dynamic. It's really only been in the last few years that we've been in the same stage of our lives."

"Oh, I still see plenty of that protective older brother–little sister dynamic," she teased. Then she looked at him curiously.

"Now who's about to be nosy?"

Turnabout was fair play. "The blonde I saw on your deck the other day, the one who said she loves you . . . What's the story there?"

"I told you, we're just friends. She's like another sister to me." He beckoned with his hand. "Don't tell me that's all you've got, counselor—the blonde on my balcony. I expected far tougher questions from the illustrious Victoria Slade."

So, that's how it was going to be.

Game on.

Victoria looked over at the bookshelves next to them. Remembering how she'd wondered what the artwork, photographs, and odds and ends said about Ford, she got up and walked over.

She spotted something. "This is new." Pointing to a silver model rocket, she looked over her shoulder. "Tell me about this."

He paused, and then walked over. "My father and I built that when I was a kid. He died about a month ago, and I found it in a box of his things that my mom gave me."

Victoria's voice softened. "I'm sorry. I didn't know."

He gave her a half smile, repeating her words from the other day, when she'd mentioned the break-in. "Why would you?"

She said nothing for a moment, just looking into those brilliant blue eyes of his. Then she returned to her perusal of his shelves.

Very aware of how close he stood to her, and trying to ignore the flutters in her stomach, she spotted a hardcover edition of *Factotum*. She opened her mouth to say something dry—*of course* he liked Bukowski—when she felt his hands on her hips.

He brushed his lips against her neck and a heady rush of sensation flooded through her.

"What is this perfume?" he asked huskily. "It drives me crazy." His mouth glided over the sensitive spot right below her earlobe.

She felt her legs go weak. When he did that, she could barely remember her name, let alone what perfume she was wearing. "The neighbor thing, Ford . . . that could get complicated."

"Not if we don't let it." His fingers slid under her shirt and skimmed over her stomach.

She arched forward when he pulled down one of the cups of her bra. "This wouldn't change anything between us," she breathed unsteadily.

He glided his thumb over her tight, sensitive nipple, making her gasp. "That's what makes it so perfect." He pulled down the other side of her bra and cupped both her breasts, his fingers skillfully caressing the sensitive peaks.

Oh, God. She gripped the shelf in front of her, fighting the urge to whirl around and climb the man like a tree.

Then one of his hands slid underneath her skirt and past the lace trim of her underwear.

"You're so wet for me, Victoria." His voice had a more guttural edge. "Have you been thinking about me fucking you?"

She was definitely taking the Fifth on that one. But then he slid a finger inside her and she had to bite her lip to keep from crying out. "Ford." She leaned back, pressing against the thick, hard ridge of his erection.

"Give me your mouth," he growled.

She looked over her shoulder, so turned on that she moaned as soon as his lips touched hers. He claimed her mouth demandingly, his tongue battling hers in a hot, erotic kiss.

Not wanting to waste another moment, she spun around. He scooped her up and she wrapped her legs around his waist as he carried her to the table.

As soon as he sat her down, both of their hands began to move feverishly. He slid her underwear down her legs, tearing them as he yanked them past her shoes. When he straightened, she tugged impatiently at the hem of his shirt and lifted it over his head.

She paused momentarily, her mouth going a little dry as her eyes took in the sleek planes of his toned, broad chest and abs, the strong, corded muscles in his arms, and the light trail of dark hair that disappeared into his jeans.

She was so going to sex this man up.

He pushed her skirt up around her waist, spread her legs, and stepped between them. After tugging her shirt over her head, he made quick work of her bra, and his eyes darkened as he peered down at her.

She went back on her elbows invitingly, feeling an almost painful ache between her legs when he plumped one of her breasts in his hand and leaned forward to suck the tip into his mouth. She threw her head back, giving into the delicious sensations washing over her as he swirled his tongue over the tight bud. He pinched her other nipple and she gasped, a shiver of desire shooting down to her toes, and then he switched to that breast and soothed the aching nipple with his mouth.

Balancing on one elbow, she threaded her fingers through his thick, silky dark hair. "Ford . . . now."

His mouth still on her breast, he yanked open the button on his jeans and unzipped his fly. Then he straightened up and grabbed a condom from the wallet in his back pocket.

She watched as he shoved down his jeans and boxer briefs. His eyes holding hers, he gripped his thick, impressive cock and slowly stroked it.

And here she'd thought her mouth had gone dry before.

His jaw clenched. "Baby, when you look at me that way . . . " Instead of finishing the sentence, he ripped open the condom and rolled it on. Planting one hand against the table on each side of her, he settled between her legs, nudged her open, and slowly entered her, inch by inch.

Her nails scraped against the wood table as she moaned, feeling incredibly, exquisitely filled. She wrapped her legs around his waist as he began to move, slowly at first, letting her get used to him. Then he began to take her harder, the table creaking rhythmically as he pounded in and out of her.

"You feel so fucking incredible," he rasped.

"Yes. Just like that." She closed her eyes, letting go for the first time in what felt like forever, forgetting all about the break-in, and her panic issues, and everything else, and focusing only on the pleasure of the moment, the strong, cocky, annoying, gorgeous man who was driving her wild as his fantastic cock thrust in and out of her, so goddamn skillfully and rough and hard and perfect that she could scream.

He slowed his pace just as she started the climb to her orgasm.

No.

"Open your eyes, Victoria," he said in a guttural voice. "Look at me."

She did, and saw his blue eyes blazing heatedly down into hers.

He moved in slow, smooth, dominant strokes, holding her right at the edge.

"Ford." She tightened her legs around his waist, trying to get the friction she needed.

He skimmed a hand possessively up her stomach and between her breasts. "You should see how beautiful you look right now." He leaned forward, and shifted the angle of his hips. "Come on my cock. I want to feel it."

She dug her nails into his shoulders, crying out as she came. His swore under his breath and grabbed her legs, pinning her against the table as his hips flexed and he pounded into her, faster and harder, until he groaned, all the muscles in his arms and shoulders straining beautifully tight as he shuddered and slowly came to a stop and finally collapsed on top of her.

Neither of them said anything for several moments as they caught their breath.

"I think I might actually be bleeding," he finally said against her breasts.

She laughed—*oops*—as he pushed up and looked over his shoulder. There were indeed several red scratches from her nails, but no blood.

She smiled cheekily. "Well, you did say that you wanted to feel it."

When he grinned down at her, looking all flushed and tousled and adorably sexy, she felt a fluttering in her stomach.

"That's not a game you want to play right before I carry you into my bedroom for round two, Ms. Slade."

Liquid heat spread low across her stomach. "I didn't say there would be a round two."

He lowered his mouth to hers, his voice husky and wicked. "You didn't say there wouldn't."

* * *

TWO HOURS LATER, feeling deliciously sore and exhausted, Victoria climbed out of Ford's bed.

Digging around in the darkness, she found her sandals on the opposite end of the room, and her skirt in the doorway where Ford had peeled it off of her. Out in the living area, she collected her bra, shirt, and torn underwear, all of which were strewn haphazardly around the table.

After getting dressed, she went back into the bedroom and sat on the edge of the bed. Ford slept on his back, one arm thrown over his head.

She reached up and gently smoothed back the lock of hair that had fallen across his forehead. "I'm heading back to my place," she said, when he opened his eyes.

He blinked and pushed up onto his elbows. "You don't want to stay?"

"I have to work tomorrow. You know how it is."

"Sure. Yeah." He ran a hand through his hair, making it all stand on end.

A few moments later, she shut his front door and walked down the hallway to her own place. She smiled to herself, thinking that someone had indeed looked well-sexed after their evening together.

Good.

Eighteen

FORD SPENT FRIDAY morning at his desk, fueled by coffee while furiously writing a follow-up piece about Darryl Moore and the probation department. And this time, the gloves were off.

He skewered the department for their incompetence in losing track of convicts, and for repeatedly overlooking curfew violations and crimes committed by offenders while on probation. The problem, he wrote, went way beyond Darryl Moore. By cross-checking the department's files against arrest records, he'd found several other examples of offenders who'd fallen through the cracks, including a car thief who'd skipped mandatory meetings with his probation officer before shooting and killing a fifteen-year-old, and a sexual predator who'd broken curfew seventeen times—without repercussion from the probation department—before raping a thirteen-year-old girl.

. . . records reveal a systemic failure to monitor felons under the department's supervision. . . . County Board president Robert Samuels said that the probation department is "understaffed and in dire need of increased funding." . . .

Acting Chief Probation Officer Reece Meisner acknowl-
edged that mistakes have been made. . . . According to one
inside source, the department has lost track of "innumer-
able convicted felons" within the county. . . .

About twenty minutes after he e-mailed the story off, his
managing editor called him into his office.

"It's good, Dixon. Very good." Marty looked up from his
computer. "Why don't you let the acting chief probation officer know that we'll be running the story on Sunday's front
page. See if he'd like to be quoted in response."

The Sunday front page—*nice*. It wouldn't be the first time
for Ford, but still. It never got old, seeing his name, and his
words, on the front page of a newspaper with a Sunday cir-
culation of nearly eight hundred thousand.

"I'll do that," he told his editor with an efficient nod.

Strutting through the newsroom back to his desk, he dialed
up Brooke at her office.

A celebratory lunch definitely was in order.

THEY MET AT The Shore, their usual place, a restaurant
owned by Brooke's company that was located right on Oak
Street Beach. They scored a prime table overlooking the
water—one of the advantages of dining with the general counsel and part owner—and toasted over a couple of Dos Equis
to his upcoming front-page feature.

Shortly after their food arrived, Brooke brought up a different subject. "Why are Charlie and Tucker sending me text
messages asking if I know what 'the real deal' is between you
and someone named Victoria the Divorce Lawyer? And more
important, why don't I know what the real deal is?"

Ford shook his head, not surprised to hear this. Charlie
and Tuck had been all over him about Victoria ever since
they'd met her—particularly Tucker, who kept asking for his
"future wife's" phone number so he could ask her out.

Clearly, in light of recent events, he was going have to tell
Tuck that wasn't happening.

Ever.

"I told you about her," he said to Brooke. "She's my new next-door neighbor."

"Ah, right. The one who *SUCKS.*"

He chuckled, having forgotten about the text message he'd sent Brooke a few weeks ago. "Well . . . I may have been a little fired up when I said that."

Brooke studied him closely, then set down her fork. "Oh my God, you've slept with her already?"

"A little louder, Brooke. I'm not sure the volleyball players on the other side of the beach could hear you."

She lowered her voice, but still looked at him like he was crazy. "Your next-door neighbor? And here I thought you were an idiot for hooking up with that chick who made you talk dirty in a Scottish accent. How is this *not* going to be awkward when it ends?"

Ford dismissed this with a wave. "Don't worry. It won't be."

Brooke rolled her eyes. "You are so thinking with your penis right now."

That part of him definitely had been all in favor of sleeping with Victoria the other night, but his head also had zero regrets. "If you knew her, you'd understand. She's different from . . . I don't know, any other woman I've met, really."

"How so?"

He took a bite of his French fries. "She's this high-powered divorce lawyer. Runs her own firm. Smart, confident, and totally snarky. The first time we had dinner together she gave me this big speech about not wanting to get married, and how she's 'self-selected out of the happily-ever-after rat race.' And it's not just a speech—the woman is truly cynical when it comes to relationships. And snarky. Did I mention that?"

"Twice."

Right. Ford ate another French fry. "Although I suppose when you get past all the sarcasm and the saucy comments, she's actually kind of . . . funny. And it is pretty cute how she's so determined to hide the fact that there's this softer side to her." He grinned slyly. "Fucking hot as hell in the bedroom. And on my dining table."

Brooke gave him an amused look. "You do realize that's the most you've ever told me about any woman you've hooked up with?"

He scoffed at that. "Get out of here. I always talk to you about the women I go out with."

"That last woman you dated? Hailey? I don't even know what she did for a living."

Ford sipped his beer, remaining silent.

"Trying to remember?" Brooke asked.

"It'll come to me."

She smiled, her point made. "I'm just saying, it sounds like you like this Victoria the Divorce Lawyer."

Christ, not this conversation. "You know what you're doing, don't you? You're married now. And that means, like every other married person we know, you want all your single friends to get married, too, so that you can have couples' dinner parties, or couples' Scrabble nights, or go on little couples' weekend trips to bed-and-breakfasts in Door County, or—"

"All right, I get the picture. And that's not what this is about." Brooke paused. "Although Cade and I were just talking about going up to Door County with Vaughn and Sidney and Huxley and Addison."

"Of course you were."

"But that doesn't change the fact that I'd hate to see *you* pass up the chance to have something good because you're too busy being a typical male bonehead about these things."

"You know, if you were a guy, and I'd just told you that I'd had fantastic, no-strings-attached sex with a hot woman, we wouldn't even be having this conversation. You'd simply high-five me and ask if she has any single friends."

She flashed him a grin. "Sorry, babe. But when they handed out best friends, you drew the straw that came with boobs and occasionally likes to talk about feelings."

Great. "I was ten years old at the time. Of course I picked the straw that came with boobs."

She laughed, and then looked at him for a moment. "Just tell me you know what you're doing."

"Don't I always? Trust me." With a confident wink, he took

a sip of his beer. "So what's going on with Cade these days? Any more crampon shopping?"

OUTSIDE THE BAY window of the kitchen, a sailboat floated by on the lake. It was an idyllic scene—a beautiful summer day, not a cloud in the sky, and the water a calm, deep blue.

Inside the house, however, the scene was anything but idyllic or calm.

"Maybe if you'd paid half as much attention to *me* as you did to all the crap you collected, we wouldn't be here," the soon-to-be ex–Mrs. Hall shouted.

"If it's such *crap*, then you shouldn't give a *crap* about getting half of it," her husband shot back. He turned to Victoria. "Does she really have to be here for this?"

They were all gathered in the gourmet kitchen of the Halls' six-million-dollar North Shore lakefront estate: Victoria and her client, Brad Hall, standing at one end of the massive granite island; Lisa Hall and her lawyer on the other. The appraiser the parties had hired hovered awkwardly by the refrigerator, trying to stay out of the fray.

The Halls, both in their fifties—him, a technology entrepreneur, her, a cardiovascular surgeon—had mutually filed for divorce after nearly thirty years of marriage, for the simple reason that they couldn't stand each other anymore. Thankfully, their two children were grown, which meant custody wasn't an issue, because the divorce proceedings had been bitter and contentious at every step.

This meeting, the purpose of which was to determine the value of Mr. Hall's sizable rare notes, coins, and stamps collection, wasn't shaping up to be any different.

Before Victoria had a chance to answer her client, Mrs. Hall jumped in.

"Oh, sure. Turn away, talk to her instead of me," she said, pointing to Victoria. "That pretty much sums up our marriage. Only before, you would talk to me through the kids. Then they left home, and we didn't talk at all."

"Can we go back to that?" Mr. Hall asked sarcastically.

"Because this conversation is reminding me exactly why we didn't talk: because you bitch about everything. It's like you don't know how to have a fucking conversation if you're not complaining about something."

"Oh, sorry if I don't get all excited about some stupid dollar bill printed in 1861." Mrs. Hall pointed to the collection of rare notes that lay out on the counter. "Because for the last ten years, that's about the only thing that seemed to get your motor running."

"Gee, another complaint. Imagine that," Mr. Hall said in mock surprise. "You know, you used to think I was cute for being so interested in U.S. history."

"I also used to think you were cute when you were a size thirty-four in pants." She smiled sweetly, gesturing to his stomach. "Things change, baby."

Okay, time to cut this off, or they would be here for hours. Victoria managed to convince her client to wait in the living room as the other lawyer corralled Mrs. Hall into the sunroom.

Unfortunately for all of them, however, the appraiser had several questions about the collection. And every time Mr. Hall came into the kitchen to answer one of those questions, Mrs. Hall bolted out of the sunroom, determined to ensure that her husband didn't screw her over "with any of his bullshit." Convinced he was hiding part of the collection, she examined every drawer and shelf in the library and master bedroom, and also insisted they open the two safes in the home. All of which was furiously contested by Mr. Hall—and for no good reason, since, as it turned out, he wasn't actually hiding anything.

Victoria finally got out of there around six P.M., and then fought Friday rush hour traffic back into the city for nearly two hours. By the time she rolled into her office to pick up some files that she wanted to review over the weekend, she was mentally and physically drained.

Given the late hour, she was surprised when she saw Will sitting at his desk outside her office. "Hey, what are you still doing here?"

He held up a white takeout bag in one hand, a bottle of Basil Hayden's bourbon in the other. "From the way you sounded when you checked in, I figured you would need it."

"I'm *so* giving you a raise."

He grinned. "Sweetie, I already gave myself a raise last month." He followed her into her office, where she dropped off her briefcase and sank gratefully into her desk chair. He handed over the takeout bag—pork fried rice that smelled delicious—and then poured two fingers of bourbon into a couple of glasses he'd snagged from the break room as she told him about her afternoon with the Halls.

When she finished eating, she leaned back in her chair, a companionable silence falling between her and Will.

It was after eight o'clock, and the sun had just begun to set. Outside the window, the Chicago skyline was set against a brilliant backdrop of orange, red, and purple.

"It's funny," she said. "Just the other day I was telling someone how in the eight years I've been a divorce lawyer, I haven't seen much that inspires me to try my luck at marriage."

On the opposite side of the desk, Will had his feet propped up on the chair next to him. He turned his head and looked at her. "I'm guessing today didn't improve that opinion much."

Indeed, it had not.

Nineteen

THE FOLLOWING AFTERNOON, Victoria proudly told Dr. Metzel about her successful train ride the previous Sunday—an achievement she'd repeated just that morning by taking the subway to his office.

He seemed pleased with her progress, and encouraged her to continue with weekend excursions, when the train cars weren't so crowded, so that she could continue to "experience the feared environment" under safer, more controlled circumstances.

"And I also took an exercise class," she told him. Granted, it had been a yoga class at seven A.M. that morning, which meant no crowd and no hot and sweaty room to trigger her fear of light-headedness, but still. Baby steps.

He walked her through another version of a relaxation technique, then tried something new: he asked her to hyperventilate, and then hold her breath, with the idea of re-creating the sensations of a panic attack.

She got about a minute into that, and then began to feel light-headed. Immediately, she stopped.

"I'm not sure about this exercise." Feeling as though her heart was racing, she tried taking a deep breath.

"It's okay, we can stop," Dr. Metzel said reassuringly. "Remember your relaxation techniques."

She nodded and closed her eyes. *I feel quiet. The muscles in my forehead are relaxed and smooth. My shoulders are loose. My legs and feet feel warm and heavy.*

After several moments, she felt better and smiled weakly at Dr. Metzel. "Guess I'm not cured yet."

"You'll get there. The point is for you to remember that *you* are in control."

She nodded, then glanced at her watch and saw they still had ten minutes left in the session.

"With the time we have left," Dr. Metzel led in, "I was wondering if we could talk about your relationship with your parents."

"Sounds very Freudian."

He smiled. "Let's start with your mother. Did her suicide attempt impact the relationship between you two?"

No beating around the bush there, apparently. "Of course. How could it not?"

"Could you expand on that a little?"

"Afterward, I felt very protective of her. My mother is an only child, and my grandparents on that side were already in a nursing home at the time, so she didn't have anyone else to look out for her. My father was no help, naturally—in fact, after her suicide attempt, his entire family completely distanced themselves from my mother and me."

"Were you worried she would try to kill herself again?"

Only every day I left for school, for about five years. "It was a concern, yes."

"That must have been very difficult on you."

Victoria paused, surprised to suddenly feel a slight burning in her eyes. *For Pete's sake, Slade.* This was something she'd resolved a long time ago. "It wasn't easy, no."

Dr. Metzel held her gaze. "Were you angry with your mother for trying to kill herself?"

She shifted uncomfortably in her chair. Okay, see, now

this was why she didn't like therapy. "I mean, what kind of question is that? You want to know how I felt? I felt *happy* when she got better. There." She pointed to his notepad. "Write that one down."

Dr. Metzel let that sit for a moment. "What's your relationship with your mother like today?"

They were moving on—good. "She still lives in central Florida, where I grew up. We see each other a few times a year. Either I'll fly down there or she'll come up here."

"How about your father? Any contact there?"

"Nope. *Nada.*" She debated whether to admit this next part. "I looked up my two half sisters on Facebook a couple years back. I guess I was just curious."

"Have you considered reaching out to them?"

She shook her head. "How do you start that conversation? I'm not sure they even know I exist."

Dr. Metzel jotted something down and then flipped through his notes. "I want to circle back to something we started talking about during our last session, before we ran out of time. You mentioned that you haven't had a relationship that lasted more than three months since high school."

Oh, brother. "The summer *after* high school. And really, I still don't see how that's relevant to . . . well, anything."

"I think if you dig a little deeper, you might find it's relevant to a lot of the things we've been talking about."

"Ah, you have a theory." She cocked her head. "Okay, I'll bite. Let's hear it."

Dr. Metzel's voice was calm and matter-of-fact. "Your father left you, started a new family, and hasn't been in contact with you since. Then your mother, the only parent you had around, tried to kill herself—leaving you fearful, as a child, that she might try to do it again. My theory, Victoria, is that because of all this, you have significant trust, abandonment, and control issues that are continuing to impact your ability to have healthy, intimate adult relationships. Issues that *you* are reluctant to acknowledge, given your near-compulsive need to always seem 'okay.'"

Victoria swallowed, and said nothing for a long moment.

Blinking back the sting in her eyes, she gave the good doctor a half smile. "Well. I asked."

DURING THE CAB ride home, Dr. Metzel's words rang again and again in her head, like a depressing emo song that was overplayed on the radio because it had angst and *meaning* and because some people, apparently, liked to focus on the crappy things in life.

The good doctor was only trying to help. She knew that. He just . . . wanted to talk about things she didn't like thinking about.

She'd been doing just fine her entire adult life. She was a successful woman; she'd worked hard to get where she was today. Back when she was twelve years old, and still Victoria Delgado, she'd started working after school and on weekends to help her mom pay the bills. Then, she'd been a cafeteria server at a retirement home, the only place that would hire her that young. Now she had people who worked for *her*, at the law firm that bore her name and her name alone.

She had two great best friends. She had sex with men when she wanted. Good sex. So *what* if she didn't have serious relationships? Was that required? What, because she was a woman of marriageable age, she was just *expected* to follow that path?

Inside her bedroom, she realized she was pacing.

See? This, too, was why she disliked therapy. In a nutshell, because it made her feel like shit.

She needed a distraction.

She couldn't call her mother; heck, with all the raw emotions she felt right then, God only knew what would come out of her mouth. Audrey and Rachel were probably available, but they would know something was wrong and, frankly, she didn't know where to start the conversation of all the things supposedly "wrong" with her right then.

She looked over at the wall she shared with Ford.

Two minutes later, she smiled when he opened his front door. "I'm early, I know. I just thought if you weren't busy, maybe we could get a jump on things."

He pushed the door open. "Sure. Come on in."

"Great. Thanks." She took a calming breath and stepped inside.

Taking her gently by the elbow as she passed by, he cocked his head. "You okay?"

It was the oddest thing, but as she stood there, feeling the warmth of his hand on her elbow and peering up into his eyes, she suddenly just felt . . . better, somehow. "I'm okay."

She touched his cheek—that was cute, this "worrying about her" thing—and then she headed in the direction of his kitchen.

Time to get back to their mission.

Twenty

THEIR FIRST STOP that afternoon was Peter Sutter Number Eight's home. Car window open, Ford watched through his camera lens as Victoria waited at the top of the front steps of the massive Lincoln Park greystone.

She rang the bell again and shifted the envelope from her right hand to her left. Watching her through the camera lens, his gaze traveled over her blue sundress, which fell just above her knees. The deep color of the dress highlighted her golden skin, and with her rich brown hair pulled back into a long ponytail, she somehow managed to look both sweet and sexy.

Then he spotted the delicate gold chain she wore around her right ankle.

Oh, man.

An erotic image suddenly came to mind, of her lying on his bed and naked except for that tiny gold chain, while he trailed his mouth up those long legs and made her moan his name in that breathless, sexy way of hers.

And . . . now he had a hard-on.

Christ. Shifting in the driver's seat, he dragged his mind out of the gutter and refocused.

After a few moments, Victoria gave up. She headed down the steps, walked back to the car, and climbed into the passenger seat. "Is this guy ever home?" Sighing in frustration, she turned and tossed the envelope into the backseat.

Hoping for better luck, they drove next to Peter Sutter Number Two's place. Ford double-parked on the one-way street, in the gap between two cars, and confirmed that his camera shot wasn't obstructed.

The front window of the garden unit was open, the blinds up, and he could see a television on inside.

He handed Victoria the envelope. "Remember, stand off to the right, so you're not in my shot."

"Got it."

As she approached the door to the garden unit, he got ready with his camera. She paused, as if looking for something, presumably a doorbell, and then knocked on the door.

As soon as it opened, Ford began snapping away.

A spike of adrenaline coursed through him when he saw that the guy had brown hair and appeared to be in his mid-to-late twenties. Wearing athletic shorts and a tank top, he was in good shape and looked "normal" enough.

Victoria smiled as she spoke, and Peter Sutter nodded in the affirmative. Ford was close enough that he could hear the murmurs of their voices, although he couldn't catch their exact words. He watched as she presumably went into her speech about living on the next block, how the package got delivered to her place by mistake, et cetera, et cetera. Then she handed over the envelope.

Sutter grinned as he took the package from her. With a friendly nod, she turned to go, and Ford spied through his zoom lens as the guy—who very well may have been the dickhead who'd bailed on his sister—leered at Victoria's ass.

Ford's grip on the camera tightened.

"Hey, wait." With a sly grin, Sutter jogged over to where Victoria stood on the sidewalk. "I didn't catch your name, neighbor. Which block did you say you live on?"

Ford set the camera down on the passenger seat, thinking it was time for Peter Sutter Number Two to take his tank top

and his pesky questions and mosey on back to his apartment.
"We all set, babe?" he called out from the car.

Sutter started at the sound of his voice—clearly not having noticed him. Victoria looked over, appearing amused by this breach in mission protocol.

"Yep, all set," she called back.

"Great." Resting his forearm on the window, Ford leveled his gaze on Sutter. "How's it going?"

"Uh . . . good." The guy mumbled a thank-you to Victoria for bringing over his package, and then hastily headed back into his apartment.

Victoria climbed into the car and raised an eyebrow at Ford. "'Babe'?"

"It felt like a 'babe' kind of moment." He threw the car into drive, took off, and parked two blocks up the street. His camera was synched via Bluetooth to his phone, so he sent the best of the photos to his cell, and then texted them to his sister. "I told Nicole to be on standby this afternoon, so hopefully she'll get back to us right away. If Peter Sutter Number Two isn't our guy, I was thinking we could try our luck charming a few doormen." He flashed her a mischievous grin. "You'll want to brace yourself for another onslaught of sexiness, since I'll be doing my reporter thing."

He chuckled as she looked out the window, shaking her head and muttering something about his ego.

So much fun.

A few minutes later, Ford's cell phone rang, sounding through the car speakers via Bluetooth. Seeing it was his sister, he answered on speakerphone so Victoria could hear. "Nic, hey. I've got Victoria in the car with me."

"Yay, my favorite lawyer." She sounded slightly winded. "Ford said he roped you into helping him find Zoe's dad. Not sure how he managed that one."

Victoria gave Ford a wry look that said *she* wasn't quite sure how he'd managed it, either.

He winked, whispering, "All charm."

Victoria turned her attention back to Nicole. "I assume you saw the photo Ford sent you? What's the verdict?"

"It's not him," Nicole said without hesitation. "This looks like the kind of guy who gets your number at a bar and then drunk texts you dick pics at two A.M."

Ford began to roll his eyes, and then paused.

Actually, he did look like that kind of guy.

"Oh, crap." In the background, the roar of an L train drowned out Nicole's voice. It took several moments for the sound to fade away—a sound that was replaced by that of Zoe crying. "Sorry, I'm out running errands—I have Zoe in the stroller and the L woke her up. Shit, and she'd just fallen asleep, too."

Zoe's crying grew louder, as if Nicole was holding her close to the phone. "I know, sweetie, that train was really loud. Anyway, like I said, it's not our Peter Sutter," she told Ford and Victoria. "Listen, I've got to go. Zoe's totally melting down here. I'll call you back later. And thank you." She said a quick good-bye and hung up.

Ford glanced over at Victoria. "She sounded okay, right?"

"Nicole? I think so. I mean, it's obvious Zoe is keeping her on her toes. Babies do that, I guess."

He nodded, making a mental note to drop by Nicole's apartment tomorrow to take her and Zoe out to lunch. He caught Victoria watching him. "What?"

"It *is* sweet, the way you're looking out for her." Her eyes held on him for a moment before she changed the subject. "So. Who's next on our list?"

Next on the agenda, in order of proximity, were Peter Sutter Numbers Seven, Ten, and Five—all of whom lived in high-rise condo buildings. Their first stop was the residences at the Bloomingdale's Building, which had an attached garage with guest parking.

"You think the guard will go for it?" Victoria asked, as they rode the elevator down to the lobby level.

"Tough to say. It's a pretty exclusive place. They should have decent security."

She adjusted her dress so that the front of it dipped a tiny bit lower, and then winked. "Just in case that reporter ID of yours doesn't do the trick."

When the elevator doors opened, they stepped out into the marble lobby and headed for the security desk. A man dressed in a gray suit greeted them. "Can I help you?"

Having spent years trying to get information from people who weren't always thrilled to provide it, Ford knew that the best approach in this situation was to act friendly and casual. "I hope so." He introduced himself, showed the doorman his *Trib* ID, and explained that, as part of a human interest piece he was writing, he was trying to track down a man named Peter Sutter who'd helped rescue a woman who'd jumped into Lake Michigan yesterday to save her dog.

"Apparently, both the woman and the dog were struggling, when this guy jumped in and saved them," Ford explained.

Victoria gave him a subtle look of approval, seemingly impressed by his cover story.

For added effect, he pulled a small notebook out of his back pocket. "The paramedics on the scene didn't get Peter Sutter's address, but they did say that he's Caucasian with brown hair, somewhere between twenty and forty-five years old. Does that fit the description of the man who lives here?"

The doorman shook his head. "Nah, unfortunately, the Mr. Sutter in this building has red hair." He looked apologetic. "Sorry I couldn't be more help—it sounds like good story."

"Should be. We want to reunite the dog and the woman with the guy who rescued them. Get some nice photos of them together." He shook the doorman's hand. "Anyway, thanks for your time."

Inside the elevator, Victoria waited until the doors shut. "You didn't even have to bribe him."

Nope, he didn't. "And that, Ms. Slade, is how it's done."

FORD'S COVER STORY about Peter Sutter, Good Samaritan, similarly worked like a charm with the next two doormen. Unfortunately, they were unable to eliminate either candidate based on the information they learned—Peter Sutter Number Ten was Caucasian with brown hair, and Peter Sutter Number Five was Caucasian and bald.

"It's been over a year since Nicole met him. It's possible he shaved his head or lost his hair in that time," Victoria said as they walked out of the lobby.

"I'll circle back to him if need be," Ford agreed.

They were in the heart of downtown, right by Millennium Park. Walking along Monroe Street, they passed by a crowd of kids playing in the Crown Fountain, a shallow pool between two fifty-foot glass towers that projected video images of people's faces while spouting water.

"Who does that leave on our list?" Victoria glanced at Ford as they walked side by side. He had his sunglasses on, and the sun highlighted the warm tones of his brown hair.

That cute stray lock had fallen across his forehead again.

"There are the guys we need to circle back to," he said. "And we also have Peter Sutter Numbers Four and Nine left. Both of them live in three-flat condo buildings with no exterior front door to their units. We'll have to get creative with those two."

"Plan D?"

"Plan D." He ran a hand through his hair, as if trying to brush the errant lock into place.

When it fell right back, she smiled. "I'll get it." Pausing on the sidewalk, they faced each other as she reached up and tucked the lock into the rest of his beautiful, dark hair. "There."

"You must have the touch." He took her hand and ran his lips over the back of her fingers.

Criminy, that was smooth. A warm feeling spread across her stomach.

"I was thinking we could grab something to eat," he said.

"You know what happens every time we do that."

His lips curved wickedly at the corners. "Indeed, I do." He tugged her by the hand, toward the street corner. "Come on."

While they waited for the light to turn, Victoria looked around. "Where are we going? There aren't any restaurants this way."

"Sure there are. Seventy of them."

Seventy restaurants? It took her a moment, then she realized they were heading in the direction of Grant Park. "Oh, no. We are *not* going to the Taste."

Every July, the city hosted the Taste of Chicago, an outdoor food festival with musical bands that brought in over two million people. Chicagoans tended to fall into two camps about the annual bacchanalia, viewing it either as a time-honored tradition or something to be avoided like the plague.

Generally not the biggest fan of teeming masses of sweaty people, Victoria considered herself among the latter.

"It'll be fun," Ford said.

"Famous last words," she grumbled.

But she allowed him to lead her across the street anyway.

IN FAIRNESS, THE scene at Grant Park wasn't as bad as Victoria had feared. Food vendors in brightly colored tents stretched along both sides of the street. Surrounded by green parkway, and with the Chicago skyline an impressive backdrop against the gorgeous blue summer sky, she and Ford grabbed some food and strolled leisurely while they ate.

She looked over and caught him eyeing her Lou Malnati's pizza. "I told you that you chose poorly." He'd given her a big speech about trying something new in the spirit of the festival—hence the smoked alligator hot dog in his hand.

When he grumbled something about it being part of the experience, she smiled and decided to take pity on him. She held out her pizza. "Here."

He leaned down and took a bite straight from her hands. "Mmm."

She felt a flutter in her chest, momentarily caught off guard by the playful intimacy of the moment. "I've been meaning to ask: how did it go the other night, when you babysat Zoe?"

"Total disaster." He proceeded to tell her all about Zoe's volcano-like throwing up and him lying half-naked on the floor outside her room.

She laughed at the story. "Aw, the mighty Ford Dixon, taken down by a four-month-old." Looking at him as they walked side by side, she was curious. "Volcanic vomiting aside, you do seem to have a way with Zoe. Is that something you want someday? Kids of your own?"

He considered this. "I'm not sure. I like kids, but there's the obvious issue of *who* I would have one with. Not all of us have stockpiles of frozen eggs lying around."

"You know, if you settled down with some nice girl, she just might give you access to her eggs," Victoria teased.

He nudged her arm playfully. "Well, if it were that easy, it probably would've happened already. And then I wouldn't be here, walking with you on this nice summer day, eating this . . . disgusting alligator hot dog." He made a face, looking down at it.

She chuckled. "Just throw it away. I'll split the rest of my pizza with you." As he jogged over to a garbage can to get rid of the hot dog, she couldn't help but think about the intriguing comment he'd dropped in there.

If it were that easy, it probably would've happened already.

"So why isn't it easy for you?" She passed him her pizza when they were walking again. "Relationships, I mean."

He shrugged. "I already told you why I'm single."

"Ah, yes. I heard the laundry list of thirtysomething male commitment angst. But I think there's more to it."

"Hmm. Do you now?" He handed back the pizza.

She took a bite, saying nothing further. Naturally, she was curious. She'd slept with him, she was working with him on a case, and, oddly enough, they were sort of becoming friends. But if this was something he didn't want to talk about, she wouldn't pry.

She, of all people, could respect someone's need to keep certain things private.

"For the record, there are some very valid reasons on that laundry list of male commitment angst." He paused. "But it's also been theorized, by some, that my 'intimacy' issues have something to do with growing up with an alcoholic parent."

As someone who knew all about having a complicated relationship with a parent, she treaded lightly with her next question. "And what do you think?"

"I think . . . that we need funnel cake." He slowed to a stop in front of a tent with a yellow-striped awning.

Apparently, they were changing the subject now.

Fair enough.

She smiled. "Funnel cake, it is."

AFTER SPLITTING A plate-sized helping of sugarcoated
fried dough, they bought a couple of beers and walked to the
Petrillo Music Shell, the outdoor amphitheater in Grant Park.
A folk-rock band was playing, so they took advantage of the
nice evening and sat on the grass to listen.

At some point around the fourth song, Ford looked over
and held her gaze, then reached out and gently tucked a lock
of hair that had fallen out of her ponytail behind her ear.

Victoria wasn't naïve; she knew exactly what he was doing.
The heated looks, the teasing, the playful touches here and
there were all part of the dance—a fun summer fling between
two people who were simply enjoying the moment.

So she leaned in and kissed him.

It was a slow, languid kiss, her lips moving over his as one
of her hands rested on his thigh. He cupped the back of her
neck, gently parting her mouth with his own. They were in a
public place, so there was only so far the kiss could go, and
perhaps that made it even more exciting. Because when his
tongue brushed against hers in a barely there tease—she felt
a zip of heat go straight to her core.

She pulled back, feeling flushed. "I think we should go."

His eyes were as smoky as his voice. "I think so, too."

Twenty-five minutes later, he had her pinned against the
inside of his front door, both of her hands trapped in one of
his as he kissed her neck and slid his free hand underneath
her dress.

"I need my hands free," she murmured, completely turned
on by the feel of his lips and hands on her.

His voice was low and sinful in her ear. "I like having you
at my mercy."

"You'll like the things I can do with my hands even more."

Just like that, he released her. "All right. Show me."

Her lips curved, she tugged his shirt over his head, dropped
it to the floor, and smoothed her hands over his chest.

So beautiful.

Then her fingers skimmed down to the fly of his jeans. She held his gaze, watching as heat flashed in his eyes when she undid the button. Slowly, she slid the zipper down, her fingers brushing against the hard length of his erection.

She got down on her knees.

"Victoria." His voice was low and guttural.

She slid his jeans and boxer briefs past his hips, wrapped her hand around the base of his cock, and took him into her mouth.

"Fuck, baby, that's so good," he groaned, flattening one hand against the front door.

After a teasing lick, she looked up to meet his gaze. "I've noticed you like to talk during sex, Mr. Dixon. Just remember, the soundproofing is terrible in this place."

He curled his fingers tightly into her hair, his eyes blazing down into hers. "I'm going to make you pay for this, you know."

She smiled wickedly.

Oh, she was counting on it.

Twenty-one

VICTORIA SPENT MOST of Monday morning in a settlement conference, working out a custody schedule for the divorcing couple's three children. It was hardly a pleasant meeting—both parties got particularly emotional when dividing up the Thanksgiving and Christmas holidays—but for the sake of their kids, everyone at least remained generally civil to one another.

In her book, that was a major victory.

When she got back to her office, Will handed her a stack of messages. "The usual suspects. Oh, and Ford Dixon called. He said he tried your cell first."

Interesting. She wasn't expecting him to call. "I had my phone on mute during the settlement conference."

"And how is our intrepid, Adonic neighbor these days?" Will asked cheekily.

Not bothering to dignify the comment, she simply gave him a look and headed into her office. She shut her door for privacy and flipped through the messages to make sure none of them were urgent.

Then she dialed the number to Ford's cell phone.

"Ms. Slade," he answered warmly. "What are you doing tomorrow between twelve and two?"

She turned in the desk chair to check her calendar on her computer. "I don't know, why?"

"I thought we might pencil in a nooner."

Seriously.

"Please tell me you did not just say that in the middle of the *Trib* newsroom."

He chuckled. "You're safe—I'm out grabbing lunch. And the real reason I called is to tell you about Plan D."

She smiled, not at all surprised to hear that there was, in fact, a Plan D already. The man was always coming up with some sort of scheme—he was rather annoyingly clever that way. "All right. Tell me."

"I went by Peter Sutter Number Four's three-flat this morning. He lives only two blocks from a Red Line stop, so I thought I'd hang out for an hour or so on the off chance I could catch a guy with brown hair walking out the front door of the building to take the L to work. But when I got to his place, I discovered something even better: a For Sale sign that says there's going to be an open house tomorrow. And since I know you're going to ask—yep, I already checked. It's for unit three, Sutter's condo."

Ooh . . . that *was* interesting news. "Is it for sale by owner? Do you think Sutter will be there tomorrow?"

"Doubtful. The place is listed with a real estate agent named Melanie Ames. But there's likely to be some photograph of him somewhere inside the place. I can snap a picture of that with my phone and forward it to Nic. And if that doesn't work, there's always Plan E."

"What's Plan E?"

"I steal his toothbrush for a DNA sample. Which brings me to the point of my call: if I have some eager real estate agent following me around, it'll be hard for me to do my thing. So I was thinking it'd be nice to have someone with me who could act as a decoy."

"That's what you were thinking, huh?" Victoria checked out her calendar. "I have a call scheduled for noon tomorrow that shouldn't last more than a half hour. Why don't you text me Sutter's address and I'll meet you there at one o'clock?"

"Actually, why don't I come to your office at twelve thirty and we can cab over together? It'll work better with our cover story if you and I arrive together."

"What cover story?"

"That we're a couple, sweetie. You and I are taking the plunge and buying a place together."

Oh, boy.

FORD COULD ONLY imagine what the cabdriver thought he and Victoria were up to.

"Okay, another worst-case scenario," she said, her body angled in the backseat of the cab so she could face him. "What if I get stuck in a conversation with this real estate agent while you're doing your thing, and she starts asking me questions about how long you and I have been dating? Or how we met?"

"I wouldn't get too complicated. Stick as close to the truth as possible. Just tell her that we met when you moved into the place next to mine, and things developed from there."

Victoria nodded. "Okay. And how long have we been dating?"

He shrugged. "I don't know. Three years?"

"Three years?" She threw him a look. "Oh, I don't think so."

"What's wrong with three years?"

"I'm just saying, *if* I were actually the type to be in a serious relationship, at thirty-three years old I would hope it wouldn't take *three years* for him and I to figure out whether we're compatible enough to live together."

Ford considered that. "All right. So we've been dating, let's say . . . six months."

"Six months? And we're already moving in together?" Victoria snorted. "How'd you manage to talk me into that?"

"Okay, why don't *you* pick a length of time between six months and three years after which you would feel comfortable *fake* living with me, and we'll just go with that?"

That got a smile out of her. "Sorry. I get a little nervous before these missions."

Yes, she did. And he found it more adorable every time they were together.

Per his instructions, the cab pulled to a stop at the end of the block. Victoria climbed out while Ford paid the driver, who—having overheard their entire conversation—gave him an odd look.

"Long story," Ford said, handing over a twenty. Then he stepped out of the cab and met Victoria at the sidewalk. Together, they walked toward Sutter's three-flat. "Remember, this is a brokers' open house, so it'll be mostly real estate agents. But you and I were driving by the other day, saw the open house sign, and thought we'd check it out. We've been eyeing this block for a while, given how close it is to both the L and Wrigley Field."

"Big Cubs fans, are we?"

"Oh, huge. We're on the waiting list to get season tickets." He crossed his fingers. "Here's hoping for next year."

"Okay, you are way too good at this." As they headed up the front steps of the building, she looked sideways at him. "One year."

He cocked his head, not following.

"That's how long I'd want to fake date someone before fake moving in with him," she explained.

"One year. Okay." With a smile, he took her hand, leading her up the stairs to the unit on the third floor.

The door was open, so he and Victoria walked right in. There were several people milling about the penthouse condo, and a handful more gathered around the kitchen island, where light refreshments had been laid out.

It was a nice space, with lots of sunlight, vaulted ceilings, and maple hardwood floors. Two bedrooms, two baths, according to the listing sheet Ford took from the dining table as part of their cover. He and Victoria meandered into the living room, where he spotted several framed photos on the fireplace mantel.

Including a wedding photo.

Exchanging glances with Victoria—she'd spotted it, too—the two of them made their way over to get a better look.

"Any questions I can answer about the place?" asked a male voice from behind them.

Ford turned around.

The man smiled and gestured over his shoulder. "My wife, Melanie, is the real estate agent, but since she's a little busy, I'm helping out." He held out his hand to Ford. "Peter Sutter."

Ford shook his hand, taking in the man's brown eyes and short brown hair. Good-looking and built, this man would undoubtedly meet even Nicole's standards of "cute" and normal looking. And there was one other thing that stood out about Peter Sutter Number Four.

He was the spitting image of Zoe.

Twenty-two

FEIGNING INTEREST, VICTORIA nodded along as Sutter talked about the upgrades he and his wife had made to the unit, and told them not to miss the private rooftop deck.

After he excused himself to greet another visitor, Ford turned to her. "Should we see the bedrooms next?"

"Definitely."

Playing their parts, they checked out the second bedroom first, which the Sutters were currently using as an office, before moving on to the master suite. Victoria smiled politely as a woman passed them on her way out. Then she turned to Ford, whispering, "I think it's him."

He nodded in agreement. "I'm pretty sure it is."

The bedroom had a contemporary-style décor, lots of clean lines and white fabrics. Victoria spotted another wedding photograph on one of the nightstands—a close-up of Sutter and his wife, smiling and looking adorably happy.

"Watch the door for me," Ford said.

She blocked any incoming traffic by putting her hand on the doorframe and pretending to study the room. Ford grabbed his phone from his back pocket and took a picture of the

Sutters' wedding photo. He checked the image, then tucked his phone away.

"What do you think the odds are that Sutter and his wife met and got married all in the last fourteen months?" she asked.

"About fifty-fifty."

She agreed, which meant they were quite possibly looking at an infidelity situation here. Maintaining their ruse, Victoria checked out the large master bedroom closet as another couple entered the room. Ford came up behind her.

"Plenty of room for your shoes," he said teasingly, in a normal volume.

The setup of the closet reminded her of the closet in her old townhome, the one in which she'd blacked out during the break-in. Remembering that moment, she suddenly began to feel slightly . . . off.

No. Not here. Drawing on her relaxation techniques, she focused on taking steady breaths from her diaphragm.

I feel calm and relaxed.

"Look there," Ford said quietly, clueless to the rising panic she felt. He moved around her, into the closet, and pointed to a row of men's red T-shirts, zip-ups, and polo shirts, all bearing the same black logo. "He works at XSport Fitness."

The comment diverted Victoria's attention and grounded her. Instead of focusing on whether she felt light-headed, the lawyerly wheels in her mind began to spin in. Knowing that Sutter worked at an XSport Fitness club was helpful—she could likely contact him at work, instead of at home, to tell him about Nicole and Zoe.

She exhaled, feeling steadier than she had moments ago, and then noticed that the other couple was waiting to check out the closet. "Oops, sorry. I'll get out of your way."

Ford followed her into the master bathroom, which had double sinks, a porcelain soaking tub, and a steam shower.

"Crap. Not a toothbrush in sight," he whispered.

Victoria paused while the other couple passed by the bathroom on their way out.

As soon as it was just the two of them, Ford quietly opened one of the cabinets. "Bingo."

"You can't take his toothbrush," she whispered.

"Why not?"

She pointed in the direction of the living room. "Because he'll notice that it's gone. And when he finds out who I am, he might put two and two together, and I don't want to get disbarred for stealing a damn toothbrush." She paused. "But, there's always Plan F."

"What's Plan F?"

She grabbed a small Ziploc bag from her purse. "Does he have a hairbrush in there, too?"

"Oh . . . I like the way you think, Victoria Slade."

She waved this off. Yes, yes, she'd become quite the super-sleuth these days, but they needed to forgo all compliments and commendations regarding her mad skills until later. "Just hurry."

Ford pulled a two-inch round brush from the cabinet.

"Not that one. That's a woman's brush. Yes—that one," she said when he grabbed a flat brush with boar bristles. She checked to make sure no one was coming while Ford yanked some hair strands off the brush.

He put the brush back, shut the cabinet with one hand, and then dumped the hairs into the bag that Victoria held open. She zipped it shut and stuffed it inside her purse.

And Peter Sutter would never be the wiser.

"Should we check out the rooftop deck?" Ford asked, getting back into character.

"Absolutely."

They nodded while passing by a man who headed into the bedroom just as they were leaving. On the upper floor, there was an alcove that contained a wet bar for entertaining, and then a door that led to the deck. Ford put his hand on the small of Victoria's back as she stepped outside.

The couple who'd been in the master bedroom was outside, as were two other women. Victoria walked to the far end of the deck and leaned against the chest-high stone ledge, as if checking out the view.

"I'd been hoping he wouldn't be married." She sighed. "It obviously makes things more complicated." She checked her watch and saw it was already after one thirty.

Ford pulled out his cell phone.

"Is Nicole on standby again?" she asked.

"She's in a class right now, but she said she'd have her phone with her." He forwarded the picture he'd taken of Sutter and then tucked the phone back in his pocket. "If she says it's him, what happens next?"

"I'll get the hair sample over to a lab I've used in other paternity cases. But that's just so *we* know that we haven't made a mistake. We'll do a second, official paternity test after contacting Sutter and telling him about Zoe."

"How long will it take to get the results from the lab?" Ford asked.

"Three to five business days, depending on how busy they are."

Ford's phone buzzed with a new text message. He took it out of his pocket, read the message, and showed the phone to Victoria.

OMG. That's him.

FORD ASKED VICTORIA to take a second look around the condo with him.

She smiled jokingly. "Why? Are you considering moving?"

"I want Sutter's wife, the real estate agent, to think we are."

She cocked her head. "You want to talk to them."

Yes, he did. Both the protective older brother and uncle in him, as well as the nosy investigative journalist, wanted to know more about this married Peter Sutter who was his niece's father.

He and Victoria went back downstairs and made their way through the place one more time.

"I love the double oven," she said as they entered the kitchen. She squeezed his hand and smiled up at him warmly. "That would come in really handy during the holidays."

An image suddenly popped into his head of him and Victoria having Thanksgiving dinner with their friends and family.

He paused, wholly caught off guard by the thought.

Fortunately he was spared from having to answer when a pretty brunette, dressed in cream linen pants and a loose-fitting pale pink shirt, walked over.

She shook hands with both him and Victoria. "Melanie Ames. I'm the listing agent, and also one of the owners. Are there any questions I can answer about the place?"

Back on his game again, Ford turned to Victoria, as if thinking. "Well . . . I guess I'd be curious to know if it's generally a quiet building? We both occasionally work from home."

Melanie nodded. "The great thing is, we're on the top floor, so you obviously don't have any noise above you. Below us, you have the middle unit, which is owned by a couple in their fifties—really nice people. Then there's the first-floor unit, owned by a single guy. Super quiet, keeps to himself. But not in a creepy, serial killer kind of way," she added quickly.

Peter Sutter came out of the dining room, chuckling. "I love how you always throw that in whenever you describe poor Toby. 'But not in a creepy, serial killer kind of way.'"

She smiled affectionately at her husband. "Because that's the first thing you think of when you hear about a guy who 'keeps to himself.'" She turned back to Ford and Victoria. "Anyway, in general, I'd say it's a pretty quiet block for being so close to Wrigley. Obviously, you're going to get some people walking by on a Friday or Saturday night who've had a few beers at the game. But I've lived here for nine months now, ever since we got married, and I practically lived here the four years before that. During that time, we've never had any serious issues with noise."

Hearing this—that the Sutters had been together for nearly five years—hardly improved Ford's opinion of the man who'd slept with his sister fourteen months ago and then had left without saying good-bye.

Melanie looked to Peter for confirmation, and he nodded. "You know me, I love being close to the stadium. We're actually staying in the neighborhood, going to a single-family home just a couple blocks over," he said to Ford and Victoria. "P.J. and I need a front yard to play catch in." He winked at his wife.

"We're expecting our first child in December," she explained, touching her stomach. "And my husband here is set on Peter Junior if it's a boy—P.J., for short."

"Because it's a cute nickname," Peter said.

"Yes, it is. For *pajamas*." Melanie turned back to Ford and Victoria. "We'll probably still be negotiating this on the way to the hospital." Then she clapped her hands, getting back down to business. "So. Any other questions I can answer for you?"

Ford glanced at Victoria, who likely was thinking the same thing he was—that Melanie Ames seemed like a nice person who deserved better than her philandering jerk of a husband.

And also that Peter Sutter had some seriously fertile sperm.

"Nope," Ford told the couple. "I think you've covered everything we need to know."

Twenty-three

THE FOLLOWING DAY, after returning from court, Victoria deliberately ignored another cheeky look from Will when he told her that a "Mr. Dixon" had called again.

When Ford answered his cell this time, she could hear chatter in the background and guessed he was in the *Trib* newsroom.

"I did some digging into Peter and Melanie," he said. "They bought a one-point-eight-million-dollar house. Five bedrooms, nice front porch and yard. All that's missing is the white picket fence."

"So they have money, obviously."

"*She* has money," Ford said. "Two years ago she left Coldwell Banker and started her own successful brokerage that represents luxury residential properties. She's like the Victoria Slade of the real estate industry."

Great. And now Victoria was about to turn this woman's world completely upside down. "Did you find out anything else about him?"

"He's a general manager at the XSport Fitness in Lakeview. Probably makes decent money, but nowhere near what his wife is bringing in." His tone turned dry. "You may get a new client out of this, once Melanie finds out what her husband's been up to."

Victoria hung up with Ford, thinking that would indeed be ironic.

On Friday morning, she received the paternity test results from the lab and called her client to give her the news.

"Inconclusive? What does that mean?" Nicole asked.

For starters, it meant that Victoria wasn't entirely the super-sleuth she'd thought she was. "It means the lab didn't have a good enough sample to get an accurate result. Apparently, you need the root of the hair to run the test, and none of the hairs we got qualified." She was quick to reassure her client. "This doesn't affect anything, Nicole. I just figured we'd run the test for our own edification. But you're sure this guy is Zoe's father, right?"

"Positive."

"Then we move forward as planned. I'll call him at work today."

Nicole sounded surprised things were moving so fast. "Wow. Okay. What do you think he's going to say? It's not every day a man finds out he has a baby with a woman he probably doesn't even remember." Her tone turned serious. "His wife is going to hate Zoe and me, isn't she? We'll always be a reminder of how he cheated on her."

Victoria said nothing for a moment, thinking back to the day when she was ten and had found her mother sitting in the living room, staring blankly out the front window.

He's leaving us. Your dad is starting a new family and a lot will be changing around here.

"You didn't know he was involved with someone, Nicole," she said. "And even if you did, at the end of the day, this isn't about you and Peter. It's about Zoe. He's her father—which means, at a minimum, that he needs to support her financially. The money will help you and Zoe, right?"

"Yes. Of course."

"Well, then, it's my job to get it for you."

Unfortunately, however, when Victoria called the gym

where Peter Sutter worked, she was put through to one of the assistant managers instead.

"Sorry, Peter's not in today. Is there something I can help you with?" the assistant manager asked.

"That's okay, I'll just call again later. When do you expect him back in?" she asked.

"Monday. He gets here pretty early, usually around seven thirty."

As much as Victoria was eager to get the ball rolling, she preferred not to call him at home, where he lived with his pregnant wife, with the news that he'd fathered a child with another woman. If for no other reason, she'd probably get a much more honest reaction from him if his wife wasn't around while they talked.

So it appeared that Peter Sutter had a three-day stay of execution.

"YOU WERE ABLE to stop the panic attack? That's excellent progress, Victoria."

As pleased as she was, she didn't want to overstate what had happened in the closet during the Sutters' open house. "It wasn't so much that I consciously stopped it," she told Dr. Metzel. "More that I became focused on something else, and that kept me from going down the rabbit hole."

He smiled. "That's a good way to describe it. Often, it's the fear of having a panic attack that can trigger another one. But in this case, when you became focused on something other than your anxiety, your body stopped acting as though it was in a fight-or-flight situation." He jotted down something on his notepad. "Have you gone to any more exercise classes?"

She nodded. "I even managed to make it through a cardio workout class. I took a water break anytime I started worrying about being light-headed. I guess it reminded me that I could just leave the room anytime I wanted to." She shrugged. "I'm not sure if that's a good or a bad thing."

"A fear of being trapped during an attack is very typical with panic disorder," he assured her.

Disorder. Heaven forbid the good doctor made it one mea-sly session without getting in the word somehow.

"And have you tried riding the L again?"

"Yes, this past Sunday."

"Do you feel ready to take the next step and ride when the train will be more crowded?"

She thought about that. Between her relaxation techniques and this new distraction strategy that had worked in the closet during the open house, she felt like she now had several solid tricks in her arsenal. "I think I am."

He seemed pleased. "Good."

"There's something I've been wondering: do you think that my panic attacks have anything to do with the fact that my mother was clinically depressed?"

Dr. Metzel set his pen down and studied her. "Are you asking if I think mental health issues run in your family?"

She paused, not one hundred percent sure she wanted the answer to that. "Yes."

"There is evidence that suggests both panic attacks and depression run in families, but I don't think the two condi-tions are linked in and of themselves. Meaning, I don't think you're genetically predisposed to panic attacks because your mother suffered from depression. But obviously, I think your childhood experiences are a large part of the reason you have control and intimacy issues."

She'd gotten that message loud and clear during their last session. "Look, I get where you're coming from. Maybe I do have a few barriers up," she conceded. "But why is that nec-essarily a bad thing?"

"You don't want to have healthy adult relationships?"

She sat forward in her chair. "But what is 'healthy'? Liv-ing with someone for twenty years who will eventually come to hate you so much that she'll go to war with you over a stamp collection that she doesn't give a damn about? Or, being mar-ried for fifteen years to someone and then discovering that he's had a mistress nearly the entire time? Day in, day out, I'm bombarded by relationships that were probably once 'healthy' but now are anything but."

"I agree that your job provides you with many examples of unhappy relationships."

Good. She was glad they could agree on that. "Yes, it does."

"But I also think it provides you with a handy excuse for avoiding relationships yourself. There *are* happily married divorce lawyers out there."

Victoria sat back in her chair. Well. Wasn't he suddenly all about the psychoanalysis today?

"Let me ask you this," Dr. Metzel continued. "The men you date: do they know how you feel about relationships?"

"Absolutely. And I purposely date men who feel the same way as I do. Not looking to settle down, just wanting to keep things casual."

"Are you seeing anyone now?"

Victoria hesitated. Part of her didn't want to open the door to this line of questioning. But something compelled her to continue. "Kind of, I guess. His name is Ford."

Dr. Metzel perked up in his chair. "Okay, good. Tell me more about Ford."

She sighed. *Here we go.* "He's my next-door neighbor. When I first moved into the building, we couldn't stand each other—that's a whole other story—but then I got roped into helping his sister with her child support case. He and I have been spending a lot of time together with that, and I guess things just evolved from there."

He began taking notes. "Is this a sexual relationship?"

"Indeed, it is." She smiled cheekily, thinking back to her and Ford's very steamy night together last Saturday. When Dr. Metzel looked up at her, she put on a more serious expression and cleared her throat.

"You said that when you first met, you and Ford couldn't stand each other. What changed?" he asked.

She shrugged. "I guess he grew on me."

"How so? What do you like about Ford?"

Victoria hadn't expected that question. "For starters, he's the most attractive man I've ever met. I mean, we're talking blushing, giggling, oh-my-God-I-can't-believe-how-gorgeous-this-man-is levels of hotness here."

"So it's a purely physical thing?" Dr. Metzel asked.

"Well, I wouldn't say it's *only* a physical attraction," she hedged. "I suppose he can be funny at times, when he's not trying to push my buttons." She smiled slightly. "Clever, too, in a quick-on-his-feet kind of way. Very good writer. I would never admit this to him, but I've been reading his stuff in the *Trib*, and you can tell he's passionate about what he's doing. Did you know one of his stories just made the Sunday front page? Pretty impressive, huh? Don't get me wrong, he knows he's good; he's got this . . . confidence that definitely gets a little out of hand at times. But beyond that, there are these moments with his sister, or his niece, when he's protective and really very sweet. I mean, he volunteered to babysit his four-month-old niece on a Saturday night. Do you know any other single man who would do that?" She smiled. "Granted, it sounds like it was a total disaster for both him and the baby, but still—that's adorable."

She stopped, suddenly realizing that she'd been going on and on.

Dr. Metzel smiled softly. "He sounds like a really good guy."

Victoria shifted uncomfortably in her chair, immediately feeling the need to clarify something. "Look, before you get all jazzed up about this, and start writing in your little note-pad, you should know that nothing will ever happen between Ford and me. And that would be the case even *if* I didn't have my alleged 'intimacy issues.'"

"What makes you say that?" Dr. Metzel asked.

"Because the guy is as messed up as I am." She half-chuckled at the truth of that. "I don't know the whole story—actually, I don't even know one-tenth of the story—but I *do* know that his father was an alcoholic who died only about a month ago and there are definitely some unresolved issues there. And besides, he *told me* he doesn't do commitment." She gestured emphatically. "Does that sound like someone I should be pursuing a relationship with? I don't think so."

Dr. Metzel studied her thoughtfully. "That's the first time

I've heard you describe yourself as 'messed up.' Granted, I don't like that term, but I find it interesting that your relationship with Ford has enabled you to be more comfortable acknowledging your own intimacy issues. Perhaps that's something we should explore in more detail."

Yep.

That's what she got for opening the damn door.

Twenty-four

THAT AFTERNOON, CHARLIE and Tucker came over to help Ford set up for his barbecue. The annual—and semi-legendary—party, which he hosted every July, reminded him of the summer barbecues his parents used to have in their townhome, when they would clear out the garage, and family and friends would mingle indoors and outdoors, sitting on lawn chairs along the driveway and in the small front yard while the kids played kickball and ghost in the graveyard in the subdivision's adjacent field.

Maybe it was the nice weather, or the company, but for whatever reason, his father had always been on his best behavior during those times.

This year, more than ever, Ford liked being reminded of good moments like that.

The three of them were moving his folding tables and chairs out of the storage room when his mother called his cell phone.

"I'm downstairs," she said. Having been in the city to visit Nicole and Zoe, she'd called earlier to see if she could drop off another box with his father's things—some photo albums he'd saved of Ford's grandparents and great-grandparents, and a huge stack of old baseball cards.

"Are you sure you don't want to come up?" he asked.

"Hey, Mrs. Dixon," Charlie and Tucker called out.

"I'm sure. Tell Charlie and Tucker I said hello," she said, having gotten to know them well in the sixteen years since they'd been Ford's college dorm mates.

He ran down to meet his mom in front of the building, where she was waiting with her car temporarily parked with the hazard lights on.

"Your dad was such a pack rat. But maybe those baseball cards are worth something. I don't know." She gave him a quick smile to cover the flash of sadness in her eyes, and handed over the box of his father's things to him.

"You don't need to go through all his stuff yourself, Mom. I'm happy to come to the house again and help."

She waved this off, only about the tenth time he'd offered. "I want to do it. It gives me something to do."

Of course that was her answer. Between her job as a teacher's aide, the second job she'd worked on evenings and weekends at Walmart for extra money after his father had injured his hand and gone on disability, and raising him and Nicole, his mother had spent the last thirty-plus years having more than enough "to do." But she liked it that way, he'd long since realized. Once his mom rolled up her sleeves and set her mind to a task, pretty much the only thing anyone else could do was get out of the way.

"Just promise me you won't try to move anything heavy. Save that for me."

She gave him a semi-offended look—at five foot ten, she was hardly a petite waif of a woman—but didn't argue. "Nicole seemed better today. Less overwhelmed."

Nicole had told their mother the truth about Zoe's father, and, at her doctor's suggestion, also had joined a new-moms support group. "I think so, too. The other day, she said that—" Ford stopped mid-sentence, spotting Victoria walking along the sidewalk in their direction, carrying two bags of groceries.

So, this was . . . unexpected. It had been years since his mom had met a woman he was involved with—and, admittedly, he hadn't been thinking he would break that habit today.

One of the inherent risks of dating a neighbor, he supposed.

Victoria saw him a moment later, and her expression immediately turned hesitant when she saw the woman standing next to him. "Hey there," she said, with a tentative smile as she approached.

"Hey yourself." Ford nodded at the bags she carried. "Need a hand?"

"I'm okay." With a grin, Victoria nodded at the large box he held. "Do *you* need a hand?"

He chuckled. "Thanks, I think I'm good." He saw his mother looking at him expectantly and made the introductions. "This is my mother, Maria. Mom, this is Victoria, my neighbor and—"

"The divorce lawyer. Oh my gosh, it's so nice to finally put a face with the name," his mom gushed, pulling Victoria in for a warm hug. "I've heard so much about you from Ford and Nicole."

"Oh—thank you. That's good to hear." Looking surprised by the hug, Victoria blushed as she caught Ford's eyes over his mother's shoulder. She gave him a little smile as she hugged his mom back, as if to say, *What can you do, right?*

And in that moment . . . something tightened in his chest.

"I can't thank you enough for helping my daughter and granddaughter," his mom said to Victoria when she pulled back. "Nicole told me all about it. And Ford, too. He says you're a very talented lawyer, and a saint to be doing all this for free."

"A saint? Really?" Victoria turned to him, her eyes sparkling mischievously as she undoubtedly recalled his skepticism over Nicole's use of that very word just a few weeks ago. "Ford, you are too kind."

He shot her a look. *Cute.* "I'm not sure *saint* was the actual word I used."

"It sure was." His mother smiled at Victoria. "And my son is not one to give compliments lightly, so if he has such wonderful praise for you, there must . . . be something to it." She paused, as if thinking about that, then turned to him with a curious look.

"I'm happy to help Nicole and Zoe," Victoria said. "It's a unique situation, so professionally this has been a nice opportunity for me."

"You have your own firm in the city, I hear," his mom said.

They chatted for a few moments about Victoria's law practice, and then she held up her grocery bags. "Well, I didn't mean to interrupt. I should probably get these upstairs, anyway. It was very nice meeting you, Mrs. Dixon." As she turned to head inside their building, she gave him a nod in good-bye. "Ford."

"So, that's Victoria," his mom said when it was just the two of them. "She seems lovely."

Through the glass door, Ford watched as Victoria stopped at her mailbox, the one next to his. Her hair, which she wore in a long, sexy ponytail again, fell over one bare, golden shoulder as she perused her mail. "She definitely has her moments."

"Sounds like you two have been spending a lot of time together."

He turned his attention to his mother, just now catching her sly tone. "Some, yes."

"Will she be at your barbecue today?"

"Yes, I invited several of my neighbors."

"Any others who you stare at like that?" She smiled knowingly when he didn't immediately respond. "I didn't think so."

He sighed, shaking his head. "You're as bad as Brooke."

"Brooke is a smart woman. Probably, you should listen to her about . . . well, whatever the situation is between you and Victoria."

Not wanting to have this conversation with his mother—because there was no "situation" between him and Victoria, at least not the kind his mom was thinking—he shifted the box in his hands and kissed her on the cheek in good-bye. "I have to get back upstairs. The grill's warming and Charlie and Tuck shouldn't be left around open flames without adult supervision."

His mom opened her mouth, likely to object—and then seemed to reconsider. "Too true."

* * *

LATER THAT AFTERNOON, Ford made his way through
the living room, where a group of die-hard fans sat watching
the Cubs game and drinking beer, and out onto the terrace. The
loft was packed, both inside and outside. Every year, the party
seemed to get bigger, although he wasn't quite sure where all
the extra people were coming from.

He had music playing on the outdoor speakers, and unlike
last year's weather fiasco—an unexpected downpour that had
driven everyone inside—it was sunny and in the midseven-
ties. He did a quick round on the terrace, going from group
to group to say hello to new arrivals and to make sure no one
needed anything. Tucker manned the grill, and in addition to
beer and wine, Charlie had made a tropical rum punch, supposedly "for the ladies," that seemed to be a huge hit.

"Hey, when's my future wife going to be here?" Tucker
asked, standing at the grill with Charlie.

"Still, with that?" Ford said.

Charlie had a question of his own. "Speaking of Victoria,
now that you two are hooking up, do you think you could put
in a good word for me with her friends? You know, the two
cute ones she was with at The Violet Hour."

"You can put in a good word for yourself," Ford said. "She
mentioned she's bringing her friends with her today."

Tucker pointed with the spatula. "Ooh—I call dibs on
whichever one looks hotter."

Ford gripped his friend's shoulder. "It's a wonder you're
still single, Tuck. Truly." Spotting a group of colleagues from
the *Trib*, he headed that way. They were in the middle of a
debate over the reasons for the mayor's recent drop in approval
ratings when Victoria stepped out onto the terrace.

Ford's eyes slowly moved over her appreciatively.

She looked fantastic, wearing some multicolored sleeveless
dress and killer turquoise heels that showed off those legs she
liked to wrap around his waist when he was inside her. But
what most caught his attention wasn't what she was wearing.
Rather, it was the white Pyrex dish she carried in her hands.

The woman had cooked for him.

He excused himself from his co-workers and made his way over to her. "You brought me a casserole. That's so . . . neighborly."

Victoria set it down on one of the fold-out tables. "Not a casserole. *Moros y Cristianos*," she said with a flourish.

He blinked. No clue.

"Cuban rice and beans," she explained.

He lifted up the lid and peeked. "Smells delicious. You actually made this?" He grinned when she gave him a dirty look—so much fun, pushing her buttons—and then he turned to her two friends. "I'm Ford." He held out his hand to the woman he hadn't met previously—Audrey, he learned—then shook Rachel's hand in hello. "And I apologize in advance for everything my friends Charlie and Tucker might say today."

"Speak of the devils and they shall appear," Tucker said grandiosely from behind him.

"Starting with that," Ford said.

After introducing themselves, Charlie and Tucker offered to show Victoria's friends around the place and get them some drinks. As the four of them walked off, Victoria leaned in toward Ford. "Don't worry—Audrey and Rachel will slap them around if they get out of line."

He looked down at her. "I think Charlie and Tuck would like that. A lot."

Victoria laughed just as Ford spotted Brooke heading over. He put his hand on the small of Victoria's back, whispering teasingly in her ear. "That would be the blonde from my cavalcade coming this way."

"Where's Cade?" he asked as Brooke approached.

"Tucker talked him into manning the grill for a while." She smiled and introduced herself to Victoria. "I hear you're a divorce lawyer."

Victoria looked at Ford. "Why is that the first thing everyone says? What are you telling people about me?"

"She met my mom earlier today," he explained to Brooke.

Brooke looked thrilled to hear this. "You met Maria? Isn't she great?"

"Oh, just briefly, out front on the sidewalk." Victoria was quick to clarify. "It wasn't like an *arranged* thing." She smiled. "So, Ford mentioned that you're a lawyer, too."

And with that, she and Brooke were off to the races.

They did their lawyer thing, the two of them talking about This Funny Case and That Crazy Thing That Happened in Court with Judge So-and-So, and as it so happened, the two of them had a mutual acquaintance, some law school friend of Brooke's who worked at Victoria's old law firm.

Wanting to say hello to a group of new arrivals, Ford excused himself from the conversation. As he headed across the terrace, he glanced back and saw both women laughing as Victoria told some story.

First Nicole had called her a "saint." Then his mom had described her as "lovely" and had given her a big hug. Now Brooke was hitting it off with her, too.

He sure hoped the women in his life weren't getting the wrong idea about him and Victoria. Sure, the two of them had fun together, good conversation, and sex that rocked his world. But at the end of the day, he was the relationship lay-over guy and she was Victoria Slade. She had frozen eggs on standby and had made the decision, long before him, to stay out of the "happily-ever-after rat race."

So if anyone *was* getting any bright ideas that this could be turning into anything serious, well . . . that would be foolish.

He paused, an odd feeling in his gut as he watched Brooke and Victoria walk over to the food table, still talking animatedly.

Yep, really foolish.

AFTER SEEING THE last guests out the door, Ford walked back to the terrace. Victoria leaned against the ledge, the sky behind her a striking mix of purple, orange, and gold as the sun set.

"No Nicole today?" she asked.

He rested against the ledge next to her. "She couldn't make it work with their schedule. She and Zoe do this single moms' playgroup on Saturday afternoons. But speaking of my sister . . . I heard you called Peter Sutter at work yesterday."

"I did."

Ford frowned. "You're not going to tell him about Nicole and Zoe over the phone, are you? I assume you plan to meet him in person?"

Victoria shrugged. "I don't know. It depends on how the conversation goes. Why?"

"Because I want to be there when you tell him."

She laughed, as if this was the funniest thing, and then cocked her head. "Wait. You're not actually serious, are you?"

Hell yes, he was serious. "I don't see why I shouldn't go—your conversations with Sutter aren't privileged. Just consider me there as Nicole's representative."

"No, *I* will be there as Nicole's representative."

He moved closer, a little frustrated that she was pushing back on this. "I'm going to this meeting, Victoria. I found the guy, and I think that earned me the right to be there when he learns about Nicole and Zoe."

"Why? So you can scowl and throw scary, no-one-messes-with-my-sister glares at him?"

That may have been part of the plan, yes. "I want to see how he reacts. Nicole is freaking out that this will make her a home wrecker, and I want to be there in case the asshole starts talking smack about her or tries laying the blame on her for getting pregnant."

"Granted, I'm a cynic when it comes to these things. But I think there's a decent chance that's exactly how he'll respond."

"Let him try to say that about my sister to my face, then," Ford growled.

"Wow." Victoria gazed up at him. "Did you know the right side of your jaw does this weird twitching thing when you go into caveman protective mode?"

He gave her a look.

She smiled innocently, then clapped her hands. "Okay. So, I understand your concerns. And you're absolutely right that I wouldn't even be talking to Peter Sutter if it hadn't been for the fact that you found the guy. With some key assistance from myself, mind you. But you still can't go to the meeting, for several reasons. You can't go because it would be unprofessional. You can't go because your presence there, as Nicole's brother, would likely put Sutter instantly on the defensive and that's not good for strategy purposes. But most important, you can't go because that's not how I operate. I don't bring big brothers of clients to meetings, or investigators, or henchmen of any sort. *I* will handle Peter Sutter, because this is what I do. And trust me when I say that if he tries to cast aspersions on my client, or shirks his responsibilities in this, he will find out very quickly just how *good* I am at what I do and how badly that can bode for him."

Ford took in the heated way her eyes flashed with determination.

"What?" she asked.

The corners of his mouth twitched. "That speech was kind of hot. Seriously, I'm at half-mast right now."

She looked up at the sky. "I don't understand how your gender *survives*. All the blood drains out of your brains the minute your penises get any bright ideas."

He laughed hard at that, and closed the gap between them. "*If* I agree not to go to this meeting, it's because I trust you to take care of my sister."

"Of course I'll take care of your sister." Her eyes met his, her mouth curved in a smile. "But *when* you agree not to go to this meeting, it's because I didn't invite you in the first place."

Always so saucy.

He rested one hand on the ledge on each side of her, trapping her in. "What am I going to do with you?"

When she opened her mouth to answer—undoubtedly, again, with some saucy response—he kissed her, hot and hard. All day and evening, he'd been waiting for this moment, when it was just the two of them. Now that he had her right where he wanted her, he didn't intend to waste another minute.

Her breath caught when he nudged her legs apart and stepped between them. He trailed his fingers up her smooth thigh and underneath her dress. "Looking at you in this dress has been torture."

She smiled coyly. "And here I'd thought you'd like this dress."

"Not when I can only look and not touch." He slid his hand into her thong and cupped her possessively, making her gasp. "But I can make up for lost time now." She was already wet for him, and that only fueled his fire. "Spread your legs a little. No one can see." The only neighbor with a view of his terrace was, well, otherwise engaged at the moment.

When she did as he asked, he shoved the edge of her underwear aside and slid a finger inside her, stroking her slowly.

She leaned into him and swirled her tongue around his in a hot, erotic kiss. Then she broke away, arching against his hand. "God, if you don't stop, we'll end up doing it right here," she panted, in a low, throaty voice.

His cock swelled as he thought about ripping her underwear off and taking her right there, hard against the terrace wall, her dress bunched up around her waist as he covered her mouth with one hand to keep the neighbors from hearing her cries.

But right then, he had other ideas.

He gave her a wicked look—after all, he'd warned her that he would make her pay. "Just remember, sound does travel in this place."

Her eyes widened. "What are you going to do?"

In answer, he got down on his knees in front of her.

She quickly glanced around, undoubtedly confirming that no one could see them, and then gripped the ledge with her hands as he lifted her dress. Bunching the material in one hand, he used his other hand to slowly pull her underwear down to her mid-thighs.

For a moment, he just looked at her. Beautiful, so ready for him, and trembling in anticipation. Something tightened in his gut, a possessive, edgy sensation he'd never felt before. "So gorgeous," he said in a guttural voice. "Now let's see if you taste as sweet as you feel wrapped around my cock."

He reached around to cup her ass in one hand and licked her.

She moaned quietly, tangling her fingers in his hair and completely giving in to him. Within minutes of using his mouth on her, her legs were shaking and he could tell she was close.

Wanting to hold her there, right at the edge, he circled his tongue around her clit, then pulled back and blew on it gently.

She spread her legs wider, her underwear still mid-thigh. "Ford, please," she begged, her voice a strained whisper.

His cock throbbed, hearing that. He loved seeing her like this, so turned on for him. Needing him. He slid two fingers in her, stroking her. "What do you want, Victoria?"

"You." She arched her back. "God, you."

Exactly the answer he'd wanted. He withdrew his fingers and stood up, and she immediately reached for the button on his jeans.

He groaned when she slid her hand into his boxer-briefs and wrapped her fingers around his cock. "Right here, baby? Is that what you want?" he rasped.

"Yes." Her eyes dark and heavy lidded, she pushed his jeans and boxer-briefs down.

Fuck, it had never been like this with anyone else, this kind of urgency and need to be inside her, buried deep as he could be. He stepped back and helped her step out of her underwear, then kissed her, wanting her mouth on his as he pushed up her dress and—

He swore under his breath, the tip of his cock right at her wet entrance. "The condoms are inside."

She groaned, then took his cock and slid it against her clit. "We need to get inside, then."

His jaw clenched as he looked down and watched her. "Yes. Now." Done with the teasing, he pulled his jeans up and took her by the hand and led her inside. She yanked his shirt off along the way to his bedroom, and when there, they quickly got her heels off along with the rest of his clothes. She climbed on top of him as he ripped open the condom and rolled it on. With her dress still on, and him sitting up, she took his cock and guided him to her entrance.

Then she sank down, both of them moaning as he filled her.

She went still then, gazing down at him, and something shifted deep inside him when he looked up into those beautiful brown eyes. As she began to move, he reached up and tangled his fingers in her hair. It was a slower pace, less urgent, but somehow even better and sweeter.

He smoothed his thumb across her cheek and something flickered in her eyes.

"It's so good with you," she breathed.

"I love being with you like this," he murmured. Seeing her softer side, so open and vulnerable just . . . did things to him.

He grabbed her hips, guiding her in slow, smooth strokes. Their eyes never left each other, until she touched her forehead to his and said his name as she came. Her body clenched tight around him, and he groaned as he followed her over, thinking he'd never felt anything as good as this moment.

Afterward, they lay side by side on the bed, catching their breath. She looked at him and said nothing, just taking him in. With a tender look in her eyes, she reached over and brushed a lock of hair off his forehead.

He reached up and linked their fingers, and they stayed that way for a moment.

Then she took a deep breath and sat up, fixing her dress. She hugged her knees, her long hair spilling over her shoulders and legs, and then turned her head toward him.

"Think there are any of those brownies left?" she asked.

Brownies.

Right.

That was all she'd had on her mind, apparently, while he'd been lying there, thinking . . . well, he wasn't sure exactly what he'd been thinking.

Obviously, it didn't matter.

So he sat up and lightly kissed her shoulder. A playful gesture, nothing too serious. "Let's go raid the fridge and find out."

After all, the relationship layover guy and Victoria Slade didn't do serious.

And they especially didn't do it together.

Twenty-five

ON MONDAY, VICTORIA waited until mid-morning to make the call.

Peter Sutter's stay of execution was officially over.

"Mr. Sutter, hello. This is Victoria Slade from Victoria Slade and Associates, a law firm here in Chicago," she led in when he answered. "I'd like to speak to you about a matter regarding one of my clients. Do you have a few minutes?"

His tone was upbeat. "Well, that depends. On the off chance this is one of those calls you see in the movies, when you tell me some rich relative I never knew died and left me millions of dollars, then sure—I have all the time you need. But if this is about a legal issue related to the gym, then unfortunately all I can do is provide you with the contact information for XSport Fitness's corporate legal department."

"Actually, this is a personal matter that has nothing to do with the gym. I represent a woman named Nicole Dixon, who I believe you met fourteen months ago at a bar called Public House." Victoria deliberately paused, waiting to see if he had any reaction to that.

He spoke after a moment's hesitation. "Um, what did you say this was about?"

Actually, she hadn't said. But she saw no point in beating around the bush. "Ms. Dixon had a child five months ago—nine months after the two of you met—and she believes you are the father. I'm calling to make arrangements for you to take a paternity test—something I hope we can handle discreetly and without need for court intervention. If that's not the case, then I'll have no choice but to serve you with a subpoena either at home or at work."

"Oh my God." He exhaled raggedly. "No, please, don't send anything about this to my home. Look, uh, I'm swamped at work this morning, but is there somewhere we can meet to talk about this? Maybe around noon?"

She thought about giving him her office address, but decided a less formal location could work better. "There's an Intelligentsia Coffee bar on Broadway and Belmont."

"I know the place. I'll be there at noon."

"You're obviously welcome to bring an attorney, Mr. Sutter."

"An attorney? I don't have— Oh, my God, I can't believe this is happening. I'll see you there at noon."

Victoria hung up the phone, thinking that the man who'd cheated on his soon-to-be wife and who'd also left without a good-bye after sleeping with her client sounded quite frazzled.

Good.

"MR. SUTTER?" SHE held out her hand. "Victoria Slade."

Peter Sutter shook her hand, staring in surprise as she took the seat across from him. He'd arrived before her and had chosen, wisely, a table in the back of the coffee shop where they could speak privately.

"I know you," he said. "You came to my open house last week, with the tall guy. You talked to me and my wife."

Victoria had anticipated this reaction and had decided that the best defense was a good offense. "Since you ran out on my client without providing her with any way to reach you, we needed to get a little creative in confirming that you were, in fact, the right Peter Sutter."

"Oh." He ran his hands over his face. "This is— I don't know what to say."

He was a good-looking guy, a fact that was emphasized by the fitted red XSport Fitness T-shirt and black athletic pants that showed off his toned physique. In light of the circumstances, the cynical divorce lawyer in Victoria assumed it was highly possible that Nicole Dixon was one of many women Peter Sutter had picked up at a bar over the last several years.

Which was why she was surprised by what he said next.

"I can't tell you how many times I've thought about that night with Nicole. I feel horrible that I left like that. I had no idea she was pregnant." He paused. "Is she, um, sure the baby is mine?"

"Yes. But we'll do a paternity test to confirm that before my client and I file a petition for child support."

"Child support." He took another deep breath. "My wife . . . Well, you were there, you know that she's pregnant. I don't know how to tell her about this." He looked shell-shocked. "Melanie doesn't know anything about Nicole."

"Yes, I gathered that," Victoria said dryly.

He cocked his head. "Wait—you think I cheated on her. No. Noooo, no. See, when I slept with Nicole, Melanie and I were on a break."

Victoria nearly did a facepalm. It was like she was at home, watching a *Friends* rerun.

We were on a break!

"Your relationship with your wife is none of my business, Mr. Sutter. I'm here solely to represent the interests of Ms. Dixon and her child."

"But Melanie and I really were on a break," he said earnestly, as if it was important she believe him. "We'd been together for around three years, and we'd started talking about getting engaged. So, one day, I went out shopping for rings and, I don't know, I started thinking about *forever* and how marriage means spending the rest of your life with just one person. And I guess I just . . . panicked."

Victoria kept her face impassive, but she was hardly impressed with the story thus far. A man panicking over the idea of sleeping with one woman for the rest of his life.

How original.

Peter held up a hand. "I know; I'm not proud of that. I'm just trying to explain. Anyway, when I told Melanie I had doubts, she basically kicked my ass to the curb. We'd been broken up for about three weeks, and it just . . . wasn't the way I thought it was going to be. I missed her. A lot. I was moping around, and my friends said I needed to get out and give being single a shot. So they dragged me out to the bar, and that's when I met Nicole. If I remember right, it was her birthday that night."

Victoria was a little surprised he remembered that. "That's right."

"I remember buying her a shot, and then she bought *me* a shot, and things just went from there. She was great. A lot of fun to talk to. We ended up back at her place and, well . . . I guess you know what happened next." He paused, his expression turning more serious. "I think we both passed out, and when I woke up and saw that I was lying in bed next to a woman, it just felt . . . wrong. I *knew* the only woman that I should be lying next to was Melanie. And it hit me that I had lost the best thing that had ever happened to me, and . . . I got choked up about that. I didn't want Nicole to wake up and see me crying and think I was some freak or that she'd done something wrong, so I just got the hell out of there." He looked Victoria directly in the eyes. "But I know that was stupid. And if I see Nicole, I plan to tell her how sorry I am about that."

Well.

She supposed that wasn't the *worst* explanation she'd ever heard.

Still, the cynic in her had some lingering questions. "You could've gone back to Nicole's place the next day to apologize."

"Actually, the next day, I went straight to Melanie's place to beg her to give me a second chance. She said she didn't want to be with a guy who had doubts, so to show her how committed I was about us, I sat on her front doorstep every night after work until she agreed to talk to me."

Okay, she'd bite. "How many nights did it take you?"

"Fourteen," he said.

"Fourteen?" Victoria smiled slightly at that. "Good for her."

"After that, everything happened fast. Melanie and I got back together and we decided we didn't want to drag things out planning a big, fancy wedding. So we flew to Santa Barbara, where her parents live, and had a small ceremony with just family and close friends. That was nine months ago." He rested his arms on the table. "As for why I never circled back to Nicole, I guess at first it was because I was so focused on getting Melanie back. Then after that, I don't know . . . It seemed a little weird, the idea of suddenly showing up on Nicole's doorstep. What was I supposed to say? 'Hey, remember me? Sorry I skipped out on you a month ago. And by the way—I'm getting married!'"

"At least she would've had the chance to tell you she was pregnant," Victoria said.

"Well, I didn't *know* that was even a possibility. I thought we used a condom. But we were pretty drunk, so . . ." With a sheepish blush, he cleared his throat. "Anyway. What happens now?"

"To start, I'll give you the address of a lab you can go to for the paternity test."

He nodded. "And then you'll call me with the results?"

"That won't be necessary. The lab will mail out two copies of the results, one to you directly and one to either Nicole or myself."

Peter shook his head emphatically. "No way. They can't send anything to my home or to work. I can't risk that Melanie would find out that way. We agreed we didn't want to know what happened while we were apart, that it didn't matter," he explained. "But now she's *pregnant*. And she's so excited about that. How am I supposed to tell her that I might already have a kid with someone else—with a woman she never knew about?" He gestured at Victoria. "I mean, how would you react if you found that out about your husband?"

"Mr. Sutter, it's really n—"

"I know, I know, it's none of your business." He shook his head, looking despondent. "I just don't want to hurt her."

Something inside Victoria softened. Yes, she thought Peter could've handled the situation with Nicole better—hell, the guy could've at least left a note before hightailing it out of her apartment. But now, at least, he appeared genuinely interested in doing the right thing.

She reached inside her purse, pulled out the business card she'd prepared, and slid it across the table. "If you like, we can tell the lab to send the results only to me. That'll give you a few days to figure out how to explain everything to your wife. My recommendation? Go with the truth, the whole truth, and nothing but."

He half-smiled, and took the card. "Thank you. I appreciate it."

That settled, Victoria grabbed her purse and stood up. "I wrote the address of the lab on the back of my business card."

"Wait," Peter said. "You didn't tell me. The baby . . . is it a boy or a girl?"

Victoria paused, the cynical divorce lawyer in her not having expected that question.

Normally, I see families as they're falling apart. I've never had the chance to bring one together before.

"It's a girl," she said.

"A girl." His eyes turned momentarily misty, and then he cleared his throat. "Right. I'll wait for your call, then."

VICTORIA HAILED A cab and called Nicole during the ride back to her office.

"You caught me just in time—I'm about to leave for an audition," Nicole said. "Did you talk to him? How did it go?"

Victoria filled Nicole in on her conversation with Peter Sutter. "He says he plans to voluntarily take the paternity test, but let's not hold our breath," she said while paying the cab-driver. "It's easy for people to *say* they want to do the right thing. Actually doing it is a whole other matter." It had just begun to rain, so she climbed out of the taxi and dashed into her building.

"Do you think he's going to tell his wife?" Nicole asked.

"He made it sound that way. But I figure he'll wait until he has actual proof that he's Zoe's father before having that conversation."

Nicole exhaled. "Right."

They wrapped up the call just before Victoria stepped into the elevator. As she pushed the button for her floor, she felt cautiously optimistic about this development in the case. Over the course of the last several weeks, she'd prepared herself for the worst with Peter Sutter. But maybe Nicole and Zoe actually were going to catch a break in this. Maybe Peter would *want* to be a part of his daughter's life, beyond just his financial obligations.

Unfortunately, she got to revel in that optimism for all of about thirty seconds.

As soon as she stepped into her office, Will handed her a stack of messages. Then one of her associates knocked on her door to discuss a client who'd spontaneously decided, mid-divorce, to spend over a hundred thousand dollars redecorating her home, and now had been hit—not surprisingly—with an emergency motion that accused her of depleting marital assets.

After addressing that mini-crisis, she spent the next few hours on the phone, going from call to call and putting out fires. Or, in some cases, starting a few fires herself.

In other words, it was a typical Monday afternoon.

But at five o'clock, after finishing an hour-long conference call, she did something that was *a*typical—for her, at least.

Will's mouth fell open when he walked into her office with yet more message slips and saw her packing up her briefcase. "Are you *leaving*? You haven't left the office at five since . . ." He cocked his head, coming up empty. "See? There is no end to that sentence."

"There's an errand I need to run." Changing the subject, she took the message slips from him. "Anything noteworthy?"

"Mr. Dixon called. This is becoming a regular thing. Perhaps I should add him to your speed dial?" Will grinned when she shot him a glare. "Oh, spare me the look—so I'm having

fun here. I like him. And so do you, even if you won't admit
it. I see the smile on your face after you talk to him."

She said nothing as she picked up her briefcase, refusing
to be drawn into this conversation.

"Don't forget your umbrella, Ms. Slade," he said cheekily.

Oops—right. She grabbed her umbrella and gave him a
slight smile. Cheeky or not, the man was a lifesaver. "Good
night, Will."

She headed down the hallway and made her way to the
elevator bank. After pushing the down button, Will's comment about Ford echoed in her head.

I like him. And so do you, even if you won't admit it.

There'd been a moment on Saturday night, as she'd been
lying on the bed next to Ford, when things had felt different
between them. Good different.

Scary different.

At the time, she'd covered up her thoughts by asking about
the stupid brownies, assuming it was just a fleeting, post-sex
thing. But here she was two days later, and the little butterflies
she felt in her stomach every time she thought about him *still*
hadn't gone away.

And that was even scarier.

When the elevator reached the ground floor, she forced
herself not to think about Ford and concentrate instead on the
task at hand—a task that already had her anxious enough.

Tonight, she was taking on the subway during rush hour.

As she cut across the building lobby, she took her earbuds
out of her briefcase and plugged them into her phone. She
scrolled through her playlist until she found the song she
wanted, and felt charged as she stepped outside into the rain
and the music began to play.

This girl is on fire.

Damn skippy.

And tonight, this girl was going to kick the ass of her teeny,
tiny panic-attack problem.

Twenty-six

FORD STOOD UNDER the red glass overhang of the Thompson Center, trying to stay dry from the rain.

He'd just finished interviewing the director of the Department of Children and Family Services for his story on parents who'd abused or neglected their children while supposedly under the agency's supervision. The interview had run longer than he'd expected—the director had been surprisingly willing to talk—and since it was already five o'clock he decided to scrap his plan to return to the *Trib* office and call it a day instead.

He checked his cell phone, hoping to have a message from Victoria.

No luck.

He was very eager to hear how her meeting with Sutter had gone, so he decided to try to catch her at work. The rain began to fall steadily as he walked the three blocks, so while waiting for a red light to change, he wrestled his umbrella out of his messenger bag.

Just then, he spotted Victoria as she stepped out of the revolving doors of her building. She opened her umbrella and began walking in the opposite direction.

He called her name, but she didn't turn, his voice undoubtedly drowned out by the cacophony of street noise as cars, taxis, and buses whooshed between them on the rain-slick street. It took a good minute for the light to change, so by the time he crossed the street he'd lost sight of her on the crowded sidewalk that was a sea of umbrellas.

Walking quickly and weaving through other pedestrians, he saw her cross the street ahead of him, and realized with an ironic smile that she'd led him right back to the Thompson Center. Seeing her head in the direction of the underground subway station, he hurried to make the light.

"Victoria!" he called, closing the gap.

She still didn't look back as she headed down the stairs to the station.

Not far behind her now, he pushed through the turnstile and made his way to the underground platform, which was even more crowded than usual because of the rain. While closing his umbrella, he spotted Victoria on the far end of the platform, her back to him as she waited for the train.

He made his way over and tapped her on the shoulder. She jumped and turned around, and only then did he see that she had earbuds in that were covered by her long hair.

"Ms. Slade. Fancy meeting you here," he said.

"Ford." She stared at him in surprise, before ducking her head to take out her earbuds.

But the strangest thing was, before she looked away, he could've sworn he saw a flicker of something else in her eyes.

Something that looked oddly like panic.

HE COULDN'T BE here.

Victoria, who'd been calm just moments ago, felt a rush of anxiety as she stashed the earbuds in the outside pocket of her briefcase, next to the umbrella. One of the reasons she'd been comfortable taking on the challenge of riding the subway during rush hour was that she'd had an exit strategy planned in the event anything had gone awry. She'd reassured herself, the same way she had during her exercise class and the time she'd gotten nervous on the elevator, that if she felt faint or panicky, she could always just get off the train and take a cab the rest of the way home.

But Ford being here changed everything. Obviously, he would know something was wrong if she suddenly decided to get off before their stop. And since she didn't want him, of all people, to know about her panic attacks, that meant one thing.

She was trapped.

Her heart began to pound, so she took a deep breath. *From the diaphragm.* Just like the good doctor had taught her.

Ford cocked his head. "Are you okay?"

Shit. He already was looking at her funny and they hadn't even gotten on the train yet.

This did not make her feel any less panicked.

Come on, Slade, pull it together. You can do this.

She forced a smile. "Sure. I'm just surprised to see you here. What are the odds, right?" At the sound of an approaching train, she swallowed hard, but maintained her nonchalant façade.

"No kidding. I just finished an interview at the Thompson Center, walked to your office and saw you leave, and basically did a loop right back here," Ford said before the train rushed into the station and drowned him out.

Victoria nodded, her attention diverted as the train came to a stop and the doors opened. She thought about bailing; she could say that she forgot something in her office, but Ford would probably offer to go with her anyway. But more important, she didn't want to run from this. She didn't want to be the person who couldn't get on a train if she had an audience. She wanted to be herself again, the unflappable, panic-free woman she'd been before the break-in had messed up everything. Because her life had been good before—and a hell of a lot less complicated when it didn't include therapy, and a pesky psychologist with pesky questions, and a summer rental with a sexy, charming next-door neighbor who made her feel things she didn't want to feel.

So if she wanted her old life back, if she wanted to get back to that person she'd been before, it started right here. Right now.

She was getting on that damn train.

That decided, she took another deep breath and stepped forward.

Trying not to be obvious about it, she let a few people pass in front of her and Ford, so that the two of them wouldn't be stuck at the back of the car. They ended up about a third of the way down the aisle, not too far from the door.

She only had to make it four measly stops, she reminded herself. Less than a fifteen-minute train ride.

"You're killing me with the suspense here," Ford said.

Victoria blinked. "I'm sorry?"

"Your meeting with Sutter," he said as the doors closed. "How did it go?"

She shifted her weight as the train began to move, drawing on the trick she'd learned during the Sutters' open house, when she'd begun to feel light-headed in the closet. If she focused on something other than her fear, her body would stop responding as if she were in a fight-or-flight situation.

Hopefully.

"It went well." She proceeded to tell Ford about her meeting with Sutter, and the distraction helped. Although she remained hyperaware of her surroundings—primarily the fact that she was in a crowded train car underground—she was able to keep up her end of the conversation.

"He could've concocted that entire story in the two hours before you met him at the coffee shop," Ford said, looking skeptical.

"Maybe. But you didn't see his face when he asked about Zoe. He was teary-eyed."

Ford grunted. "Probably freaking out over how he's going to pay child support for two kids, *and* for a divorce lawyer, once his wife hears about this alleged 'break' they were on and kicks him to the curb for good."

She nudged him. "Let's just see how this plays out."

This is Chicago, said the train's automated PA system as they pulled into the station. *Doors open on the right at Chicago.*

Victoria exhaled. She was halfway home, with only two stops to go. Reassured by this, she began to feel proud of her progress, when—

The doors sprang open and all hell broke loose.

A large group of teenagers wearing yellow camp T-shirts clambered onto the train, laughing, chanting some kind of cheer, and pushing each other around.

"Stay together!" someone called out as the group shoved their way inside the already crowded train. To make room, the people at the front of the aisle moved toward the back of the car.

Having no choice, Victoria moved back, too.

It was an extremely tight fit. The people in the aisle were packed in with barely enough room to breathe, awkwardly jostling one another as the train began to pull away from the station. Ford put one hand on her hip, steadying her. With her shoulder pressed against his chest, he shrugged off their situation with the ease of a commuter who'd been in this situation many times before.

"Beats trying to find a cab in the rain," he said.

Yes. Sure. For normal people.

"That's true," she managed to say. She gripped the handle on the back of the seat next to her, suddenly feeling as though it had become uncomfortably warm in the train car.

Please, not now.

She forced herself to say something—anything. "So what was your interview about?"

Ford chatted on, while she silently tried to pull herself together. But every time she'd get into her relaxation techniques—*I feel quiet, my shoulders are loose*—he would ask her a question, or pause for her to comment. And of course he would, because to him this was just a normal, everyday conversation between two people riding the subway home—not exposure therapy for a goddamn mental disorder.

My legs and feet feel warm and heavy.

As they pulled into the Division station, she had a decision to make. She could get off the train now, which would look really odd since they lived only one stop away, and clue Ford into the fact that something was amiss. Or she could suck it up, and stay put.

The Division station and her stop, Damen, were so close. Only about a two-minute train ride apart.

She made up her mind.

She was going to finish this thing.

A few people got off at the Division stop, but somehow the group of rowdy teenagers just subsumed that space, giving her no respite. When the train began moving again, she took a deep breath.

My neck feels relaxed. My breathing is soft, full, and easy.

The Damen station was aboveground—the Blue Line continued on an elevated track from that point—so any moment now she would notice the train ascending, she would see the gray haze of natural light and hear raindrops on the windows. And then she would know she was home free.

My entire body is relaxed and comfortable.

Ford peered down at her, his lips curved in a coy smile. "Are you around tonight? I thought maybe we could grab something to eat."

She knew what she was supposed to say in response, the expected quip—*You know what happens every time we do that*—but her lips felt like they were moving slower and she'd just started to form the words when—

The train came to a sudden stop.

The guy in front of Victoria bumped into her, pushing her back into Ford. She swallowed, and waited for the train to start moving again.

It didn't.

"Come on. What now?" the guy in front of her complained.

She tried to remain calm—they were probably just waiting for another train to clear the station. But then her mind began racing. What if this wasn't a momentary delay? What if she were stuck here for a while, in this enclosed underground metal box that had no exits? She'd never make it; she'd already been hanging on by a thread, so the train needed to start moving—*now*—before she fainted or caused a scene, before everyone started staring at her, because everyone on the train was going to realize that something was wrong with her, and worst of all *Ford* would know that something was wrong with her, and—

"I have to get out of here." She tried inhaling, but it wasn't working; the air in the train car felt oppressively stuffy.

Ford looked down at her, and a flicker of understanding crossed his eyes. "The train," he said quietly, as if something about this registered with him. He put his hand on her elbow reassuringly. "It's okay. We'll be moving any moment now."

The train lurched forward, but it was too late; she felt light-headed and oddly disconnected from her body, as if this had become a dream, and Ford was saying something to her but all she heard was a rush of white noise as her vision narrowed and darkness closed in.

"I think I'm going to faint," she murmured.

The last thing she felt before blacking out was his arms closing around her.

SHE HEARD THE sound of a man's voice, commanding and authoritative.

Coming out.

It took her a moment to recognize the voice as Ford's, to remember where she was, and to realize that she was moving.

He was carrying her off the train.

She felt the firmness of his chest against her cheek, the strength of his arms cradling her. When a rush of cooler air hit her, she breathed it in, slow and deep.

Ford shifted her in his arms, and she heard murmurs. Other voices.

"We're off the train, Victoria." His tone was reassuring. "I'm going to call 9-1-1 and get you some help."

Please, no. She was already making enough of a scene. She gripped his shirt with one hand. "No. Just . . . don't move."

Forcing her eyes open, she saw that she and Ford were on the train platform, and that a small crowd of people had gathered around them.

All staring at her.

"I'm fine," she said to the crowd. She went for a weak joke, to minimize the weirdness of the situation. "Guess I probably shouldn't have skipped lunch today."

"I think it would help if she could get a little space," Ford told the spectators, not unkindly. Then he lowered his voice. "Victoria. Look at me."

Really, she wasn't sure she could face him right then. But, figuring she had to bite the bullet sometime, she finally tilted her head back and met his gaze.

His eyes were a warm blue, his expression a mixture of relief and reassurance. "You're okay now. I've got you."

She felt a sharp tug in her chest and opened her mouth to thank him for getting her off the train—but then she noticed something. "You're soaked."

The back of his hair and neck were all wet, the water having spread along his collar and shoulders, and even beginning to creep down the front of his shirt and the leather strap of his messenger bag. She saw then that they were only partially covered by the overhang above them, and realized that he was using his body to protect her as he held her in his arms.

Shielding her from the rain.

He peered down with a soft smile, his voice husky. "Well, you said not to move."

She swallowed hard, the butterflies that had been lingering in her stomach suddenly having multiplied into a full-fledged swarm.

Oh, God. No.

She looked away from Ford, focusing instead on the rain dripping down from the overhang as she fought back the tightening in her chest.

Breathe, Slade.

"Victoria—are you okay?" Ford asked. "Say something."

She took a moment to collect herself, and then faced him. "I just . . . want to go home."

Twenty-seven

WHEN THEY GOT to Victoria's front door, Ford noticed that her hand was trembling as she put the key in the lock.

"I can get that." He gently took the key from her, then unlocked the door and led her inside the loft. He set down both his messenger bag and her briefcase, which a helpful passenger had carried off the train after she'd fainted.

"I should change into some dry clothes," she said. They'd both had umbrellas for the walk home from the L station, but it was pouring outside and the legs of her pants were soaked.

He combed his fingers though his wet hair. "Me, too. I'll just prop your front door open with the deadbolt so I can let myself back in."

She paused at that, but then nodded. "Okay."

Grabbing his messenger bag, he headed back to his own place. After letting himself in, he ran a hand over his mouth, needing a second to clear his head.

That moment, when Victoria had gone limp on the train and had fallen unconscious into his arms, was something he wouldn't forget for a long time. If ever. The fear he'd felt thinking something might be seriously wrong, and then the utter relief when she'd opened her eyes, peering up at him with an expression that was so wholly, uncharacteristically vulnerable, it had brought forth a near-violent surge of protectiveness from somewhere deep inside him . . . Those kind of raw, powerful emotions were unlike anything he'd ever experienced before.

He exhaled, not at all sure what to do about that.

For now, however, he needed to focus on her. He quickly stripped out of his wet clothes, toweled off his hair, and threw on jeans and a T-shirt. When he let himself back into Victoria's loft, he saw that she was still in her bedroom. He didn't know if her trembling hands meant she was cold from the rain, or in some kind of shock after blacking out, but he figured that drinking something warm would help either way. After rummaging through her kitchen cabinets, he found a mug and chamomile tea, and got a teakettle going on her stove.

She came out of her bedroom, with her hair pulled back into a ponytail and wearing jeans and a loose lightweight sweater. She took a seat on one of the island barstools and watched him pour the hot water over a tea bag in the mug.

"Thank you," she said.

He noticed she was acting subdued, which was unusual for her. Then again, she'd just fainted on the train—he hardly expected her to be turning cartwheels right then.

He sat down on the barstool next to her and watched as she wrapped her hands around the mug. "You're shivering. I'll get you a blanket." He looked around the room, beginning to wonder whether he was going to have to override her insistence that she didn't need medical attention. She could fuss and holler all she wanted, but if he got the sense that anything was even slightly off, he'd throw her over his shoulder and carry her to the damn emergency room if he had to.

She shook her head. "It's fine. The shaking will stop in a few minutes. This happened the last time I fainted, too."

He was quickly putting the pieces together. Obviously, what had happened today wasn't simply the product of her skipping lunch. He recalled seeing her on the L platform that Sunday morning a few weeks ago, acting a little oddly, and now realized that she'd been talking herself into getting on the train.

He figured he might as well be direct. "Are you claustro-
phobic?"

She cocked her head. "Huh. That seems less weird. Sure,
let's go with that."

He reached out and tucked a lock of hair behind her ear.
"How about if we just go with the truth?"

She met his gaze, and then looked down at her tea and took
a sip. "The truth. Right."

VICTORIA AVOIDED FORD'S gaze, finding it hard to look
into his eyes when she knew what was coming.

"So, I've been having these . . . panic attacks," she began.

"Panic attacks. Okay." He exhaled, nodding. "Do they only
happen when you're on the train?"

"In my exercise class, too, and once on an elevator. And
the other day, I got a little freaked out when we were in the
closet at the Sutters' open house. But the train has been a
particular challenge for me. As you saw firsthand."

"Is this something that started recently?" he asked.

She smiled slightly. Of course he would have lots of
questions—the man always asked questions. "A couple
months ago. I had the first one when I was trapped in my
closet during the break-in."

His jaw tightened. "I should've asked more questions about
the break-in. You didn't seem to want to talk about it, so I—"

"It's not about the break-in," she said. "Apparently, that
was just the catalyst that brought all these bigger issues to the
surface."

He cocked his head. "What issues?"

"That's the million-dollar question, isn't it?" She took
another sip of her tea, buying a moment. Part of her was
tempted to just BS her way out of this conversation. But
another part of her wanted—maybe even needed—him to
understand why she was the way she was. "According to my
therapist, I have a 'near-compulsive need to always seem
okay.' And also trust, abandonment, and control issues that

apparently impact my ability to have healthy relationships." She shot him a quick glance to see how he reacted.

He exhaled, undoubtedly processing all that. "Okay."

She gave him a self-deprecating smile. "You asked."

He appeared to consider his next question carefully. "And did this therapist say why he thinks you have these issues?"

"My childhood. Cliché, right?" she asked, trying to sound glib. Then she turned more serious. "My father leaving, for one thing. And also that my mom tried to commit suicide shortly afterward."

Ford slid his hand over hers, his voice softening. "Victoria . . ."

"It's *fine*," she said defiantly, out of habit. "It was a long time ago, it happened, and my mom and I dealt with it. It's just that there was this moment during the break-in, when I was on the phone with the 9-1-1 dispatcher, that somehow stirred this stuff up all over again. But I don't want you to think that I'm this person who went through this big tragedy, and that that means—"

He cut her off right there. "What I think is that a lot of people have shit they have to deal with from their childhood. And sometimes, that shit messes you up a little, whether you want it to or not."

She went quiet as the words fell between them.

He was right. She *was* messed up. Sure, on the outside, she looked like she completely had her shit together. That was what she wanted people to think, after all—the only side of her she allowed them to see. Yet here she was, the supposedly tough, unflappable, confident Victoria Slade, so afraid of losing control that she'd sent herself into a full-fledged panic attack and had actually *blacked out* in front of an entire train of people.

Yeah, not exactly "unflappable" there.

She laughed humorlessly, her words dry. "Wow. I could've saved myself a ton of money in therapy bills and just talked to you instead." She slid her hand from Ford's grasp and stood up. Walking toward the windows, she ran her fingers through her hair and exhaled.

She heard him get up as she looked out the window, and closed her eyes when she felt his strong arms come around her.

"If you and I were alone for an hour in some therapy room, I'm not sure how much actual talking would've occurred," he said.

She felt a bittersweet pang, knowing that he was trying to get a smile out of her. And of course that's what he would do. As much as it killed her to admit it given their less-than-auspicious start and his quite healthy ego, he *was* a good guy. A great guy, actually. In addition to all the things she'd told Dr. Metzel, he had a protective streak a mile wide for the people he cared about—and it was that quality, not his eyes or his incredible body or even his wicked, sly charm, that she found most attractive of all.

In an alternate universe, albeit one where a lot more was different than simply the night they'd almost met at The Violet Hour, she could imagine that Ford would be exactly the kind of man she would— Well . . . anyway.

Taking a deep breath, she turned around and met his gaze. "Here's the thing. After what happened today on the train, I think . . . I probably need to focus right now on this panic stuff and getting my act together."

"I agree that you should take care of yourself." He smiled. "But even with the 'panic stuff,' you have your act together more than anyone I've ever met."

If you only knew. "No, I mean I need to focus on *just* these panic attacks. And work, obviously." She paused. "Meaning, this probably isn't a good time for me to be involved with anyone."

For a long moment Ford said nothing, simply studying her with those piercing blue eyes. "You just decided this now?"

She tried to sound nonchalant. "Well, yes."

"Why?"

"Like I said, after this panic attack, I think I should focus on therapy and—"

"—work," he finished for her. "Right. The same therapy and work you've been doing these past few weeks, the whole time we've been involved. But suddenly, *now*, you need to focus exclusively on that."

The comment put her on the defensive. "Did you see what just happened to me on the train? Oh, I'm sorry, it must've been somebody else who had to carry me off when I was *unconscious*. I think it's safe to say that whatever I've been doing these past few weeks, it isn't working."

She tried walking away, because once again he was too close and she needed to get away from his knowing reporter eyes. But he caught her hand, stopping her.

"Victoria." He moved closer.

She thought about backing up, but then it really *would* look like she was running from him. So she held her ground, forcing herself to remain stoic and stifling the urge to lean into his hand when he touched her cheek.

He gazed down at her, his voice husky. "Why are you so afraid of this? Of us?"

She felt an unexpected stinging in her eyes. Instantly, she fought back against her emotions and shoved them down deep. "Ford, I'm so sorry if I led you on in some way." Her tone was gentle, but firm. "But . . . there is no us."

He took his hand from her face and backed away a step.

"We agreed this was just a casual thing," she continued.

"We did," he said. "And if it *is* just that, I don't see why there's suddenly a problem."

She tried to play if off. "I'm not saying there's a problem. But after what happened today, I just . . . want some space."

"Space." He ran a hand over his jaw and then nodded. "Okay. Sure. I don't like the idea of leaving you alone right now, but if that's what you need, I'll come back later. How about if I check on you in a couple hours?"

She felt a lump in her throat. That was . . . a really sweet thing for him to offer. "That won't be necessary, but thank you."

He pulled back, his eyes searching hers. "What the *fuck* is going on, Victoria?"

She blinked, caught off guard by his sudden anger. "I told you what's going on."

He stepped closer, his expression a mixture of confusion and something else she couldn't read. "Everything was fine until tonight. But then you faint, and suddenly you're shoving me out the door." He paused. "Did I . . . do something wrong?"

"No," she said emphatically, feeling terrible he would even ask. "Not at all."

"Then help me understand what's happening." His expression softened. "Victoria, talk to me."

She looked down at the ground, needing a moment, and then met his gaze. "I don't want to fight with you, Ford."

He stepped closer, his lips curved in an affectionate smile. "Shockingly, this time I actually don't want to fight with you, either."

"But I do want you to go," she said softly.

He stopped, hearing that.

She saw a brief flicker of emotion in his eyes, but then his expression turned stony. His voice was cool as he backed away from her.

"You know what? Fine. I spent years living with someone who ran hot and cold. Someone who would be my best friend—my fucking hero—one day, and then the next morning he'd wake up hungover—or sometimes even still drunk—and tell me to get the hell out of his face, or backhand me for making too much noise while playing basketball on the driveway."

She took a step toward him. "Ford."

"Don't." He held up his hand. "You don't want me around, Victoria? No problem. I'll get the hell out of your way, no more questions asked."

Without so much as a second glance, he turned and walked out of her loft, slamming her front door behind him.

When he was gone, Victoria put her hand on her stomach and inhaled slow and deep, just like the good doctor had taught her.

Breathe, Slade.

Just breathe.

Twenty-eight

THE FOLLOWING FRIDAY morning, Victoria caught herself once again staring out her office windows when Will came in with his update.

She sat upright in her chair and put on a smile. "So? What's the word?"

The day's mail had been delivered and, notably, once again there hadn't been any paternity test results for Peter Sutter. Wanting to keep the momentum of the case going now that she had Sutter's attention, she'd asked Will to call the lab and find out how much longer it would take them to process the results.

"Get this: the lab says Sutter never showed up to take the paternity test," Will said.

"You're kidding," Victoria said.

She was so going to light this guy up.

"Thanks, Will." After he left her office, Victoria reached for her phone and dialed Peter Sutter's work number. "Well, Mr. Sutter, it appears we're going to do this the hard way," she said when he answered.

"No, no—we're good," Peter said immediately. "I planned

to call you today to explain. I'm going to the lab on my lunch break, I swear. It's been a crazy week—Melanie got an abnormal result on her quad screen test, so we had to do an ultrasound, but that was still inconclusive, so then she had to have an amniocentesis . . . and luckily, everything's okay with the baby. But with all the medical procedures and everything going on at home, I didn't get a chance to get to the lab."

Either Victoria was losing her touch, or Peter Sutter was the best damn bullshit artist she'd ever encountered. Because, despite his extremely spotty track record, she actually believed the guy.

Which was a shame, really. Given her mood, she'd rather been looking forward to biting someone's head off.

"Today, Mr. Sutter," she said, in no uncertain terms. "It's a cheek swab, not brain surgery. Get yourself to the lab or I'll come down to that gym with a Q-tip and get it myself."

She hung up the phone, debated whether to call Nicole with the update, and then ultimately decided to wait until after lunch to see whether Sutter actually did go to the lab as promised.

Then her mind drifted—as it had several other times this week—to the *other* Dixon. The one who'd stormed out of her place four days ago.

You don't want me around, Victoria? No problem. I'll get the hell out of your way, no more questions asked.

Feeling terrible about their argument, she'd texted Ford the morning after and apologized for the way things had ended. His reply, several hours later, had been short and not especially sweet.

Don't worry about it.

She hadn't seen him since, although she knew he was around. She could hear him through their shared wall at night, watching the news per his routine, while she lay in bed trying to pretend she was actually reading whatever the heck book she had open on her e-reader.

She'd thought about knocking on his door to try to smooth over the awkwardness, but in the end she'd decided it was probably better to just let things go. He clearly had zero interest in talking to her, which she undoubtedly deserved. She *had* ended things out of the blue, after the man had carried her off a train and gone above and beyond to take care of her.

You asked for this, girlfriend.

Ah, good. She and her sassy subconscious were on speaking terms again. Seemingly miffed about the fight with Ford, the pesky voice had been giving her the cold shoulder all week.

But for once, her sassy subconscious was right—she *had* asked for this. And she still wanted this, she just . . . hadn't expected to feel so off her game afterward.

Obviously, she simply needed to get back to her routine. She had no doubt that this lingering ennui or whatever would dissipate in a few days, so until then, she would keep marching ahead, doing her thing.

So when Will walked into her office a few minutes later to let her know that her eleven thirty appointment had arrived— the very contentious, snide, and argumentative opposing counsel who'd once called her a "ballbuster" in open court—she smiled and mentally cracked her knuckles in anticipation.

"Send him in."

THAT EVENING, FORD nursed a beer at Estelle's, a neighborhood dive bar. He sat at a high-top, staring up at the small TV above the bar that was playing *Vanilla Sky* and only half listening to Charlie and Tucker's latest erudite debate—the animal they'd least like to encounter in the wild: shark, bear, or lion.

"What kind of shark are we talking about?" Charlie asked.

"Great white," Tucker said.

"How about the bear? Brown or grizzly?"

"Doesn't matter. Grizzly."

Charlie considered this. "I gotta say lion."

"You'd rather face a great white shark than a lion?" Tucker scoffed. "Fuck that. Man is helpless in the water against one of those things."

"Yeah, but of the three, sharks and bears don't *want* to eat you," Charlie countered. "A lion would."

Tucker waved this off. "Lions are lazy. And males don't do the hunting, anyway. If he's just eaten, I bet you could walk by while he's chilling and he'd be all, 'Sup, dude. Got some impala leftovers under that acacia tree if you want them.'"

Ford shook his head, taking another sip of his beer.

"Who said it had to be a male lion?" Charlie asked.

"Um, I did. 'Cause if I meant female, I would've said 'lioness.'"

"What are you, fucking *National Geographic*? Who says 'lioness'?" Charlie turned to Ford. "What about you? What animal would you least want to face off against in the wild: bear, lion, or shark?"

"Crocodile."

"Crocodile. Another contender emerges." Tucker flagged down the waitress. "I'll get this round." He looked at Ford's beer, only half-empty, and grinned. "You pacing yourself? Got a hot date with my future wife after this?"

Ford gave him a look. "Actually, your future wife and I aren't seeing each other anymore."

Tucker's mouth fell open. "What? When did this happen?"

"Dude, she was just at your barbecue six days ago," Charlie said. "How'd you manage to screw things up since then?"

Tucker hit him in the arm. "Nice, Charles. Real sensitive."

Charlie glared back. "Like you know what to say, either." He pointed to Ford. "Brooke always handles the sensitive stuff."

"True." Tucker eyed Ford for a moment, then leaned over and whispered to Charlie, "Maybe we should text her. He looks a little . . . broody."

For chrissakes. "No one is texting Brooke," Ford said. "For one thing, she's out of town for work, and for another thing, I'm not broody." Seeing Charlie's and Tucker's skeptical looks, he felt the need to continue. "Come on. I always knew it wasn't going to be a long-term thing with Victoria. She said she needed space, so we agreed not to see each other anymore. It's not a big deal." Granted, that was the whitewashed version of last Monday's events, but he saw no reason to share the details of Victoria's panic attack—nor the argument afterward—with Charlie and Tucker.

Besides, as he'd come to realize these last few days, it was probably a good thing that he and Victoria were no longer hooking up. Things between them had been starting to feel a little . . . real. And he didn't *want* real. He'd just been caught off guard on Monday, not having expected her to end things so suddenly.

But that was neither here nor there now.

"So you're cool with this?" Charlie asked.

"Definitely cool," Ford assured him.

Tucker raised his beer glass. "Dude. You're back."

Pfft. Ford raised his glass and grinned. "Who said I ever went away?"

He finished his beer, joking around with Charlie and Tucker and having a good time. His friends found some women to talk to—of course they did—and just as Ford was debating whether to order a second drink, out of the corner of his eye he caught a flash of a long, chestnut-brown ponytail.

Immediately, he turned . . . and saw that it was a woman in her mid-twenties. She caught him looking and walked over with a smile.

"Sorry," Ford told her. "I thought you were someone else."

"Oh." Pretty, and with legs that went on for days in her short skirt, she pointed to his empty glass. "Well, how about I buy you a drink while you're waiting for your someone else to show up?"

Ford appreciated the gesture. And on a different night, perhaps he'd take her up on that offer. "Thanks. But I'm just hanging out with my friends tonight."

"Sure. No problem." With a carefree shrug, she walked back to her group of girlfriends.

A few minutes later, Tucker was at his side. He nodded at the brunette. "Huh. I thought you were in there."

"Nah, she was just asking me for the time. Said she has a boyfriend." Ford made a big show of shrugging. "What can you do, right?"

Tucker looked at him. Then he reached out and squeezed Ford's shoulder, his voice turning uncharacteristically serious. "Hey. You win some, you lose some, right?"

Ford smiled slightly. "Indeed you do, Tuck."

A moment passed, neither of them saying anything further. Nothing else *to* be said, really.

Then Tucker cocked his head and grinned. "So can I talk to the brunette, then?"

Ford chuckled. Some things, at least, never changed. "She's all yours."

Twenty-nine

ON SATURDAY AFTERNOON, for once, Victoria had plenty to say during her weekly session with the good doctor.

She paced in his office while describing her panic attack, cross-examining him about the effectiveness of his supposed techniques and her alleged progress—both of which seemed highly debatable given recent events.

"I can tell that you're upset," Dr. Metzel said calmly when she'd finished her rant.

She snorted. A regular mind-reader, this one.

He gestured. "Please. Have a seat."

After debating—she'd been on the fence about coming to this appointment at all—she sat down in the chair across from him.

Yes, she was angry with Dr. Metzel because of her setback. And she *needed* to be angry with him—or with someone, at least. Because if she didn't have her anger to focus on, she'd start thinking about the fact that these panic attacks weren't going away as easily as she'd hoped, and that scared her.

She'd never been cowed by anything in her life, and she'd be damned if she'd start now.

"I understand your frustration," he said. "But I do think you're still making progress."

"Tell that to the seventy people who saw me faint on the train. Or to Ford, who had to carry me off, like I'm some damsel in distress. Do you realize how embarrassing that was?" She pointed to her chest, her emotions raw. "I do *not* need rescuing."

He studied her for a moment. "Why didn't you just get off the train at an earlier stop? That would've solved your problem instantly."

"I told you, I didn't want Ford to know about the panic attacks."

"Why not?"

She exhaled. Always so many questions. "It doesn't matter. Ford and I aren't seeing each other anymore. I ended things Monday night." She pointed. "Go ahead. I'll wait while you write that down in your notebook." *Patient shows zero progress and continues to be a general pain in the ass.*

She pictured him stamping the top of her file with one word written in red ink: *hopeless.*

But instead, Dr. Metzel held her gaze. "Why did you end things with Ford?"

"I don't want to talk about him."

"I think you do. You didn't have to tell me you weren't seeing him anymore."

She paused at that. This whole week she'd been trying to cover up the fact that something was off. And, frankly, it was getting a little exhausting.

Dr. Metzel slid his chair closer to hers and leaned forward earnestly, resting his arms on his knees. "I know you see me as the enemy here, Victoria. But believe it or not, I really do want to help you. And I think I *can* help you. If you'll let me."

She shook her head, knowing that opening this door would mean saying things out loud that she didn't even want to acknowledge to herself. "I can't have these kinds of feelings for Ford."

"Why not?" Dr. Metzel pressed.

She met his gaze. "Because I can't need anyone that way." She saw him waiting for her to continue. Fine. She'd go there, just this once. "You asked how I felt that day when I came home and found my mother unconscious. At first, while I was waiting for the ambulance, there was mostly shock and fear and a lot of promises that if she pulled through, I'd be strong enough for the both of us from that point forward."

You're going to be fine, Mom. I'll take care of you. Just please, please don't leave me, okay?

Victoria cleared her throat, needing a moment to fight back the prickling sensation in her eyes.

"But when we got to the hospital, after I watched as they wheeled her off on a gurney, there wasn't anything I could do except wait. And sitting there, all I kept thinking was that she'd *wanted* to leave me. My own mother. And that realization was so much worse than anything I'd felt when my father had left, because she didn't bother to say good-bye. Didn't even leave me a note."

She met Dr. Metzel's eyes. "You asked before if I was angry with her. I wasn't angry—I felt *betrayed*. I was ten years old at the time, and she was all I had left. What the hell did she think would happen to me if she'd died? Did she even think about that?"

"Did you ask her that?"

"Sure, because that's all she needed: more guilt. I couldn't ask her; I was terrified that if I made a wrong move she'd relapse. So instead, I did what I promised I'd do if she pulled through: I sucked it up and stayed strong, for the both of us." She set her hands in her lap. "I realize now, as an adult, that my mother's suicide attempt had nothing to do with me—it was a product of her depression. And I also think that she deliberately chose to take those pills before I came home because, deep down, she wanted to be found. She wanted help." Victoria's voice turned quieter. "But I remember how it felt sitting in that hospital waiting room, all by myself. I remember the pain of being abandoned by someone I loved more than anything. Someone I thought would never leave me.

"Every day, I see the hurt on people's faces as their relationships fall apart. So I ask them what they need to be able to move on, and then I fight as hard as I can to get them those things. But what I never tell my clients is that I *know* what they're going through. I know the rejection and the hurt and the fear that grips you by the throat when you realize that you're going to have to get by on your own, but have no fucking clue how to do that." She looked Dr. Metzel in the eyes. "So here's my question for *you*, Doctor: knowing that kind of pain, and having lived through it once, why on earth would I ever allow someone to be able to hurt me that way again?"

He seemed ready for the question. "Because not everyone leaves."

"Nearly half of all marriages end in divorce. That's a lot of people who decide they want out of something that was supposed to last forever."

He continued on, speaking more passionately than she'd ever heard him. "Because you decide that the good moments are worth it, no matter what might happen down the road. Because you find someone who's worth facing your deepest fears for, someone you're willing to take a chance on."

Victoria looked away, shaking her head. "You make it sound so simple." After a long moment, she continued. "You do realize this is all a moot point, right? Even if I was willing to take a chance—and I'm not saying I am—none of this changes the fact that Ford has his own issues with commitment."

"It's true that telling Ford how you feel means taking a risk." Dr. Metzel smiled. "But believe it or not, Victoria, you're not the first person to be afraid to put yourself out there when it comes to relationships."

That got a small smile out of her. "And here I wanted to be such a trailblazer for the fear-of-intimacy-and-abandonment crowd." She paused, feeling the need to set the record straight about one other thing. "And I don't think you're the enemy. Just . . . a big pain in the ass."

Dr. Metzel laughed, giving her a nod in acknowledgment. "I'll take it."

* * *

THE FOLLOWING MONDAY, after a morning court call, Victoria returned to the office to find that Peter Sutter had left a message for her.

"He wanted to know when the results of the paternity test would be in," Will said. "He sounded really anxious."

She rolled her eyes. Oh, sure, *now* Sutter was eager to get answers, after keeping them all on pins and needles last week. Fortunately, to keep the ball rolling, she'd called the lab after Sutter's visit last Friday and had asked if there was any way they could expedite the results.

"Sure, we can fax them over in one business day for an additional fee," the case manager at the lab had informed her.

Figuring the money came out of her own pocket anyway, she'd given them the go-ahead.

"I have to jump on another call," Victoria told Will. "Can you call Sutter back and let him know that the lab said they'd get me the results by noon?"

Will nodded. "Will do."

An hour later, he walked into her office while she was on yet another call, and put a note on her desk.

Peter Sutter is here.

Surprised, she mouthed, *Here?* as her opposing counsel continued talking on the other end of the line. When Will nodded, she wrapped up her call as fast as possible and then headed out to his desk.

"He's in the waiting area," Will said. "And apparently, he's not alone."

Victoria cocked her head. "He brought a lawyer?" Perhaps Sutter was preparing for a fight, after all.

Bring it on.

"The receptionist only said that he was with a guest," Will said. "Do you want me to check it out?"

"No, I'll go out there myself." She headed down the hallway to the waiting area, wondering if she was going to find one of the usual suspects in the Chicago family law scene sitting next to Sutter. And when she rounded the corner, she did, indeed, see a familiar face.

Just not the familiar face she'd expected.

Victoria blinked at the sight of Peter and his wife, Melanie, sitting side by side in two of the waiting area's leather chairs. She walked over and extended her hand as they stood up. "Mr. Sutter, Ms. Ames . . . this is a surprise."

Peter looked incredibly nervous. "I, um, told Melanie everything over the weekend. The truth, the whole truth, and nothing but."

Melanie smiled tentatively at Victoria. "Sorry to drop in unexpectedly like this. I'm sure you're very busy."

"We're anxious to hear the test results, so when your assistant said you'd have them by noon, we thought we'd come down and get them in person," Peter explained.

Admittedly, Victoria was surprised by this turn of events—the cynical part of her having assumed that Sutter would hold out as long as possible before telling his wife about Nicole and Zoe. She checked her watch. "Actually, it's almost noon now, so we should have the results any moment. Why don't we head to my office and wait there?" She led them through the hallway, catching Will's eye as they passed by his desk.

She raised an eyebrow at him. *Anything from the lab yet?*

He shook his head.

Inside her office, she gestured to the chairs in front of her desk. "Please, have a seat." She sat down across from Peter and Melanie. "Can I get you something to drink? Coffee, tea?"

Both of them asked for a glass of water. After gulping down half the glass, Peter looked at his wife, then at Victoria.

"I guess we'd forgotten about the awkwardness factor when we decided to storm down here and wait," he joked, shifting anxiously in his chair.

"How's the sale of your condo going?" Victoria asked, going for a neutral topic.

"We just had a couple come back and take a second look this weekend. I think they're very interested." Melanie smiled at Victoria. "Then again, I thought you and your boyfriend were interested in the place, too, so maybe I'm losing my touch."

"Oh, the guy with me at the open house wasn't my boyfriend," Victoria was quick to clarify. "Actually, in the interest of full disclosure, he's Nicole's brother."

"Nicole's brother?" Peter ran a hand over his mouth. "Great. He must think I'm a jerk."

"Really? You two aren't dating?" Melanie asked Victoria. "Huh. I could've sworn I got a vibe."

Thankfully, they were interrupted by a knock on the door.

All three of them looked over as Will walked into Victoria's office, carrying what appeared to be a fax printout.

"This just arrived from the lab." He handed it to Victoria and left.

She glanced at Peter, who bounced his knee nervously, and at Melanie, who gripped the arms of her chair.

Without looking at it, she slid the fax across the desk to them.

Peter peered down at the document and took a deep breath. Melanie reached over and took his hand. "It's okay, Peter," she said softly. "No matter what it says, you and I will be fine. We'll figure this out. Together."

Peter stared right into her eyes. "You know how much I love you, right?"

"Yes." Melanie smiled tenderly. "I knew it the thirteenth night you sat on my doorstep."

"I sat on your doorstep for fourteen nights."

"I know. I kept you out there one more for good measure."

Peter laughed, then brought his wife's hand to his mouth and kissed it.

Watching this scene from behind her desk, Victoria couldn't help but feel as though she were intruding on a private moment.

But she also felt surprisingly touched.

For eight years, she'd watched and listened as couples argued and fought. She'd seen the demise of so many relationships, she couldn't possibly count them all. Her office, Victoria Slade & Associates, was the place where marriages died and happily-ever-after came to its bitter, ugly end.

But not today.

Peter and Melanie looked at her and blushed, as if they'd just remembered she was in the room.

"Sorry. This week has been an emotional roller coaster. All right. Here goes." Peter picked up the fax, skimmed the top cover sheet, and then flipped to the next page and read the results.

"She's mine," he said to his wife. "I have a daughter."

Melanie's eyes filled with tears. She squeezed his hand. "Okay."

Peter turned to Victoria, his voice thick with emotion. "What's her name?"

"Zoe."

"Zoe," he repeated. "That's pretty." He went quiet, as if unsure what to say next.

"I'd asked Nicole to e-mail me a photo of her. Would you like to see it?" Victoria offered.

"Yes. Please."

Victoria pulled up the picture of Zoe on her iPad, and then handed it over to Peter.

Melanie covered her mouth. "Oh my gosh, she looks just like you."

Peter wiped his eyes. "She really does." He took a moment to compose himself, and then he looked at Victoria. "When can we meet her?"

They spent the next few minutes discussing schedules, and Victoria promised to get back to them with some possible dates and times as soon as she'd spoken to Nicole. Obviously, conversations about child support and custody arrangements were on the imminent horizon, but for now, she was content to simply let Peter and Melanie process everything.

As she walked them out to the waiting room, Peter turned to her. "Thank you for tracking me down. This is a lot to take in, but nevertheless, I can't imagine having a daughter out there and not being a part of her life."

Victoria smiled, even though the comment hit a little close to home. "You're welcome. But honestly, most of the credit for finding you goes to Nicole's brother."

Melanie shook her hand next. "We'll wait for your call."

She paused on the way out the door, then gestured between her and Peter. "Oh, and for the record . . . we *were* on a break."

We were on a break!

Victoria smiled and gave Melanie a nod.

"So you were."

THAT AFTERNOON, FORD met with his editor to discuss the possibility of bringing on another reporter to work with him on both the Department of Children and Family Services and probation department investigations.

"You wouldn't believe how many examples there are of convicts slipping through the cracks. And worse, in the case of DCFS—*kids* slipping through the cracks. There are a lot of stories to tell here—I just can't keep up with all of them."

"What about Castellon? You've worked with him before," Marty suggested.

"He's swamped with the pension-fund crisis series. How about Pearson?" Ford suggested.

Marty considered that. "She'd be a good fit for this. I'll talk to her today."

When Ford got back to his desk, he saw that he'd just missed a call from Nicole on his cell phone.

"Did you hear?" his sister answered, when he called her back.

No clue. "Hear what?"

"Victoria met with Peter Sutter and his wife today. She gave them the results of the paternity test and apparently everything went well. Like, really well. They want to meet Zoe. This is actually happening, Ford—she's going to have a *dad*."

Hearing the excitement in his sister's voice, Ford smiled. So Victoria Slade had gotten her man, after all.

Good for her.

"That's great, Nicole." They talked for a while about the logistics—apparently, Victoria had suggested that Nicole and Peter get together to "catch up" before he met Zoe.

"Can you imagine how awkward that conversation will

be?" Nicole asked. "'Hey, Pete, good to see you again. Funny thing, huh, you and me having a baby?'"

As least there was going to *be* a conversation. Ford was still reserving judgment on Sutter, but so far, the guy seemed to have his heart in the right place.

Shortly after he hung up with his sister, Samantha Pearson stopped by his desk. Even though she'd only joined the Watchdog Team last year, she already had a reputation at the *Trib* of being tenacious and extremely thorough when it came to investigating a story.

"I just talked to Marty about the DCFS and probation department series," she said. "He says that if I help you, I'll probably piss off a lot of government bureaucrats."

"That's true," Ford said.

Samantha smiled. "Then I'm in."

Ford wrapped up for the day at five thirty and took the Blue Line home. The train was crowded, typical for rush hour, and as he stood in the middle of the packed car while holding on to the railing above him, he realized that it had been exactly one week since Victoria had her panic attack.

He'd been doing some research into panic disorder—not that he was sitting around ruminating over her or anything. The investigative journalist in him was just . . . curious. And his research had helped him understand that it was the panic attack itself that the person feared—not necessarily the environment, like a train car—and that while the attacks were not dangerous, they could be terrifying to the sufferer because he or she felt so out of control.

His fingers clenched around the steel railing when he thought about how afraid Victoria must've felt that day. He'd been standing right next to her, rattling on about his interview with the director of the Department of Children and Family Services, and he'd had no clue that anything was wrong until the moment right before she'd fainted. If only she'd said something, maybe he could've—

Well, anyway. The point was, he sure hoped this fancy, expensive therapist of hers was helping her out. Not that it was any of his business anymore.

Obviously.

Oh—and also that her therapist was familiar with the benefits of cognitive restructuring and interoceptive exposure. Because from what Ford had read, people with panic disorder were having a lot of success with those therapies.

Yep. So not his business.

He stopped at home and changed into his workout clothes, then headed to the gym a couple blocks from his place. He stayed for two hours, running and lifting weights to the point of exhaustion. After toweling off in the locker room, he walked back to his building.

He slowed down as he approached the glass door.

Victoria stood in the foyer, next to the mailboxes. Judging from her pantsuit and the briefcase slung over her shoulder, she'd just gotten off work.

He paused, watching for a moment as she flipped through her mail, and then headed inside.

"Long day?" he said.

"Oh! Hi." She started, and then smiled hesitantly at him. "Just a typical Monday. You know me." She bit her lip, as if regretting her choice of words.

Yes, he did know her.

He smiled to cover the awkwardness. "I heard the news— Nicole told me that things went really well with Sutter and his wife today."

"It did. We still have a lot of details to talk about, but you know . . . I think it's going to work out." Her lips quirked. "Although Sutter looked a little nervous when he heard you're Nicole's brother."

"Is that right?" Ford considered that. "Good."

She smiled, and then a silence fell between them.

He pointed toward the elevator. "Are you heading up?"

"Uh, yes, actually." She shut her mailbox and they walked together to the elevator. Ford caught her eyeing his damp T-shirt.

"Sorry. I just came from the gym," he said as they stepped into the small elevator.

She pushed the button for their floor. "It's not like I haven't seen you sweaty before."

He looked at her.

She blushed, as if just realizing what she'd said. "That was awkward. Sorry." She shook her head self-deprecatingly.

And despite everything, they shared a smile.

The ice broken—at least, in part—she turned toward him, speaking genuinely. "I'm really sorry about Monday, Ford. The way things ended, I mean."

She'd texted him a similar apology six days ago, and at the time he'd been kind of a dick in return. But now, standing across from her in the elevator and seeing the sincerity in her eyes, he found himself softening.

Yes, it was over between them. And that realization stung a little. Maybe more than a little, although he wouldn't allow himself to go there. But other than the abruptness of their breakup—if one could call it that—he really had no reason to be *mad* at Victoria. Not once, the entire time they'd been hooking up, had she given him any reason to believe that their relationship was anything except a fun, casual fling. So if he'd been starting to think . . . Well, he didn't know what he'd been starting to think, and it didn't matter now. The point was, she was his next-door neighbor, at least for the rest of the summer, and it was inevitable they would run into each other. He wasn't going to be a jerk and make the situation even more awkward.

"It's fine. Really," he said. The elevator stopped at their floor, and they both stepped out. "I mean, we both knew this was going to run its course eventually, right?"

There was a flicker of something in her eyes, but then she smiled. "Right. Absolutely." She gestured. "After all, you have your laundry list of thirtysomething commitment angst."

"And you have . . . what was it again?" He rubbed his jaw, as if trying to remember. "'Self-selected out of the happily-ever-after rat race,' was it? No obligations, expectations, or endgame of a marriage, two-point-five kids, and a minivan in the suburbs."

She laughed. "I really laid it on thick that night, didn't I?"

"Oh, there was quite a speech."

They reached her door. When she turned to face him, he

took his keys out of the pocket of his workout shorts and gave her a soft smile, one that she returned. And as they stood there, looking at each other, on that doorstep where they'd first met and also had their first kiss, they both understood exactly what this moment was.

Closure.

"Good night, Victoria."

Her voice was soft. "Good night, Ford."

He left her standing there and turned toward his own place. When he heard her front door shut, he briefly closed his eyes.

And kept right on walking.

Thirty

THE FOLLOWING FRIDAY, one of Victoria's associates, Nadia, rushed into Victoria's office with an excited smile.

"Got a question for you," she said. "I'm in the middle of the Ciotta deposition, and he just said that he recorded some phone calls between his wife and her co-worker, trying to find out if there was anything 'flirty' going on between them. When I asked, he admitted that neither his wife nor the co-worker knew that he was recording them." She cocked her head. "Isn't that wiretapping without consent? Did the guy actually just admit on the record that he committed a *crime*? Can we use that as leverage against him?"

Victoria considered this. "Maybe. *If* that does constitute an illegal wiretapping."

"And does it?"

Victoria smiled. "No clue. But I agree it's worth looking into. How long before you have to get back to the dep?"

Nadia checked her watch. "Two minutes."

Hearing that, Victoria got down to business. "All right. Here's what you're going to do: grab Joaquin and explain the situation. Tell him I said to start his research with People versus Melongo. I know that the Illinois Supreme Court recently struck down the state eavesdropping law as over-broad, but I'm not sure how the case law has shaken out since then. That's the first thing we need to figure out. And tell him to also check into whether there's any kind of exception if the eavesdropper owns the phone line on which one of the parties was talking—like some kind of implied consent."

"Got it."

"When you get back to the dep, don't mention the wiretap issue yet," Victoria said. "Take another break in forty-five minutes, and then you, Joaquin, and I will discuss whether we have a move here. Sound good?"

Nadia nodded. "Yes. Thanks."

Moments later, Will walked into her office. "I'm going to Perry's for lunch. Do you want me to pick up your usual?"

Always a lifesaver, this man. "That would be great—thank you. And keep my schedule clear at one o'clock. I'll need fifteen minutes to meet with Nadia and Joaquin."

The rest of the afternoon was nonstop, between advising Nadia and finalizing a marital settlement agreement in one of Victoria's own cases. It was after seven o'clock when she finally got home, stripped out of her suit, and changed into jeans and a flowy, sleeveless shirt. Luckily, she had a quiet evening planned. She'd probably just rent a movie since her trusty e-reader had been failing her as of late—nothing she read seemed to grab her attention these days.

After unpacking her briefcase, she realized she'd forgotten to check her mailbox on the way up. Sticking her keys into her back pocket, she headed down the hallway and waited for the elevator while scrolling through all the work e-mails she needed to catch up on over the weekend.

Ding!

As the elevator doors opened, she looked up from her phone and saw Ford standing inside.

With an attractive blond woman next to him.

It took Victoria a moment to find her voice. "Hi."

"Victoria—hi." He smiled awkwardly at her while holding the elevator door open for the blonde, who gave Victoria a polite *hello* as she stepped out.

Ford followed the blonde out of the elevator, then—always the gentleman—he held the door open for Victoria, too.

"Thanks." She stepped inside, and then turned around and looked at Ford.

As their eyes met, the elevator doors slid shut between them.

Swallowing, Victoria pushed the button for the ground floor. Then she looked up as the elevator descended.

Her lip began to tremble.

Shit.

Her stomach rolled. Covering her mouth, the instant the elevator doors opened she bolted out and pushed through the front door. She ran straight to the alley behind her building and dry-heaved while holding on to the brick wall with one hand.

Afterward, she leaned against the wall, catching her breath.

She couldn't go back to her place. She couldn't risk that she would hear them laughing, or—God—hear the bed squeaking or banging against the wall, or the blonde moaning his name, or worst of all, *Ford* moaning as some other woman touched him, kissed him, stroked him, and figured out all the ways to drive him crazy, like Victoria once had.

She pushed herself off the brick wall and started walking.

Several people passing by on the sidewalk did a double take when they saw her. Victoria ignored all the looks, for once not giving a shit what anyone else thought. Seven blocks later, she walked into Rachel's boutique shop, ringing the chime on the door.

Standing behind the counter while tagging a dress, Rachel looked over. Her eyes widened. "Oh my God, Victoria, what happened? Are you okay?"

Victoria caught sight of her reflection in the mirror behind Rachel. Thick black rivulets of mascara streamed down her face, mixing with her tears.

She gave her friend a wry smile. "I think it's safe to say I'm definitely *not* okay."

AUDREY ARRIVED AT the shop ten minutes later with a bottle of bourbon in hand.

"Holy shit, Rachel wasn't kidding. You are a mess." Audrey sat down next to Victoria on the couch by the dressing rooms. "What happened?"

Victoria went for a joke. "Well, for starters, apparently I *do* like Ford."

"Oh." Audrey smiled. "I hate to break it to you, sweetie, but Rachel and I figured that out at the barbecue."

Rachel came out of the back room with three coffee cups and set them down on the table in front of the couch. "He brought home another woman tonight."

Shocked, Audrey turned to Victoria. "What?"

"I ran into them at the elevator," Victoria said.

"And then she puked in the alley," Rachel added.

Audrey's head spun. "You puked in the alley? Wow. You must *really* like him."

"Oh, God. Don't say that." Victoria bent her head over her knees and took slow, deep breaths.

"The vomiting seems to be her way of expressing her feelings toward Ford," Rachel told Audrey.

"Aw. And they say romance is dead."

Her head against her knees, Victoria groaned. "Don't make me laugh—my stomach already hurts enough." She sat up. "I keep picturing him with that other woman, and thinking about what they might be doing right now." She looked at her friends. "I did this."

"You? Um, no, *he* did this," Audrey emphasized. "He's the asshole, bringing home another woman while you two are seeing each other."

"We're not seeing each other anymore. I ended it almost two weeks ago," Victoria said.

Now it was Rachel's turn to look surprised. "You did? Why?"

"Well . . . that's kind of a long story."

Rachel reached out and squeezed her hand. "We have all night."

Audrey held up the bottle. "And we have bourbon."

That got a smile out of Victoria. "Okay." As the three of them sat there, drinking bourbon out of coffee cups in the middle of the store, she proceeded to tell Audrey and Rachel everything: the flashback she'd had during the break-in, her mom's attempted suicide, her panic attacks, the therapy with Dr. Metzel, and, ultimately, her breakup with Ford.

"It's a lot to take in, I know," Victoria said.

"Why didn't you tell us about all this earlier?" Audrey asked gently. "Vic, we're your best friends. My God, after my divorce you moved me into your place and let me stay there for almost a month."

Victoria smiled sheepishly. "I'm good at handling other people's problems. Just . . . not so much my own."

Rachel put a hand to her heart. "I'm still stuck on the part when Ford carried you off the train."

"It was either that or leave me there, clogging up the aisle at his stop," Victoria joked. When Rachel gave her a look, she turned more serious. "I know. He was really sweet and I . . . freaked out and pushed him away."

"So? What are you going to do about it?" Audrey asked.

Victoria pulled back. "Do about it? There's nothing I can do. Whatever we had between us, he's obviously moved on to some other woman."

"You don't know what that was," Rachel said. "You were wrong that other time, when you saw him with the woman who turned out to be his friend."

"Even if that were true, he's not looking for a serious relationship," she pointed out.

"That's what you said, too, once," Audrey said.

"And I'm still saying that." Victoria paused for a moment. "Maybe." When her friends smiled, she pointed, quick to cut them off at the pass. "No. Whatever you're thinking, just . . . no."

"I'm thinking you have to tell Ford how you feel," Audrey said.

Oh, God.

Feeling her stomach clench, Victoria bent over, her head between her legs. "Yep. Here I go again." Breathing deep for several moments, she turned her head to the side and peeked at her two friends. "You can't be serious. Look at me." She sat up. "I'm supposed to ignore the fact that Ford says he doesn't want anything serious, *and* the fact that he may have already moved on to someone else, and just walk up to him and lay my feelings on the line, without having the faintest idea whether he feels the same way? Do you honestly think—even on my best day—that I'm capable of putting myself out there like that?"

Audrey and Rachel both looked her dead in the eyes. "Yes."

Victoria blinked, not having expected them to be so unequivocal.

Then Rachel grinned. "Although on your worst day, you might end up puking on his shoes. So choose your moment wisely."

Right. Helpful.

SEATED AT HIS dining table, Ford looked over when he heard a front door close in the hallway.

He went momentarily still, and then realized that the sound was too muted to be coming from Victoria's place.

Turning back to his laptop, he tried to focus on his research. He was working on yet another follow-up piece in his probation department series, cross-checking arrest records against the list of nearly one thousand convicted felons who hadn't been seen by their probation officers for two or more months. It was turning out to be a massive investigation, although at least now he had someone to share the workload.

He and Samantha, his co-worker on the Watchdog Team, had planned to meet that afternoon to divvy up the names of lost convicts. But then her one year-old son's nanny had called in sick and Samantha had taken the day off. Eager to nevertheless get a jump on things over the weekend, and seeing how she lived only five minutes away in Bucktown, she'd offered to drop by Ford's place that evening, after her husband got home from work, so that Ford could bring her up to speed on the investigation and give her copies of his files.

It was a wholly platonic meeting—obviously—but he knew what Victoria must have been thinking when she saw him and Samantha heading to his place. And he couldn't decide what bothered him more: that Victoria would assume he was already hooking up with someone else, or that *he* found it so incredible that *she* might actually think that. Because he and Victoria were done. Finished. And they'd never had any kind of commitment between them even when they were together. So if he wanted to go on a date, or meet a woman for drinks, or bring a whole goddamn bachelorette party back to his place for a wild orgy, he was perfectly free to do so.

But there'd been that *look* that Victoria had given him when she saw him with Samantha.

And that look was bullshit.

That look had pissed him off all over again, because they'd had their nice talk last week. They'd had their closure and they'd parted ways on good terms and they were supposed to be done but that look, that fleeting, brief, probably meaningless look of hers . . . had given him hope.

And he didn't want to have hope.

Not when he knew exactly how this would turn out.

He checked his watch and saw that it was nearly ten o'clock at night. Swearing under his breath—so much for not sitting around ruminating over Victoria—he grabbed his phone and nearly texted Charlie and Tucker before stopping himself. He knew they would be at a bar, and he had zero interest in the bar scene tonight. Texting Brooke also was out of the question, because the only reason a single man would ever text his married female friend at ten o'clock on a Friday night was to *talk*, and he didn't want to *talk*. He just wanted to get out of his place and burn off some energy.

So he changed into his workout clothes, went to his twenty-four-hour gym, and just . . . ran. On the treadmill, for an hour. Afterward, he lifted weights, and by the time he got home it was after midnight. He took a long, hot shower that sapped every last bit of mental and physical energy out of him, and then he crashed hard.

He slept until nine o'clock, then dove back into the research he'd started the night before. All morning long, there was this nagging sensation in the back of his mind, and at noon, when he broke for lunch, he finally figured out what it was.

No hair dryer.

Granted, there'd been a couple other weekend mornings when Victoria had skipped her interminable hair-drying routine. But now that he thought about it, he hadn't heard *any* sound coming from her place for nearly the last eighteen hours. No hair dryer, no heels on the hardwood floors, no shower, sink, or bathtub running, and no front door opening and closing. Not even a toilet flushing.

And that was the moment he started to get a little worried.

He thought about texting her, but to say, what, exactly? *Are you okay? Did you come home last night? Because I've been sitting here like a loser wondering why I never heard your hair dryer or your bathtub running.*

Yeah, because that wouldn't be creepy and stalker-ish at all.

He went into the bedroom and pressed his ear against the wall, listening for any signs of life.

Nothing.

He'd slept hard last night; he supposed it was possible she'd come home after he'd gone to bed—or, maybe, while he was at the gym—and he'd missed that. And then, perhaps, he'd somehow also missed all sounds of her stirring this morning. Maybe on some subconscious level, he'd wanted to tune her out, so that he didn't have to think about her.

Or maybe she'd just been missing for the last eighteen hours. *Fuck.*

He went to her front door and knocked.

No answer.

Once back inside his loft, he told himself to keep calm, that there was no reason to believe Victoria was in any trouble. Still, to be on the safe side, he grabbed his phone, having thought of a plausible reason to text her. He would say that he planned to install a new faucet and towel bar in his master bathroom, and wanted to make sure this wasn't an inconvenient time for her since there would be a lot of noise. It was a short, polite question, and she would write back some short, polite response. And then he would know she was okay and could move on with his day.

He was halfway through typing the message when he heard her front door open.

Thank God.

He exhaled in relief—both that she was safe and that he didn't have to go dig out the towel bar in his closet and start drilling away in order to maintain his cover story. Realizing he never had grabbed that lunch, he stuck his wallet, keys, and phone in the pockets of his jeans, tucked his sunglasses into his shirt, and headed out.

As he was shutting his door, Victoria's door opened. She stepped out into the hallway carrying a bag of garbage.

And wearing the same shirt and jeans that she'd had on the night before.

She spotted him and blushed, her hand instantly smoothing down her wild-ish, wavy hair. "Hi."

Feeling as though the wind had been knocked out of him, Ford momentarily had no words.

Right.

Understood.

Judging from her hair and clothes, it was pretty clear that Victoria the Divorce Lawyer had *not*, in fact, slept in her own bed last night.

He somehow managed to keep his tone casual. "Hey there."

She smiled hesitantly, probably worried he was going to say something that would make this *really* uncomfortable. "Heading out?"

"Uh, yes. I'm meeting someone for lunch, actually." He even threw in a sheepish smile, as if he, too, was acknowledging the awkwardness of the situation. Because at this point, screw it. He might as well let her think he was dating Samantha. It was better than letting her think the alternative—that he was the fool who'd been worrying and waiting for her to come home all night.

"Oh." She shifted the garbage from one hand to the other. "You know, I was—"

"Sorry." He cut Victoria off, feigning an apologetic smile. He wouldn't make a scene, or say anything to make her feel awkward. But he couldn't stand there, talking like everything was normal. Not right now. "But I'm actually running a little late, so . . . " He pointed to his watch.

"Right—of course." She swallowed and waved him on with her free hand. "Have a good lunch, then."

"Thanks." With a nod in good-bye, he headed down the hallway. Not bothering with the elevator, he pushed through the stairwell door and kept walking, down four flights of steps, and then out the building's front door and into the bright summer sunshine.

He put his sunglasses on as he headed down the sidewalk, ignoring the ache in his chest.

So much for that last shred of fucking hope.

Thirty-one

THE NEXT MORNING, there was an unexpected knock on Ford's front door. When he answered, he found Brooke standing there, one hand on her hip and the other one holding a ticket.

Ford frowned. "Didn't you get my text? I said I'll pass on the game."

"Oh, I got your text." Without waiting for an invitation, she bulldozed her way into his place and walked straight into his kitchen. She grabbed his phone off the counter and used it to turn on a satellite radio station. Music suddenly filled his entire loft, piping through the built-in speakers.

He raised an eyebrow. "Are we . . . having a party?"

She nodded in the direction of Victoria's place. "Background noise." She set his phone down. "Free skybox tickets to today's Cubs/Sox game and you'll pass? There isn't a man in Chicago who would turn that down."

"With you and Cade, Vaughn and Sidney, and Huxley and Addison? No, thanks—it's all couples." And while normally he would jump at the chance to watch the Crosstown Classic from one of Wrigley Field's luxury suites, today he wasn't in the mood to be the odd man out with a bunch of happily married or engaged twosomes.

"Fine. I'll invite Charlie and Tucker, too," she said.

"They might as well be a couple," he said dryly.

She looked at him for a moment, and then pointed. "You told me men don't do this."

"Do what?"

She walked around the counter, speaking animatedly. "Two years ago. We were at Firelight, having drinks. Cade and I had split up and *you* said that men don't mope around after a breakup. You said that men avoid issues, get drunk, and pick up a new girl to forget the old one—but that you *don't* brood."

Ford held out his hands in disbelief. "How do you remember that? And I'm *not* brooding."

She folded her arms across her chest and looked at him.

"I know you're my friend," he said. "But please, for once, can you just act like you have a penis? Because I don't want to talk about this."

She shrugged. "Fine. We'll just sit here and listen to music." She reached for his phone again. "Have you heard Taylor Swift's new song?"

"No."

"Well, you're going to—on endless repeat until you start talking."

Kill him now. "Fine. It's over with Victoria. What else do you want me to say?" Despite his frustration, he was careful to keep his voice low. "She ended things two weeks ago, and yesterday she came home in the afternoon wearing the same clothes she'd had on the night before. Life moves on, I guess." He threw up his hands. "There—is that enough of a heart-to-heart?"

"The same clothes?" Brooke looked surprised. "So, you think—"

He cut her off. "Actually, I'd rather *not* think about that. At all."

"But . . . you two were getting along great the last time I saw you. What am I missing here?"

Ford sighed. Sensing that there was no way of getting around having this talk, he took a seat on one of the barstools and pulled out the other one for Brooke. After she sat down, he filled her in on everything—except for the stuff Victoria had told him about her mother's suicide and her trust and abandonment issues. That seemed too personal for him to share with anyone else.

"So, Victoria saw you with another woman, and then, as far as you know, she didn't come back to her place until the following afternoon." Brooke looked at him. "Did you ever think that maybe *she* didn't want to think about *you* being with someone else? So maybe she went to stay at a friend's or something."

As a matter of fact, he had considered that—more times than he wanted to admit. And the thought of Victoria being jealous and actually caring that much about him being with another woman gave him another one of those stupid flashes of hope.

Which he instantly quelled.

"Maybe." He shrugged. "Anything's possible."

Brooke grinned, as if that settled that. "I think you need to find out if it's more than a possibility."

"No."

She cocked her head, speaking more definitively. "Yes, you do. You have to talk to her, Ford."

He pushed away from the counter and stood up, not wanting to hear this. "No, I don't."

Brooke stared at him like he was crazy. "Why not?"

"Because it wouldn't make a difference!" he shouted. When she blinked in surprise, he turned away, furious that she'd pushed him into this conversation. "Dammit, Brooke."

He walked over to the window and ran a hand over his jaw. After taking a moment, he turned around. "Even if it's all true—even if Victoria didn't sleep with someone else, and she left for the night because she didn't want to see me with another woman—it wouldn't matter. I can't . . . be with someone who won't let me in." His humorless smile was wry. "And, yes, I know that's ironic, coming from me. But if I ever were to go down this road, and let myself fall for someone, it can't be halfway. I have to know that she's in, too. I can't spend my life waiting and hoping for the next good moment, giving everything and loving someone who pushes me away and can't love me the same way back. I won't let anyone mess with my head again like that." He shook his head. "I can't."

Brooke's expression softened. She stood up and joined him by the window. "No. And you shouldn't have to."

She put her arm around him and rested her head on his shoulder. They stayed that way for a long moment.

"Sorry I made you talk about feelings," she finally said.

He kissed the top of her head. "Yeah, you're kind of a jerk that way."

"I could always go next door and kick her ass," she offered.

"Babe, you're, like, five-two."

"Not in heels." She nudged him. "Come on. Come to the game with us. It'll be fun. You know you love it when they bring the dessert cart around."

He couldn't argue with that. Besides, if he didn't say yes, Brooke would probably stage a damn intervention and then he'd just have to talk more about feelings. "All right. If Charlie and Tucker can make it, count me in."

Brooke did a little clap. "Yay."

"I said *if* Charlie and Tucker can make it."

She gave him a look. "What are the odds that Charlie and Tucker have something better to do today?"

Fair enough.

MID-MORNING ON MONDAY, Nicole called Victoria's office to check in after her meeting with Peter Sutter. Per Victoria's arrangements, the two of them had met at a coffee shop close to Nicole's work, so they could reconnect and smooth over some of the "Hey, we had a baby together!" awkwardness.

"So? How did it go?" Victoria asked.

"Pretty good, actually. The first thing he did was apologize for leaving that morning without saying good-bye. And he also said that he really regretted missing the first five months of Zoe's life. He's a nice guy. I can see why I slept with him," Nicole joked.

"And you're still on for tonight? Peter and Melanie will be at your place at six to meet Zoe?" Victoria asked.

"That's what he said. But I wanted to talk to you about that. I'm starting to freak out about this meeting."

Uh-oh. "How so?" Victoria asked.

"It's Melanie. What if she doesn't like me? What if she decides that Peter should be focusing on her pregnancy and their baby instead of Zoe? Or worse, what if she decides to get a lawyer involved because she thinks she and Peter should raise their baby *and* mine?"

"Based on my interactions with Melanie, I don't think any of that will happen," Victoria reassured her. "But if it does, we'll handle it. *I* will handle it. That's what I do, Nicole."

Nicole still sounded hesitant. "Can you come tonight? I'd feel so much better if you're there, too."

The request surprised Victoria—she'd planned to stay out of everyone's way tonight and just check in with Nicole afterward. But after hearing the nervousness in her client's voice, she couldn't refuse. Especially since Nicole wasn't just any client.

I trust you to take care of my sister.

Of course I'll take care of your sister.

"I'm happy to be there, Nicole. Absolutely."

After she hung up with Nicole, Will walked into her office with a stack of message slips.

"All these came in during one phone call?" Victoria asked.

"That's Monday for you," he said matter-of-factly.

"Speaking of which, can you move my afternoon schedule around so I can be free by five o'clock?" When Will gave her a look—*You've got to be kidding me*—she smiled. "Thanks. You're a god."

He snorted disdainfully as he walked out of her office.

And then he worked his magic and had her free at five minutes *before* five o'clock.

When she stopped by his desk on her way out, he checked his watch. "Time for the big meeting, huh?"

"Almost time. I'm going to stop at my place and drop off my briefcase. Since this is supposed to be a casual get-together, I was thinking I should look less lawyer-y."

Will looked her over. "Better lose the suit, then."

Pfft. Now they were just getting crazy. "It's still a business meeting."

"Just saying," he said in a singsong tone.

She caught a cab in front of her building and made a quick pit stop at home. Grumbling to herself that Will was probably right—because, really, when *wasn't* he?—she changed out of her light gray pantsuit and into a cream, V-neck sleeveless dress. Then she grabbed another cab and gave the driver Nicole's address.

The cab pulled up in front of a vintage apartment building in Lincoln Square. There were six units on the second floor, and Nicole's was the closest to the stairwell, on Victoria's right. She knocked on the door and waited. After a brief pause, she heard someone approach, and then the door opened.

Victoria blinked. "Ford. I . . . didn't realize you would be here."

He stood in the doorway, looking surprised himself. "Nicole asked me to come for moral support. She didn't mention you were coming, too." For a split-second, he seemed to hesitate, and then he stepped back from the door. "Come on in."

Nicole's living room was cozy, but small and packed tight with baby paraphernalia. Not sure whether she should sit or stand, Victoria hovered by Zoe's swing and watched as Ford shut the front door.

He gestured in the direction of the bedrooms. "Nicole's getting Zoe dressed. They should be out any minute." He tucked his hands into the pockets of his jeans and silence fell between them.

Victoria tried to fill the void, keeping her tone light. "How's work going?"

"Good. Busy. You?"

"The same. Good. Busy."

Another silence.

Victoria met his gaze, her chest pulling tight as she fought back the words hovering on the tip of her tongue. *Oh, God, did you sleep with that woman? Or worse—do you have feelings for her?*

Since this was hardly the place to have that conversation, she simply smiled.

He gestured to her outfit. "You're awfully dressed up tonight." Despite his easygoing tone, his jaw twitched. "Big plans after this?"

Just then, Nicole walked into the room carrying Zoe, who looked adorable in a pink sundress with a white lace collar. "Yay, Team Nicole is all here." She smiled at Victoria. "Thanks for coming."

"You didn't mention that you'd asked Victoria to be here, too," Ford said offhandedly.

"I didn't?" Nicole cocked her head. "Huh. With you two being next-door neighbors and spending so much time together lately, I guess I figured you would talk among yourselves." She looked between them. "No?"

Victoria and Ford shifted uncomfortably, neither of them wanting to take a stab at answering that one.

"All right, I want you two to be honest with me about something." Nicole turned first to Ford, then Victoria, giving each of them a long look. "No bullshit." She paused. "Does this dress make Zoe look like a pilgrim?"

Victoria exhaled, having been braced for something else. "I don't think I've ever seen a pilgrim wearing pink."

"But it's too fancy, right? Like we're trying too hard?" Nicole asked.

Seeing the anxious look on Nicole's face, Victoria pushed aside her own feelings and did what she did best—focused on someone else's problem. "She looks perfect, Nicole." Walking over, she tickled Zoe's tummy. "Because she is perfect. And Peter and Melanie are going to love her."

Sitting on her mother's hip, Zoe just stared up at Victoria with those big, brown eyes.

"Not even a smile for me, kid? Tough crowd," Victoria teased.

Zoe held out her arms.

Nicole *aw*-ed and handed Zoe over. As Victoria smiled and bounced Zoe on her hip, Ford walked out of the room and headed into the kitchen.

"Huh. I wonder what's gotten into him?" Nicole said.

Victoria glanced at Nicole, suddenly noticing that the younger woman's gaze seemed rather knowing.

Luckily, she was saved from having to answer by a knock on the front door.

"Okay. Show time." Nicole took a deep breath and then exhaled. She opened the door with a smile, introducing herself to Melanie and inviting her and Peter in. The couple looked very nervous—but also excited—as they stepped inside the apartment.

Peter's eyes softened the moment he saw Victoria holding Zoe.

"There she is." Swallowing, he walked over and touched Zoe's hand. "Hey there, Zoe. It's really nice to meet you."

In response, Zoe squirmed and reached for Nicole. Victoria handed her over, and everyone chuckled when Zoe ducked her head against her mother's shoulder and peeked at Peter with one eye.

"She gets a little shy around strangers." Nicole blushed, quick to amend that. "Not that you're a *stranger*, stranger."

"Well, I suppose I am a stranger," Peter said gently, still smiling at Zoe. "But we're going to change that."

Not wanting to be in the way, Victoria moved off to the side as Nicole, Peter, and Melanie took seats around the coffee table and began to talk among themselves. She watched for a moment and then, thinking that everyone seemed to be getting along just fine without her, she headed toward the kitchen.

Looking out the window over the sink, Ford turned around when she walked in. "Sounds like it's going well in there."

"Aren't you going to say hello to Peter and Melanie?" she asked.

"Sure, on my way out. The room felt a little crowded." He leaned against the sink, gripping it with his hands. "So, you did it, Ms. Slade. You brought your first family together."

She remembered that moment in the car, when he'd been

teasing her. *That is an unexpectedly beautiful way to describe what we're doing here, Victoria.*

"*We* did it," she corrected him.

"Right." He smiled, but it didn't quite reach his eyes. Then he looked away, and the only sound in the room was the chatter of Nicole and the Sutters talking in the background.

And it was in that moment, standing across from Ford on the opposite side of the kitchen, that Victoria realized something.

She *hated* this distance between them.

She had done this. She'd pushed Ford away and now she very well may have lost him for good. Or maybe she'd never had him in the first place. Maybe what they'd had was always just a casual fling for him, and he'd already moved on. Maybe she would only make things even more awkward if she told him how she felt. And maybe, quite possibly, she was going to end up crushed at the end of this.

But there was only one way to find out.

Why on earth would I ever allow someone to be able to hurt me that way again?

Because you find someone who's worth facing your deepest fears for.

Indeed she had.

Thirty-two

THE DRESS WAS killing him.

Not only did Victoria look incredible in it—the cream color showing off her silky, golden skin—but it looked like the kind of dress a woman would wear on a date. And he didn't want to think about Victoria going on dates, because that got him wondering, again, where she'd been on Friday night. Or more important, who she'd been with.

His jaw tightened every time he thought about another man touching her. But what bothered him even more—if she had, in fact, been with another guy—was the fact that she'd spent the night. Because not once, during the entire time Ford had been sleeping with her, had she done that with *him*. Sure, she'd stayed late, but after they'd had sex every which way and were both so spent they could barely move, inevitably she'd gotten dressed and had made some excuse about sleeping better in her own bed. And he hadn't pushed back, because on some level it made sense—her bed *was* only ten feet away, after all—and also because, at the time, he'd figured that her not sticking around until morning would make everything less complicated in the long run.

Yet here they were, nevertheless. With her wearing a dress that some other guy might be unzipping later tonight and Ford gripping the sink so tight at the mere thought, he was lucky he didn't dent the stainless steel.

Still, he kept his tone light. "So, you did it, Ms. Slade. You brought your first family together."

"*We* did it," she said.

"Right." They *had* made a good team, and the proof of that was in the next room over. But that was done, and now, apparently, the only thing that he and Victoria did together was make small talk. And while he could fake his way through a short conversation as they passed each other in the hallway, or at the mailboxes, he had a feeling that if he stayed in this kitchen with her for much longer, he would say something he'd regret.

Their eyes met across the room.

Did you moan his name the way you used to moan mine?

Yep. Something like that.

"So, it seems like everything's going well here." He pushed off from the sink, careful to keep his expression neutral. "Since you guys don't need me, I think I'll head out."

Victoria pulled back in surprise. "You're leaving?"

He shrugged this off. "You've got this covered, Slade. I'm not sure why Nicole even asked me to be here in the first place."

She took a step toward him. "But . . . I was thinking we could share a cab home together."

Good for her, that she wasn't fazed by all this polite small-talk. But the idea of sitting next to her in a car for twenty minutes, pretending that everything was just peachy, held zero fucking appeal for him.

So he lied.

"Actually, I'm not going home. I have plans."

"Plans. Oh." For a moment it looked like Victoria was going to say more, but then she bit her lip and fell silent.

Right.

Moving past her, he walked into the living room and smiled at Peter and Melanie, both of whom seemed surprised by his unexpected appearance. "Peter. Melanie. Good to see you again. Don't mind me, I'm just on my way out."

"You're going?" Nicole stood up from the couch, holding Zoe, and shot a look at Victoria, who'd just come out of the kitchen.

"I think you all can manage without me," he said, with a light chuckle to underscore the fact that he was fine—of course he was—everything was cool, he just had places to be.

Then he opened the door and left, taking the stairs down and exhaling as soon as he got outside. He ran a hand over his mouth as he walked along the sidewalk in the direction of his parked car, and made it almost a block before he heard someone call him.

"Ford."

He glanced over his shoulder and saw Victoria following him, walking briskly in her dress and heels and carrying a small leather purse. The sight pissed him off, because whatever this was, whatever she wanted to talk about—his semi-terse behavior, or perhaps the fact that he'd left without saying more to make Peter and Melanie feel "welcome"—he didn't owe her any answers. "Go back inside, Victoria."

When she kept right on following him, he shook his head and turned into the alley that led to the side street where he'd parked his car.

"Ford, hold on."

He spun around. "What?" She stopped at his brusque tone, and stood a couple feet from him in the alley. When she hesitated, he gestured impatiently. "What, Victoria?"

She lifted her chin. "Are you dating that woman who was with you in the elevator?"

Fuck that. All his frustration boiling to the surface, he took a step closer to her. She had no right to ask him that, not anymore. *She* had kicked *him* out of her life. "Would it make any difference if I was?" he asked sharply.

Victoria held her ground, peering up at him and taking a moment before answering. "No."

His shoulders slumped.

Well. He'd asked.

"That's what I thought," he said tersely. He spun around and started walking toward his car.

"Because I'd fight for you anyway."

He stopped.

His heart pounding, he turned around to face her.

She stepped toward him, speaking determinedly. "This was not supposed to happen. My whole adult life I have avoided exactly *this* happening. I had things all mapped out, I knew what I wanted, and I was set. But then you came along, and you messed up all of that, with your little quips, and your jaw that twitches when you get protective, and the way you somehow manage to always be so infuriatingly unfazed no matter what I throw at you. And now I'm stuck. I can't get back to my old life and, even crazier, I don't *want* my old life anymore." She held his gaze. "Because that life doesn't have you in it."

She moved closer. "These past two weeks without you have felt . . . wrong. And I miss you. So much." Her lip began to tremble, but she swallowed and kept going. "I know I pushed you away. But not because I don't care. It's because I care so much that it scares me." Her voice softened. "But losing you scares me even more. And I thought, maybe, if you felt the same way, that we could start over. Only this time . . . we'd do it for real."

She fell quiet then, standing still as she waited.

His throat feeling tight, Ford needed a moment before he could answer.

If I ever were to go down this road, and let myself fall for someone, it can't be halfway. I have to know that she's in, too.

And that speech, coming from her, said everything.

He moved closer and cupped her face in his hands. "I love you."

Her eyes filled with tears, her expression suddenly so hopeful and vulnerable it made his heart ache. "Really?"

"Yes." He smiled softly. "Like, crazy, awful, miserable-without-you kind of love. Hell, even Tucker was trying to cheer me up."

Victoria bit her lip. "But the blonde in the elevator—"

"—was just a co-worker." Ford stroked his thumb across her cheek, wiping away one of her tears. "See, apparently, that's how these crazy, miserable-without-you things work. It means you're the only one I think about. Ever since the day I first knocked on your door."

She smiled and touched his cheek. "You weren't the only one who was miserable. Friday night, I had to sleep at Rachel's because I couldn't stand the thought of you with another woman."

"Ah . . . Rachel's. *That's* where you were."

In his head, he did a little victory dance.

"Where else would I have been?" She cocked her head. "Wait, did you think—"

He cut her off. "Still don't want to think about it. Ever."

Her lips curved. Then she looked at him for a moment, her expression softening. "You know I love you, too, right?"

He pulled her closer, his voice thick with emotion. "I do now."

He bent his head and kissed her, tenderly at first, and then more heatedly as they leaned against the building, her purse falling to the ground, and his forearms pressing on the brick as he held her face in his hands.

When she finally pulled back, her cheeks were flushed. "I think we need to get out of this alley."

His thoughts exactly.

Ford scooped up her purse and they hurried through the alley. But then Victoria stopped in her tracks when they got to his car. "Shoot. I forgot about Nicole. She's still with Peter and Melanie."

"Nicole will be fine."

"I was so distracted when you left, I'm not sure I even said good-bye. Not my usual level of client relations," she said with a sheepish grin.

He took out his phone. "I'll text her and explain everything." He read out loud as he typed. "'Victoria left with me. She says good-bye.'" He hit send and winked at her. "Now can we go have make-up sex?"

A guy passing by them on a bicycle looked over sharply and nearly crashed into a parked car.

"Seriously," Victoria said to Ford.

But he noticed that she climbed into his car lickety-split.

"I got a funny vibe from Nicole earlier," Victoria said as she buckled her seatbelt. "Do you think she knew something was going on between us?"

As Ford got behind the wheel, his phone buzzed with a new message. He shook his head while reading it. "Well, at least now I know why she asked me to come tonight."

He held out the phone so Victoria could see his sister's reply.

You're welcome. Now stop brooding.

IN HIS BEDROOM, as the evening summer sun filtered in through the shades on his windows, Ford kissed the back of Victoria's neck. He slowly inched down the zipper of her dress, thinking how, a mere hour ago, he'd been going out of his mind at the thought of some other man doing exactly this. But now here they were.

And she was all his.

He pressed his mouth to the top of her shoulder as he pushed the dress down her arms and let it fall to the floor.

"Ford," she murmured, leaning against him.

He picked her up and carried her to the bed. After setting her down, he stripped off his clothes as she kicked off her heels and took off her bra. Then he climbed onto the bed and swept his mouth over hers in a long, possessive kiss. When his hands finally moved to her underwear, she sighed. But instead of yanking them off, he pulled them down just an inch and slowly kissed his way down to her stomach.

She groaned. "You're driving me crazy."

He smiled wickedly against her skin. "Better get used to it, Ms. Slade. I have two weeks' worth of driving you crazy to make up for."

Afterward, they lay face-to-face on their sides, looking at each other as the fading sunset cast a soft orange glow around the bedroom.

She reached out and slid her hand over his.

"Don't even think about asking me for brownies," he growled.

She laughed. "I was just going to say that I'm really glad those assholes broke into my town house. Because that led me to you."

He slid a hand down her back and pulled her close once again. "You slay me, Victoria. You know that, right?"

She sunk her fingers into his hair and smiled.

"I do now."

LATER THAT NIGHT, Ford woke up to the sound of his front door creaking shut.

He sat up and saw that the other side of the bed was empty. Frowning, he quickly threw on his jeans and went out into the living room.

No Victoria.

Then he noticed a dim sliver of light filtering in through a crack between his front door and the wall, and realized that someone had left the door propped open with the deadbolt.

Seconds later, that someone tiptoed back in, bare-legged and wearing his shirt.

Victoria smiled when she saw him standing there. "Sorry. I was trying not to wake you." She held up a skinny travel container. "Toothbrush."

Ford's mouth curved. Saying nothing, he walked into the kitchen and opened one of the drawers.

She rested her hip against the counter, watching him. "You are awake, right? This isn't some creepy sleep-walking thing, is it?"

He gave her a look as he walked over. Then he set something down on the counter in front of her.

A spare key to his place.

She smiled softly, looking down at it for a moment, and then picked it up. "Well. I guess we'd better alert the cavalcade that unit 4F is officially closed for business."

"Had to get that in, did you?" He scooped her up as she laughed, and set her on top of the counter, liking this look of her in his shirt and not much else.

She looked again at the key in her hand. "It's been years since I've had an actual boyfriend."

That made him go soft on the inside all over again. "It's going to be even longer before you have another one."

Her expression turned almost shy. "This happily-ever-after stuff . . . marriage, two-point-five-kids, and the minivan . . . I never thought those things were in the cards for me. This is all very new."

It was new for him, too, but it also felt very right. He wrapped his arms around her. "We have plenty of time to figure out those things. And we always have the frozen eggs."

She peered up at him. "We?"

"Yes. *We*." No hesitation.

"We," she repeated, not a question this time. Then she slid her arms around his neck, her voice husky. "I like the sound of that, Ford Dixon."

He lowered his head and kissed her, not worrying about what would happen tomorrow, or three months from now, or even thirty years down the road. All that mattered was that she would be by his side.

And that was the happiest damn ever-after of them all.

Epilogue

TWO WEEKS LATER, Victoria sat side by side with Ford, trying not to smile when she saw him run a nervous hand through his hair.

Ah, had she ever been there.

"So, this is Ford," she told Dr. Metzel, with no small amount of isn't-my-boyfriend-so-cute pride.

Two days ago, when she and Ford had been talking about their weekend plans, she'd offhandedly remarked that she had her therapy appointment on Saturday. Much to her surprise, he'd offered to go with her.

And then her heart had melted when she'd heard why.

"It's nice to meet you, Ford," Dr. Metzel said with a warm smile. "As I told Victoria on the phone, I'm happy to explore therapy options for the both of you. Normally, in circumstances like these, I'd recommend a combination of couple's sessions and individual sessions. But let's see how things go today, and then we can figure out a plan of attack. Okay?"

When they both nodded, the good doctor picked up his pen. "I think we should start with you, Ford. What is it that you would like to accomplish in these sessions?"

"Wow." Ford exhaled, shifting uncomfortably in his chair. "We're just diving right in with that one, are we?"

Victoria patted his knee. "It's okay, babe. He already knows you have issues, too."

"Right." He held out his hands, going for a joke. "I guess Dad didn't play enough catch with me growing up."

Victoria turned to Dr. Metzel. "Clearly, he's going to have to dig a little deeper."

Ford shot her a look. "Smart-ass." But when they shared a smile, he eased back in his chair, seemingly more relaxed.

Dr. Metzel pointed between them with his pen. "Ah. I see how this works." He began scribbling in his notepad.

Ford glanced sideways at Victoria, speaking under his breath. "Does he always write everything down?"

"You get used to it after a while," she whispered back.

Dr. Metzel looked up and folded his hands on his lap. "So, Ford. You were about to say what you would like to accomplish in these therapy sessions."

"Well . . . I think we all can agree that Victoria and I aren't the best at letting down our guards. A few weeks ago, after her panic attack, both of us held back instead of opening up and we nearly lost each other because of that." He looked at her, his blue eyes holding hers meaningfully. "And I think, basically, we both know that this is a really good thing, and don't ever want to be in a place where that happens again."

Victoria linked her fingers through his, feeling her throat tighten with emotion. "Well said."

I'm not about to cede control to Fate, waiting around for Mr. Right to show up on my doorstep.

But apparently, Fate had gone and done her thing, anyway. That sneaky little bitch.

Keep reading for an excerpt
of another irresistible novel
from Julie James

Love Irresistibly

Available now from Berkley Sensation

BROOKE PARKER STEPPED up to the bar at The Shore restaurant, ready to place her lunch order. The bartender, however, beat her to the punch.

"Hey, it's my favorite customer—Chicken Tacos, Extra Pico." He flashed her a grin. "That's my nickname for you."

Yes, she got that. "I suppose I've been called worse," Brooke said as the bartender moved to the cash register to ring her up. She was indeed a regular, and she took pride in that. The restaurant was only two blocks from her office, right on Oak Street Beach, which made it the perfect midday escape. And it had the best chicken tacos in the city. Not that she was biased.

Okay, maybe she was a *little* biased.

She handed over a twenty-dollar bill. "I'll take a strawberry-mango smoothie, too."

"Ooh, a smoothie. Getting a little crazy today, are we?" In his early twenties, with blond hair and a tanned face, the bartender had the look of a recent college grad who planned to spend a lot of time playing beach volleyball this summer.

He called Brooke's order back to the kitchen, and then

looked her over. "I'm starting to feel like I should know more about you, Chicken Tacos, Extra Pico." He winked. "Since we've been seeing each other on a weekly basis for nearly a month now." He took in the tailored gray suit she wore. "I'm thinking that you are a . . . lawyer."

"Good guess."

"I knew it. I bet you're one of those ballbuster types in court."

Brooke fought back a smile. Really, she should just spare the poor guy the embarrassment, but this was kind of fun. "Actually, I'm not a trial lawyer." She decided to give him a hint. "I'm general counsel for a company based here in Chicago."

He made a big show of being impressed. "Look at you, Ms. Thing. What kind of company?"

"Restaurants and bars."

"What a coincidence. We're both in the restaurant business." He leaned his elbows on the bar, giving her a smoldering, sexy look that likely helped him rake in big tips with the female clientele. "It's Kismet."

Or . . . maybe not so much. Brooke raised an eyebrow. "Are you supposed to be flirting with the customers?"

He brushed this off with an oh-so-cool smile. "Probably not. But for you, Chicken Tacos, Extra Pico, I'll break the rules. Just don't tell any of those stiffs in corporate."

Brooke had to bite her lip to hold back a smile at that one. Aw, she definitely couldn't clue the poor guy in now. Then a voice called her name.

"Playing hooky for the afternoon, Ms. Parker?"

Brooke turned and saw Kurt McGregor, one of the managers of The Shore. "Unfortunately, no. Just sneaking out for a quick break."

Kurt gestured to the bartender. "I hope Ryan here is treating you well."

"Ryan has been most charming," she assured him.

The bartender pointed between them. "You two know each other?"

Kurt chuckled at that. "You could say that. Ryan, this is

Brooke Parker from corporate. She's general counsel of Sterling."

The grin on the bartender's face froze, replaced by a look of panic. "Oh, shit. Sterling Restaurants. As in, the people who sign my paychecks?"

"The one and only," Brooke said.

The bartender looked like he'd swallowed a bug. "I just called you a stiff."

"And Ms. Thing."

"Please don't fire me," he whispered.

Brooke pretended to think about that. "It's tempting. But firing someone involves a *lot* of paperwork. Not something I want to do on a Friday afternoon. I'll hold off until Monday instead." She saw his eyes widen. "I'm kidding, Ryan."

Kurt cleared his throat pointedly. "Ryan, maybe this would be a good time to check on Ms. Parker's order?"

The bartender straightened up, clearly relieved to be dismissed. "Good idea. One order for Chicken Tac—uh, Ms. Parker—coming right up." With that, he bolted for the kitchen.

Kurt turned to her after the bartender left. "Okay, seriously. Should I fire him?"

"Nah. He sneaks me extra pico on the side. He's a keeper."

Kurt chuckled at that, then gestured to the terrace. "Are you sticking around? I'm sure I can finagle you a table with a view of the lake if you want to eat in."

Brooke looked out at the umbrella-covered tables on the sunny terrace, tempted by the idea. It was a gorgeous June day, and the view from the terrace was undeniably one of the best in Chicago: skyscrapers towering majestically against the shimmering blue of Lake Michigan. Today, however, duty called.

Actually, duty called every day. Duty had her on speed dial.

"Wish I could. But I've got a conference call in"—Brooke checked her watch—"yikes, twenty minutes."

Ryan the bartender came out of the kitchen with a carryout bag and a smoothie. With a sheepish look, he set both on the bar in front of Brooke and scurried off.

"By any chance would this conference call have anything

to do with a certain deal you're negotiating with the Staples
Center?" Kurt asked in a sly tone after Ryan disappeared.

Brooke's face gave nothing away. "I can neither confirm
nor deny the existence of any such deal."

"Spoken like a true lawyer."

Brooke winked as she grabbed her smoothie and tacos and
headed for the door. "Always."

BROOKE BRISKLY WALKED the two blocks from Oak
Street Beach to the elegant eight-story building on Michigan
Avenue that was home to Sterling's corporate offices. Tacos
and smoothie in hand, she pushed through the revolving doors
and waved hello to Mac, a retired Chicago police officer who
manned the front security desk, as she passed through the
lobby and headed toward the elevators.

When Ian Sterling, CEO of Sterling Restaurants, had
approached her two years ago about coming on board as general counsel—or "GC" as the position was commonly called—
he'd been very candid about his vision and plans. He'd started
the company with one restaurant, an American bistro in the
heart of downtown Chicago, and within eight years had opened
six more restaurants that ran the spectrum from summer hot
spot The Shore, to an Irish pub on the south side of the city,
to Sogna, the company's "crown jewel" that had just this year
earned a coveted three-star Michelin rating.

Many restaurateurs would've been satisfied there, but not
Ian Sterling. He was aggressive, he was driven, and he had
plans. Big plans.

A friend of a friend knew the owner of the Chicago Cubs,
and Ian convinced the owner to consider letting Sterling Restaurants take over the food and beverage service for the Stadium Club and skyboxes at Wrigley Field.

"Should you choose to accept the position," Ian had said
to Brooke, à la *Mission Impossible*, on the evening he'd for-
mally offered her the job over dinner at Sogna, "your first
task as GC will be to close the Wrigley Field deal."

"And then what?" Brooke had asked.

"You'll be part of a team that will build an entire sports and entertainment division of Sterling," he'd said. "Ballparks. Arenas. Stadiums."

Brooke had to admit, she'd been impressed with his ambition. She'd been working at a law firm at the time, in the corporate department, and had been the associate with primary responsibility over Sterling Restaurants' non-litigation matters. Having known Ian for several years by that point, she'd been aware that he'd contemplated hiring an in-house attorney. What she hadn't realized, however, was that he'd planned to ask *her* to fill the position. "You're not concerned that I only have five years' experience?"

"I've seen you in action many times, Brooke. You're tough when you need to be, and you can charm the pants off men who have three times your experience."

"Well, yes. Although I try not to take advantage of that too often. Very awkward negotiating with people who are sitting around in their underwear."

Ian had grinned. "I like your style—and just as important, I like you. So the better question is, do *you* think you can handle the job?"

A direct question. Luckily, Brooke had never been one to mince words, either, and Ian's enthusiasm and drive were infectious. It was an opportunity to take a chance, to get involved with a young company that was on the rise. So in answer to Ian's question, she'd looked him right in the eyes. "Absolutely."

Because Brooke Parker was a woman who was going places. She'd made that promise to herself a long time ago.

Two years later, she had zero regrets about taking a chance with Sterling. The company had grown steadily since she'd come on board as GC, most notably in their sports and entertainment division. After finalizing negotiations with Wrigley Field, Brooke and the other two members of Ian's "dream team"—the VP of sales and the VP of operations—had spent a lot of time schmoozing and wining and dining prospective clients. And when they'd landed a contract to take over the food service at the United Center—home of the Chicago Bulls and Blackhawks and the fifth-most-profitable sports venue in North America—they'd all partied like it was 1999 at the Sterling corporate office.

A few months after that, they'd headed down to Dallas, where Brooke and the two VPs had given their best sales pitch and negotiated a deal with the Cowboys. A short while later, they landed the contract for Dodger Stadium, too.

During the Dodger negotiations, the general counsel, a woman with whom Brooke had formed a friendly relationship, just so happened to let it slip that she'd heard whispers that the folks at L.A. Arena Company—who owned the Staples Center, aka home to the Los Angeles Lakers, Clippers, Kings, and Sparks—were also unhappy with their food and beverage vendor and looking to make a change as soon as their current contract expired.

So the dream team had struck while the iron was hot.

And now, assuming there were no hiccups in the deal Brooke was finalizing today with the lawyers representing L.A. Arena Company, Sterling Restaurants would soon be adding the Staples Center, the number one most profitable sports venue in the country, to their roster.

In a word, they were hot.

Sterling was an exciting, demanding, absolutely exhausting place to work. Sure, that meant long hours for Brooke, but she believed in the company and her role there. Whether negotiating a multimillion-dollar contract with the GC of the Dallas Cowboys, or investigating an internal complaint that one of their pastry chefs had a problem playing grab-ass with the waitresses, there was never, ever a dull moment.

After exiting the elevator at the third floor, Brooke turned down the hallway that would take her to Sterling's offices. She pushed through the frosted-glass doors and said hello to the receptionist. According to the clock on the wall, she still had fifteen minutes to eat lunch before her conference call. Plenty of time.

"I'm back," she told Lindsey, her assistant, who sat at the desk outside Brooke's office.

"A couple of calls came in while you were out," Lindsey

said. "The first one was from Justin. He asked that you call him back as soon as you get in."

The message took Brooke somewhat by surprise. She and Justin, aka the Hot OB, had been dating for a little over four months now, and she could count on one hand the number of times she'd talked to him at the office. Both of them were always so busy during the day, it was simply easier to e-mail or text him on her way home from work. "Uh-oh. I hope he's not calling to cancel tonight. We've got reservations at Rustic House," she said, referring to a nearly-impossible-to-get-into restaurant on the north side that was *not* in the Sterling family.

"Traitor," Lindsey said with a grin. She handed Brooke a piece of paper with a phone number on it. "And you also received a call from Cade Morgan at the U.S. Attorney's Office."

Now that got Brooke's attention.

Just about anyone who followed the local news knew who Cade Morgan was. One of the top assistant U.S. attorneys in Chicago, he'd made a name for himself by prosecuting several high-profile government corruption cases—and, a little over a year ago, the famous "Twitter Terrorist" case that had garnered international attention. He had a reputation of being smart, disarmingly charming in front of judges and juries, and tough as nails against opposing counsel.

And what he might possibly want from Brooke, she had no clue.

"Did he say what this was in regards to?" Brooke asked.

"No. Only that he'd like you to call him back as soon as possible. He was very firm about that."

This unexpected message from the U.S. Attorney's Office had Brooke feeling a bit . . . uneasy. Cade Morgan was a prosecutor who handled big cases that got a lot of media attention. Whatever this was, it wasn't a social call. And as general counsel for Sterling Restaurants, her hackles were up.

"Thanks, Lindsey." Brooke went into her office and shut the door behind her, trying not to get too rattled by Morgan's message. She didn't know what he wanted, she reminded herself, so there wasn't anything worth worrying about. Yet.

Never a dull moment, she thought again to herself as she

settled in at her desk and unwrapped one of the tacos. Double-tasking per usual, she took a bite while dialing Justin's number on speakerphone.

"Hey there," she said when he answered his cell phone. "I wasn't sure I'd actually catch you." She could picture him looking cute in his scrubs right then—an easy image to conjure up since she'd seen him wearing them a few times late at night after one of his shifts.

"I stepped out of the office for a short break," Justin said. His obstetrics practice was located a few blocks from Brooke's office, which was nice if they wanted to meet for lunch. Although come to think of it, they'd only met for lunch once, back when they'd first started dating.

He sounded apologetic. "I just sent one of my patients to the hospital to be induced. She's only a half-centimeter dilated, but she's forty-one weeks with gestational diabetes. Since it's her first baby, this could be a long night. Sorry to have to cancel on you like this."

"Darn babies. Somebody needs to explain to them about date night," Brooke said jokingly. While she was disappointed not to see Justin tonight, she understood that work conflicts sometimes came up. Heck, she'd had to reschedule two dates so far this month because of last-minute emergencies she'd needed to handle at the office.

"Yeah. Right." He cleared his throat as if hesitant about whatever it was he wanted to say next. "You and I sure seem to be missing each other a lot these days."

Aw, the Hot OB missed her. And he was right; it had been a busy month. She'd been in Los Angeles for nearly a week, working on the Staples Center deal, and then had been swamped trying to catch up with everything at work after that. Lately, it seemed the only times she and Justin were both free was between eleven P.M. and five A.M. "So let's not miss each other tonight, even if we can't do dinner," she suggested. "Why don't you text me when you're finished at the hospital and come over to my place?"

"That'll probably be around two A.M."

"I know. But since that's the only time we both seem to be available, it's either that or nothing," Brooke said.

"Yes, that certainly does seem to be how it works with us. Heaven forbid we ever go on an actual date."

When she heard the frustration in his voice, Brooke got a sinking feeling in her stomach.

Not again.

She tried to smooth things over. "Look, I know that things have been crazy for me with these back-to-back deals in Los Angeles. You're a doctor, you know how it is—your schedule is just as bad." Admittedly, she was feeling a bit defensive right then, and felt the need to note that for the record.

He sighed. "I know. Tonight is my fault. And then next time, something will come up for you."

"We talked about this when we first met." Given her less-than-successful track record with relationships, she'd been up front with him from the beginning about the demands of her job.

"You're right, we did," he said. "And frankly, back then I thought I'd hit the jackpot. It was great that you never got mad when I had to cancel plans, or when I forgot to call. And you never complain that I don't take you out enough. Hell, in some ways it's like dating a guy."

Alrighty, then. "I don't need to be wined and dined, Justin. I can walk into eight restaurants in this city and have every employee practically tripping over themselves to make sure I'm happy."

"I'm sorry, Brooke," he said contritely. "But this . . . doesn't work for me anymore. I like you. You're a great girl, and you have awesome Cubs skybox tickets. I love it when they bring that dessert cart around."

Glad she scored high when it came to the important things in life. "But?"

"But you seem to be really focused on your career right now—which, don't get me wrong, is totally fine—except, well, I'm thirty-four years old. I'm starting to think about getting married, having kids, the big picture. And I guess what I'm trying to say is . . . I don't see a woman like you in that big picture."

Brooke blinked. Wow.

A woman like you.

That stung.

"Fuck, that came out harsh," Justin said. "I just meant that you're so independent, and I don't even know if you want to get married or have kids, and half the time I think you just like having a warm body to cuddle up with every now and then—"

"Hold on. This is the *non*-harsh version?"

"Sorry," he said, sounding sheepish. "I just think we're looking for different things. I want—"

"A big-picture girl," Brooke interrupted. "I got it." She definitely didn't need to have it spelled out for her any clearer than that.

When both of them fell awkwardly silent, Brooke glanced at the clock on her phone. "I hate to say this, since it's apparently what makes me a *small*-picture kind of girl, but I have to go. I've got a conference call with a bunch of other lawyers in Los Angeles that can't be rescheduled."

"I understand. You do your thing. Good-bye, Brooke."

After hanging up, Brooke stared at the phone for a long moment.

Another one bites the dust.

That was her third breakup since starting at Sterling. She seemed to be in a pattern with her relationships, where everything was great in the beginning, and then somewhere around the four-month mark things just kind of fizzled out. The men would give her some speech about not getting to the "next level," or about wanting "more" than hot sex at midnight after a long workday.

"Hold on. A *guy* said this to you?" Her best friend, Ford, had looked both shocked and appalled by this when they'd met for drinks after Breakup Number Two. "As in, someone with an actual penis?"

"Two guys now," Brooke had said, her pride admittedly wounded at being dumped again. "I don't get it. I don't put any pressure on these men, I'm happy to give them all the space they want, and the sex is good enough. What else could your gender possibly want in a relationship?"

"Beer and nachos in bed?"

"This is the advice you offer, your sage insight into the male perspective? Beer and nachos in bed?"

Ford had flashed her an easy grin. "You know I'm not good at the relationship stuff. Even other people's relationship stuff."

And, judging from today's turn of events with Justin, Brooke wasn't all that much better.

I don't see a woman like you in that big picture.

The intercom on Brooke's phone buzzed, interrupting her thoughts.

"I have Jim Schwartz, Eric Keller, and Paul Fielding on the phone for you," her secretary said, referring to L.A. Arena's in-house counsel and the two outside attorneys who represented them. "Can I put them through?"

Right. Back to work—no time for a pity party. As Brooke shoved her now-cold tacos back into the bag and reached for her phone, she spotted the note on her desk and belatedly remembered the call from the U.S. Attorney's Office. Well, Cade Morgan would just have to wait.

She told her secretary to put the call through and forced a cheerful note into her voice. "How are my three favorite Los Angeles lawyers today?" she asked.

As they said in Hollywood, the show must go on.

"Julie James writes books I can't put down."

—Nalini Singh, *New York Times* bestselling author

FROM *NEW YORK TIMES* BESTSELLING AUTHOR

Julie James

THE FBI/U.S. ATTORNEY SERIES

Something About You

A Lot Like Love

About That Night

Love Irresistibly

juliejames.com
facebook.com/juliejamesfanpage
facebook.com/LoveAlwaysBooks
penguin.com